PRAISE FOR
THE NOVELS OF MARY BLAYNEY

COURTESAN'S KISS

"Blayney crafts a powerful story with an outspoken modern heroine (à la Elizabeth Bennet) who wins readers' hearts. All of Blayney's characters leap from the pages into fully realized people you care about. . . . The twists and depth of emotion [are] unforgettable."
—*Romantic Times* (four stars)

"I can't praise this book enough. . . . I'm highly impressed with the skill that is used to take diverse characters [and] have them fall in love while intertwining the story with a perfect rendition of Regency England. . . . Thankfully there will be another wonderful story coming."
—Night Owl Romance

"A highly enjoyable love story, full of warmth and wit."
—All About Romance

"The fourth 'Kiss' Pennistan Regency romance is a terrific entry."
—Genre Go Round Reviews

STRANGER'S KISS

"I couldn't wait to see what happened next and I loved it. If ever someone wanted a perfect Regency romance, this would be it. I can't think of any emotion that wasn't seen and I can't think of anything more that I could possibly want."

—Night Owl Romance

"An emotionally charged story of revenge, loss, passion and redemption. Blayney plays readers like a virtuoso, allowing laughter, tears and every emotion in between to claim your heart."

—*Romantic Times*

"A terrific entry in a great Regency saga . . . *Stranger's Kiss* is another winner from marvelous Mary Blayney."

—Genre Go Round Reviews

TRAITOR'S KISS / LOVER'S KISS

"Taut and daring, an emotionally charged tale that satisfies from beginning to end. *Traitor's Kiss* will steal your heart!"
—GALEN FOLEY

"Reminiscent of Regency masters Putney, Balogh and Elizabeth Boyle . . . [Blayney's] consummate storytelling completely involves readers."
—*Romantic Times*

"Danger, deception, and desire blend brilliantly together in these two deftly written, exceptionally entertaining Regency romances."
—*Chicago Tribune*

"Mary writes with a quiet beauty and great confidence."
—Risky Regencies

"These two exhilarating Pennistan family Regency romances are well written, filled with plenty of action and star great courageous lead characters. . . . Fans will enjoy both super tales."
—Genre Go Round Reviews

"This beguiling pair of novels from author Mary Blayney delivers a double dose of romance and intrigue."
—Fresh Fiction

By Mary Blayney

Traitor's Kiss/Lover's Kiss
Stranger's Kiss
Courtesan's Kiss
One More Kiss

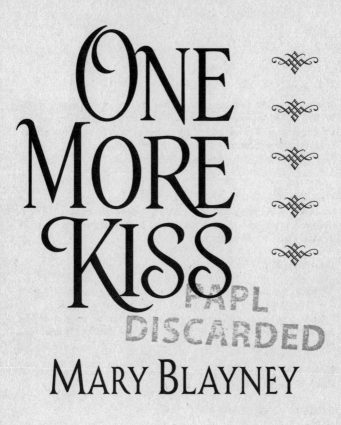

ONE MORE KISS

MARY BLAYNEY

BANTAM BOOKS
NEW YORK

Copyright © 2013 by Mary Blayney

Published in the United States by Bantam Books, an imprint of The Random House Publishing Group, a division of Random House, Inc., New York.

BANTAM BOOKS and the rooster colophon are registered trademarks of Random House, Inc.

ISBN 978-0-553-59314-3
eISBN 978-0-345-53574-0

Cover design: Lynn Andreozzi
Cover illustration: Aleta Rafton

Printed in the United States of America

www.bantamdell.com

9 8 7 6 5 4 3 2 1

Bantam Books mass market edition: May 2013

Dedicated to Owen Thomas Blayney

Prologue

JESS PENNISTAN WAS in a world of trouble with no one to blame but himself. He rubbed his neck as he stared at the losing play, then looked at Crenshaw, acknowledging the bastard's win with a nod. He forced himself to maintain his façade of bored patience even as a string of curses echoed through his head.

Bigger fortunes had been won and lost at this very table. What had just been wagered, a tract of land, seemed innocuous enough, but in his family wagering land was simply not done. More than not done. To wager land left to him by his mother was akin to spitting in his family's face.

No one else seemed to be aware of this drama. Play went on accompanied by shouts of triumph, the occasional groan of loss, and the laughter of men and women who were playing an entirely different game.

The place was overheated, which exaggerated the cloying perfumes that only partly covered the stink of

men and women who had decided that washing was
an unnecessary annoyance.

Baron Lord Crenshaw was the exception. Despite
the amount of brandy he'd imbibed and the hours he'd
spent gaming, Crenshaw looked refreshed, his linen
still spotless, his smile an invitation to play on.

"If you will accept my voucher, Lord Crenshaw, I
will bring you the land's worth in gold within a fortnight." Surely he was due for a big win soon.

"Perhaps," Baron Crenshaw allowed, swirling the
brandy before drinking it down in one swallow.

Jess waited, well aware that Crenshaw was hoping
to test his tolerance to the breaking point.

"I tell you what, Pennistan, I will hold the voucher if
you will include with it the whore beside you. She's the
one that you won from Delcroft earlier this evening, is
she not?"

Jess nodded and did not have to look at Sadie to feel
her anxiety. "Damn it, Crenshaw, she is barely sixteen."

"Del tells me the bitch needs someone with my talents to broaden her experience," Crenshaw said, ignoring Jess's objection. Then the man closed his eyes,
smiling at some private thought. The idea alone
aroused the sadistic pig, and the slut next to him whispered something in his ear. Crenshaw grabbed her
hand and pushed it into his crotch. Jess turned away.

Sadie was watching him and Jess gave her the slightest shake of his head to reassure her. Tears began to
leak from her eyes and trickle down her cheeks. How
had this silly, stupid girl wound up here? She should be
wife to some farmer in the Midlands, spending her

days tending children and baking bread, not in London spreading her legs for anyone with money.

"If you do not care to share, Pennistan, then I refuse the voucher and will take the land. I assume the acreage is worthless but, oh, the joy it brings me to know that your brother, the duke, will be enraged."

Yes, Jess thought. This had been Crenshaw's goal all along. And what did it say about Jess himself that he had been bored enough to take the risk of gambling with a man whom the world thought he had cuckolded?

"Unless you wish to wager something else of value, I will be going upstairs to allow Merribeau to finish what she has so delightfully started. Would you and your whore care to watch? It adds a certain piquancy to the experience especially when there are ropes and chains involved."

Crenshaw stood up and pulled the willing Merribeau by the hand. "You see, Pennistan, I am more than willing to share. Indeed if you had not been so set on freeing me of my wife through divorce, I do think the three of us could have come to a very interesting arrangement." With a shrug of indifference Crenshaw moved past him.

That last comment was more than Jess could stand. He pulled Crenshaw around to face him. The man might be famous for his pugilistic skills, but Jess had surprise on his side and years of practice in the boxing ring at home with his brothers.

Before Crenshaw could raise his hands, Jess swung at him, connected, and sent the man crashing onto a table, which collapsed under his weight.

Crenshaw was dazed, or perhaps unconscious; Jess didn't care which.

He took Sadie's hand and tossed some coins at Foxley, who appeared outraged, to cover the cost of the furniture. His "outrage" was only pretense. Such a show was good for business. Jess urged Sadie out the door anyway and decided that he was done with gaming hells for the rest of the Season.

He would send Sadie wherever she wanted to go, take himself off to see his brother David, and convince him to go to Sandleton House for some fishing. It would be easy enough for their brother, the duke, to find him there and consign him to some level of Dante's hell for this biggest of missteps.

And maybe, just maybe, a few days of fishing and the quiet of Sandleton would give him a chance to think of a way to win the land back from Crenshaw.

Chapter One

Havenhall Manor
Kent
August 1820

"DO COME TO the window, Beatrice," Cecilia Brent urged her sister without turning around. "Tell me if you know who this is. It must be someone important. He's riding the most impressive horse and has a red scarf around his neck."

Beatrice could feel Cecilia's anxiety as clearly as she could see it in her eyes. They might not look alike but the closeness they shared as twins made it easy for Beatrice to know what her sister was thinking. *Do I look as good as possible? Is my dress the right style, the right color? Will people like me?*

How was it that even when she wasn't smiling Cecilia still managed to be more beautiful than any woman for ten miles? And what in the world could she do, Beatrice wondered, to convince her anxious twin that this house party could be fun?

"I do believe the countess gave us the best suite in the house. We can watch everyone arrive."

"I wish Papa had given us the guest list instead of insisting we memorize it," Cecilia said as she clasped her hands together.

The sitting room's cream and gold colors with pale green accents were lovely and very calming, but they did not seem to be doing anything to allay her sister's nerves.

"Papa meddles entirely too much. Even Roger agrees with me on that, Ceci." Beatrice put her arm around her sister's waist as they both watched the people below perform the practiced choreography of greeting and being welcomed.

"He is your best friend. Of course Roger agrees with you."

"That's true, but he also works with Papa so he agrees with me at his own peril. Roger says that Papa approaches everything as though it were a business merger."

"Some marriages are."

"Yes, but we are here for a *party*," Beatrice emphasized the word, "and not for a husband."

Cecilia gave her halfhearted nod, the one she used when she wanted to avoid an argument.

Beatrice abandoned the subject. There would be time enough for it later. She concentrated on the man below.

"I do believe that's the heir to the Bendas dukedom. He is on the list as Viscount William Bendasbrook, but I think he has a new title now. His grandfather died last year. Do you recall the gossip? His grandfather was that crazy duke who was always at odds with the Duke of Meryon."

"And then Meryon married his daughter. Yes, I recall. It was like a fairy tale." Cecilia was silent for a moment. "Just think, Bitsy, a man who will be a duke is at our house party!"

"Ceci, Papa could easily buy a dukedom if they were for sale." Beatrice bit her lip again to keep back her next thought. *As heiresses we are at least as valuable a commodity as any titled heir.* If she spoke aloud it would only add credence to Ceci's idea about marriages as mergers. "This will be fun," Beatrice insisted. "It's the beginning of our lives among the ton."

"Hmmm."

Which was another thing Ceci said when she did not agree. No big loud arguments for Cecilia Brent, Beatrice thought. It was odd because Beatrice herself quite liked a rousing argument now and again.

Beatrice waited until Ceci looked at her. "But it will only be fun," she added, "if you stop fretting."

Her sister nodded and sighed. "I will try."

"Consider it this way. The next two weeks will be our entrée into a world where every sort of adult intrigue is commonplace. Watching it will be fascinating. And we are the ones to decide if we want to be a part of it."

"You think we are the ones who choose? Not at all. This is a test," Cecilia said flatly. "To see if we fit in."

"Stop, Ceci." Beatrice tried to hide her exasperation. "Of course we fit in." *Or at least you do.* "We've had an education equal to theirs, clothes from London, a sponsor who is a countess. What more do we need?"

"Better birth? A father who is not a mill owner?"

Ceci did have a way of arrowing to the truth. The Season they had such hopes for was where they would meet the ladies and gentlemen of the ton who measured everyone by their birth, not just by their wealth.

So they were, and always would be, a mill owner's daughters.

"We can only hope that the countess's influence will be an adequate substitute." Besides, once the gentlemen of the ton saw Cecilia, her parentage would be the last thing they thought about. Beatrice kept that to herself.

"Hope and pray that I do not break out in spots," Cecilia said with a little laugh, which made Beatrice feel five times better. When Ceci joked about her looks all was right with the world.

Cecilia leaned a little closer to the window as if that would improve her view. "I thought that the viscount was older than we are, but he seems rather small."

"I am even shorter. Perhaps you think I should flirt with him and the two of us should make a match?"

"Not at all, dearest." Ceci's tone was all apology. "Your diminutive size seems perfectly natural for a woman, but for a man it is a bit odd, is it not?"

Beatrice considered him again. "He is said to be unusually short, but the red scarf is actually how I recognized him. Viscount Bendasbrook, or whatever his title is now, always wears one." As she spoke he disappeared from sight. "According to the countess, despite his size he is manly in every way. Quite an adventurer both in the bedroom and out of it. That's the way she described him."

"How would she know that?" Cecilia asked, and then sighed. "I wish I did not sound so shocked. We are nineteen and I should be more sophisticated about such things." She walked over to the dresses that were spread out across the sofa. "Do you think he and the countess had an *affaire du coeur*?"

"No, I do not. The countess is old enough to be his mother and besides, she was happy in her marriage and has only been widowed for just over a year. I do not think she has taken a lover yet." A blush spoiled her try at a sophisticated comment. "Ladies gossip. Just like we are right now."

"But this is not gossip." Ceci paused and then went on. "Even your Roger would agree with that. This is an exchange of vital information. In fact it would be rude if we did not know as much about our fellow guests as possible. Just imagine what they must know about us." Cecilia examined the dresses and shifted a gown from one end of the row to the other.

Beatrice surveyed the collection of dresses with her sister. The more natural waistline was very flattering on Ceci, on both of them really, and the apricot color of this particular gown would show off her sister's perfect complexion.

"What do the other guests know about us? That we are newcomers to society and are late making our appearance among the ton because we were in mourning for Mama, God rest her soul."

"And that our dear mama," Cecilia finished, "was a school friend of the countess who kindly consented to be our godmother."

Beatrice nodded, for her part desperately wishing that Mama was part of this adventure. The pang of loss still haunted her, but a little less each day. She did not know whether to feel guilty or relieved.

"You make it all sound so simple, Beatrice. What if they think we are posers? What if they think Papa is not enough of a gentleman to associate with? We will be ignored from the first."

"The countess would never invite guests who would treat us that way." Maybe it would be better for Cecilia to worry about their clothes. "Now, tell me what dress I should wear tonight."

"I have no idea." Ceci began to wring her hands again. "Do you think we have the right clothes? Can we wear jewelry or are we too young for anything but pearls? Oh, I do wish this first meeting with the ton was over. A fortnight is a long time to look and be perfect. I do so miss Mama."

"Sweet, dear sister." Beatrice hugged her, rocked her back and forth. *So do I, so do I,* she thought. She'd always been able to calm everyone, whether the upset was caused by nerves or temper. "Mama is with us in spirit, and you could wear a flour sack and look lovely, and these gowns are perfection. The countess approved of them and even supervised the needlework herself."

She patted her sister on the back before letting her go.

"I'm sorry. I am so sorry, Bitsy. You are right."

Most of the time I am, Beatrice thought, but did not dare say it aloud.

"I am being silly."

"Soon these people will be our friends," Beatrice insisted, devoutly hoping this was another one of those things she was right about. "And then when we go to London for the Season we will know people."

"I will be relieved if they acknowledge us in London. Friendship is too much to ask."

At the sound of wheels on gravel, Beatrice went back to the window, grateful for the distraction. Ceci was considering the dresses yet again.

"Who do you think this is?" The awe in her voice drew her sister's attention instantly.

A singularly handsome gentleman had jumped out of the impressive coach. He was blond, well built, and lithe. He offered his hand to a woman. An older woman. Old enough to be his mother. Then he gave his hand to help a much younger woman down.

"Are they a couple?" Beatrice was surprised at the disappointment she felt as she stepped back from the window, no longer particularly interested.

"No," Ceci said. "At least I don't think so. My guess is that the older woman somehow talked him into escorting them and he is trying to free himself from their grasp already."

"How in the world do you know that?" Beatrice moved back and stood next to her sister. "Yes, I do believe you're right. He's smiling and all that is polite but somehow he has already detached himself from them." How had he so clearly conveyed his lack of interest without being rude? "I have no idea what his name is, but he is surely a gentleman of the ton. He has that way of dismissing someone by his very air."

"Yes. Where do they learn how to do that?"

"It's not an ability that is limited to men born to rank. Papa can do it."

"Yes, he can, Bitsy, but not like this gentleman. With Papa it is quite final. With this man there is an air of regret that hints at next time."

"I think it's called charm," Beatrice said, and they looked at each other, neither willing to say aloud that charm was one thing their dear papa lacked completely. They both returned their attention to the scene below. "We will meet him soon enough."

No sooner had Beatrice spoken than the gentleman looked up.

"Eeek" was all that Ceci said before stepping back, out of sight.

Beatrice did not move, caught by the way the gentleman's smile grew into a grin. He did not look away, but kept watching her.

Beatrice returned his smile, wishing that she could draw. She wanted to catch his delighted expression, his appeal, the way he made her skin tingle. Instead she kept staring at him, committing his face, his smile, to memory, before remembering that she was going to see him any number of times over the next weeks.

Beatrice raised her hand, not quite waving, in a gesture of greeting.

The nameless man swept off his hat and bowed extravagantly without taking his eyes from hers.

Beatrice's smile froze. That was not what she'd intended at all. She had only wanted to make a small sign of friendship. His outlandish bow acknowledged her tiny wave as if she had invited him into her life or even into her bed. She answered his gesture by abruptly pulling the drapes closed.

Still standing in front of the velvet panel, Beatrice concentrated on the elaborate fringe as she instantly banished the mental picture of him naked in the pose of Michelangelo's *David*.

"Why did you do that?" Cecilia asked.

"Why must some men think every gesture is an invitation to a flirtation? Every man except Roger."

"He is a perfect gentleman," Cecilia agreed.

She wished Roger were one of their party. She would have much more fun with him nearby to discuss ideas and her current readings. But no, he and Papa *had* to go to London this week. Papa insisted it could not wait. Now she would have no escape from unwanted flirtation. Best not to dwell on it at all, she decided.

"That dress will look awful on you," Beatrice said with as straight a face as she could manage.

Ceci turned to her, panic in her eyes, and then relaxed. "Oh, stop teasing me. It's lovely. But is it too much for the first night?"

"Perhaps we should let the maid the countess hired give us her opinion. She has served the ton for years and I'm sure we can depend on her."

Ceci's long silence gave Beatrice hope.

"Yes, that's a very good idea."

It was as much enthusiasm as her sister had shown all day.

Beatrice kept her expression solemn but mentally clapped her hands and wished she could jump up and down. If Cecilia kept on being this reasonable and listening to her suggestions, this house party would be as much fun as she insisted it could be. Beatrice relaxed for the first time since their arrival.

There was a tap at the sitting room door and a footman came in at her "Enter."

"I beg your pardon, miss, but Mr. Brent would like to see you and your sister before he leaves. He is in the front hall salon if you would like me to escort you there."

The twins exchanged a look and then Cecilia stopped at the looking glass to check her appearance, and Beatrice gathered her spectacles. She could only hope that whatever Papa had to say would not ruin all her efforts at cheering Ceci.

Chapter Two

"I'VE SENT FOR Beatrice and Cecilia so I can give them the written guest list as you asked, but before they arrive I want to know why in the world Lord Jessup Pennistan has been added to the list." Abel Brent set the paper down. Still standing, he folded his arms and waited for the countess's answer.

"Because it is impossible to say no to him." The dowager Countess of Haven folded her arms, imitating him, ready for an argument. When Abel stayed silent, a shocked look on his face, the countess laughed instead.

"Not in that way, dearest. At least not for me. I am almost old enough to be his mother." An outright lie. Her own son was two years older than Lord Jessup. "Jess is a charming rogue whom I've known since he was in swaddling clothes."

"But his reputation, Jasmine. He was involved in a divorce."

"Yes, he was, and Jess is so charming that the man who brought the suit still sees him socially. And as you well know, the baron will be a guest at this very house party."

"I don't know." His hesitation was all she needed.

"But I do, Abel, and I would never do anything that would endanger Beatrice and Cecilia. I think having Lord Jess to flirt with will be excellent practice for the Season."

"Then you think they will have a Season? That the guests here will approve? I am not worried about Lord Crenshaw. I do believe he has a slight *tendre* for Beatrice. There is Mrs. Wilson and the Earl of Belmont, and even Nora Kendrick has some influence." Brent shook his head, looking even more uncertain.

"What is there not to love about your girls? The two are bound to be welcome wherever they go."

"We are prejudiced, Jasmine. Their father and their godmother can hardly be expected to harbor any objectivity."

"You do know that I have enough cachet, even as a dowager, to present them? I am only hoping for them to know a few people before we arrive in town. It will make the girls so much more comfortable from the start."

"It could happen." Which was what Abel said when he knew he was being stubborn, but did not want to say so aloud.

"Which brings me back to Lord Jess." She had best clear that up now. "There will be rogues aplenty dangling after them in London and a small flirtation with someone like Jess will teach them how to handle it."

"But what if he seduces one of them?"

"Have some faith in your daughters." Jasmine could not quite control the edge in her voice. "Besides, I have warned Jess to be on his best behavior."

"His brother the duke must be disgusted with him."

"I have no idea," Jasmine lied again. "His sister and her husband will be joining us. Perhaps you can ask them when you return."

Brent laughed, as the countess had intended. "I wonder how Mrs. Wilson will handle Lord Jessup's presence with a chick of her own to launch."

"They seemed to be on the best of terms when they arrived. He came in the coach with them since her husband was unable to come and Jane dislikes traveling alone."

"He came with them?" Brent's expression was incredulous.

"I told you he was charming."

"Now you see, that is what makes me nervous. My girls have no experience with men like that."

"Well, they will after this next fortnight, won't they?" And that was the last of it, the countess decided. "I am going to greet the latest arrivals. The girls should be here any moment."

As Beatrice followed the footman she saw the countess leave a room up ahead, walking purposefully in the other direction. As she expected, the footman opened the door to the room the countess had just left.

"Papa!" Cecilia exclaimed, hurrying over to her father before the footman had even closed the door. "Is everything all right?"

"Why are you still here?" Beatrice asked with much less tact. "Where is Roger? Is he still here, too?"

"Roger is in the study on the first floor, where he cannot find anything but books to flirt with."

Abel Brent dominated the space with his size and the aura of power he carried with him. He had the kind of presence that made people stop on the street and ask each other who he was. Not a gentleman by birth, he was still a man who commanded respect.

"Roger never flirts! He is a complete gentleman. The finest I have ever met."

"So you remind me whenever I want to dismiss him." Papa folded his arms and looked down at her.

Beatrice mimicked his stance but had to look up, which did spoil the effect. "You would never find another machine designer half as talented as he is."

"Precisely why I let you convince me to keep him on."

His smile made Beatrice smile in return. She did love her papa, even when he was annoying.

Cecilia came between them and took her father's arm. "Did you have us come so you could wish us well one last time, Papa?"

"Of course," he said as if that thought had just occurred to him. "And the countess insisted that I give you the guest list. She says one's memory is never perfect when dealing with so many new faces. A dozen guests in all. I have added two and scratched out one who had to send a regret at the last minute. So it's to be twelve," he said again, "though not all are arriving today."

He pulled the thrice-folded list from his pocket. "Now tell me the names you recall," Papa demanded, draining a little more fun from the air.

"There was a gentleman with a red scarf. Ceci recognized him." Beatrice prompted her sister with a nod.

"Yes." Cecilia's panicked expression eased. "It was Viscount Bendasbrook, who has another title now."

"He is the Marquis Destry. His father is the Duke of Bendas. Destry is his heir."

"I do believe we saw Mrs. Wilson and her daughter," Beatrice went on, guessing at the two women who had arrived with that flirtatious man.

"Miss Wilson is not yet out and this will be her first exposure to the ton. I want you girls to be kind to her."

Papa did have a soft spot for the newcomer, being one himself.

"Papa, we would not be anything but kind," Cecilia insisted. "After all, we are in the same position."

"Baron Crenshaw, of course," Beatrice said. They all knew him a bit. His estate was near Birmingham and she had danced with him more than once at the Assemblies.

"A fine gentleman," Papa acknowledged, "even if he has spent most of his time in London until recently. Birmingham society is lucky to have a man of his stature in residence these days."

"The Earl of Belmont," Beatrice continued, though she knew nothing about him but his name.

"Who is not worth a guinea," their father said, consulting a seemingly ever-present mental ledger. "His father invested in hot-air balloons as a means of transporting goods. A disaster in more ways than one. Still, an earl would give you an entrée to society."

Both girls nodded. They knew what was coming next.

"Your dowry and his title would make a nice package, eh? I think that's entirely possible."

"Yes, Papa," Ceci answered as Beatrice tried to control her annoyance at such an absurd suggestion. How many times would she have to tell her father that she was not interested in marrying someone with a title, if she married at all? And Ceci should not be subjected to such a fate, either.

"Not that I would have you marry for a title," he added, giving Beatrice a knowing look. "But I want you both to be secure and comfortable in society, for I will not always be with you."

"Oh, Papa," Ceci said, as if everyone knew Mr. Brent would defy death forever.

Her father briefed them again on the good and bad points of the rest of the men and women on the list. He was such a mix of sensibilities. He loved them, Beatrice knew that without a doubt, but he was so attuned to business that he hated to see an opportunity pass him by.

"And there is a new addition to the list, Lord Jessup Pennistan," Papa said as he shook his head, a confused frown replacing his usual certainty. It was so rare an expression that Beatrice leaned closer so as not to miss a word.

"Lord Jessup has nothing to recommend him except that he is the son and brother of a duke. He has been involved in several tawdry incidents which I will not even discuss with gently bred girls, and his main occupation is gaming."

Never mind the gambling, Beatrice thought, it was the "tawdry incidents" that intrigued her.

"Why, Papa," Beatrice said, recalling where she had

heard Lord Jessup's name before, "he is the one who came with Ellis when you called him home from London, is he not? I never met him but I recall that Ell could talk of nothing but what a fine fellow he was."

"Being called 'fine' by a man not yet twenty-two carries no weight with me. Have nothing to do with him," her father said with his sternest expression, "but I want you both to consider all the other gentlemen carefully. Even Lord Belmont. It would be most excellent if one or, praise God, both of you made a match here. Men who would be willing to invest in the mills and the canals and even consider the new train engines under discussion would be even better."

"No, Papa," Beatrice said firmly, even as Cecilia nodded. "We are not here to be bought and sold like two bolts of cloth. We are here to see how the ton suits us and if we would like a full Season in London."

"That's what the countess said, but I am also sure she agrees with me."

"No, she does not," Beatrice insisted. Cecilia gasped at her boldness.

"Beatrice!" her father snapped. "Now is not the time for one of your battles for independence. You will go into this house party with an open mind and make a good match."

It was such an absurd statement that Beatrice laughed. She could not help it, even though she knew it would infuriate her father.

"Papa," Cecilia interrupted, ever the peacemaker. "Please do not upset Beatrice. You know how splotchy her complexion becomes when she loses her temper. And we both want to look our best."

"Yes, very well," her father said, grabbing at the

peace offering. His daughters made to curtsy but he gave each one a crushing hug instead, whispering to Beatrice, "Find someone and be engaged before this is over."

Beatrice stared at the closing door, gritting her teeth and doing her best to control her temper. She would make sure that Cecilia was distracted and then she was going to see Roger. If he agreed, she would be able to silence her father once and for all. She seethed all the way back to their suite, a plan forming in her head.

When they were in their sitting room with the footman on the other side of the door, Beatrice gathered up the dresses and went through the bedchamber into the dressing room, Cecilia following, just as she'd hoped. "What are you doing, Bitsy? I have not finished deciding what to wear."

Inside the narrow space, their new maid was putting away the rest of their things, but she stopped the moment they came to the door.

"Darwell," Beatrice began, "we want to know what dresses to wear and how to wear them to our best advantage. We need your advice."

"Advice, Miss Brent?" the maid asked, with a hauteur that was somehow reassuring.

"Yes, exactly. Cecilia had hoped to devise a list before we left Birmingham, but the gowns arrived too late. I think it is a blessing in disguise, as your advice is just what she needs."

The woman had such a superior demeanor that Beatrice was half afraid she might refuse.

"If you want to prepare a dressing plan, Miss Cecilia, I would be delighted to help you both."

"Yes, if you please." Cecilia was so meek that even Darwell shook her head.

"You never need to say please to me, miss. I work for you."

Cecilia gave an uncertain nod and followed Darwell into the dressing room.

Perfect, Beatrice thought. She forced herself to walk away slowly despite wanting to run, patted her pocket to be sure she had her spectacles, and was at the door to the bedchamber before she announced, "I'm going downstairs to find out what time dinner will be and where we are to gather beforehand."

"Bitsy, Darwell should do that!" Cecilia called from the dressing room, but Beatrice pretended not to hear.

If Papa was so set on an engagement then she would present him with one this very night.

Beatrice hurried along the hallway and down one flight of stairs to the first floor. The footman directed her to the library and she waited impatiently for him to knock on the door and for Roger to call "Enter."

Storming into the room, Beatrice struggled to calm herself enough to keep from launching into her tirade until the door was closed. "For the love of God, Roger, marrying some dandy because he has money or a title is completely unacceptable." Beatrice waited until Roger Tremaine glanced up from the plans he was fiddling with. "I will not even do it to please Papa."

"Then you are not staying for the house party?" Roger paused in his work to await her answer.

"Of course I will be staying. Cecilia needs my support. However—" She straightened and announced firmly, "I am going to stay as a betrothed woman."

"You're engaged?" Roger put down his pen and stood up.

"I will be by the end of this conversation."

"To whom?" Roger looked around as if there were another eligible gentleman with them.

"To you, dear idiot." She smiled at him.

Roger did not return her smile.

"You can't be serious, Beatrice."

It was not the response she had hoped for. "Yes, yes I am. I cannot imagine anyone more perfect for me than you."

"Nonsense. We are friends. And nothing more. Besides, your father would not hear of it. You know he has his sights set on someone from society."

"Your father is a retired general, Roger. You would be accepted in society if you wished to be."

"But the fact is that neither my father nor I are at all interested in the ton. And I would not consider being part of it even if you and I shared a passion that was not to be denied."

"I have no interest in titles and dandies, either, and I think your work is very important. And it is design. You are not in trade at all, you know."

He waved that distinction aside. "More and more gentlemen, titled and not, are making investments in a number of ventures."

"Yes, so you see, you are actually a far-thinking revolutionary."

"Spare me that, Beatrice. I am pursuing my own interests. No more. There are men among the 'dandies,' as you call them, who are the real revolutionaries. Gentlemen who see that land is not the only avenue to wealth, that manufacturing and mining are the way of the future."

She had just proposed to him and Roger was discussing economics. With defeat certain, Beatrice stood firm on her original thought. "I will not always do what Papa insists."

"So this is actually about defying your father and not some abiding love for me." He came around the table and took her hand. "Beatrice, I love you. Like a sister. And you love me like a brother."

She snatched her hand away, angry even though she knew it was true. "I wish men would stop telling me what I think."

"But it is so obvious, my dear girl."

She wanted to yell at him to stop being so patronizing.

"Beatrice," he spoke softly, "using me as a way to defeat your father is unfair to all of us. It is not one of your better ideas."

"Perhaps not," she admitted. "But when will Papa realize that Cecilia and I have enough sense to manage this on our own?"

"He is your father, which means he will do all he can to make sure you are safe and happy. And for Abel Brent that means managing every detail he can."

"Mama was the only one who could convince him to leave well enough alone." Beatrice bit back the plaintive *I wish she were here.*

"The countess cares deeply for you and Ceci. Maybe you can talk to her about your father."

"I suppose, but would that be disloyal to Papa?"

Roger laughed. "Hardly. The countess knows his failings as well as you do."

"Really?" Roger would not make that up, but how often had the countess and her father been together? "All right. I will talk to her." She touched his arm. "Thank you, Roger."

"You have a fine mind, Beatrice, even if you are given to rashness. I am sure some man will find that charming."

Beatrice laughed and this time punched his arm. "It would drive you insane in a wife, admit it."

"Indeed, yes," he said cheerfully. "But in a friend it is vastly entertaining."

"I hope you have a safe trip to London."

"Thank you, Beatrice." He sat down again.

"What are you working on?" Beatrice pulled her spectacles from the drawstring pouch attached to her sash, and came to stand behind him.

She stared at his drawing, but even wearing her spectacles it made no sense to her. It did have a certain artistic appeal, she thought, and she tried to pick out a section suitable for study as a work of art.

Roger did not answer her. She could see that something had caught his attention and he was no longer even aware of her presence. Papa was lucky to have Roger in his employ. Design meant more to him than anything else. Including an ill-advised marriage proposal from his best friend.

Feeling aggrieved for her whole sex, Beatrice left the room, resisting the urge to slam the door. Men persisted in thinking that they ran the world. At times like this Beatrice suspected they might be right.

Chapter Three

"ARE YOU HIDING from Mrs. Wilson or her daughter, Pennistan?"

Lord Jessup Pennistan took the proffered hand and made his bow to the new Marquis Destry. Impeccably turned out, complete with his signature red scarf, the former Viscount Bendasbrook might have a new title but he was still as friendly as a ten-year-old, and about as short as one, despite his thirty years.

"Neither, but after traveling with Mrs. Wilson, I thought it only fair that Belmont and the other guests have an opportunity to find out where 'everyone that counts'—that was her phrase—plans to spend the summer, the winter, and the Christmas holidays. Plus the chance to learn about the health and well-being of her other children. All are doing as well as can be expected under the circumstances."

"What circumstances?" Destry asked.

"I have no idea. I believe I fell asleep. Why don't you go ask her?"

Destry shook his head, obviously too wise in the ways of the ton and its mamas to fall into that trap. "You know, the countess never mentioned you would be attending."

"I was a last-minute replacement to even the numbers since Mr. Wilson was unable to break away from the demands of the estate."

"So no pending announcements from that quarter?"

"What quarter is that, Des? And have you been at the wine already?"

"You and Miss Wilson." Destry tried to look as though he thought that was possible.

"No, it has been made perfectly clear to me that I am not an eligible *parti*," Jess said firmly. "I could not agree more."

The two looked over at Mrs. Wilson and her daughter. The mother was chattering away while Miss Wilson stood nearby with the polite smile of someone who was used to waiting.

"She is the sort who can talk on without ever taking a breath," Destry observed. With unspoken agreement the two men turned away from the ladies and found a spot out of their line of sight.

"I guess we are by way of relatives now," Destry went on. "Since my aunt is married to your brother and all."

"And the happy ending to that tale was more than welcome," Jess agreed, though he had yet to meet the new duchess. That was not a subject he wanted to pursue. "How lucky for me that the countess invited you to this house party. It's been awhile since we matched wits over cards."

Destry smiled, rising up and down on the balls of his feet. The man found staying still a challenge. "It would be my pleasure, Jess. At least you understand it's all a game and not some personal insult when I relieve you of a few guineas."

"More than a few, last time we met. I hope you enjoyed it. This week luck will sit on my shoulder and it will be your pockets to let."

"Name the place and the game and we will see who has the luck. Perhaps with a few side wagers on what alliances might be formed here."

"It's a party, Destry. I thought we established that I'm not looking for a match. Are you?"

"Not likely."

Now that they had both stated the obvious disclaimers Jess wondered if Destry was as disinterested as he claimed to be. He was set to inherit a dukedom and would someday have to consider an heir.

Before Jess could sound the man out on his true intentions, the countess approached them, all cheerful greetings for Destry. Then it was his turn, and a chill radiated from her as surely as warmth had for the marquis.

"Your ability to enliven any party is well known, Lord Jess. I trust you will do your best to see that everyone is entertained without leaving them paupers."

She gave him a cool smile before moving on to the next group.

There was a long silence before Destry spoke.

"And what did you do to earn that snub? You did say she invited you to stay."

Jess shrugged, unwilling to go into details while the countess was still within hearing. They both watched the countess, who had left her hauteur behind as she spoke with two other gentlemen.

"I'll mind my manners. The only reason I'm here is because Crenshaw is coming and I welcome any chance to best him at play."

"Crenshaw, here? Won't that be a problem? I know you meet socially but this is a small group and for an extended period of time."

"We are quite civil to each other."

"Despite the fact that you cuckolded him and were named in his divorce."

"Ancient history, Destry." Jess's gambler's ability to control his countenance came in handy at times like this.

"Is he courting again?" Destry asked.

"Crenshaw and I are not *that* civil, Des, and you can be sure that is one question it would be wiser for me not to ask."

"Er, yes, I can see where any interest on your part might be misconstrued."

"I want the land back. The land he won from me. That's my only reason for being here."

"The loss still rankles, eh?"

"Yes." Which was all he was going to say on the subject, even to a friend of such long standing.

"Indeed, the estrangement between you and the duke over that wager is a source of some distress for the duchess."

And there it was, no secret after all. "You gossip like an old lady, Destry. The next time you write to the duchess tell her that I am doing my best to rectify the error."

The countess spared him the need to discuss the subject any further by choosing that moment to address the assembled guests. "Welcome, welcome, dear friends. It seems that almost everyone has arrived at the same time." She took a moment to nod and smile at her guests individually before she went on. "It will be a few minutes before we have you settled in your rooms," she continued. "But if you would like to move into the Square Salon, we can begin the introductions, renew acquaintances, and have some food and drink as well."

"Excellent! I am off to say hello to the others," Destry said, with a promise to find Jess in the game room later.

A footman led the guests down the passage. Jess, the Wilsons, the countess, and two others brought up the rear of the party.

"I beg your pardon, my lord." Miss Wilson stood at his elbow and his first thought was to check if her mother was standing beside her. No, she was still on the other side of the hall, but was watching her daughter closely. And him.

"Miss Wilson." Jess bowed to her.

"Can you identify the lady near the Earl of Belmont? Mama does not recognize her." Miss Wilson stood with her back to Belmont and spoke very quietly.

"That is Mrs. Kendrick. She is a widow who is only now back in society. Her husband was an admiral in His Majesty's navy. He survived a life at sea during a war but died in an accident at home upwards of three years ago."

"How unfortunate." Miss Wilson raised a hand to

her mouth, her distress genuine. Jess wasn't sure if that was because she understood the pain of losing someone or because Mrs. Kendrick's presence added a note of sophistication with which she could not compete.

Which was totally unfair to the girl.

She was pretty and amiable, and this was her first house party. The only mark against her was that she was so very young. Seventeen, as her mother had said at least three times on the ride in. He recalled being seventeen and was rather happy that it was so far in his past.

With a quiet "Thank you, my lord," Miss Wilson turned to rejoin her mother. Mrs. Kendrick's dog, which resembled nothing more than an armful of fur, jumped down from her arms, began barking, and raced toward the grand staircase where a young woman hastened down.

The dog and the girl met at the bottom of the steps. She scooped up the animal, welcoming his very sloppy greeting even as Mrs. Kendrick hurried over to reclaim him.

Jess ignored the mixed cries of concern and laughter as he realized that this was the woman from the window. The one who had waved at him. Now he could see she was as lovely up close as she had appeared from a distance, with diminutive but promising curves in all the right places. Her brown hair was alive with gold highlights, her eyes a lively brown, and her mouth eminently kissable. Indeed, he thought, she was the very definition of a "pocket Venus."

Her expressive smile captivated him, both serious and adventurous at the same time.

She held the dog away from her cheeks. The sound of

her laughter faded, but the joy of it still lit her face. What a treasure. Closely guarded, no doubt, as Jess realized that she must be one of the mill owner's daughters for whom the countess was hosting the party.

This little Venus was blessed with a joie de vivre that would eclipse her lack of birthright, and a fortune that would make everything else irrelevant to an impoverished peer. Which he most definitely was not, neither impoverished nor a peer.

And he also had long since lost interest in innocents, he reminded himself. Seducing the unschooled was like making love to someone who spoke a different language. Even flirting brought too great a margin for misunderstanding, tears, and angry fathers. All of which he had grown tired of a lifetime ago.

She laughed again and lowered the dog to the floor. As she did, something dropped from a pocket and the ever-playful dog snatched it up.

"Do catch him, please!" The girl raced after the dog, who was heading straight for Jess. He made a grab for the animal and caught it by the black silk collar it wore. As he lifted the creature and tucked it under his arm, he bowed to the girl.

With the girl at his side, he turned toward Mrs. Kendrick, who was looking as distressed as a mother with a misbehaving child.

"Don't move!" the little Venus ordered.

Before her words registered, Jess continued toward Mrs. Kendrick, and as he completed that first step he felt a crunch beneath his boots.

"My spectacles!" Venus cried.

Irritated by his own clumsiness, Jess handed the dog

over to its owner and bent down to retrieve the mess of metal and glass fragments. He pulled out his handkerchief and wrapped the remains so that she would not be cut by the glass.

"I told you not to move," the girl said with quiet disappointment.

"I do apologize." He gave her another exaggerated bow as he handed her the linen-wrapped glasses. Their hands touched. It was that simple, but he felt a jolt of awareness and knew she did, too, by the way her eyes flew to his.

"Why is it that men simply do not listen?" she asked him, still holding his hand and looking as though she truly wanted an answer to that question and a hundred others. He wished he knew. He wished he could give her all the answers. But that was not his role at this house party.

"Because I was blinded by your smile and deaf to anything but your laughter."

"Really?" She let go of his hand, accepting the pathetic bundle of her broken spectacles, her disappointment at the glib answer apparent. She then curtsied with a flamboyance that matched his. "I imagine you have used that excuse before."

"Only when it is the truth." Innocent, yes, but not naive. That was refreshing. "I offer my apologies for the distraction, but then I do think it is you who should apologize to me. For the distraction, that is, since it's your beauty that caused it." There, he had coaxed a smile out of her finally. "I am most sincerely sorry to have ruined your spectacles."

"It's quite all right, sir. I have another pair."

The little Venus smiled over her shoulder at him as

she turned away, taking a step or two toward their hostess.

That smile, he thought, was the most charming invitation. It was not, should not be, what he wanted at all.

"My lady, my apologies for causing such a commotion," she said to the countess.

"There is nothing to apologize for. This is Mrs. Kendrick, and she tells me she is the one who should have kept better control of her dog."

Jess watched the girl make a pretty curtsy to Nora Kendrick and accept the dog's lick of apology. He was not the only one impressed with her manners. Then she turned to Mrs. Wilson and her daughter.

"I do so beg your pardon and apologize for such an inappropriate greeting."

To Jess's surprise Mrs. Wilson made a dismissive sound and her daughter did the same.

"There is nothing to apologize for, miss. We have dogs ourselves and they are endless mischief."

Lord Belmont and Mrs. Kendrick had gone on down the passage. Mrs. Wilson and her daughter followed.

"Dearest." The countess put her hand on Venus's shoulder and patted sympathetically. "I am so sorry. What will you do without your spectacles?"

"I do have another pair; it is only that they are even more unflattering than these were, if that is possible." She shrugged. "It's not as if anyone will pay attention to me once they meet Cecilia."

Jess was set to escape, had moved toward the passage when the countess called him back. He came to her side and bowed.

"Beatrice, this is Lord Jessup Pennistan. And Jess,

this is Miss Beatrice Brent. She and her twin sister are my very special guests this fortnight."

"Miss Brent." Jess bowed, wondering if she had a brother. The name was familiar, but Jess was sure he'd never met this "very special" guest before.

"I do believe her father knows your brother Lord David and his wife."

Miss Brent stared at him and he was not sure if the intensity of her gaze was because she was missing her spectacles or because she was waiting to gauge his reaction to her paternity.

"You are Lord Jessup Pennistan?" Miss Brent asked as though she was hard of hearing as well as short-sighted.

"Indeed, yes, since birth," he said glibly, bowing slightly.

"You know my brother, Ellis Brent," she stated, and then turned to the countess. "He brought Ellis home after he lost his allowance and more in London while gambling and," she paused before adding, "and engaging in other activities."

His pocket Venus was Ellis Brent's sister? God help him. His time with Ellis had made him consider giving up the gamer's life altogether. He had not only lost the land to Crenshaw at that time, but had been down to his last guinea.

Ellis had not fared any better. Worse, in fact. He'd ended up with no money and in debt to a particularly wicked group of moneylenders.

Jess had hoped that taking him home would help Ellis's chances of surviving a brutal retribution.

"I never heard from your brother again, Miss Brent. I trust he is well?" No longer gaming at least.

"Yes, he is. He seems to have learned his lesson and is now settled, married, and living in Scotland."

"I am happy to hear it." *Better him than me*, Jess thought. *Married and living in Scotland in less than a year.* Marriage was bad enough but living in Scotland sounded like hell.

The countess was anxious for him to be gone, if the stone-cold expression in her eyes was any indication. Then why had she introduced them? He aimed his smile at his hostess and bowed.

"If you will excuse me, my lady and Miss Brent, I will join the other guests and look forward to seeing you later."

Chapter Four

"I KNOW FATHER disapproves of Lord Jess," Beatrice said to the countess after she was sure Lord Jess was out of hearing. "But don't you think Lord Jessup did entirely right in insisting that Ellis return home before he lost more than money? He even escorted him."

"Yes, my dear, I am sure that is how it appears to you," the countess said. "However, Lord Jess was equally responsible for introducing Ellis to all manner of debauchery."

"My lady godmother, we both know that Ellis had discovered those sins well before he left Birmingham."

"Do not champion Jess, Beatrice. He can handle his own defense," the countess said.

"He was such a gentleman just now," Beatrice insisted. "Yet Papa says we are to have nothing to do with him. But you invited him, so he must be socially acceptable. And you did make a point of introducing him to me." It made no sense at all. If this was what ton life would be like she was not sure she could manage its peculiarities.

"I allowed him to attend so that you could learn a lesson. An important one. You will meet any number of men like him when you go to London. Full of charm, but little else. Socially acceptable, but not at all desirable."

"Why not?" she persisted, willing to risk a snub for an honest answer.

"Because your papa and I say so."

Which was no answer at all. This was a pointless conversation. "I wish Mama were here. She would never keep me in the dark like this." Beatrice was appalled at the hint of tears in her voice.

"Beatrice, sweetheart." The countess paused. "I know you still miss her and no one can take her place. But in this case even she would insist that ignoring Lord Jess is the wisest course of action."

"Then why is he here?" Beatrice asked again, this time with a vehemence that demanded an answer.

The countess laughed. "You are the most stubborn chit. I will not say any more. Go dress for dinner while I settle the new arrivals into their rooms. And promise me you will avoid Lord Jess Pennistan."

Miss Beatrice Brent stood on tiptoe and kissed her godmother's cheek. "If it will make you happy. I promise to ignore him as best as I can at such a small house party."

She dashed up the steps. She was inexperienced and a little too curious but not stupid. She rubbed her hand against her skirt, remembering the amazing way his touch had made her feel, as though she were being awakened from a sleep with the promise of something wonderful. But once she had released his hand, her normal sensibilities had returned. It was that easy.

THE COUNTESS CORNERED Jess before he could join the other guests in the salon.

"Jessup," she began in the most dampening tone. "I am having serious second thoughts about allowing you to stay. Did I not make it perfectly clear that this house party is being held to introduce my goddaughters to respected and influential members of the ton?" She paused and gave him a withering look. "You are neither respected nor influential."

"Yes, my lady." Jess absorbed the snub, the downright insult, with a mental shrug. The countess was only telling the truth. "And as I told you, the only reason I am here is to win my land back from Crenshaw. This gathering seems an ideal opportunity."

"It had best be that simple," the countess replied, "because I do not like being used."

"I am being honest with you." Jess tried to keep the desperation from his voice. "It *is* that simple. If you are not willing to allow me to stay, then it will be after Easter in London before I have another opportunity to best him, and by then he will have added it to his entail or made the land otherwise impossible to win back."

The countess pursed her lips, which did not become her. Small lines around her mouth hinted at her age, something he knew she never told anyone. Forty or fifty or somewhere in between, he guessed.

"I did not ask before, but now I'm wondering why this land is so important to you."

Honesty was all that would serve. "My mother left

me the land and made me promise never to sell it. I was caught up in a game where one could wager anything but money. It seemed amusing at the time."

"Until you lost it."

"And Crenshaw would not accept my word that I would pay him the cash."

The countess nodded as though she had heard of such games. "I assume there was a lady involved."

"Yes, a woman. Not a lady."

The countess shook her head. "So you were coveting yet another woman of Crenshaw's. At least this one was not married to him, was she?"

"No, my lady." Jess tamped down the spurt of anger, sorely tempted to tell the countess the truth of what had happened.

"One would think that experience would have taught you that those efforts never end well, at least not for you."

"Yes." He kept his true opinion to himself. He hated everything that Crenshaw represented, and removing Sadie from his influence had given Jess some satisfaction. A lot of satisfaction.

"So, young man, this visit is not about winning the hand of a wealthy heiress?"

"No, it is most definitely not, my lady. God spare me that complication. I prefer to stay unmarried."

She moved away from him. "Then what was that interlude I just witnessed?"

Jess smiled. "Miss Brent is an artless, charming little bit of a thing. But now that I have the measure of her I will be on my guard."

The countess laughed. "Artless and charming, but with a fine brain that is endlessly curious. Be careful."

"Yes, my lady." It seemed a wiser answer than what he was really thinking. Was his pocket Venus going to try to seduce him? He was still doing his best to forget the surge of lust that had swept through him at the mere touch of her hand.

He knew better than to think that lust was something either one of them could control. He would regard it as the warning it was and keep his distance.

The countess sighed heavily. "All right, you are welcome to stay. You heartless rogue," she added with a smile that was both resignation and anticipation.

"Thank you, my lady." He nodded his appreciation and bowed soberly.

"However did you convince Jane Wilson to allow you to accompany her?" the countess asked.

Jess smiled and the countess held up her hand.

"Say no more. That smile has been the undoing of more women than I can name."

He took her hand and bowed over it. "I will be on my best behavior. The land is all I wish to claim."

"Yes, well, tell your valet to unpack and dress you for dinner. Do not be late!"

BEATRICE HURRIED ALONG the passage, trying to puzzle out how she could give the appearance of ignoring Lord Jess while still finding out all she wanted to know about him.

What was the scandal no one would talk about? How much did it have to do with Ell's behavior while in London? And what exactly did "debauchery" entail? Was it something worse than going to a brothel? For the love of God, that was quite bad enough.

Pausing outside the door to her suite, Beatrice calmed herself. She knew that if Ceci saw her, she would instantly guess that something had roused her twin's curiosity and would plague her with questions. And it was nothing, really.

When she pushed through the door she found Ceci seated at the dressing table, while Darwell tried several different hairstyles on her.

"Beatrice, you will never guess what the countess has given us." Cecilia did not move her head so much as an inch, but her excitement was obvious.

"Then you had better tell me." Beatrice smiled at her sister's reflection in the mirror and then moved out of sight, settling into a nearby chair. Cecilia could not see her, but Darwell stopped her work for a moment as if she sensed something was afoot.

"When the countess was in London . . ." Cecilia paused and started again. "She ordered a signature fragrance for each of us. Darwell just gave me mine. It's perfect. A mix of floral, mostly. Come test it. Darwell has yours in the dressing room and will not let me sample it before you do."

The countess is a genius, Beatrice thought, as she went toward the dressing room. It was the kind of gift that would give Cecilia a boost of confidence when it was most needed.

"Come smell mine first, Bitsy," Cecilia insisted.

"I already can. It's in the air and it is a wonderful scent. It reminds me of you in the garden, moving among the flowers, stirring their scent so it fills the air. I do wish I could paint. It would make an exquisite picture." *It announces there is more to you than beauty*, Beatrice thought.

Cecilia read her expression. *Thank you, dearest,* she answered in the wordless way they had communicated since earliest childhood. Then she laughed with delight.

In the dressing room, on the tall, narrow chest that held their stays and stockings, Beatrice found an amethyst-colored bottle. Her name was written on it with more curves and swoops than she had ever seen.

Doing her best to still her expectations, Beatrice pulled out the delicate glass stopper and sniffed at the fragrance. There was a floral element here, too, but a spicy jasmine and cinnamon scent dominated. It was beautiful but much too sophisticated for her.

She took the bottle into the bedchamber and let Cecilia smell it. "Why, Bitsy, it is exactly right."

"Really? Do you think so? You know I count on you to always be honest with me."

"It's perfect. Truly."

"Ladies." Darwell interrupted them with the one word. "We are to keep country hours, so you will not have much time to rest. Come here, Miss Beatrice. Let me undo your buttons and stays so you can put on a dressing gown."

Darwell put down the pins and comb, spun Beatrice around, and made short work of the task. Beatrice went into the dressing room and sat down on the chaise. The scent, her scent, filled the little room. She could only wish she was as intriguing as the fragrance hinted.

Pulling off her chemise, Beatrice reached for the fresh one that Darwell had set out for her.

The chemise was still in her hand when Darwell came through the door. "Do you like the dress, Miss Brent?" she asked in a loud voice and then added sotto voce, "What are you up to, miss? You have the devil in your eyes."

"Not the devil, surely." Beatrice did not have to pretend insult. "I am only curious about the guests we will be meeting this evening."

"I have worked as a lady's maid for longer than you have been alive, and I will go immediately to your father if you do anything to upset your sister or behave in a way that would endanger her Season."

"I never would, Darwell. Never." She was angry now, and offended by Darwell's harsh criticism.

"Very well, miss. Perhaps I have overreacted."

Her contrition lasted a mere second. "Sit and let me do your hair." The brusque Darwell was back. "What do you think of the dress I put out for you?"

"It's quite nice, thank you," Beatrice said dutifully, as though the maid had a direct link to the countess *and* her seamstress.

"Flounces would not suit you at all."

"Really?" How had the woman guessed that she wanted flounces?

"No, miss. You do not have the height for them. The simple braid trim is all you need. You may be short, miss, but you are beautifully proportioned."

"Thank you," she said, surprised at the compliment. She wondered if Lord Jess had noticed her proportions.

Darwell left but came back momentarily with a wet cloth.

"Lie down on this chaise and put this compress on your face, not just your eyes, and try to rest. Forget all about the intrigues here."

Beatrice nodded and lay back on the chaise, as directed, touched by Darwell's remorse. The cloth was

dampened with more than water. It smelled of laven-
der and perhaps chamomile and was almost as comforting as Mama's hand on her brow. She did doze but
she had a strange dream. In it, Artemis walked through
a hallway, her nose buried in a book. She was surrounded by amazing Greek statues, one of a man and
the rest of women. The man's face echoed Lord Jess's
and all of the women's marble faces were turned
toward him, some with longing expressions and others
with satisfied ones. Artemis remained, engrossed in
her book until the male statue stopped her progress.
With an elaborate bow he spoke, "Which group do
you wish to join? It is your choice, Artemis."

Before she could decide, Beatrice woke up. She knew
the answer, could feel it in her heart and lower, but
was relieved that no one else could guess. She liked the
idea that she was Artemis in the dream, for the goddess was strong-willed and powerful even though she
had never married.

An hour and a half later Darwell pronounced them
"dressed to perfection." Hair done up, modest jewelry
donned, cheeks pinched until they were pink, they
were ready to make their first bow among the ton.
"You are glowing, Beatrice," her sister gushed. "Isn't
this exciting?" She paused, then added, "And terrify-
ing at the same time."

"Concentrate on the idea that this is but practice for
the Season with a group of the countess's friends. How
can they be anything but lovely?"

The countess herself came to collect them, fussing
over their gowns and general appearance amid their
thanks for the perfumes.

While the countess adjusted one of the flowers in

Ceci's hair, Darwell whispered, "Hold your head up, Miss Beatrice, and watch out for your sister. That will keep you out of mischief."

Beatrice took the chivvying with a firm nod and descended the steps to join the party for the second time that day.

Chapter Five

JESS DID NOT intend to be the last to join the party, but his valet had dawdled and insisted on shaving him, and then ruined three lengths of linen tying his cravat.

"Who the hell are you trying to impress, Callan? None of the gentlemen here need a new valet."

"Yes, my lord." Those were his three favorite words. Followed by "Thank you, my lord" on the rare occasions when he was paid on time.

"Begone. You will be late to the servants' table."

"Yes, my lord," Callan said, ignoring the order and giving a final brush to the dark blue coat that was Jess's favorite.

With Callan's directions he found the Long Porch easily enough, following the sound of laughter as it echoed down the corridor.

He had no idea whether the countess favored a structured sort of house party or if they would be left to find their own entertainment. Destry and Belmont could be counted on for a challenging game of cards even if Belmont did prefer more modest stakes than he did.

Were any of the ladies so inclined? The stakes would escalate when Crenshaw arrived, but for now gaming would be as cordial as the guests who were present, which meant altogether delightful.

The others were outside on the terrace. The Long Porch was not a porch at all, but a room with a wall of glass doors that opened onto a generous terrace. The stone terrace overlooked a carefully natural garden, clearly the work of Repton or one of his more talented students.

Jess had stopped at the drinks table to garner a glass of sherry when a woman emerged from the door leading to the terrace. It was Venus, or perhaps her twin.

The scent she brought into the room hinted at secrets and magic and made him want to draw her closer. This sister was even more tempting than the other. He took a step back.

"You and your sister are amazingly alike, Miss Brent."

"Oh!" she said, raising a hand to her throat, apparently surprised by his presence. When she stepped fully into the room and saw who had spoken, her good humor returned.

"I assure you, my lord, my sister is far more beautiful than I am. As a matter of fact everything about her is beautiful."

"I beg your pardon, Miss Brent, but when I met her this afternoon, the only difference I noted is that she wears spectacles."

"I don't understand. Who are you talking about?"

She came up to him, a confused smile replacing the flirtatious one.

"Your twin, I met your twin earlier today."

"You met me, my lord." She took yet another step, as though twelve more inches would make that clear, and then added, "Though she is my twin, my sister does not look anything like me."

"Were you able to find your extra pair of spectacles?" Her scent enveloped him, her innocent eyes urging him on. Attraction replaced caution.

"Yes, but I only need spectacles when I am going to do close work or read."

"Ah, I see. And is close work or reading important to you?"

"Both are, my lord." She leaned closer and whispered, "There is a rumor about that I am a bluestocking."

A rumor she did not deny or seem to find offensive.

"Then remind me not to play any games with you." It was just as well that he had never been attracted to overeducated women. And yet he still enjoyed standing close to her.

"You already are playing games, my lord," she said with a directness that should not have surprised him.

He took a deliberate step back, but her scent lingered between them. "You see, that is why I find educated women so unappealing. They have no sense of humor." He winced at the snub even though it was deliberate.

Beatrice Brent looked as though he had slapped her and he felt such regret. Surely he could have nudged her away with something less hurtful.

"I have a friend, a gentleman friend, who maintains

that educating women would double the development of new ideas and inventions."

"Miss Brent, my greatest fear is that a woman will discover exactly how uneducated most gentlemen are."

"Do you number yourself among them, my lord?"

"Yes, and rather proud of it."

She looked disappointed.

"You see, I am able to live happily in my ignorance and enjoy the pleasures of life without a worry for troublesome ideas and debates." That was better, he thought, and drank his sherry in one gulp. "While those who think and study develop wrinkles and worrisome tics and are still not able to change what is wrong with the world."

"You do not really mean that, do you?" Her eyes were wide with dismay.

He poured himself another tot of sherry, then faced her once again. "Yes, I do. The world is what it is, and the sooner we accept our place in it the happier we will be. These endless efforts to improve ourselves, to care for the poor, and to teach everyone their letters are misguided attempts to prove that we are not innately selfish at best and little better than animals at worst."

Beatrice blinked and slowly shook her head. "I am so sorry for you, Lord Jessup. Your life must be singularly empty. Do you have any friends?"

He slapped his glass down and was relieved when it did not break. "You were not listening. Another failure of educated women. I am doing exactly what I want to do and am exactly where I want to be. Can you say the same, Miss Brent?"

She had no answer for him. Not in words at least,

but he had hit a responsive chord. He could read it in the way she lowered her eyes from his.

Jess was sorry if he had damaged her sensibilities but he was not going to apologize. This was exactly one of the pitfalls of meaningful conversation. There was too much potential for offense. In this case that was just what he had intended.

The silence stretched between them, and in it was a more honest answer to his question than anything she could have said. He resisted the urge to soothe and comfort, to placate with winning words and honeyed charm. What he really wanted to do was draw her into his arms and show her what pleasure they could find if she would just stop thinking so hard. Of course doing that would completely upend this painful effort to put some distance between them.

The door from the corridor opened and someone came into the room. Before Jess could turn to see who it was, Miss Brent called out. "Lord Crenshaw! How lovely to see you." She hurried across the room and curtsied to the gentleman. His equally happy welcome indicated that they were of some long-standing acquaintance.

Crenshaw took her hand and bowed over it, lingering a moment longer than necessary.

She withdrew her hand but still retained a welcoming smile equal to any she had shared with him. The minx. So she was that friendly with everyone.

"Do you know Lord Jessup Pennistan?" Miss Brent asked with guileless pleasure, apparently unaware of exactly how well the two knew each other.

"Yes, I do."

The man's curt answer drew a mystified glance from Miss Brent, her gaze shifting from him to Jess.

"Pennistan" was the extent of Crenshaw's greeting.

Jess answered with a nod of his own and silence.

Miss Brent's brow wrinkled with curiosity, but she chose to relieve the tension by taking Lord Crenshaw's arm. "We must announce you to the countess, my lord. And Cecilia will be so pleased to see you."

"I bask in your joy alone, Miss Brent."

Little Venus blushed at the effusive compliment and Jess wondered if Crenshaw was courting her. An educated woman was not his usual flirtation, but then Miss Brent's fortune might make him willing to overlook her bookishness.

That could not be permitted.

Jess watched the two of them go out to the terrace and fortified himself with another tot of sherry, doing his best to convince himself that Venus did not need to be rescued. And if she did, there was time to consider how best to save her from the bastard.

BEATRICE WATCHED AS the countess welcomed Lord Crenshaw. After a brief conversation she excused herself and turned to her other guests. Crenshaw scanned the small group and moved purposefully back to Beatrice's side.

Before he could speak, the countess clapped her hands and waited for everyone's attention. Only those closest to her heard. Beatrice saw Cecilia jump at the sound and knew her sister's nerves were winning. Even as she tried to think of a way to excuse herself from Lord Crenshaw she felt someone tap her arm.

"Excuse me, Miss Brent. Could I stand with you? My mother is ill this evening and I am not at all comfortable on my own."

"Of course." Beatrice wound her arm through Miss Wilson's, wondering why this girl thought she herself was any more comfortable. She and Cecilia might be two years older than Miss Wilson but they were not at all used to society.

"Miss Wilson, do you know Baron Lord Crenshaw?" She stepped back so that she stood between the two but not in front of them. She heard the countess try for everyone's attention one more time and winced at the poor timing of her introduction. Neither Miss Wilson nor Lord Crenshaw seemed to be aware of the countess's efforts.

"Lord Crenshaw," Miss Wilson murmured with a curtsy.

"Lord Crenshaw, this is Miss Wilson," Beatrice went on.

Crenshaw bowed to her. "I know your parents and your older sister. How lovely to have the second of the Wilson trio out in society."

"There are actually four of us, my lord. But Betty is still in the nursery."

"My apologies for neglecting your sister." He bowed again and Beatrice thought his manners a little too precise. In this gathering Lord Crenshaw was not as informal as he was at the Assemblies. Beatrice considered what that might mean. Did he view her differently than he did Miss Wilson?

The sound of breaking glass drew all their attention.

"Neither conventional nor economical but it worked, did it not?" the countess called out in the silence that followed. "I am delighted that you are all such enthusiastic conversationalists and trust that by now everyone knows everyone else."

The company looked around, nodding and smiling. Beatrice had met everyone and had been disconcerted to see that her father had stayed on with the group for the time being. But not Roger. No, Papa had probably sent him on to London. How disappointing.

"Lord Crenshaw has joined us just in time for dinner," the countess continued.

Everyone turned to him, bowing and curtsying, except Lord Jessup, who stood near the terrace doors. It confirmed in her mind that there was some sort of bad blood between them.

Who would know? Whom could she ask? It was more than curiosity, she decided. She and Cecilia needed to be armed with all the information possible as they made their way through the unknown that was the ton.

She scanned the company and decided to wait until she found out who was most inclined to gossip, just a little. Suddenly it occurred to her: Darwell, their maid. She had lived among the ton for years, her whole life. Beatrice imagined that as a maid there was probably not much she didn't know about the principal players at the party. About Lord Jessup, the Earl of Belmont, Baron Crenshaw, and Marquis Destry. *Perfect,* she thought.

"We are also joined this evening by Mr. Abel Brent, who will be leaving soon for London and will return later in the week. His daughters, Miss Beatrice Brent and her sister Miss Cecilia, are my honored guests and as welcome as my own children would be if my son and daughter-in-law were not abroad on their wedding trip."

Several in the group applauded lightly and the countess smiled at their good wishes.

"After dinner we will gather in the Gold Salon and I will tell you what I have planned for the week, and you can discuss what entertainments you can contrive for yourselves and each other."

Beatrice heard someone laugh a little and saw Marquis Destry press his lips together.

The countess gave him a look of reproof, undermined by the amusement in her eyes. "In a few minutes dinner will be announced. I would like to invite the Marquis Destry to escort me, and the rest of you may follow as informally as you wish."

JESS WATCHED THE Brent sisters, as Destry elaborated on how they could "contrive to amuse" themselves. Lewd comments to which Jess refused to respond with anything more than a laugh. He was already the countess's least favorite guest. No reason to risk being sent home like a misbehaving schoolboy.

"The Brent sisters are intriguing," he said at last.

Destry nodded, distracted from his bawdy game. "The taller one, Miss Cecilia, is one of the loveliest women I have ever seen."

"Blond hair, blue eyes." Jess made the inventory as though he had not noticed her before. "Quite pretty."

"Pennistan, that's like saying a Rembrandt is quite nice. She is a diamond and will take society by storm."

Destry was right. Cecilia's blond hair was thick and beautifully coiffed, her skin that lovely peaches-and-

cream shade that looked sun-kissed even on the raini-
est of days. Her very blue eyes were friendly enough
and her mouth was a pink bow of perfection.

"Maybe," Jess half agreed. "But look how uncomfortable she is. You can see the tension in her body, the
way she stands so still as though she's holding a pose.
She's not easy here. She looks like she is afraid someone will look beyond her beauty and find her wanting."

"Then credit her with brains enough to realize that
there is more to a woman than beauty."

"Defending her, are you?" Yes, Jess could see the
little man was quite taken with the angel of perfection,
not just by his words but by the way he kept glancing
around to see where she was or who she was talking to.

It was more than his usual restlessness. This was focused.

Marquis Destry and Miss Brent. What an odd couple they would make.

"Miss Beatrice is lovely in her own way," Jess observed. "She has a quiet beauty that one does not notice at first. I expect her looks will only improve as she
ages."

Destry nodded, still all but dancing on the balls of
his feet. "They each have much to admire."

"You can't marry both of them, Des," Jess said, annoyed. A besotted Destry could grow to be a bore.

"Don't want to marry both," Destry answered shortly.
"Just proving I am not blinded by Miss Cecilia's
beauty. Most likely they are different in more ways
than their size."

Jess watched Destry watch Miss Brent, the beauty,

and turn away the moment she glanced in his direction.

"I would wager a quid that they're as different as it is possible to be," Jess mused.

"A bet I will not take for a number of reasons, not the last of which is that I can guess what method you would use to win." Destry's gaze drifted to the Brent sisters again, even though he could only see their backs.

The man was already becoming predictable.

"You don't think she will give me the time of day, do you, Jess?"

"I have no idea, Des; attraction is strange and indefinable. Who would have thought that my oh-so-proper duke brother would marry a woman who had spent her life among musicians in Italy, even if she was the disinherited daughter of a duke?" Belatedly he remembered that the new duchess was Destry's aunt.

"When you see them together you know it is a love match."

"I have no doubt of it," Jess said, relieved that Destry was not offended, even if the man was beginning to see the whole world through the prism of the lovesick. He had barely even met the woman. "Or that my brother David would marry such a lively ingénue as Mia Castellano."

"She is that. Did you know we were engaged for a time?"

"You and Mia Castellano?"

"Certainly not me and Lord David."

"Good God." Jess felt more shocked than mortified at his second gaffe. "I'm sorry if mentioning her brings painful memories."

"Not at all. She is a delightful woman," Destry said

with apparent goodwill. "We both agree now that we are too much alike for a marriage to have worked with anything less than a shouting match on a daily basis. As a matter of fact, the disagreements had begun even before our engagement ended."

"She and David do seem to thrive on their frequent arguments."

"As you said, there is no accounting for what will make a marriage work."

Which was not what he had said at all, but before he could correct Destry the butler announced dinner. Thank God. They were nattering on like a couple of old ladies observing the dance floor.

As he watched, Mr. Brent approached his daughters. Cecilia look relieved, Miss Beatrice a trifle vexed. Jess smiled to himself. Would she be as vexed if he had offered her his arm?

Chapter Six

AS THE COUNTESS took Marquis Destry's arm, Mr.
Brent offered an arm to each of his daughters. Beatrice
accepted, but felt compelled to whisper, "Papa, escorting us totally defeats the purpose of finding out who is
interested in knowing Cecilia better. And I was looking forward to spending more time with Baron Crenshaw."

He patted her hand. "There will be plenty of time,
daughter. This way the gentlemen know that I will be
alert to their behavior, even Crenshaw despite our
recent association. The two of you are precious to me."

Cecilia breathed "Oh, Papa" at this sweet declaration, and Beatrice herself was touched. This would be
the first time that he had left them alone among strang-
ers. It only now occurred to her that it might be difficult for him. She leaned her head on his arm and he
gave her hand a little squeeze.

To her surprise, instead of turning into the house,

and the dining room that could easily seat fifty, the countess led them through the garden and into a copse of trees that hid a summerhouse from view of the main residence.

This summerhouse was one large room decorated like a fairy bower. Made almost entirely of windows and doors, most of them left open to the gentle summer air, the supports between the windows looked like gnarled trees that bloomed into faux leaves painted on the ceiling. The room itself was lit with dozens of candles set in masses of moss with small vases of summer flowers scattered about, on the ledges of the windows and the mantel of a green, marble-fronted fireplace now filled with potted ferns. Beatrice thought it both fanciful and seductive.

The countess spoke in a loud voice until she had the attention of all her guests. "In the last century the third earl constructed a banqueting platform in one of the old lime trees. It actually had a staircase so one could easily reach the space and share a meal with the birds."

There were gasps and sounds of amazement from her guests.

"Some time ago, a storm rendered it unsafe for more than one or two at a time, but the last earl and I had this room built to recreate the feeling of dining in nature."

A table that could comfortably seat their party of ten was elegantly laid. A large branch of some flowering tree—which Beatrice was sure that Cecilia could name—ran the length of the table as the centerpiece. Very unconventional but in keeping with the theme. Small figurines, the tiniest of boys and girls—made from some type of clay, Beatrice supposed—were placed in various poses along the branch.

Every one of the countess's guests, even Beatrice's pragmatic father, expressed delight at the charmed setting, though Beatrice wondered if she was the only one who did not see how the food could arrive warm. They were a significant distance from the house and, perforce, the kitchen.

"How long before one of the gentlemen fiddles with those innocent-looking figures and puts them in a not-so-innocent pose?" Beatrice whispered to her sister as they waited to be seated.

Cecilia pressed her lips together for a moment. "Do be quiet, Beatrice." Cecilia turned to their father. "Papa, wasn't it clever of the countess to contrive this gem and also to give us all a topic of conversation?"

"Yes, it was," Beatrice answered for him. "I was just asking Cecilia"—Ceci stepped on her foot, and despite the flash of pain, Beatrice ignored the warning and kept on talking—"what she thought the table fairies were made of. Do you think spun sugar or clay?"

"It hardly matters, does it?" Papa looked impressed. "The countess is an amazingly talented woman, a veritable magician, is she not? Excuse me, girls. I want to tell her how lovely this is." He did not wait for an answer but made his way to the countess's side.

Cecilia and Beatrice looked at each other in some confusion. Papa so rarely was effusive in his praise. "Of course, he is so very grateful to the countess for her kindness to us," Ceci offered.

"That's one explanation" was as close to agreement as Beatrice would allow.

The table seating was not as random as the progress

to the summerhouse had been. The countess had Lord Destry to her right, but instead of the Earl of Belmont on her left, as was proper etiquette, she had given that seat to Mr. Brent.

Lord Belmont sat at the foot of the table with Miss Wilson on his left, taking the place of honor her mother would have been given if she had not been ill. That change led to Beatrice's being seated next to Lord Jess. Beatrice was delighted with this seating arrangement before recalling that he had snubbed her not twenty minutes ago.

Mrs. Kendrick was seated on the other side of Lord Jess. Across from her and next to Miss Wilson were Lord Crenshaw and then Cecilia, which put her twin between Lord Crenshaw and the marquis, Lord Destry.

Beatrice watched her sister. The marquis was an unknown, but Lord Crenshaw was an acquaintance of a year's standing. Beatrice was sure Cecilia was nervous but equally certain that her sister was well prepared for this modest challenge.

Before she could turn to the Earl of Belmont, Lord Jess bent to her. "Miss Brent, do you see that one of the little people on the branch is wearing spectacles?"

Beatrice looked in the direction he indicated and saw that he was not teasing. Next to the miniature in spectacles was another little person holding a dog and talking to a gentleman wearing a red kerchief.

"Why, she has each one of us represented. I wonder where Ceci and Papa are?" She looked up and down the table as the other members of the party made the same delighted discovery.

"After dinner, the fairies will be moved to the mantel

in the Square Salon, where we will meet later so that you can admire them. Please feel free to take your fairy as a favor and a reminder of this party." The countess's face showed how much pleasure she took in this scheme.

Lord Jess leaned over and touched the figure with the spectacles. "I imagine some of us might like to have someone else's fairy as a token."

Beatrice shook her head and then said exactly what she was thinking. "Not an hour ago you all but gave me the cut direct and now you seek to charm. Why?"

"I saw how much Lord Crenshaw values you and I decided that I should not abandon a chance to know you better."

What did that mean? Beatrice wondered. She was sure the two had no use for each other. Her first thought was that she did not wish to be a bone they fought over like two dogs, then almost as quickly she decided it might be interesting to be in the middle. It would certainly be good preparation for London.

"My answer is as honest as your question," Lord Jess insisted.

"You will excuse me if I will now wonder which Lord Jessup Pennistan I am seated next to. The one who charms or the one who challenges."

He laughed at her asperity, which made her blush. Did he think she was flirting? Or did he just never take anything seriously?

She gave him her back and turned her attention to the earl. "Your fairy is easy to identify. That shock of white hair is as unique as it is distinguished. But why is his chin in his hand in such a contemplative pose?"

The earl laughed quietly. "The countess is a clever

woman. But I do wonder who fashioned these. A doll maker, perhaps?"

"We could ask her after dinner."

"Where's the fun in that, Miss Brent? I should rather investigate and work it out ourselves, then ask the countess if we are right."

That was a little odd, Beatrice thought, and moved to change the subject. "Tell me, my lord, what are your interests beyond Parliament and your estates?"

"Can you not guess? I love a puzzle, a riddle, even deciphering codes. If there is a mystery to be solved, I'm the one for the job."

"So your figure is mulling over some conundrum as you sit on the branch." It explained his inclination to seek out the answer rather than ask. He was not like any gentleman she had ever met, but then she had never met an earl before. He was, most likely, unique among his peers as well. What fun it would be to come to know him better.

"I do believe the Belmont on the branch has solved a puzzle and is ready for a new one."

"Truly? Here is a conundrum for you." Beatrice began to explain what she called "the mystery of the false Rembrandts."

The earl looked sincerely interested and Beatrice did not even think of Lord Jess for the next little while.

CECILIA COULD NOT believe she was seated next to Marquis Destry. At least Lord Crenshaw was known to her, but the rule of table etiquette meant she would have to speak with both of them for an equal amount of time.

She would be so much more comfortable where Mrs. Kendrick was sitting, between her father and Lord Jessup Pennistan. Lord Jess might be unacceptable to her father but he had been kind when she met him earlier in the evening and not nearly as intimidating as a man who was heir to a dukedom.

Cecilia held her hands tightly in her lap and waited for the footman to serve the first course. Her fairy looked back at her, seated on an elegant chair surrounded by flowers but otherwise unremarkable.

Was she the only one who had no distinguishing characteristic? How awful. She examined the miniatures more closely. The baron's figure was coatless with his fists raised, ready to fight anyone who might round the branch, and Lord Destry wore his signature red kerchief.

"The countess has the right of it with you, Miss Brent." Lord Crenshaw nodded toward the figure.

"Do you think so?" She did not mean to sound coy but was curious about what his interpretation might be.

"But of course. You are seated on a throne, queen of all you survey."

"Oh, my goodness. That cannot be." She looked from the baron to the marquis, making an effort to include him in her conversation with Lord Crenshaw. "Surely our hostess is queen of this realm."

"I imagine you could interpret Miss Brent's figure in a number of ways," Lord Destry said. "It could be—"

"There is no doubt of your representation, Destry," Lord Crenshaw interrupted. "Your figure is the smallest on the table. We might have overlooked it were it not for the red scarf you use to call attention to yourself."

Lord Destry ignored the comment and continued to

speak. "It could be that a woman of Miss Brent's obvious refinement needs no more entertainment than to sit and observe the world pass by. Look, even the flowers gather around her."

"I do love the garden and spend as much time there as I can. Perhaps that is the symbolism the countess intended."

"The flowers are only a frame for your beauty," Lord Crenshaw added.

"I think the flowers rest at your feet in homage," said the marquis.

Was this a contest to see which one of them could embarrass her the most? "One thing I observe," Cecilia tried, desperate to turn the conversation away from her avatar, "is that we will be served in the Russian style this evening."

"Ah, yes," Lord Crenshaw said, "the centerpiece would hardly allow for the placement of the French service."

"I prefer the Russian," Destry added. "The food is usually warm and you have more to choose from than the few dishes arranged in front of you in the French service."

"Yes," Cecilia agreed, "but with the Russian service I am always tempted by every dish offered and end up with enough food for a glutton."

"Miss Brent," Lord Destry began, "I suspect that there is not an unkind bone in your body if you are even afraid of offending the food that is offered you."

At a word from the countess the marquis turned to her, leaving Cecilia to wonder if what he'd said was a snub or a compliment. She blushed. She might wish it was a compliment but could not doubt it was a snub.

Chapter Seven

"So you believe that the false Rembrandts are not a deliberate fraud, but rather artists of Rembrandt's school who were attempting to emulate him?"

"Yes, exactly, Lord Belmont." Miss Brent sat back in her seat, smiling at his quick grasp of her idea.

"But how can you tell the true old masters from the fakes?" Jess asked before he recalled that he was not part of the conversation, just an eavesdropper. She had drawn him in with her scent, the intensity in her voice, the way her enthusiasm radiated from her body. He felt like a hapless player ensnared by a game of luck.

Belmont did no more than raise his eyebrows at the interruption. Beatrice Brent did not seem to take offense, but that may have been because she was so enthusiastic about art.

"As I explained to Lord Belmont, my lord, there is a certain style that only Rembrandt maintains. He has a way of seeing the world that is only his and cannot be duplicated." She picked up her fork, then put it down again without sampling the beef on her plate.

"But is that not only a matter of opinion?" Lord Jess went on. "There is a Rembrandt at Pennford Castle and I wonder if it would meet your criteria."

"It is not my criteria only, my lord. This has been a discussion among true experts, not just students of the subject like me."

"But could a supposed expert not tell the owner it is a forgery and then buy it at a reduced price and resell it as an original?"

"You suppose everyone has as devious an imagination as you do, Jess." Belmont signaled for more wine even as the footman came forward with the decanter.

Beatrice tilted her head to one side. "I've thought of that myself," she said to Belmont with a mischievous smile. She leaned back to include Lord Jess. "I prefer to think of it as a clever construct and not devious at all."

"And I meant no offense, Miss Brent." Belmont returned her smile with one of his own. "To you or to Jess."

"None taken, Belmont," Jess acknowledged. Belmont was hardly the only one who thought his actions were motivated by ill will. His brother the duke had once asked him if gaming was his way of defaming the Pennistan name.

"It would be fun, though, would it not?" Miss Brent went on. "I mean to see if one could carry off the idea of claiming a true Rembrandt was a forgery." She had such a charming way of leaning toward him as she spoke, as if confiding a secret. He stayed where he was, close enough to count the gold flecks in her brown eyes, enjoying the exquisite torture. He nodded in answer to her question.

He might have considered flirting with her as a way of distracting her from Crenshaw's possible suit, but at the moment he was doing it solely because she was irresistible. Later, he told himself, later he would come to his senses, but for now discussing Rembrandt and forgery was far more innocent than it sounded and the dinner table was a perfectly safe place to allow himself to be captivated.

"The problem is," Belmont spoke, ending the reverie, "one would have to be an expert on Rembrandt and willing to jeopardize one's own reputation if the trick did not work."

"Only if you were caught, my lord." Beatrice looked from one of them to the other. "I would think that the risk would be part of the fun."

Belmont raised his eyebrows yet again, which Jess read as an unwillingness to commit himself one way or the other.

Jess nodded slowly as it occurred to him that this gently reared young woman may have a good bit of her brother's wildness in her, very carefully tamped down, which made him think of any number of things it would be "fun" to do with her.

"Exactly how would you undertake the fraud?" Lord Belmont asked. Jess feared that a question like that was similar to lighting a fuse.

This time Beatrice ate some of the pâté before speaking, though Jess was willing to wager she had no idea what she was chewing so thoroughly. He watched her expression as her clever brain worked out the perfect crime. From puzzlement to idea to wicked certainty.

He glanced at Belmont, who was watching her too, but with a smile that could only be called avuncular.

"I would choose someone who is not well schooled in art, someone who only bought the Rembrandt painting to impress others."

She must know many who fit that description among the circle of newly rich mill owners in Birmingham, Jess thought.

"Then I would hire a competent forger to create a copy. I would confront the owner of the original about its authenticity, using my knowledge, which would certainly be far superior to his. I suppose that is prideful to say, but do you not think that someone who has spent years pursuing an interest is naturally more informed than a newcomer?"

"Yes, I do," Jess agreed, thinking of his passion for gaming and the way he was torn between educating newcomers or taking all their money.

"That's true for many of us at this very table," Lord Belmont said with a serious face. "Your father when it comes to business, the baron and fisticuffs, Lord Destry and riding, the countess and entertaining. I do not know your sister well enough to guess what her expertise is, but it is the rare person who does not excel in some area."

"Thank you, my lord. Somehow that is very reassuring to me. Lord Jess, what is your area of expertise?"

"Gaming," he said, and waited to see how she would react.

"Yes, you and Ellis shared that interest for a while, but you did bring my brother back to us. For that I am grateful." She searched his eyes as if she was trying to find that goodness. Generosity and guilt she might find, but very little goodness.

"So you are now confronting the owner of the Rembrandt and are about to convince him it is a fake," Lord Belmont reminded her. Jess was grateful to have her vivid imagination focused on her "clever construct," as she phrased it, and away from his virtue or lack thereof.

"I will not bore you with the technical details but I could easily convince him that someone had duped him. His pride would be savaged by the thought and he would willingly let me take it away for further study." She paused and gave them a look. "Does this work so far?"

Jess pretended offense, matching her mood. "Theft is not one of my areas of expertise. Belmont would know better." His inference was quite deliberate and Miss Brent gave all her attention to the earl.

Belmont shook his head. "What Jess means is that I have helped several friends find lost items. As I told you, I can never resist a puzzle." Belmont finished off his wine before adding, "It sounds plausible so far, Miss Brent. Pray, continue."

She closed her eyes as though that would fortify her as much as the wine was fortifying Belmont. "I would replace the real painting with the forgery and return it to the owner with the sad news that it is not truly a Rembrandt—the advantage being that when I am able to sell it, the buyer could announce the discovery of the original from which my owner's forgery was copied. Is that too complicated?"

"Not at all complicated, my dear," said the earl and

then waited for the footman to step back after refilling his glass.

Despite the amazing amounts of wine the man imbibed, he was never foxed. The only sign that Jess could find was when he began to call the ladies "my dear." Was it because he drank only wine, never brandy or other spirits?

"Not too complicated," Belmont repeated, "but it does involve at least one other person who could attempt blackmail at some later point."

"Do you think so?" Beatrice said with some disappointment, but after a brief pause she shook her head. "But I would know that he is an art forger, which is an equally valid basis for blackmail. It would be quid pro quo."

Her naïveté was showing here, Jess thought. "Yes, but that would end the moment either one of you admitted the forgery and theft to someone else," he said.

"I am sure neither one of us would be foolish enough to do that," she insisted with a firm shake of her head, as if she knew the forger as well as she knew herself.

"So you think you could keep your own counsel. Never speak of it to anyone, not even your sister, your twin?" *Or your lover?* He kept that one to himself.

"Yes, I am sure I could keep the secret. There are many things I never tell Ceci. She does worry so much. About everything."

"I can see why, if constructing clever ways to steal art is one of your hobbies." He smiled.

"The earl did ask, my lord."

"You mean all one must do is ask in order to lead you into a life of crime?" *Or sin?*

Belmont's bark of laughter drew both their attention. "Jess, you deserve to be in her black books to even hint that Miss Brent would so easily stray from the right path."

"Belmont, you are a devil. How do I answer that? It would be rude of me to say that Miss Brent is too sensitive or that I was not teasing at all."

"Which was it, my lord?" Miss Brent asked, without a smile now. She moved in her seat so that even her skirt was not touching him.

"Neither," he insisted, feeling trapped.

Miss Brent turned to Lord Belmont. "So here is another mystery for you to solve, my lord."

Belmont smiled. "Lord Jess's behavior is no mystery at all, my dear Miss Brent. But I will leave you to decipher it from the clues you have."

Miss Brent looked from one to the other, clearly wondering what Belmont knew that she did not.

"In the meantime," Lord Belmont went on, "do tell me how you can tell a real Rembrandt from his lesser imitators. I find I am fascinated and want details, if you please, my dear."

Jess turned to Mrs. Kendrick, reminding himself that Miss Beatrice Brent was a woman he had no business trying to charm.

LORD DESTRY FINISHED his opening conversation with the countess and, before he turned to her, Cecilia watched him take the salt and sprinkle some into his wineglass. Puzzled, she wondered exactly what that would do to the wine. Anxious to fit in, she took some salt from the cellar nearest her and did the same thing.

"Miss Brent, do tell Miss Wilson that I speak the

truth when I say that Birmingham is a far lovelier town than Manchester."

The question from Lord Crenshaw made Cecilia start, but before she answered, she realized why his questions were always worded like an instruction with only one possible answer. Still, it was an easy enough subject and she was grateful for the escape.

Cecilia leaned forward and spoke to Miss Wilson, who was seated just beyond Lord Crenshaw. "Oh, indeed it is. At least, I think so. Birmingham has such lovely gardens, and a river runs through the middle of the city. There are walking paths and the shops. While it is not at all equal to London, it is far superior to any other city in the Midlands."

Lord Crenshaw turned to Miss Wilson, who smoothed her hair before answering. "I do believe you show some prejudice, Miss Brent, as Birmingham is your home."

"We cannot all live in London," Lord Crenshaw teased. "And Mr. Brent must remain close to his interests in Birmingham."

All gentlemen had "interests" to attend to. What a nice way of *not* saying that her father ran mills.

Cecilia sipped her wine while trying to think of a topic of conversation and almost choked at the hideous element the salt flavoring added. She glanced at Lord Destry, who shrugged a shoulder, before returning her attention to Lord Crenshaw.

Miss Wilson was now speaking with the earl, and Lord Crenshaw was watching the girl with an intensity that made Cecilia question his recent interest in Beatrice. He sensed Cecilia's study of him and turned to her.

"What holds you close to London these days, my lord? We miss you at home." That was a neutral enough question.

"London has amusements that cannot be duplicated anywhere." He showed his teeth in a smile that was more suggestive than flirtatious.

"You mean the theater and opera?"

"Indeed, as you will find when you have your Season. London knows no bounds when it comes to entertainments."

Cecilia had no idea why the image of a bordello should pop into her head but was much relieved when Lord Crenshaw went on.

"Gaming is how I spend most of my evenings when I am not in the Midlands."

Now she felt silly. His expression was filled with an apologetic demeanor as he admitted his weakness.

"Indeed," Cecilia said. "Do you prefer cards, games of chance, or horse racing?"

"All of them," Crenshaw said with an encompassing sweep of his hands. "In fact, I wager a quid we will have trout for the fish course."

Lord Destry leaned forward. "I wager a quid that we are served trout and turbot."

"You're on!" Crenshaw nodded.

"And you, Miss Brent?" Destry asked. "What do you think we will be served? Would you care to join our little wager?"

Knowing exactly what her father thought of gambling, Cecilia smiled demurely and looked down so they could not see the lie. "It would not be fair, as I already know what is going to be served."

They were interrupted by a footman serving soup

and when the server moved on Lord Destry picked up his fork and began to eat. His fork, Cecilia thought. Why his fork?

The others were talking over their soup so she once again followed his behavior. One could hardly enjoy the soup with a fork but if it was the way it was eaten in fashionable society then she would not be caught out. Perhaps it was a new trend. She watched as Lord Destry speared a small piece of asparagus from the bowl and ate it.

The marquis looked directly at her and smiled. It was not a comfortable smile, but the kind one used when teasing or testing.

"Tell me, Miss Brent, if I took my serviette and tied it around my neck would you do the same?"

"That is ridiculous," she said with more sharpness than was polite. "I mean . . . ," she corrected herself, trying for a less severe voice, "of course not." She hoped he could not tell how strained her smile was.

"Then why do something as silly as try to eat your soup with a fork?"

"Because you did," she said, feeling her smile die. "And was that a test to see exactly how gullible I am?"

Cecilia was proud of the fact that she had a mild temperament, but at the moment she had to fight the urge to pour her soup in the man's lap.

"Miss Brent, just between us, if you please." Lord Destry leaned closer and lowered his voice as he spoke.

Cecilia nodded, though she was not sure she wanted to share a confidence with the man.

He looked away, clearing his throat before he spoke. "I put salt in my wine so that I am not tempted to drink too much. I love the juice of the grape, but have learned that I have a lower tolerance than most."

"I see." Horrified that she had mimicked him, she wanted to shrivel into a little ball of mortification and die.

"Please believe me," he said, "those who make up the ton are no more than men and women born in lucky circumstances with just enough wit to pretend that they are better than the rest of the citizenry."

"I suppose," Cecilia said with a slight nod.

"If there is one thing I know, Miss Brent, it is that anyone taken in by the way they act, no matter if it is salting their wine or something more egregious, like shunning someone, that person is as much a fool as they are."

Cecilia was struck silent by the snub and looked away lest he see the tears filling her eyes.

Chapter Eight

WILLIAM, YOU IDIOT, he shouted to himself. He tried to find a way to apologize for his affront, a completely unintended one. His words were aimed at men like Crenshaw and women like Mrs. Wilson. Sweet, too-cautious Miss Cecilia Brent was only trying to fit into this new circle. Besides, her looks guaranteed that she could eat her peas with a knife dipped in gravy and still be welcomed anywhere.

"I did not mean to insult you, Miss Brent," he said anxiously. Her eyes were fixed on Crenshaw even though the man was fully engaged in conversation with Miss Wilson, but he knew she could not turn her ears off and must hear him. "I am well aware that you are a newcomer and hope to find a place in the ton this Season. I only wanted to help."

She glanced back at him. "Thank you, my lord." She spoke stiffly, as if good manners were an innate part of her, but her eyes shimmered with tears.

He spoke quickly, so that he would be talking to her face and not the back of her head, though even that managed to be as beautiful as the rest of her.

"The fact is that you have complete control of this gathering."

When she gave him that not-quite-convinced half nod she had used before, he went on. "Yes, even though you are the least experienced in the ways of the ton."

He read skepticism mixed with a good bit of hurt still lingering in her eyes. He hurried on.

"Observe, if you please. When you turn from me, Lord Crenshaw must perforce abandon Miss Wilson to speak with you. Belmont will turn from whatever puzzle your sister has presented him with to speak with the much more ingenuous Miss Wilson, so she is not left alone with her soup.

"Of course, Lord Jess will have to entertain your sister with the more genteel of his gaming tales, and Mrs. Kendrick, who has been laughing at the more risqué of them, will don her lady's airs and talk to your father. The countess will sigh in disappointment at the interruption and speak with me. There, you see? It is all in your control. Shall we test it?"

With a slight, cold smile of agreement, she turned from him. He was worse than an idiot. His title was the only thing that kept him in such good company. William pushed aside all hope of something as ludicrous as a shared love with Miss Brent. *What a fantasy, you undersized moron.*

William turned to the countess, who patted Mr. Brent's hand as she turned away. Destry noted the personal touch and wondered, but kept his polite gaze focused on the countess as he asked, "Who will be arriving later in the week, my lady?"

"IT WAS EXACTLY as he said, Bitsy. When I turned away from him, Lord Crenshaw turned to me and the entire party changed partners as if it were a dance and I had called a new step."

The two sisters stood a little apart from the other ladies as they waited for the gentlemen to join them. Miss Wilson played the pianoforte with quiet precision while the countess and Mrs. Kendrick fussed over Mrs. Kendrick's dog.

"I assume that's the way all dinner parties are, Ceci. Tell me, why were you so offended by his behavior?"

"He uses his understanding of people to amuse himself. No one is ever pretty enough or charming enough to be spared his snubs. I am not the slightest bit interested in knowing him better."

Beatrice wondered what the gentlemen were discussing over their port. For the love of God, if Cecilia was right they would both be the prefect targets for his insults. But the marquis did not seem that sort of person at all. She wanted to find a quiet corner and think this through.

"Why can't he be more like Lord Crenshaw? He does his best to make us feel as though we are as welcome as anyone with a title."

Beatrice shrugged, afraid that any answer would only upset her overwrought sister more. This was why she liked studying paintings so much. They could not talk back or insist on their own interpretation. She was relieved when the door opened and the gentlemen joined them.

Soon after, the tea arrived and the countess asked Mrs. Kendrick to pour while she invited everyone to take a cup and listen to her ideas for entertainment.

"I have an activity planned and I invite all of you to participate as you wish." The countess waited a beat.

Her guests nodded.

"I would like each one of you to tell us about what you enjoy most. You may demonstrate a talent, give us a lecture, or teach us a skill."

Beatrice leaned closer to Cecilia and whispered, "Aren't we lucky that the countess warned us of this in advance?"

Cecilia nodded with some force. "Yes. Look at Miss Wilson, she is as terrified as I was at first. Even the Earl of Belmont looks uncertain."

"Your idea is perfect, Ceci, asking each guest to bring you a plant to identify."

"Now I only have to decide what the prize will be if I am bested."

"You won't be." Beatrice's confidence was sincere. "No lady knows plants half as well as you do."

"Ah," said the countess. "I see a mix of enthusiasm and dismay."

"I must reassure Miss Wilson. She does play quite beautifully." Beatrice left her sister and made her way to where Miss Wilson sat near Lord Crenshaw.

"Come, Lord Jess," the countess urged. "We would all like a lesson in billiards or perhaps on the finer points of vingt-et-un."

Everyone looked about for Jess Pennistan. Beatrice knew exactly where he was, standing near the door, something stronger than tea in his hand, watching the gathering but not really a part of it.

Lord Jess came forward, a lazy smile in place as he bowed to his hostess. "As you wish, my lady. I was thinking of challenging everyone to race rabbits. I am sure I can come up with an appropriate prize."

The company laughed.

"Even better, my lord," the countess said, "perhaps playing in twos would mean less of a drain on the rabbit population."

"Perhaps two teams only. Men against women?" He looked at the ladies with an expression that implied they were not up to the challenge.

"You're on, my lord," Mrs. Kendrick called out in such a strong voice that her dog barked at the upset. She calmed her pet and then added, "Of course, no lady or gentleman should be required to participate."

"Soon we will have enough rules to rival those that overwhelm a bill in Parliament," Crenshaw grumbled.

"In which case I want to assure you that rain or shine we will not lack for entertainment," the countess said. "Now, please, enjoy your tea and each other."

The gathering dissolved into smaller conversational groups and Miss Wilson turned to Beatrice.

"But what will I do about the lecture?" she all but wailed. She looked from Lord Crenshaw to Beatrice as if she had no skills or talents whatsoever.

"You will play your favorite piano piece and tell us about the composer," Beatrice suggested.

"An excellent idea, Miss Beatrice. You are brilliant." Lord Crenshaw beamed his approval and Beatrice shrugged, uncomfortable with the extravagant praise.

"I could do that quite easily." Miss Wilson's voice

was no longer panicked, her whole demeanor much more relaxed.

"Or you could make a game of it," Beatrice suggested, "and play pieces and ask who the composer is. That puts the burden on the audience and not on you."

Miss Wilson glanced at Lord Crenshaw, who nodded thoughtfully. "A clever suggestion, but you do not want to tax your audience. Or embarrass them."

"Yes, I suppose you are right, but it would be a great game."

"Well, you could play a piece, then talk about the composer a little. After that you could ask the others to name the composer, making it a game of sorts."

"Miss Brent, does that brain of yours ever stop working?" Lord Crenshaw asked. Beatrice was sure he meant that as a compliment but she could not quite control the blush of embarrassment.

"Now, now, dear girl," Crenshaw said, taking her arm, "do not be upset. It is not at all what I intended."

"Thank you, my lord," she said with some relief, and withdrew her arm from his. "I do think that Lord Belmont is waiting to speak to you," she added, for the earl was bearing down on them with an eye on Crenshaw.

"Miss Wilson." Beatrice drew her aside. "Let's collect Cecilia and discuss what pieces you should consider playing."

"Please do call me Katherine," Miss Wilson urged. "I would so value you as a friend."

Beatrice smiled and returned the compliment. This was going to be as much fun as she had hoped it would be.

* * *

JESS WATCHED BEATRICE Brent tend to both her sister and Miss Wilson.

"And what are your further observations on the Brent sisters, Jess?"

Destry had stepped up onto the hearth, which brought his height close enough to Jess's ear that their conversation would be between them alone.

Jess didn't hesitate. "It looks as though Crenshaw is trying to curry favor. And Miss Brent seems politely interested. I cannot decide if that is a good or a bad sign. Is she just being coy or is she angling for a closer connection?"

"So that's the direction of your thoughts." Destry took a quick look at the three young women.

"I am wondering if I should undermine his possible courtship."

"Ever the defender."

"Not a hardship when defense means a flirtation with someone as tantalizing as Beatrice Brent."

"Tantalizing? Oho, so you are interested."

Jess wished he had chosen a less revealing term. But it was true, Beatrice Brent was as tantalizing as champagne.

"No," he said with his best blank expression, trying to climb out of the hole he had dug for himself. "She has no need of my help in any form. Look at her. Miss Beatrice Brent is a woman with strong opinions and protective instincts."

"How do you know her so well?"

"I don't at all, but at dinner she went on and on about Rembrandt's genius and when not talking about that she was looking down at your end of the table. She went immediately to her sister's side as they were leaving the dining room."

"The countess told me their mother died just a year ago; perhaps Miss Beatrice Brent has taken on a more maternal role with her sister. They do seem very close," Destry said, his eyes on the young ladies.

After a long pause, during which they both watched the three young women, who were also being studied by Crenshaw, Destry asked, "Why did you not challenge him to a duel all those years ago?"

"Because my brother insisted that Crenshaw's lack of honor would not guarantee a fair fight."

"So he remains loose to find a woman easily wooed and led to the altar." Destry's words were edged with disgust.

"Yes, I know. But I have played the savior before and once was entirely enough for this lifetime."

"Admit it, Jess, you would never let it happen again."

"Damn it, Destry, stop playing at being my conscience. You go save someone."

"I think I just might."

With that, Lord Destry hopped down from the hearth and sought out the three ladies. Jess watched him do his best to charm them. Miss Wilson's attention was easily won, but then her cheeks blushed with uncertainty when both Miss Brents were decidedly cool to Destry. Ah well, Jess thought, the man's love life was not at all his problem. He turned to find Mrs. Kendrick watching him. Her dog slept draped over her arm.

She curtsied to him. "Does the joy of observation in closer quarters not define a house party?"

"Indeed, it must, since you were watching us watch the young women who were wondering whom they should watch. The question is, Mrs. Kendrick," he bowed to her, "who is watching you?"

She laughed and shrugged. Her dog whined a little at the interruption of his rest. "Ah me, to be young again," she went on. "Their longing is palpable, is it not? You are close enough in age to them not to feel as I do. To be that age with the wisdom I've gained since then would be a great gift."

"My dear Mrs. Kendrick, you are much too young to speak that way. That said, I fear I have learned much too little and would make the same mistakes all over again."

"We each harbor those regrets, my lord." She did not speak for a moment. "Speaking of regrets, I must ask, if only to relieve my own discomfort, how it is that you and Lord Crenshaw can be in the same room?"

At least she did not blush or look away, and she waited for his answer rather than trying to answer for him. "The fact that he still tolerates my presence even after I was named in his divorce is proof of how little the marriage meant to him." Jess paused to swallow the rage that came with the memory. "You will note that when we are not gaming we each pretend the other does not exist."

"Then how is it that you are both guests at the same house party? It is too small a group to avoid each other all the time."

"I am willing to wager that you will never see us any closer than the width of a room, unless we are playing cards at the same table."

"So it would be accurate to say that you cordially hate each other."

If Mrs. Kendrick noticed that he did not explain why they both happened to be here, that suited him perfectly. "There is nothing cordial about my hatred, madam. I will shed no tears when his death is announced."

"Please, do tell me exactly how you feel, my lord." Mrs. Kendrick's laugh made him smile. "Now, tell me what you know of Lord Belmont. I do find him a fine figure of a man."

"Belmont?" Jess drew a breath and considered how to describe the earl. "The Earl of Belmont is unique, perhaps even eccentric."

"Eccentric? Truly? Do you know, that is my favorite sort of friend." She smoothed her dog's coat and added, "You know him from your gaming?"

"No, Belmont enjoys play as long as it is not deep. And I fancy a greater challenge." What was the point of gambling if you did not risk more than you could afford? "The earl lives near Portsmouth, not far from my brother Gabriel and his family. Gabriel marvels at the earl's support of any number of unusual charities. And my brother is not easy to impress. One might call him unconventional."

"Your brother or the earl?"

"Both, I suspect."

"And what sort of charities?"

"I think you shall have to ask him yourself. But beware; for all his generosity he is as poor as a church mouse, a fact that is well known."

"Then how fortunate that I am not."

Mrs. Kendrick moved away with a languid grace

that made Jess think of the bedroom. She did not approach Belmont, however, but rather went back to the countess.

What an entertaining group this was. He eyed Crenshaw. Unfortunately, not all of the entertainment was as amusing as Nora Kendrick, or as tempting as Beatrice Brent. Crenshaw had sought Beatrice out again, he could see, and had tucked her arm possessively through his.

The familiarity of it made Jess's gut roll. He closed his eyes and prayed for calm. Though Beatrice let go of Crenshaw's arm soon enough, she did give the man her complete attention, as though what he was prosing on about fascinated her as much as the artist she had discussed at dinner. Was it pretense or was she really intrigued by him?

It did not matter, he insisted to his nobler self. He was here to reclaim the land and not to play the hero, no matter how appealing the heroine in distress was.

Chapter Nine

THE COUNTESS CALLED for their attention and several conversations faded as everyone turned to her. "Mrs. Kendrick wants to share her talent this evening. She claims she will be awake all night worrying if she does not. Of course there will be more guests in a few days, but she would prefer to entertain you now."

"I could help her sleep."

Beatrice pretended she had not heard Lord Crenshaw's comment, certain that it was meant for Lord Belmont's ears only.

"Did you hear what Lord Crenshaw said?" Ceci whispered to her sister.

Beatrice nodded.

"And the earl laughed. How could he?"

"What else would he do? I expect men make those sorts of comments all the time."

"Not Papa!" Cecilia said with shocked certainty.

"No, not Papa," Beatrice lied, allowing a flash of annoyance at her sister's naïveté. After all, Papa was a man, not even born a gentleman.

"It was a comment no gentleman should make in the presence of ladies." Cecilia blushed. "Mayhap he does not think of us as ladies."

"Of course he does, Ceci. He did not think we would hear him. Now stop buying trouble and let's watch Mrs. Kendrick."

Cecilia gave a halfhearted nod, pretending that she believed her sister.

"If you would all have a seat in the chairs gathered in this semicircle." The countess gestured toward the seating.

Most took the seat nearest to them, though a few of the gentlemen remained standing, moving to the edge of the circle.

Mrs. Kendrick stood in the center of the gold-tone Turkey carpet. Her dog was wide awake now. With a word for his ears alone she set him on the carpet and waited while he sat up and looked at her.

"Good dog." Her voice had a singsong quality to it when she spoke to her pet, and Beatrice suspected that the dog responded to the tone as much as her words.

Mrs. Kendrick went through a series of conventional commands including "Sit," "Roll over," and "Shake." The dog performed all on cue and everyone made appropriate sounds of approval.

"That, my friends, was to prepare you and Finch, my dog, for the real performance."

She looked at Finch, who sat, shaking with nervous excitement. "Finch, find the tallest man in the room." Without hesitation he ran over to Lord Jess, who was standing on one end of the semicircle of chairs. Jess made a bow to the dog and the assembled guests.

Mrs. Kendrick's "Good dog!" brought him back to her for a reward. He sat up, accepted the treat, and then moved in a gesture that looked amazingly like a bow. The company laughed and applauded lightly.

"Finch is not a purebred but is every bit as refined in his behavior as any gentleman I know." She glanced at Beatrice and added, "Most of the time."

Beatrice ran her fingers over the old spectacles she was carrying in her reticule and nodded with what she hoped looked like gracious dismissal.

"Finch! Find the man who wears a red scarf."

He arrowed straight to Lord Destry, who was not wearing his scarf this evening, and everyone applauded.

With each success Mrs. Kendrick rewarded Finch with the tiniest tidbit of meat, after crooning the familiar "Good dog!" and entertaining the other guests with tales of Finch's extraordinary daring.

"Now find the Earl of Belmont." Finch looked at the two remaining men and went over to sit at the feet of Belmont, who laughed with the rest of them.

"Finch spent most of the first three years of his life on my husband's ship. We were both amazed that when the admiral retired Finch was happy ashore."

"My guess is that he took his cue from your husband," Belmont suggested.

What a lovely thing to say, Beatrice thought, and watched the earl. He wasn't smiling but there was a twinkle in his eyes that made Beatrice wonder if he was attracted to the young widow.

Mrs. Kendrick gave the earl an almost melancholy

smile. "How kind of you, my lord. No doubt Finch has grown attached to me these past two years. I am wondering how he will like London."

"Given what the earl surmised," the countess said, "I imagine he will enjoy London as much as you do."

"I hope so. I am looking forward to next Easter and the Season, even though it will not be my first. You three will have such an adventure. You must be over the moon with anticipation." Mrs. Kendrick looked at each of the young ladies in turn as she spoke, and Beatrice did her best not to grin back, though she did smile and nod with perhaps too much enthusiasm. It made up for Cecilia's half nod and Miss Wilson's blush. Yes, they had not yet been invited to participate but surely Mrs. Kendrick's obvious approval was a goodwill gesture no one could ignore.

"Now, Finch," Nora Kendrick said, returning her attention to her dog. "Find the youngest guest among us." He went to Miss Wilson unerringly.

"Find the twins. One and two." She held up her hand, showing one finger and then two, and Finch trotted over and nosed Beatrice's shoe, and then Cecilia's. After praise and reward, Mrs. Kendrick gave another command and with that she curtsied to the party.

"I will now give Finch one final command." She looked at her dog and held out her arms. "Show everyone who you love best."

With a bark of understanding, Finch jumped into her arms. Everyone laughed and applauded with enthusiasm.

"That was delightful, Nora, and a fine example of what I am hoping each of you can entertain us with over the next week."

Beatrice went over to congratulate Finch and his owner, hoping it would show that there were no ill feelings left over from their first meeting.

Lord Jess came up beside them and offered his congratulations, too. Beatrice could *feel* him next to her. Even though they were not touching, his presence heightened all her senses, and made her feel restless. She wondered if he felt the same way. Would their connection grow even stronger if she reached out and touched the back of his hand?

Oh dear, he made her feel reckless, not restless. Beatrice was trying to think of a gracious way to move away when the Earl of Belmont approached. "A fine trick, Mrs. Kendrick."

"Thank you, my lord." She gave him a mere sketch of a curtsy.

"Tell me, how is it that you gave such a fine fellow a bird's name?" Lord Belmont reached out to stroke the dog, a gesture that brought his hand rather too close to Mrs. Kendrick's breast.

Beatrice noted that Mrs. Kendrick did not seem to mind the close contact. Indeed, she stepped a little closer, just a half step but a step nonetheless. Lord Belmont scratched Finch's chin and smiled down at the dog.

Beatrice looked at Lord Jess, whose amusement made her feel like a child among adults. To walk away now would be rude. Besides, it would be good for her to watch a flirtation between a sophisticated couple.

When Lord Jess glanced at her, Beatrice gave what she hoped looked like a knowing smile and turned her attention to Mrs. Kendrick, ignoring the fact that his glance made her feel ever more reckless.

"My dog is named Finch because as a puppy he liked to chase birds so much I thought he wanted to be one. Naming him for a bird was as close as I could come to giving him his heart's wish."

"I see." Lord Belmont stood his ground but folded his arms across his chest, which was as good as moving closer. They were barely a hand's width apart. Beatrice noticed that Lord Jess started to imitate the earl's stance, but changed his mind and clasped his hands behind his back.

"Finch being so much more refined a name than Vulture or Egret?" Belmont asked. When Mrs. Kendrick nodded he went on. "But what about Falcon or, perhaps, Robin?"

"Falcon is much too pretentious for such a small fellow and Robin better suited to a girl, I think."

"I was able to puzzle out the trick," the earl announced. "For we all know that it is quite impossible for a dog to know who has a habit of wearing a red scarf and which two are twins."

When Mrs. Kendrick would have protested, the earl stayed her with a raised hand, with one finger almost, almost pressed to her lips.

"I will keep the secret, but it will cost you, Mrs. Kendrick."

"Will it?" she asked with a smile, not so much flirtatious as amused. She finally had enough mercy to include the two onlookers. "Do you have any suggestions, Lord Jess, Miss Brent?"

"For what Belmont should charge," Lord Jess asked, "or what the secret to Finch's tricks is?"

Beatrice laughed. She could not help it. She spluttered an "I beg your pardon," and pressed her lips together to silence her giggle.

"Please, do not," Lord Jess urged. "I so enjoy an appreciative audience."

"Nevertheless, my lord," Mrs. Kendrick said, with laughter in her voice, too, "I think the earl and I can determine payment quite on our own."

"Then we shall leave you to it." Jess bowed and took Beatrice's arm and there was an explosion of feeling that bolted to her belly and lower. He did not react at all. Did he not feel the same way?

Before they could walk away, Mrs. Kendrick stopped Lord Jess with a hand to his sleeve. "No, please stay." She made no further explanation of her request.

Jess turned to Belmont. "We are staying."

"I would just as soon have you leave but will bow to the lady's sensibilities."

Holding her arm still, Lord Jess said, "Miss Brent confided in me that she is desperate to know the explanation for Finch's tricks."

"I said no such thing," Beatrice insisted, then decided to try her hand at the game of flirting. "But Lord Jess read my mind." She lowered her eyes. "I am endlessly curious." Rather pleased with her own attempt at a phrase with double meaning, she looked up at her small audience. "About almost everything."

The earl laughed. Lord Jess dropped her arm to cover a convenient coughing spell and Mrs. Kendrick nodded at her with approval. "We have among us a fine student of the arts." She did not specify exactly which arts she meant, and for some reason a bedroom popped into Beatrice's mind.

"I will disclose the secret of Finch's genius," Lord

Belmont said, "but only if you wish to have the illusion of the dog's intelligence spoiled."

When no one objected the Earl of Belmont went on. "The first person you asked Finch to identify was Lord Jess, who was standing at the end of the half circle of guests. The next was beside him and so on. You introduced enough distraction in between your commands that I am sure most did not notice the order was quite precise."

"You are too clever, my lord." Nora Kendrick hugged her dog close as if consoling him. "I thought I was quite circumspect."

"That you are, my dear lady, but I am quite observant."

At that moment Crenshaw and Miss Wilson approached them. As Beatrice had observed, whenever Lord Crenshaw approached a group Jess excused himself or left without a word.

After watching them carefully since their mutually curt greeting, Beatrice had decided that they were at odds over something. Perhaps a game that had gone wrong. Or a quarrel over a woman. Or even something as simple as a horse one had purchased even after the other had made his interest known.

She would dearly love to know the details.

AS HE STEPPED away, Jess heard Miss Wilson say, "How ever did you train your dog, Mrs. Kendrick? Our dogs can do no more than fetch sticks."

He moved toward the window, withdrawing from the conversation. From his new vantage point Jess watched as Mrs. Kendrick allowed Belmont to take her dog and cuddle him in his arms. Now there was an interesting duo: a wealthy widow and an impoverished earl. An association that would be best served by marriage for the earl, and yet Mrs. Kendrick was decidedly independent. How entertaining. He wondered if Destry would care to wager on who would win.

Miss Brent, or the little Venus, as he still thought of her, was now in earnest conversation with Destry with the same intensity she had shown with Crenshaw. It could just be her way. He wondered how that intensity would show itself in the bedroom. He smiled at the thought and banished it as quickly. He was not shopping in the marriage mart. Not this week or this year. Maybe never. And Miss Brent was not suited to anything less than lifelong commitment.

He forced himself to avert his eyes, and immediately caught sight of Miss Cecilia Brent. Beatrice's sister was a beauty and would have no trouble garnering all the attention she could crave, even if she was alone at the moment, staring out the window. He took a step in her direction as he eyed the last couple.

The countess and Mr. Brent stood together talking to a young man who had just come in, not one of their party. The countess and Brent were a pairing he never would have guessed, but the way they stood so close, their clothes touching, if not their bodies, told him that they were deep into an affair and still delighted with it.

Jess recalled the countess's husband, who had been more interested in directing the farming of his land than in London or Parliament. As a husband he had regarded his wife with an offhand affection. They had lived apart for months at a time, the countess spending the entire season in London while the earl was on his estate. The arrangement had seemed to suit them both.

Mr. Brent could not be more different. He was intense and dogged in his pursuit of whatever he wanted; at least, that was what Jess's brother David had told him. Thinking back to how Brent had escorted his daughters into dinner, Jess decided he was either as controlling as Crenshaw or very protective of those he loved. Perhaps both.

Venus finally saw the man who was talking with the countess and her father. With a word to Destry they both joined that group. She greeted the young man with such enthusiasm that Jess realized they were friends of long standing. Perhaps more than friends.

It didn't matter to him. He was a confirmed bachelor, Jess reminded himself, for the second time in as many minutes. He looked about at his fellow guests, several of whom were also watching the tableau by the door. Relieved he was not the only one fascinated by Beatrice, Jess moved across the room to Miss Cecilia, who would surely know the newcomer's identity.

Chapter Ten

CECILIA DID NOT give him a chance to ask about the new member of their group, but launched immediately into conversation without her usual blush of embarrassment. "There is the loveliest night-blooming jasmine on the patio."

"Flowers are not my forte, Miss Brent. Exactly what is lovely about it? Are not all flowers lovely?"

"Yes, but what I thought was—" She paused and then started again. "What I meant was that it is unusually thriving and lush." She turned and looked at him for the first time. "It has found the perfect spot to bloom. Do you know the scent of the jasmine?"

"Only from perfumes."

"Let's go outside and you can experience it. I would love a closer look."

With a glance at the party behind them, Jess opened the door and they stepped out onto the patio. The night was still warm and the air carried the scent of the profusely blooming plant's hundreds of small star-shaped flowers.

Miss Brent turned to him. "The fragrance of the jasmine reminds me of summer nights and secrets, mysteries even."

"Exquisite," Jess said. The same could be said of the woman before him. While her sister was the one who captivated him, he had to acknowledge that Cecilia Brent had the kind of beauty that made one look again. At the moment she was especially lovely, and the flowers that surrounded her paled by comparison.

She smiled. Ignoring the intimacy of the moment, indeed unaware of it, she walked over and stooped down to touch the soil of the plant.

Jess stayed within sight of the window and as far away from the young woman as courtesy would allow. This was no attempt at flirtation for Cecilia. Who would have known that she had such a profound interest in flowers? So serious was her interest that the possible impropriety of their situation had not ever occurred to her.

Though he was certain that she was not interested in anything but the plants, he still wished they were not alone, and he breathed a sigh of relief when her sister, Destry, and the stranger came through a door farther along the patio.

"I see, they are out here so Ceci can look at some plant." There was relief in Beatrice's voice as she made the announcement.

Jess sauntered over to them. "Your sister wished to see the night-blooming jasmine and have me experience its unique scent."

As he finished speaking, Cecilia confirmed his statement by announcing to no one in particular, "Aha! I thought so. It's planted in some special potting mix and fertilized, too. And the urn can be transported into the greenhouse on cool nights or for the winter. How perfect."

"My lord, plants are her passion," Beatrice began, but Jess would not let her continue. The code she was using could be easily translated: *My sister did not lure you out here for a flirtation.*

"Yes, that is quite evident, Miss Brent. I have learned a great deal in just these few minutes."

The little Venus narrowed her eyes. Good, she found his response as opaque as he'd intended.

Recalling her manners, she stepped back and announced, "Lord Jessup, this is a friend of the family, Roger Tremaine. Roger, this is Lord Jessup Pennistan. Roger works on machine design for Papa. He came to say good-bye to us since he leaves for London in the morning."

Each took the measure of the other before exchanging bows. Cecilia turned to Tremaine and wished him well with an absentminded affection. It was clearly Beatrice whom the man was most intent on seeing, or perhaps it was Beatrice who was intent on seeing him.

Nothing there but friendship on Tremaine's side, Jess decided. As for Beatrice's interest, why did he have the feeling she was using her friend as protection?

Destry rescued them from continued conversation. "So, Miss Brent," he said, speaking to Cecilia, "why are you so fond of this particular flower?" Destry shepherded them over to the flowering shrub, which was fully as tall as he was.

"It blooms at night, which makes it unique and

somewhat mysterious. It seduces one with its fragrance as surely as the moon and stars do with their distant light. It is from a tropical clime but flourishes here if it is well tended."

It was the longest speech the beautiful Miss Brent had given before them. Jess was struck by how much more her intelligence appealed to him than her classic blond loveliness. But despite both, he still found Beatrice's curiosity and liveliness far more appealing.

"And it was Mama's favorite scent," Beatrice Brent added.

"Yes," Roger said. "You could always tell when she had been to visit Mr. Brent—that lovely scent would stay in the air for hours."

Beatrice nodded, as her smile grew a little strained.

"Is it not a wonder how scent plays with our memory?" Jess said, doing his best to turn the conversation from dead mothers, though he did recall that his mother had favored a fragrance laced with violets. To this day he found the flower's scent both melancholy and comforting. "I walk into a card room and the very smell of the place reminds me of the thrill of a wager and the absurd importance of a turn of the card."

"Do you enjoy gaming, Miss Cecilia?" Destry asked, all eager interest.

"Gaming? I suppose it could be entertaining," she began, and then hesitated. "I am, however, not quick with numbers so I would do better not to consider it."

"There are all sorts of games that do not involve counting. I would be delighted to teach you some of the simpler ones."

Jess could see, as Destry did, that Miss Cecilia Brent was going to say no.

"Why not include Miss Beatrice, too?" Roger suggested.

"And I will add my counsel as well," Jess said.

Destry so clearly needed his help that Jess could not resist offering it, even though he was supposed to be avoiding the Brents.

Beatrice rescued Destry's proposal by answering for her sister. "That's a wonderful idea, Roger." Then she turned to him. "And it would be great fun to learn from an expert."

Jess was not sure if that was an insult or a compliment.

Beatrice went on without giving him a clue. "We should wait until Papa leaves as he does not approve of gaming." She turned to her sister. "Ceci, I do think it is one of those aspects of London social life that we should understand, if not actively pursue."

Despite the reasonable tone of her voice there was that mischievous twinkle again. It gave Jess an itch between his shoulder blades. Usually that itch meant trouble.

"Excellent," Destry exclaimed. "How long is Mr. Brent staying?"

Beatrice glanced into the room at her father, but it was Roger who answered. "He was planning to leave this afternoon but the countess convinced him to stay for the opening dinner." He looked at Beatrice. "It gave me an extra few hours to work."

She nodded. "And you ate at your desk."

As they all watched, Mr. Brent whispered something to the countess and she nodded in return. Then she took up a pose in the center of the room and the four of them reentered the salon.

"It has been a long travel day for most of you," the countess began, "so I did not plan any entertainment for this evening beyond Finch's wonderful performance. Mr. Brent tells me that a storm is brewing but if you would like some exercise before you retire to your bedchambers, I have had the Long Gallery lit. You are welcome to stroll through it and admire the art collection housed there."

"Yes, let's go to the gallery." Beatrice made to take Tremaine's arm. "I cannot wait to see the Rembrandts, the drawings especially."

Tremaine took a step away from Beatrice and shook his head. "I am to leave at first light, Beatrice. So I will say good-bye now."

"And I am much too tired, Bitsy."

Beatrice would have argued but Nora Kendrick, who was standing next to them, said, "I will be delighted to meet you in the gallery after I hand Finch off to my maid."

"Wonderful and thank you, Mrs. Kendrick." Beatrice gave her sister a kiss on the cheek. "Tell Darwell that I will not be late."

"Roger," she said, turning to him. "Good-bye, and come back for a day or two when you are finished in town, will you? I know the countess would love to have you stay awhile."

"I'll try, but your father wants the plans for the new threading machine as soon as possible, so I think I will be immersed in the plans for at least ten days."

"Which should put you here just in time for the last few days of the house party and a holiday you have more than earned."

Much like brother and sister, Jess decided as he

watched the two of them bicker over his duties and her wishes. Finally Tremaine broke away, promising to return as soon as work permitted. Beatrice appeared to be pleased with that, so Jess decided the man must be the sort who was true to his word.

BEATRICE ALL BUT skipped to the Long Gallery. The countess had hurried her through it the day before but that had been like teasing a child with a toy, then withholding it.

She made her way to the room that ran the length of the house, so long that she could not see the other end. Of course the clerestory windows that gave extra light during the day were dark now and the chandeliers could only provide so much light.

One of the Rembrandt drawings was in a well-lit spot and she pulled her ugly spectacles from her reticule to set about examining it, delighted to be within breathing distance of a work by the great master. The small landscape featured cottages, meadows and, if you looked carefully, a distant windmill. The brown wash over the paper was as much a part of the drawing as the lines and shadows.

At the sounds of footsteps she wheeled around to see Lord Jess and the marquis approaching.

"Have you come to see the Rembrandt drawing, too?"

DESTRY HAD INSISTED this was a shortcut to the card room. Now it wasn't. There was no way they could graciously ignore Venus's longing to share her favorite subject with someone, anyone, even two philistines who would rather be playing cards.

"You are a student of art?" Destry asked.

"Yes," Jess answered for her, "and particularly of Rembrandt." He could tell by her expression that she was not sure if his comment was a tease or a compliment. He just smiled.

"I enjoy his work, my lord, though I am hardly an expert."

"Excellent," Destry said with unfeigned enthusiasm. "We have two of his paintings at our house in the north. Perhaps you and your sister could visit sometime and see them."

"Thank you, my lord. That would be wonderful."

Jess had no idea if there were any Rembrandt drawings at Pennford. One of his paintings, yes, but he had never paid that much attention to the art collection. What did it say about his life that the last drawings he had studied had been in his mistress's bedchamber? They were drawings of her in poses that were designed to arouse his body more than his artistic appreciation. Being with someone as young and eager as Miss Brent made him feel jaded beyond redemption.

"I will grant you, Miss Brent," Lord Jess said, this time minding his manners, "Rembrandt is a wonderful artist. He draws quite beautifully. But what makes him great? Indeed, a 'great master'?"

"Are you truly interested, my lord? Or are you teasing me?"

"You had best grow used to it, Miss Brent," Lord Destry said, rising up and down on the balls of his feet. "Most of the time it is impossible to tell. I am not sure he even knows."

Jess waved away the caveat with a half laugh. "I am truly interested, and wish to hear your explanation." He expected it would include words more educated than "pretty" and "romantic."

"I will take you at your word, my lord, and give you an art lesson whether you *truly* want one or not." She pointed to the lower left corner of the small drawing. "Tell me what you see there."

Jess peered closely, looking for a trick, and then shrugged. "I see a walking path defined by plants growing on either side."

"Yes, that is what it looks like but in fact it is just a series of vertical lines and a darkened swipe of brown wash. Not a trail or plants at all."

Lord Jess looked again and nodded slowly, impressed when he had been prepared to be sarcastic.

"An economy of style is an important part of Rembrandt's genius in drawing," she said, not trying to contain her excitement. "He draws a series of lines, a very few lines, and we see crops ripening in the field."

Lord Jess stepped back.

"And do you see those four diagonal lines and the small rectangle in the distance?"

"A series of carefully spaced lines that is the veriest hint of a windmill," Lord Jess said, hoping that she found his awe gratifying.

"Amazing, Miss Brent. Will your lecture be on Rembrandt?" the marquis asked.

"Yes, hopefully not a prosy, boring lecture. I am trying to find a way to make it interesting."

"Your own enthusiasm will be contagious, I'm sure."

Jess meant that as sincerely as he ever meant anything but he hoped that neither she nor Destry realized it.

"I am sorry to keep you waiting, Miss Brent." Mrs. Kendrick arrived breathless. "Finch would not cooperate at all."

"That's quite all right, Mrs. Kendrick. I could study Rembrandt's drawing for hours without boredom. And I had Lord Jess and the marquis for company." Beatrice's smile beamed with pleasure and a healthy dose of invitation. The woman was either a natural teacher or had the makings of an outrageous flirt.

Jess and Destry bade good evening to the two ladies and headed back to the game room.

"She certainly is enthusiastic about art," Jess said as he turned to watch the two ladies progress down the hall. They chatted together, stopping periodically when Beatrice called Mrs. Kendrick's attention to another work of art.

"Jess, I know that expression. Do not tell me that you are going to seduce her."

"Never. Nothing has changed."

"She is not in your usual style."

"What is my usual style?" It was a warning and he saw that Destry recognized it.

"No insult intended, Jess, but you have always preferred more sophisticated ladies." Destry stopped short, thunderstruck. "Are you planning a courtship?"

"God, no. Are you mad? Neither one of us planned that meeting. You suggested the route to the game room. We talked to her for less than ten minutes and now you have me walking down the aisle. There is a world of intent between being impressed with her knowledge and a flirtation, much less a courtship."

"I like her sister," Destry said, which would have been a non sequitur if Jess was not used to the way Destry's mind jumped around. "I suppose it cannot hurt if you and Beatrice are on amiable terms, in case the four of us should like to have a picnic together or some such outing."

"An outing? That would be carrying friendship too far."

So Destry was planning a courtship. Jess glanced at him again to gauge his sincerity and found his friend watching him as though waiting for a verdict.

No, the new marquis wasn't joking.

"Stop thinking that I have already failed," Destry admonished and then clapped Jess on the back. "Now let's find Belmont and set up play for the evening."

All they could interest anyone in was billiards. Mr. Brent and Belmont agreed, both insisting on modest stakes, for what Jess suspected to be completely different reasons. Brent only played to be sociable. Hadn't his daughter said he disliked gambling? And Belmont could barely afford even modest stakes.

Abel Brent played with an intensity and focus that explained his success in business, though it did not carry over to the billiards table. He lost completely, not helped at all by Destry's brilliant play.

Jess thought, more than once, that the marquis's short stature was the key to his success, though he was not stupid enough to share the thought with anyone else.

As they collected the balls to ready them for the next round, Brent came over to where Jess was standing at the drinks table.

"The countess tells me that you invited yourself to this gathering."

That was blunt, if true. Brent spoke softly but there was an edge of steel in his voice.

"Yes, sir," Jess said, feeling as though he'd been called before a tribunal of one. He could hear Destry and Belmont laughing over something and wished he were with them.

"If you are hoping to ensnare one of my daughters, I will tell you right now that I will have none of it. They are well-brought-up young ladies and know nothing of wastrels like you."

Jess pursed his lips. He straightened but did not bow to this man, who was, after all, his social inferior. "The countess knows why I am here and she also knows that I would do nothing to annoy her, which includes dangling after any young woman not yet out."

Brent gave him a curt nod and, without another word, shoved his cue into the rack and left the room.

"Poor loser, eh?" Destry asked as he rose up and down on the balls of his feet.

"I think he has another appointment," Belmont said, saluting the two with his glass.

"An appointment?" Destry asked, then smiled. "Ah, with a lady." He thought a moment more. "With the countess."

Even though Belmont did not confirm it, he did not deny it, either. Jess became even more certain that Brent and the countess must be having an affair.

It was bad enough to have a corner on Brent's ill will, but now he was sure that the countess would be watching his every move. Not that it mattered, Jess reminded himself. He was here to win the land from Crenshaw. No other reason.

As for distracting Beatrice Brent from Crenshaw, he would have to tread carefully there. It might be a mistake to flirt with a woman who was too young to understand the game.

Chapter Eleven

As THEIR MAID was combing out her hair, always her last preparation for bed, Beatrice judged it just the right time for a little gossip.

"Darwell, tell us what you know about the marquis Destry, would you? Please." Beatrice added the last word as a gesture of goodwill.

Darwell paused a moment. "I do not gossip, miss."

"Of course not, Darwell, I am not asking for gossip." Belatedly Beatrice decided that what she wanted was information and that was not gossip, was it?

"I would like to know more about him. Papa could only tell us that he is to inherit the Bendas dukedom someday. Surely there is more to him than that, just as there is more to us than that we will inherit money when Papa dies."

Darwell finished with her and patted her shoulder. She changed seats with her sister and Darwell began the same routine with Ceci as Beatrice settled on the bed and braided her hair.

"His parents spent most of their time in London and I would often see his nursemaid in the park. He was ever a sickly baby. He grew out of that phase, but his nurse fretted constantly that he was not growing as he should. Finally she told me that they were going north to the family seat in the hope that the bracing Northumberland air would be good for him."

Darwell shook her head and continued to brush Cecilia's hair. Beatrice looked at her sister's reflection in the mirror. Cecilia shrugged her shoulders.

"Do you know the Earl of Belmont?" Beatrice asked.

Darwell brightened at the change of subject. "Not well, but I do know he never misses a trick. He is just the man to go to if you have a puzzle to be solved. I think he could even solve a murder, if the need arose."

"A murder?" Her hair half braided, Beatrice sat up on her knees, absolutely fascinated.

"That is not all imagination on my part, miss. His valet says that the earl has a theory that Napoleon did not die of a stomach ailment but was poisoned."

"Poisoned?" Cecilia said, incredulous.

"I am going to ask him about it." Beatrice was intrigued. "Lord Belmont is a fascinating man."

When she caught the speculative look in Darwell's eyes, she added, "Though being old and poor makes him less than appealing for anything more than the most ladylike flirtation."

That made Cecilia laugh, and even Darwell's lips twitched in a half smile.

"Bitsy, what in the world is a 'ladylike flirtation'?"

Beatrice thought it over. "When one makes it perfectly clear that one is enjoying a gentleman's company."

"But that's the way one should treat every gentleman. Is that not right, Darwell?"

Their maid considered the question carefully. "Not always. There are some gentlemen it is wise to avoid altogether."

Beatrice frowned. "Like Lord Jessup Pennistan?"

Darwell's expression changed from thoughtfulness to one that hinted at deeply repressed anger. "Not Lord Jessup, miss. He is one of the finest gentlemen in the world. Let no one ever convince you otherwise. I know it. I have seen his goodness."

The two waited for Darwell to go on. Cecilia's eyes were wide with surprise at the maid's vehemence as much as her words. Beatrice began to ask for details but Darwell raised her hand holding the brush.

"I will say no more. When I am no longer in service to you, you will both appreciate the fact that I am not a gossip." She lowered the brush and inspected Cecilia. "Your hair is finished, miss. Now go to bed. I will clean the brushes, put your clothes away, and see you in the morning. Your riding habits will be out and ready before breakfast, which will be served beginning at nine o'clock."

When she left the room Cecilia and Beatrice looked at each other. *What was that about, do you think?* Cecilia asked, her eyes narrowed in speculation.

I have no idea, Beatrice thought, even as she tried to guess.

Bitsy, I am not even sure I want to know.

Beatrice widened her eyes. *I do. I truly do.*

Finally Cecilia spoke aloud. "Just be careful who you choose to ask about it."

Beatrice nodded.

"You know, Bitsy, it's an inconvenient blessing that she doesn't gossip. For we are much too open around her."

"But I will find someone who's willing to tell me everything they know," Beatrice said.

"Of course," Cecilia agreed.

"Not the countess. She is too close to Papa and, besides, she would wonder at our curiosity about a man Papa has ordered us to avoid."

Each climbed into her own small but elegantly canopied bed.

"Did you have the servants move the beds closer together?" Beatrice asked.

"Yes, it was only a matter of moving the table that was between the beds. This way we can whisper as long into the night as we wish without waking Darwell."

"Wonderful," Beatrice replied. "But Darwell is our maid, not our governess."

"I know, Bitsy, but I can't help but feel that she would report to Papa, or at least the countess, if we did anything of which she did not approve."

"I think you may be right." They were both silent a moment, Beatrice listening for Darwell. "Can you hear her?" she whispered.

"No," Ceci whispered back. "I do think she has gone to bed."

Beatrice nodded and hurried on in a hushed tone. "Who can we ask? Katherine Wilson might have overheard her mother and her friends discussing the matter."

Ceci's nod lacked conviction.

"Ceci, you know how Mama loved to share tea and news with her friends. That's how we found out about any number of things she would just as soon have kept from us."

"I am sure Katherine has had the same experience," Cecilia agreed, "but I am much less sure she would share anything with us."

Beatrice thought Cecilia might be right. Katherine Wilson was trying so hard, too hard, to be perfectly well behaved. She and Cecilia had that in common. Still, their new friendship might make it possible for them to share confidences.

"Mrs. Kendrick. *She* would be one to tell all she knows, and welcome all we know." Though Beatrice wondered what they could possibly have to share that was likely to be as intriguing as Lord Jess's story.

Ceci responded with a low "hmmm" and Beatrice was sure her sister had not heard a word.

Sighing softly to herself, she turned on her side, wound her leg around the bed linens as she was wont to do, and followed her sister's example. It took her several moments to relax. She was distracted by the memory of Darwell's final words to them—she and Cecilia would be riding in the morning. Beatrice fell asleep trying to devise a way to excuse herself from an exercise that she abhorred and her twin loved.

CECILIA SMOOTHED HER dark green habit and raised her face to the sky, risking freckles to be one with nature for just a minute. What was that bit of Wordsworth that Bitsy so favored? *"All that we behold is full of blessings."* Today was such a day.

The storm of the previous night had made for a clear sky and it was the perfect morning for a ride. She looked around for her sister and saw that she had not moved from the head of the trail.

"Oh, do come on, Bitsy. That horse is the most placid animal, but surely she can move faster than that. She can eat later." Cecilia's much livelier mount jiggled his bridle in agreement. She soothed him with a hand to his neck and watched her sister.

"I do not care to ride in the wood. It's too easy for a horse to stumble."

"Calling this a wood is like calling your horse a champion." Cecilia considered the copse of trees. There was a wood beyond and a river which she hoped to reach sometime before noon.

"You go on ahead, Ceci. I'll catch up, or maybe you can stop and collect me on the way back."

"Why did you even come? You could have read or spent time in the gallery."

"I keep thinking that if I ride more I will grow to like it better."

"Like it? I would be pleased if you didn't look like you were facing a death sentence every time you mounted."

"It could be a death sentence for someone my size. I'm too small to have any control at all."

The words were barely out of her mouth when the sound of hooves moving at an alarming rate caught Cecilia's attention. She shifted her horse closer to Beatrice and the sweet slug that was her mount for the day

as a man on a great black horse came over the first rise
beyond the stables and went thundering by them.

The red scarf around his neck announced the rider
as Marquis Destry, but he was moving so fast there
was no time to exchange greetings. In fact he did not
even acknowledge their presence.

"You see, Bitsy, size has nothing to do with the ability to control a horse. Or enjoy a rousing gallop." Despite Destry's lack of manners, Cecilia could not resist
making the point.

"Go join him, Ceci. Please. I will go back to the stable soon and the groom can accompany you."

Cecilia desperately wanted to ride off, but she could
not leave her sister alone. She rode back to the groom
who was waiting just out of hearing distance.

"My sister has remembered an invitation she does
not wish to be late for. Would you escort her back to
the stable? She is not sure of the way." With a look of
complete understanding, the groom nodded and followed her back to where Beatrice was waiting.

"Dearest," she began, and explained the lie to her
sister. Beatrice did not even attempt to disagree. Cecilia thought she saw some relief on her sister's face, but
that might have been her imagination.

Cecilia headed out at a sedate walk, moving into a
more satisfying canter as Beatrice and the groom vanished from sight.

When she was into the deeper wood, she slowed her
horse. Determined to avoid Marquis Destry so she
could enjoy the flora and fauna, Cecilia watched
the ground and moved away from the trail he'd left.
She identified the trees as she rode and delighted in the
ferns that grew at the edge of the path.

If she could choose to be a plant she thought it would be a fern, with elegant fronds that opened themselves to the gentle sun that filtered through the trees, which sheltered them from the harshest of weather. Her father would be an oak, she was sure, and Beatrice a violet. Small and delicate, but with its roots digging in everywhere to make itself known and felt.

Lord Destry would be a thistle or some other irritating plant.

Her meditation was cut short by the sound of water. She returned to the well-traveled trail, heading toward the gurgle of water over rock, and found something bigger than a stream but smaller than a river.

There was a ford across it but she was not about to attempt that alone, though her horse showed no hesitation. He lowered his silky neck to drink and she used a nearby rock to aid in her dismount. She dipped her handkerchief into the water, wiped her face, and then found a comfortable seat on the rock, or as comfortable as one could be on a rock. From her new vantage point she surveyed the plants that lined the bank.

Hoofbeats from across the stream drew her horse's attention before she even noticed them herself. Lord Destry appeared on the other side of the ford and moved through it with confidence.

"Good morning, Miss Brent!" He stopped in the middle of the ford while his horse drank. He did not wait for an answer. "If you would like to cross the ford, I can lead your horse for you."

"No thank you, my lord. I was enjoying the solitude but must return to the house in a moment."

He either did not hear, or chose to ignore, the word "solitude," because he rode up beside her, jumping off his horse with practiced ease. There was no doubt that men had the advantage of women when it came to riding. Someday she was going to risk it all and don a pair of trousers so that she could try riding astride herself.

He sat on the rock next to her and began pulling off his boots. "It's a perfect day for wading. The cool of the stream will feel marvelous. Care to join me?"

"My lord!" Cecilia stood up, horribly embarrassed by the suggestion that she show her ankles in public. Not exactly in public, but to a man who was not a relative or even a close friend.

"Miss Brent," he said with a sigh. "I had hoped that any woman who was willing to venture out unaccompanied would not be beyond the very slightest of improprieties."

"You are wrong, my lord, and I am only alone because Beatrice recalled another commitment and the groom escorted her back to the house. I wished to spend a little more time in the wood."

"And would not be deterred by convention, which is my point exactly. You know," he went on, "this is what house parties are for. It is a break from the burden of London rules and prying eyes."

"I would not know, my lord." And if they did go to London, she would hardly be traveling in the same social circle as the heir to a dukedom.

"You will know London soon enough, Miss Brent. And I promise you will look back on this lost adventure with great regret." He had pulled off his boots and stockings. He stood up and waded into the water, his very pale feet quite clear through the gentle wash of the stream.

"Ahhh," was all he said, but he made the sound a long, drawn-out groan of pleasure.

They were perfectly normal, ordinary feet. His was a perfectly ordinary reaction. But still she blushed. Climbing up onto the rock she seated herself on her horse before she said, "I will leave you to your childish play, my lord."

"I will catch up with you!" he called out as she left, which only made her more determined to be back at the stables before he could join her.

She could have made it, she was sure, if she had not been stopped by Lord Crenshaw and her sister who were themselves headed to the river.

"I met your sister on her way to the house and she agreed to ride with me. We are going to cross the ford and meet up with Mrs. Wilson and the countess, who have taken her dogcart the long way round to the old banqueting platform she mentioned last night."

"I'm not sure about the ford," Beatrice began with atypical caution. What she really meant was that she was not sure about trusting the horses to cross the ford without tumbling them into the water.

"Nonsense," Crenshaw said. "I'll be with you and you will be quite safe."

"Of course you are right, my lord," Beatrice said with a firm nod.

"I would never let anything happen to you, my dear girl."

Cecilia watched the scene play out before her. *He would never let anything happen to her.* Now there was a grandiose thought. A tree could fall and kill them both. The horse could be stung by a bee and bolt.

Lord Crenshaw was charming, but his words represented the perfect example of a man's pride taking the place of common sense.

"Of course not, my lord." Beatrice looked away with a knowing grin on her face.

Cecilia watched them ride off, convinced that Beatrice's grin meant that she and her sister were of like minds when it came to men and their pride. Still, it appeared that Lord Crenshaw had some particular interest in her sister.

Cecilia moved on, mulling over whether she was in favor of such a match. Well, there was no point in making a decision on that until she found out if Beatrice herself would consider it.

Chapter Twelve

CECILIA WAS DOING her best to dispel her specula-
tions about Lord Crenshaw and Beatrice when she
heard a mad gallop, apparently the speed at which
Lord Destry did everything.

Lord Destry was almost beside her, still moving at
an unwise speed, when a rabbit darted into the path in
front of his mount. The horse took exception to having
company on the path and reared up. Destry held on
with amazing skill, but just as the horse was settling
yet another rabbit raced after the first. It was too much
for man and horse. Destry was thrown and he landed
on the dirt path with an alarming thump.

With a screech that she swallowed before it became
a full-born scream, Cecilia leapt off her horse and ran
over to Destry who was, ominously, not moving. His
eyes were open and for the most hideous of moments
she thought he was dead.

Then he blinked and her terror resolved itself into anger, close to a wholly unreasonable rage.

"You stupid, stupid man! Why were you riding so fast? Are you hurt?" She put her hands on her hips to still their shaking. His body looked as it should, no arms or legs at odd angles. She waited. When he did speak she understood.

"No breath," he rasped painfully. He closed his eyes and they both waited.

He was a fine figure of a man. When he was lying down and one was not so conscious of his height, he was handsome and very well formed. She blushed a little at the thought but his eyes were still closed so there was no one to tease her about it. Why was it that a tiny woman like Beatrice was not remarked on, but a short man, at least one as short as Lord Destry, was considered an oddity?

"You look as though you are in one piece, my lord," she said with a return of her usual calm. "That is, unless you have broken your back and will be crippled for life."

His eyes flew open at her bluntness and he wiggled his legs and feet.

Relieved, she knelt beside him. He seemed to be breathing more normally. "Are you recovering?"

He nodded. "My horse."

"Enjoying some grass until you are ready to remount."

"Good." He raised himself on one elbow, ignoring the hand she offered. She withdrew it. He would have to beg before she offered him her hand again.

* * *

WILLIAM, YOU IDIOT, he thought. He wanted to swear and was just as glad that he did not have the breath for it since it would dig him deeper into Miss Brent's bad graces. He looked like some schoolboy trying to impress a girl, which he certainly had done but not in the way he'd hoped.

"I am quite all right, Miss Brent." Except for a raging headache and wickedly wrenched shoulder. He sat for a moment, letting the world settle around him, and brushed at his trousers as if that would remove the dirt stains.

He began to stand but stilled when he felt her hands on his shoulders. "Please do not try to stand, my lord. I can see you must still be dizzy."

Yes, he was, but a good part of that came from the sensation of her hands on him, her lovely scent so close, the feel of her breath in his hair. "All right," he said, leaning his head back into the comfort of her breasts. He bit back a smile and groaned a little.

Miss Brent was quiet for much too long. William turned to look at her. She regarded him through narrowed eyes, as though she was not sure whether to trust him or not.

He raised a hand to his temple and rubbed his aching head. "Thank you. Thank you very much. I cannot recall the last time I was thrown from Jupiter."

"We can blame the rabbits. One, any good rider could have handled, but two was quite unexpected."

"Maybe," he allowed, closing his eyes to escape her gaze, but her beauty was now permanently etched in his memory. There was more to the woman than her perfect skin, her white teeth, her beautiful blue eyes, her perfect mouth, and her burnished gold hair. She had handled his fall with calm and sense and had not made a bad toss worse with histrionics. He valued that as much as her looks.

"Shall I find someone to help you?"

He heard concern in her voice, not impatience with his clumsiness, or anger at him for ruining her outing.

"No, I will be fine once I am over the mortification of looking a fool."

"But, my lord, that comes so naturally to you, I would hardly think it mortifying."

There was a set-down that was unexpected. Her air of sweetness hid a touch of acid that surprised him and made him wonder what else she hid behind her lady-like demeanor.

"Then I am in good company." He straightened as he spoke. "As I often think that myself."

Before she could answer, insult him more, or, God forbid, apologize, he hurried on. "I am more sorry than I can say for teasing you last night and then making my observation of the company sound so personal. It was not intended that way."

There was no answering smile, her face remained neutral. *Leave it at that, idiot.* "I can manage now, and thank you again for your help." He rose to his feet.

She stepped back, watching anxiously as he moved toward Jupiter. His arm still ached as much as his head, but he felt steady enough as he looked around for his hat. He spotted it and bent to grab it, ignoring the spin of dizziness, and whistled for his horse. Jupiter came but stopped short of where he was standing.

William turned to Miss Brent, who was still studying him, apparently fearing a faint was not far off.

"No comfort from my horse. I expect he thinks me worse than a fool. We've known each other much too long for him to mistake me for anything but a human subject to absurd behavior on a regular basis."

Miss Brent flushed a little, but did not apologize. Good for her. He liked spine in a woman.

"Can I offer you a leg up onto your horse before I go?" He asked the question and bowed with as much deference as he could muster.

"No thank you, my lord. This stump is all the help I need." She proved it by using the nearby rotting piece of wood to mount. She settled herself and looked back at him.

"Our brother Frederick was killed when a horse threw him," she added. "He was sixteen. Years later my sister was thrown herself and has not ridden comfortably since. You are very lucky, my lord. If you are not at the stable shortly I will send one of the grooms to find you." With that Miss Brent urged her mount toward the stable.

William watched her as she turned away. *Even more wonderful,* he thought with a hefty dose of sarcasm. Not only had he looked too stupid for her to ever consider dancing with him, much less kissing him, but he had reminded her of a heartbreaking loss.

How could he ever hope to redeem himself in her eyes? No need to figure out why it mattered. He could still feel heat where his head had rested against her. Only a bigger fool than he was would deny the attraction.

*   *   *

"I DO NOT know who was more embarrassed, the marquis or me. And I was terrified for a moment." Cecilia stopped her washing-up and looked at her sister.

"Yes, I can imagine only too well."

"I know, dearest, and I am sorry to have even mentioned it. It is only that I do not know how to behave with him now."

"I'm sure you're not the first one to call him a name, Ceci. Someone as hell-bent on adventure as he is would hardly be humiliated."

"Bitsy, I'm the one who is humiliated," Ceci all but wailed. "He is a marquis and I called him stupid!" She wrapped herself in a robe and began to pace the room. "How will I behave around him now?"

Beatrice stood in front of her sister to make her stop moving and then took Ceci's tightly clasped hands in her own. "Calm yourself," she commanded. When she had her sister's complete attention, Beatrice went on in a softer voice. "Why should anything change? Do you like him better for falling off his horse?"

"Yes, I do. What I mean is that at least I see him as more human, more like a normal person, which is probably why I spoke that way to him. But when I remembered his rank, his place in society, I could not even find the words to apologize."

"Then let me remind you what you told me he said last night." Cecilia nodded and Beatrice went on. "Luck and chance are all that separate the heir to a dukedom from the rest of mankind. Or something like that."

"And," Cecilia added, "they have 'wit enough to

pretend that they are better than the rest of the citizenry.' I recall that part exactly."

"Keep all of it in mind and treat him just as you would those would-be gallants at the Assemblies in Birmingham."

"Oh, I could never do that."

"For the love of God, Ceci, he is not a royal, and has proved that even he can be thrown from a horse. He is not any more special than Papa or Roger."

"Hmmm" was all Cecilia said. Beatrice gave up trying to convince her and turned her full attention to her own toilette.

By the time they were abed twelve hours later, Cecilia realized that she need not have worried. At dinner that evening she was seated between Lord Crenshaw and the earl, as far from the marquis as was possible.

The evening's amusement involved a theater troupe brought from London to perform for them. The play, Sheridan's *The Rivals*, was familiar to everyone, but the actress who played Mrs. Malaprop brought such humor to the role that even those most familiar with the story were entertained.

Over tea and brandy the countess invited them to try to converse like Mrs. Malaprop, whose defining characteristic was her hilarious tendency to confuse similar-sounding words. It was amusing, especially when Lord Crenshaw suggested it was an effort for Mr. Brent to fend off the "gallons" who wished to court his daughters. But the best of all was when Lord Belmont insisted he was not under the "affluence" of wine or brandy.

Cecilia thought she could do something with "pity"

and "pretty" but decided not to call attention to herself.

Neither the marquis nor Lord Jess joined in this game. They were deep in conversation with Mrs. Kendrick and missed all but the last bit when the laughter over Lord Belmont's phrase drew their attention.

"What did we miss?" Destry called out as he joined them.

"It will be our secret for 'old' time," Beatrice told him, and they all laughed again with Destry none the wiser.

As she fell asleep that night Cecilia decided that it would be easy enough to avoid Lord Destry the next day by the simple expedient of not riding.

FORGOING HER MORNING ride was an excellent strategy for avoiding the marquis, but what Cecilia had failed to take into account was how bored she would be without the exercise. She was also constrained by the need to avoid places where he might be found. That meant she spent an inordinate amount of time with her sister doing things Bitsy loved but Cecilia found monumentally dull.

"This is ridiculous, Ceci," Beatrice insisted as they explored the library after spending an hour in the chapel examining the stained-glass windows. "You are so good at seeing to the heart of the matter. Would it not be easier to apologize than to be looking over your shoulder every minute?"

"You think I should apologize?"

"No! What you have to do is stop avoiding him or

soon he will notice and that will make it even more uncomfortable."

Why must Beatrice be right so often?

BEATRICE FELT NOBLE for insisting that Ceci stop being foolish. She'd rather liked having her sister for company all day. They had explored the library and found a folio of drawings of flowers and shrubs of Kent which both of them had enjoyed examining. Cecilia even forgot about hiding from the marquis for long enough to ask a footman to carry the folio onto the patio so they could examine it in better light.

In the end Cecilia was no more relaxed than she had been the day before and Beatrice knew she had to convince her twin to speak to the marquis.

They were both distracted from their concerns when Darwell was late and they needed to help each other dress for dinner.

The maid finally came into the room looking less composed than usual and Beatrice looked at her sister. *Has she been crying?*

Ceci gave her a nod of agreement. *Do not ask. Pretend everything is normal.*

Darwell tried to act as if nothing was amiss, but her distraction was obvious. They were ready to put on their dresses when she came to her senses and, without apology, announced: "No, no, those are not the right gowns for this evening. There is a theme to tonight's dinner and you both will look perfect in these."

For Cecilia she drew out an off-white dress with black lace around the flounces. It was a very sophisticated dress for an ingénue, but according to Darwell perfectly acceptable for a private country party. Beatrice's dress was even more dramatic, a white gown with a Greek key trim on the skirt made with a fine braid, deftly woven.

Darwell misbuttoned Beatrice's dress twice and finally Cecilia could not stand it anymore. "Darwell, please, tell us what is wrong. You seem upset."

"Not at all, miss," she said, stiffening.

"Nonsense," Cecilia said with unexpected sharpness. "We can be as discreet with your confidences as you are with ours. Has someone offended you?"

"It's nothing, Miss Cecilia."

Cecilia waited, and Beatrice turned to look at Darwell even though her dress was not yet entirely done up.

Darwell closed her eyes. "Lord Jess's valet."

"All right," Beatrice encouraged, "what about him?"

"This is ridiculous. I am a grown woman. I am near fifty years old. I will discuss it no further."

Cecilia did not think she needed to. She looked at her sister, who nodded agreement.

Beatrice handed Darwell a comb. "Very well, as long as you can assure us that the valet is not insulting or, God forbid, assaulting you."

Cecilia added, "You must know we would not . . ." She paused and began again. "None of us, including Papa and the countess, would tolerate any abuse of someone so close to us."

Gathering her dignity once again, Darwell curtsied. "No, Miss Brent. Callan has done nothing to offend or insult me. He never would."

Having only half the story did nothing to alleviate the constraint among them, but Darwell was in fine

form once again and did a masterful job of styling
their hair to suit their dresses.

Tonight the countess did not come for them. Darwell
told them that a footman would escort them to the library, where the group would congregate. They had
been there earlier in the day, but they were grateful for
the guidance. It was too easy to lose one's way in such
an enormous building.

All the way down the stairs and around the main
floor the two discussed Darwell. Surely it was a love
affair that had their maid so flustered. Very romantic,
they agreed, and Beatrice decided she would try to
wheedle information about Callan from Lord Jess.

Before they reached the door to the library Beatrice
halted their progress. "Tell me how you are going to
handle the marquis."

"I will forget about it, if he does."

With a nod of acceptance, if not outright agreement,
Beatrice gestured to the footman to open the door.

Beatrice slowed as she entered the room. It was so
poorly lit that it had a completely different atmosphere
than it had had earlier in the day. At that time the
room had been filled with light from the windows at
each end, with candles lit for close reading.

Now the curtains were drawn, even though it was
still light out, and the only light came from the chan-
delier overhead.

At Beatrice's "Are we in the right salon?" the footman nodded. She and Cecilia went fully into the room
where another servant offered them a glass of sherry.
They both declined the spirits, and Beatrice looked
around the room, hoping they were not the first guests
to arrive.

Thank goodness Lord Crenshaw was there. He hurried over to them with a conspiratorial expression.

"This is a bit of a mystery, is it not?"

"Yes, indeed," Beatrice agreed.

"The countess is famous for her creativity," Crenshaw went on. "And I think we are about to experience it firsthand."

Mrs. Wilson and her daughter came in right behind them. Mrs. Wilson stopped short on the threshold. "This cannot be right!"

"Come in, come in," Crenshaw said, as though he knew exactly what was in store for them and could not wait to share it.

"Why is the room so dark?" Miss Wilson asked. Was that a tinge of fear Beatrice heard in her voice? Really, the girl was much too easily frightened.

"Lord Crenshaw tells me it is part of the grand scheme for the evening," Beatrice reassured her.

The other ladies seemed inclined to stay in a group around the baron, so Beatrice stayed with them even though she knew what would happen. Mrs. Wilson would prattle on for hours about her life, about people and places her audience had never heard of or met.

"The vicar verily invites himself to dinner," Mrs. Wilson started, "and then annoys everyone with his bodily noises. My husband insists it is a compliment, but I would prefer even a poorly worded thank-you letter."

Beatrice was not sure how he managed it, but Lord Crenshaw turned from the other ladies and took her arm, and in a moment they had escaped the group and were seated on the sofa on the other side of the room.

"How did you do that?" Beatrice asked.

"Do what, my dear?" he answered with a half smile.

"Manage to remove us from Mrs. Wilson so deftly and without insult? I must learn such tactics before we go to London."

"I could teach you that and so much more if you would like."

Beatrice answered with a cautious nod, suddenly feeling discomfited by his tone if not his words.

Crenshaw laughed and patted her hand. "Lord Jess is the rake, Miss Beatrice. Not I. I mean to instruct you in any number of social niceties that can spare you boredom and embarrassment during your time among the ton."

"Thank you, my lord," Beatrice said, relaxing more, though now *she* was distracted. The mere mention of Lord Jess's name made her wonder where he was. "I am sure there is more to learn than dance steps before we are ready for the London social world."

The marquis came into the room and Beatrice watched as he approached Mrs. Wilson, her daughter, and Cecilia.

CECILIA WAS ACTUALLY happy to see Lord Destry. The truth was she would have been happy to see anyone who would rescue her from Mrs. Wilson's pointless chatter. Mrs. Wilson stepped back to make room for the newcomer but did not break off her story.

Destry smiled and nodded in all the right places, and Cecilia wondered if he was registering a word the woman was saying. Was that the secret to enduring this inanity?

"My husband insists that some estate emergency is keeping him away from the house party."

"I can completely understand your husband's wish to stay home, alone," Destry answered, proving that he was listening after all. Cecilia had to bite her lip to keep from laughing.

"I wish you would tell me why, my lord," Mrs. Wilson said, her aggrieved air even more pronounced.

Destry glanced at Cecilia and she added, "Please do, sir," as though she were desperate for an explanation of the inner workings of the masculine mind.

His words were addressed to Mrs. Wilson, but he did not look away from Cecilia as he said them.

"Because the quiet of nature is so appealing after the chaos of family life."

Cecilia smiled at the private joke and decided the man liked to tease everyone and not just her. It was a peculiar sort of relief to know she had not been singled out.

The word "chaos" was all the invitation Mrs. Wilson needed to launch into a discussion of the various illnesses and inconveniences of her household staff. Really, it was enough to put one off marriage entirely.

"Good evening, Miss Brent. Destry." Lord Jess appeared beside her, dressed all in black. The small pearl-and-diamond stickpin that decorated his cravat was the only relief from the effect of midnight.

"I imagine that your valet must have discovered the theme for this evening as well," Cecilia said by way of welcome.

"Something to do with night or darkness?" Destry guessed, then added, "Why wasn't my valet given the information?"

"I have no idea, but Darwell was insistent that we wear these particular gowns."

"Leonie Darwell is your lady's maid?" Lord Jess asked. His surprise was tinged with something else she could not name.

He knew Darwell well enough to know her Christian name, Cecilia noticed. She took a step back, wondering if she had stumbled onto an ill-advised topic of conversation. "Yes, she is," she began, then paused and began again. "That is, the countess arranged for her to care for us for the Season."

It struck Cecilia that this was the perfect opening to find out how well Darwell knew Lord Jess's valet. "Darwell seems to know your valet very well. His name is Callan?"

"Yes, Callan." He considered the statement and then laughed and addressed Lord Destry. "That explains how he knew what the theme was. Darwell passed it on to him."

He looked down at his coat as though noticing it for the first time. "He has been excessively meticulous with my appearance the last day or two. I accused him of trying to impress someone. If it is Darwell then I congratulate his good taste."

That wasn't much help. The *tendre* was news to Lord Jess. There would be no information from him after all.

"As for you, Miss Brent, Darwell is a loyal and talented maid. You and your sister could not have chosen better."

It sounded as though he knew Darwell better than his own valet. What in the world did Lord Jess and Darwell have in common? Not that she dared ask.

Without an immediate response from her the silence grew awkward with the unasked question hanging in the air between them. How fortunate that he could not read her expressions the way Beatrice could.

Cecilia was spared the onslaught of complete embarrassment by the countess's entrance. *Finally.*

Chapter Thirteen

THE COUNTESS DID not have to break a glass to draw their attention this time. Destry noted that even Mrs. Wilson stopped talking mid-sentence. The countess was dressed in a black gown, but it could never be taken for a mourning outfit. Diamond-like crystals glittered in the light from every inch of the fabric.

Two footmen followed her, carrying large, well-shaded flambeaux. Their presence and the uneven light from the torches added to the guests' mood of cautious uncertainty.

"She is a dark fairy who has deigned to join us," Destry announced to the room, giving the countess an opening with which to commence.

The countess curtsied to him. "One can always count on you to play the game, my lord."

"With pleasure, my lady." Destry bowed to her.

"What in the world is she planning?" Cecilia whispered, most likely to Beatrice, who had joined the group. The low hum of voices echoed the question.

"I have no idea," Beatrice answered and then turned a questioning look at Destry.

"Something very, very different," Destry said, stating the obvious. *God help me,* he thought. After not seeing Cecilia all day he'd managed to be clever for exactly one minute.

Before he could say anything else which was bound to be equally inept, the countess spoke again.

"Good evening, everyone! Tonight we are going to experience the dark and dread world of Dr. Frankenstein. Is that name familiar to any of you?"

Destry looked around the room and saw Belmont nod and Mrs. Kendrick raise her hand a little. Cecilia Brent edged closer to her sister. Destry stepped toward the duo as well, since no one had told him not to.

CECILIA WOULD NEVER raise her hand but Beatrice knew she recognized that name and the story.

"It's the book that Ellis brought us from London." Beatrice widened their circle a bit to include Lord Destry in their conversation. "He only brought the first volume. I've always wondered how it ended."

"Perhaps we will find out tonight," Destry said with obvious delight.

"In the novel, Dr. Frankenstein attempted to create a human being." The countess caught the eye of each of her guests. "He succeeded, but not entirely, as the creature he gave life to was more a monster."

Belmont raised his hand. "One could argue that it

was the way mankind treated him that made him a monster."

"Yes, indeed, my lord. I should have said that he had the physical look of a monster."

Belmont nodded and the countess went on.

"Tonight we will hear a reading of highlighted parts of the novel after dinner. We are expecting other guests, welcome and unwelcome, as the evening progresses."

"Who could she mean?" Cecilia was not fond of surprises.

"Maybe she has discovered the author of the book and he will attend." Beatrice thought that would be fabulous. "But it's probably just a way of establishing a mood, especially for those who have not read the book."

The countess walked across the library to stand near the fireplace. "Now follow me, please. We will make our way through a hidden passage, from here to the dining room."

"What fun!" Beatrice said, not in a whisper, drawing the attention of the assembly.

"I hope so, dear Beatrice," the countess said as all the guests drew closer to her.

Beatrice could easily hear the pause in Miss Wilson's voice when she said, "A secret passage?"

"There is no need to be afraid. It's probably just a back way for the servants," Lord Crenshaw reassured her.

"But I hate small enclosed spaces."

"No, you don't. I will see that you are safe."

Despite his gallant offer to secure her safety, Beatrice thought that Lord Crenshaw's denial of Katherine's fear was an absurd statement from a man who had made her acquaintance only a day ago.

Beatrice noticed Lord Jess's reaction, and was taken aback by the anger she saw in his face. She squelched her own criticism and tried another tack, announcing to no one in particular, "I would imagine that a house as old as this one must have several secret passages."

"And ghosts," Lord Destry added. "Excellent!"

Everyone laughed at Destry's boyish enthusiasm. Even Lord Jess, whose expression was now more relaxed, though he did keep glancing at Lord Crenshaw with an air of interest, if not calculation.

The countess nodded to the butler. "Mervis, open the door to the hidden passage."

With some effort, the older servant pulled on a ring that decorated the edge of the mantel. Soundlessly, the entire bookcase swung out to reveal a short flight of steps and a passage that dissolved into darkness.

"It would have been better if it had creaked," Lord Jess whispered into Beatrice's ear.

"I find it reassuring to know that someone has maintained it," Beatrice answered.

"You're not afraid, are you?" he asked with a laugh.

"Only of breaking my leg," she answered. She took a step away from him. He was standing too close, so close that she could feel him even when he was not touching her.

He matched her movement, restoring the nearness of their bodies. "It's your scent," he whispered, bending down so that his breath tickled her ear. "The fragrance you wear, it's . . ." He paused and thought for a moment. "It's captivating."

Like his eyes, she thought, and could not decide whether to abandon her new perfume or bathe in it.

"I should like to go first," Lord Belmont announced, stepping to the front of the line.

"I knew this would capture your interest, my lord earl," the countess said, "but one of the footmen with a lighted torch will take the lead and I will follow. Marquis Destry, will you be the last of our party with the other torch behind you?"

Destry bowed with a flourish.

"If anyone should prefer not to follow this route, Mervis will show you a more conventional way to the small banquet room."

Mrs. Wilson stepped closer to the butler, but was the only one to do so. Her daughter looked doubtful, but with an encouraging nod from Lord Crenshaw, she took his arm.

"This is not my idea of entertainment," Cecilia whispered to her sister. "But I am not going to act like some old lady."

"Bravo, Ceci." Beatrice patted her arm. "I will go in front of you and Lord Destry will be behind you, so there will be help should you need it." It would give her sister a chance to be near him without needing to maintain a conversation.

"His idea of help would probably be dousing the torches so that we could only feel our way through the passage."

"Ceci, he is right behind you."

"Indeed I am, and what an excellent suggestion, but since it is your idea, I do think I will have to come up with one of my own."

"I beg your pardon, my lord," Cecilia said, sounding both embarrassed and annoyed.

"No need, Miss Brent. You have my measure already." He would have gone on, but Mrs. Wilson began a soliloquy on why she could not join them, as if everyone wished to know.

Beatrice pulled her sister close and whispered. "I do believe the marquis forgives you all real and imagined insults."

"Do you think? He does not seem to mind." Cecilia let go of a sigh and Beatrice could see her mood lighten considerably.

When Mrs. Wilson finished and the countess sent her on her way with Mervis, the rest lined up as Beatrice suggested, with Lord Jess in front of her. Better than being in front of him and pretending she did not care how she looked from the back.

The lead footman descended the four steps into the passageway that sloped gently but inexorably down. They moved slowly and, as she stepped into the passage, Beatrice lifted her skirt with one hand and reached out the other to touch the wall. It was dry and smooth and cold to the touch.

When she reached the bottom of the short flight of steps, Beatrice noticed that lit torches were set high on the wall for as far as she could see, but they just cast confusing shadows, adding to the haunted feel of the dim space.

"This is not so bad," Cecilia whispered.

Apparently the whisper carried in the narrow space.

"No, no, Miss Brent," Destry said. "A comment like that is just asking for trouble."

No sooner had he spoken than Beatrice heard the scuttling sound of something small and four-footed.

Destry's "You see? What in the world was that?" was not at all reassuring.

Lord Jess turned and spoke over his shoulder. "Have no fear, ladies. I am sure that sound is only for effect."

"We're not afraid, are we, Cecilia?"

"No," said Cecilia. Her single word was so loaded with doubt that Beatrice had to bite her lip to keep from laughing.

"I will step closer to you, Miss Cecilia," Destry said. He must have, for Cecilia moved closer to her sister. A moment later Cecilia made a sound of distress, and began a dance of frantic movement. "Something just brushed my hand."

"I'm sure it was only the tip of my scarf, Miss Cecilia," Lord Destry said. "It's nothing to be afraid of."

"Your scarf? It was your scarf?" She was almost crying and then, with what Beatrice knew was a supreme effort, Cecilia went on. "Then perhaps you are standing a little too close, my lord."

Mrs. Kendrick's laughter echoed back to them and Beatrice relaxed a little. "Think of us as a troop of soldiers, Miss Brent," Mrs. Kendrick called out. "We are made comrades by the unknown, determined to protect one another no matter what happens."

"I was thinking," Beatrice said, "that we are like a group of children who have very mixed feelings about this adventure but are reassuring ourselves of a nice treat at the end."

"No, we are adults who are playing and frightening ourselves in the process."

"You are marvelous, Miss Cecilia," Jess said from

his position directly in front of them. "Cutting right to the truth of the matter."

"Let's move on," the countess ordered kindly.

"Ladies," Jess turned and whispered to the sisters, "I wager a guinea that Miss Wilson screams first."

Neither of them had a chance to accept or decline the wager before an unfamiliar masculine voice echoed along the passage and they all froze. It was heavily accented. German, perhaps.

"Dr. Frankenstein," the voice called out in a macabre bass. "Help me. Help me. Help me." The last was a long drawn-out wail that did, indeed, make Katherine Wilson scream.

While the voice chilled Beatrice to the bone, she was rational enough to find amusement in the theatrics.

Then someone ahead of them stumbled, and the reaction echoed down the line. Beatrice lost her footing on the descending path and wrapped her arms around Lord Jessup so she did not fall or push him into Miss Wilson who was in front of him.

Jess wrapped his hands around hers as they cinched his waist, her face pressed into his back. Surrounded by darkness, she could barely see, but she could feel his breath sharpen, the muscles in his back ripple. She wished there was more light and that they were face-to-face so she could raise her eyes to his and see what he was thinking, whether he was as aware of her as she was of him.

Instead she pulled her arms out of his grasp with a whispered, "Thank you, my lord. I only needed a moment's support." Then wished she had come up with something a little more flirtatious.

"And here I thought you were flirting with me."

"No!" she protested. "I was afraid that if I fell, others would, too."

"How thoughtful," he said agreeably.

She didn't have to flirt; he was good enough at it for both of them. She pressed her lips together, not that anyone could see her smile.

They moved forward once again, but now they could hear someone crying and Lord Crenshaw's voice, reassuring but edged with frustration. "Calm yourself. It's only a party game."

Lord Jess reached forward and put his arm around Miss Wilson's waist. "Forgive my impertinence, Miss Wilson, but close your eyes and hold on to me. Think of being in a meadow or some other large open space. Let your imagination go there and we will be in the dining room in just a moment."

How kind of him, Beatrice thought, his thoughtfulness pushing her interest in him one notch higher. Maybe he used teasing and flirtation as a way to hide his more generous nature.

I want to know this man better. I want to know what he thinks, how he sees the world, how I would fit into his arms, and what his kiss is like. It was a truth she would keep to herself for now.

A few more steps, a turn around a sharp corner, and a glowing light announced the end of the trail. Within a minute they joined the party at the back of a room, lit with the same flambeaux in tall stands. The ladies stood apart from the gentlemen and took a moment to shake out their skirts The gentlemen brushed off their sleeves, though there was no sign of dust or insects.

Beatrice turned to Katherine Wilson. "Are you quite all right now, Katherine?" She cared for the girl, but was also grateful for the excuse to avoid Lord Jess's distracting presence.

Katherine nodded, but she was still shivering and Beatrice wondered if she should offer to take her to her mother.

"I am so sorry, my dear," Lord Crenshaw said, "and I apologize to you, too, Miss Brent. I had no idea her fear was so real."

Beatrice knew he valued her good opinion and though she thought him in the wrong, she nodded her acceptance of his apology. Lord Crenshaw offered her his arm and they moved away from the end of the passage.

While the countess fussed over Katherine Wilson, full of apologies, Lord Crenshaw escorted Beatrice over to Cecilia and then stood with them.

"How many more such passages are there?" Destry asked, his enthusiasm obvious, giving everyone a happy distraction.

"I am sure there is one less passage than Lord Destry would like," Cecilia breathed to her sister.

"Mervis could tell you," the countess said. "I can never quite recall."

Flanked by the two footmen with their flambeaux, the countess approached the table. Before she could take her seat the disembodied voice called out, again.

"Dr. Frankenstein. I need you. I am begging. Please." The last word was an agonized plea. After a moment of silence the voice called out, "I will make you pay for this!" This pronouncement was thunderous and everyone jumped. At least all the ladies did.

"Who is that?" Cecilia whispered with some vehemence to no one in particular.

"Is the voice familiar to you?" Lord Jess asked, looking at her with a calculating eye. "Care to wager? I will take Mr. Wilson, who is a practical joker of the highest order. He has decided to join us and that is why his wife did not come with us through the secret passage."

"I accept that. One guinea, my lord?" Beatrice said with a coquettish tilt of her head.

"Bitsy! Papa would never approve of that," Cecilia whispered. "You know how he dislikes using money for such things."

"But I know it's not Mr. Wilson," Beatrice whispered back. "Even Papa would agree that wagering on something you are certain of is like a wise business decision."

"Hmmm" was all Cecilia said, apparently unconvinced.

"Who do you think it is, Miss Beatrice?" Destry asked.

"I do not have to say the name aloud, do I?" Beatrice turned to Lord Jess. "Only to you."

"Yes, that will be sufficient for me as long as no one else accepts the wager." Beatrice came close to him and whispered the name. Lord Jess smiled like a pleased tutor.

"Your gaming had best end with this, Bitsy," Cecilia whispered with unusual sharpness.

"Have we not already agreed to be taught after Papa leaves?" Beatrice murmured, and then added, "I am not sure how I will find out if I am right."

"Where is he speaking from?" Destry asked, rising up and down on the balls of his feet as if that would help him see better.

All four of them scanned the walls of the room. Only

then did Beatrice notice the artwork. The space had a vaulted ceiling with the ceiling panel painted as the heavens. The walls were a single continuous mural depicting something monumental and Roman. She must come back and see this in better light.

"He could easily blend in with the life-size men in the mural, especially with the room so dimly lit." This contribution from Lord Jess.

The rest of the party stood in another group except for Lord Belmont, who was making a circuit of the space.

"Lord Belmont may find out for us," Beatrice observed. "For him it is another mystery to be solved."

"Ladies and gentlemen."

The three words called their attention to the countess, who was now seated at the head of the table with the two footmen standing on either side of her. The crystals on her dress caught the light, the glow making her look intimidating as it proclaimed her majesty.

With a silent gesture to Destry to seat himself at the foot of the table she acknowledged him as the ranking nobleman present.

"Isn't it interesting that, without a spouse, the countess can devise a number of different seating arrangements that honor us by rank?" Cecilia was twisting her hands together, trying to hide her nerves.

"So that guarantees we will always be in the middle," Beatrice added with logic. "But you watch and see if we do not always have a different gentleman seated next to us."

"Oh, do you think that's what she intends?" Cecilia looked down at her dress and smoothed a nonexistent crease.

Before Beatrice could answer her sister, indeed before she could admit that she had no idea what the countess intended, the disembodied voice spoke again.

"Sit down, now, my lord." His command was whispered and was all the more threatening for it.

Belmont bowed in response and left his study of the darker corners of the room. He sat to the countess's right, Crenshaw to her left, and the footman guided the others to their seats.

The countess raised her glass. "Here's to an intriguing evening."

Chapter Fourteen

TONIGHT BEATRICE WAS again seated next to Lord
Jess. Was that an answer to her unspoken wish to
know him better? Lord Crenshaw was on her other
side for the first time since they had all dined together.

Dinner was served in the French style and they began
to help themselves from the platters arrayed around
the table. Beatrice was relieved that the salmon was
not near and considered the haricots verts enough of a
penance. Did they never go out of season?

"Have you heard of this novel, my lord?" Beatrice
asked Lord Crenshaw, earning a smile of approval
from the countess.

"Yes, and I do not think *Frankenstein* an appropriate book for a young woman to read."

His comment made Beatrice all the more glad that
she had not admitted to any familiarity with it. "You
have read it then?"

"No," he said. He ate some trout and went on. "A

woman's sensibilities are too delicate to deal with monsters of any kind."

"Yes, I can see that you would like to protect those you care about from all the horrors of the world."

"Indeed, I would protect anyone I cared for and I have."

Beatrice heard something in his voice she could not quite identify, but went on anyway.

"How noble of you, my lord, but surely you know that is impossible. Childbirth is a monster all its own and one women have been forced to face alone since Adam and Eve."

"That is not a subject to be discussed at dinner, or ever between a man and a woman who are not married." Lord Crenshaw's tone would have made ice shiver. Beatrice flinched.

Now she recognized the edge in his voice. Anger. He was incensed about something. Was it what she had said? She looked up, desperately wishing for someone to rescue her from her mistake.

Lord Jess was watching them with an intensity that was as unsettling as Lord Crenshaw's anger.

"How many think it is possible for monsters to exist?" Lord Jess's raised voice drew everyone's attention.

Relief overwhelmed Beatrice's anxiety, and she felt even more charitable toward Lord Jess. She smiled at him, meaning only gratitude, but she could read Cecilia's expression. *Stop grinning at him like a lovesick milkmaid.*

Milkmaid. Surely not. But she tamed her smile. Her relief was short-lived.

"The idea of monsters is nonsense," Lord Crenshaw

responded, with unnecessary vehemence. The two men stared at each other as though they would prefer to be dueling with swords and not just words. And Beatrice was in the middle.

"Not necessarily." Belmont's calm voice added a much-needed dose of reason. "Let's start with ghosts. How many here accept them as possible?"

The countess spoke up promptly.

"I went through the attics here when the earl and I were first married," the countess began, "and in one of the larger closets I walked in on a man reading near a window. He looked most annoyed with me and I hurried out of the room apologizing profusely. As I walked back down the passage I realized that I could see through him. Yes, I believe in ghosts."

Beatrice could tell that Mrs. Wilson was not convinced, but was polite enough not to cast aspersions on her hostess's story.

"I have heard compelling stories of monsters deep in the coal mines in Wales, and even one in a loch in Scotland." The earl sipped his wine and smiled, waiting for the other guests to react.

"Told by illiterate men who drink too much blue ruin." Crenshaw waved his hand as though to dismiss the conversation and added, "There are more worthwhile subjects to discuss."

"This is a party, my lord," the countess chided with a charming smile. "We can leave those 'worthwhile subjects' to you gentlemen over your brandy."

"I saw something odd once," Miss Wilson began, rather tentatively. "At my grandfather's house, a week or so after he died."

"A ghost?" Beatrice encouraged.

"No, it was something in the night sky. It resembled a star but was the size of a cricket ball. It moved with amazing speed."

"It was a falling star." Crenshaw spoke as though he had been there.

"No, my lord, it was not." Her voice was filled with such urgency that the man started in surprise. "It moved in an uneven pattern, up and down and east to west, then west to east. It grew larger as it came closer to the field in which I stood. Finally, it chose a spot and settled to the ground."

She had the complete attention of everyone at the table. Beatrice half smiled at the footmen standing at service. They had lost their usual air of indifference. Indeed they were more wide-eyed than the dinner guests.

"What happened next?" Destry prompted.

"I don't know. I ran away." She covered her mouth for a moment. "You see, I did not want to know."

"Every time you tell that story it grows more strange." Mrs. Wilson was trying to look amused but was not very successful, her eyes darting from one guest to the next to see what they thought.

"But I have only told this story once before, Mama, and that was to you and Papa," Miss Wilson whispered, her discomfort growing.

"I think it was no more than a very vivid dream." Mrs. Wilson ignored her daughter's comment and spoke to the others.

"Undoubtedly a dream, and women have such vivid imaginations." Lord Crenshaw made it sound like imagination was a terrible weakness. Beatrice was seeing a new side to him this evening—one that had little appeal for her.

"If it was a dream, Miss Wilson, then you have the beginnings of a fine novel yourself." Lord Belmont looked thoughtful. "But there have been other such reports in different parts of the country and even the world."

Conversation exploded among the group, as the company considered Belmont's words.

"What do you think of that, Miss Brent?" Lord Jess asked, leaning close, which she appreciated, for she did not wish Lord Crenshaw to hear her answer.

She could see the brown streaks in his blond hair, his surprisingly long eyelashes and blue eyes that were almost always lit with a smile. What was his question? She could not quite recall.

"I'm fascinated," she said finally, hoping it was an adequate answer.

"Do you think Miss Wilson's night visitor could have been from another world?" He did not move closer but his serviette slipped and his effort to grab it brought his face next to hers.

"Are you implying that there are worlds we have yet to discover here on earth?" She moved a little away from him, trying to decide if he was flirting, then reminded herself that she and Roger had proved that a man and woman could carry on an intelligent conversation without it being called a flirtation. "Or do you just wish to prove that women are subject to absurd conjecture?"

"Never. That is Crenshaw's area of expertise." He spoke without looking up, settling his serviette on his lap and taking up his fork.

Yes, she thought. There was a difference between his testing, or was it teasing, behavior and Lord Crenshaw's imperious statements.

Beatrice nibbled on some chicken, while she watched Lord Jess handle his fork. His fingers were long and elegant, with short and brutally clean nails. It was only in contrast to the white of his shirt cuffs that she noticed how bronzed his skin was, as though he spent more time than most in the saddle or not wearing gloves.

"Miss Brent," he began again, "I think we have discovered all intelligent life on this planet. But what about the other planets in our solar system? Or in our universe? My brother David is a man of science and the thought of life from beyond our world fascinates him."

"I have never heard that idea before." She still wondered if he was teasing her. "Dealing with this world is enough of a challenge. Look at the damage Napoleon caused, and even at peace there is enough dissent here in England to demand all our attention. No, we do not need visitors from beyond our world."

"Perhaps Miss Wilson's visitors feel the same way, for they have not made themselves known in a general way, have they?"

"Do you think Miss Wilson truly saw something from another planet?"

"No, I do not. I think it was some comet or meteor. I think she was upset by the death of her grandfather. There are any number of explanations much more sensible than a visitor from the stars."

Beatrice could not have said why she felt relieved by Lord Jess's certainty but she did. Or maybe it was only because she recognized his kindness in not making his thoughts known the way Lord Crenshaw had.

"Shall we take a walk one night, when the moon is new?" he suggested. "We can search the sky for another such visitor. It would go some way toward convincing Miss Wilson that we believe her."

That would be fun, she thought, but kept it to herself since it would be terribly inappropriate.

"We would invite the others, naturally."

Lord Jess sounded as though he felt his reputation would be threatened if he was alone with her.

"Any guests that you think might be sympathetic."

She gave him a searching look and found only polite suggestion in his expression.

"Which would mean neither Lord Crenshaw nor Mrs. Wilson."

"Exactly, I see we are like-minded in that."

She looked away from him and he laughed.

"Now why should the suggestion that we think alike make your color rise?"

"Because I cannot think of anything further from the truth. Not that I mean that as an insult. But our experience of life could not be more different." *And I am curious about you. Too curious for my own good.*

"Don't you think that the countess intended for this party to give you some familiarity with people whose lives have been very different from your own? Mrs. Kendrick, Lord Belmont."

"Practice. I told Cecilia this is practice."

"Life in a city like London will be filled with new adventures every day."

She could not restrain a smile. "It will be so much fun."

He smiled into her eyes. "I wish I could see it through your eyes. It's been too many years since any of it was new to me."

Lord Jess served himself from a platter on his right, and Beatrice found herself relieved that he had looked away. For a minute she had thought she could read his mind. He seemed to feel regretful, to wish that life could be different.

"You will have to make a decision quickly on a gentleman's suitability. Your advisers will not always be readily available."

Now he sounded like a tutor. It was patronizing and she would have none of that. "And I suppose you are the type I should avoid, my lord?"

"Only in London, Miss Brent. Here I am as safe as your maiden aunt or the countess would not have invited me."

"Then, yes, my lord. I should love to scan the night sky for unusual stars. It would be fun." Her enthusiasm was tempered to a ladylike timbre, but she really did want to do it. And she did not want company when they did. Just the two of them, the night sky, and a million stars.

"I do not think your sister would be inclined to go," Lord Jess said in a considering tone, "but I am sure Lord Destry would, and Mrs. Kendrick and Lord Belmont."

"Mrs. Kendrick and Lord Belmont would be perfect company."

Lord Jess speared a bite of duck with his fork. "It will have to be late in the evening when it will not interfere with any plans the countess might have."

"But that's ideal as well. I noticed last night that

there is a new moon and it will have set by then." Beatrice thought the plan perfect, but then realized that one element was not in their control. "The weather must cooperate and that is always a challenge."

"You think visitors from beyond earth are discouraged by a little summer rain? We can search from the protection of the summer house if the night is wet. Or are you afraid that it might be boring?"

The smile that tilted his lips was a silent dare. She decided he was teasing. And she was not up to his weight in that arena. It was best to change the subject. "Why do we even need to consider visitors from another existence when our own writers can conjure up the fantastical for us? Have you read *Frankenstein*?"

"Never heard of it," he admitted blithely. "Is that terribly crass of me?"

"Not at all, my lord." He was still teasing her. She was sure of it. His tone made it sound like being crass was something he would love to be accused of. "There were only five hundred copies printed. In three volumes."

"You are a bibliophile *and* a student of art?"

"Yes, my lord," she said, making her eyes go wide. Then she leaned closer to him. "Now you will be convinced I am a bluestocking?"

She did not wait for an answer but straightened in her chair and went on. "My sister and I have read the first volume, but when I tried to order the other two they were no longer available. Even the subscription library was unable to buy a copy."

"What a disappointment." His tone implied it was anything but.

"Be serious, my lord," she scolded. "How would you

feel if you were in the midst of a compelling game of cards and you were made to stop before you knew who would win?"

"It would be frustrating, to say the least. Especially if there was a wager involved. I do see your point."

How could he be so absolutely intriguing when they had nothing in common? Or was that why he fascinated her? But then what was she to him? Just another flirt. Not his usual style but all that was available to him now. That hurt a little, since it was probably the truth. She began to turn away.

Once again, Lord Jess leaned toward her, whispering, "I should like to learn more about Rembrandt."

She turned back to him, their faces close, much too close. "I'm sure there are some excellent books in the library on that very subject."

"Well done. You are mastering the set-down."

Without giving him a chance for further comment, she turned to Lord Crenshaw, suggesting he sample some of the chicken in cream sauce that was at her right hand, determined to ignore Lord Jess for the rest of the meal.

At the end of the service the countess announced that the ladies would withdraw," and when the gentlemen join us we will hear highlighted portions of *Frankenstein* with musical accompaniment by Miss Wilson, who is sharing her talent with us this evening."

Lord Jess moved Beatrice's chair back for her, and when she thanked him with barely a glance he laughed and whispered, "It is the least of the ways I would like to serve you."

The way he said "serve" gave the word a whole different meaning. One that involved kissing. Beatrice faced him. Now that she had determined why he was interested in her, she no longer wanted to play. "I've had quite enough practice at flirtation for one evening, my lord."

"You wound me," he said, clearly amused and not at all annoyed. He raised her hand and kissed it. "I will have to keep practicing."

She pulled her hand from his, wiped the back of it on her skirt—though there was nothing to remove other than the feel of his lips—and gave up besting him at his own game. She could feel her face growing red and blotchy and hated him for it.

THE GENTLEMEN MOVED about the dining room, Belmont apparently still searching for the hiding place of the unexpected dinner guest. Crenshaw went behind the screen. Before the footmen brought in the brandy, Destry cornered Jess.

"Tell me what you were about with Miss Brent. Her sister could not concentrate on her food, or worse, give me her undivided attention, she was so distracted by the intimate conversation you two were having."

"Intimate conversation?" Jess repeated. "We were whispering so that damn Crenshaw would not give us his unwanted opinion on everything we said. We were discussing Miss Wilson's story."

"You're trying to tell me you were not flirting with her?"

"Is it possible for a man and woman to have a conversation without flirting?" Especially with someone as engaging as Beatrice Brent, he added to himself. "A smile and a look, yes, but we were not discussing how to have an affair in the midst of such a close party."

"As long as she knows the difference between a flirtation and a courtship." His voice trailed off. "Jess, were you serious about dangling after her because Crenshaw is interested?"

"No, of course not," Jess lied. The truth was she did need to be distracted from even the idea of so disastrous an alliance.

"Well, there is a difference between flirting and forming an attachment," Destry reminded him, apparently unconvinced.

"And the countess trusts that I know the difference."

"Then you had better hope that Miss Brent does as well."

Jess thought back to the little Venus's parting shot. "I have no doubt that she does."

A footman came in with a large tray loaded with decanters and glasses. Lord Crenshaw came from behind the screen still buttoning his fall, and Belmont joined them.

"I found the space where the speaker hid," Belmont announced, "but there are no clues about his identity except for a cone made of stiff paper that would have served to amplify his voice." The others joined him in speculation.

DESTRY APPRECIATED THE neutral subject. Crenshaw and Jess were in too small a company to avoid each other for long. He had a feeling they would be joining the ladies quickly, which suited him. Jess might not have seduction on his mind, but he did.

Chapter Fifteen

"WHAT IN THE world were you and Lord Jess doing?" Cecilia asked, not bothering to hide her dismay.

The ladies were in the music room, where chairs were set up facing the piano, which held pride of place even though not quite in the middle of the room.

"Isn't this a lovely salon?" Beatrice asked. It was clear to Cecilia that her sister was trying to change the subject.

That wouldn't work. But the room was amazing. There was a harp with a stool, with music on a stand in front of it as though someone had only just left off playing. There were cases in which other instruments were stored—or was it displayed—including some that looked so old she would not dare touch them.

"Yes, the best part is the gorgeous flower arrangements in those wall niches. They add color and life." She pulled her sister by the arm. "Come, let's examine this one."

She tugged her sister toward an unoccupied corner of the music room. Once they were out of hearing, Cecilia confronted Beatrice again.

"He was practically in your lap, Bitsy," Cecilia admonished. "What I mean is, you looked as though you were welcoming his advances." She paused and then held up her hand. "I'm not even sure you should tell me. If that was not a seduction then I do not know a violet from a rose. Do the two of you have plans for a midnight assignation?"

Beatrice shook her head. "Of course not! We were discussing Miss Wilson's night-sky visitor and he suggested that we gather a party of guests and go out to a field to see if we can find it again." Beatrice decided it would not be a good idea to tell Cecilia that she rather hoped the party would be small and willing to leave them to their own interests.

"That was what you were talking about?"

"Yes. What else could it have been?"

"He has a reputation, Beatrice." Cecilia tried to calm herself with a deep breath. "What I mean is, Lord Jessup spends all his time in London. There is no doubt in my mind that he is an expert at seduction. Everyone at the table was watching you."

"They were?"

"Yes, and it did not look as though you were discouraging him."

"Yes, we were flirting a little. I was practicing, just as we are supposed to. And it's not nearly as awkward as I thought it would be."

"Beatrice, exactly when did the countess tell us we should practice flirting? What I recall is Papa telling us to have nothing to do with Lord Jess. You know he was the one who brought Ellis home when he lost all his allowance gaming."

"Yes, yes, I do," Beatrice admitted, as though it was a tiresome bit of old news. "And I feel grateful for it. Listen to me, Ceci. Have you noticed how kind Lord Jess is?"

"Kind? No, I have not. It is hardly the first word that comes to mind when I think of him."

"What is the first word?" Beatrice asked, distracted from her main point.

"Detached. Dangerous. Cynical."

"That's three words, and they are each a little of the truth except for dangerous. I don't think he is dangerous at all, only misunderstood. I think he behaves as he does to hide his kindness, perhaps even his goodness."

"Beatrice, you are not smitten, are you?" Cecilia made it sound like a dread disease.

"No. Really, not at all." Not so much smitten as attracted. That was the only way to describe how she felt when she was near him, as if being right next to him was not close enough. "Ceci, I have seen his kindness a number of times in just these three days."

"Perhaps he is only acting that way to seduce you."

"You don't believe that any more than I do."

Cecilia agreed with a reluctant nod.

"Lord Jess has assured me he is on his best behavior here."

"Then I would hate to see him at his worst. He looks as though he is ready to beat Lord Crenshaw to a pulp whenever the baron says something the slightest bit patronizing."

"He may look like he wants to but he does not. So I

think he deserves credit for controlling his sensibilities."

Before Cecilia could comment further, the giant doors to the room opened again and the gentlemen joined them.

As soon as the gentlemen found seats there was a crashing sound from the pianoforte—a single melodic strike that arrested everyone's attention.

Miss Wilson proceeded with a piece that Beatrice did not recognize but that suited the provocative mood of the evening. Cecilia was seated on one side of Beatrice and Lord Destry was on the other. She looked around for Lord Jess and found him standing near the doors.

"Ladies and gentlemen," the countess called. "First I would like to make the voice of the monster known to you." She gestured to the doors. "He is our own Mr. Brent."

She raised her hands to applaud his performance as Abel Brent came into the room.

"PAPA!" CECILIA COULD not believe it was her father who had played the part of the monster. Her father was not an actor, or had never been before.

Beatrice did not appear surprised at all. She clapped her hands.

Mr. Brent strode to the front of the room, taking a bow before the countess and the assembled party. Then he came over to take a seat near where the countess was standing.

"I knew it was Papa!" Beatrice looked back toward the double doors and Lord Jess bowed to her. Cecilia watched the exchange and knew that no matter what Beatrice said, her sister was as infatuated as any innocent could be.

"How? How did you know?" Cecilia asked, doing her best to draw her sister's attention away from the only man in the room of whom her father did not approve. *Please let Lord Jessup exercise some discretion and not pay his gaming debt in Papa's presence,* she prayed.

"Beatrice!" Cecilia nudged her sister. "Turn around and act like a lady, please."

Beatrice settled facing front once again.

"How did you know it was Papa?"

"That deep sonorous voice is the one he uses when he is speaking in public. I heard him once, when the second mill opened. Mama and I attended the tea after the inspection and Papa spoke to all the new workers."

"Why didn't I go?"

"You had the headache."

Oh yes, Cecilia remembered. She had suffered such awful cramps in those days when her courses had first started. She was often abed for a day or two. Thank goodness that had passed.

"He is willing to do anything to see us properly launched," Cecilia whispered to her. "Including becoming an actor."

"Or perhaps he is just very fond of the countess," Beatrice whispered back. Her eyes widened. "The most shocking idea just occurred to me. Do you think they are having an affair?"

Cecilia gave a couple of short sharp shakes of her head and tried to banish even the mental image that brought to her. "No!" she said with more shock than denial. "He is a successful mill owner, a respected personage in Birmingham, a generous benefactor to several workhouses."

"None of which means he does not have a personal life."

"Yes, but it's hard to think of him being involved with someone other than Mama."

Beatrice took her sister's hand and gave it a squeeze, as much as saying, *Let us not think about it.*

Cecilia squeezed back. *I have already forgotten it.* It was not the truth but she hoped it would be once their attention was distracted.

The countess stepped up to the music stand beside the piano. "Our reader this evening is the Reverend Michael Garrett, vicar of the church at Pennsford and Lord Jessup Pennistan's brother-in-law. He is a gentleman very familiar with public speaking."

Reverend Garrett strode into the room, stopping to grasp Lord Jess's hand warmly and bow to the company. He took his place at the music stand set next to the piano.

Beatrice nudged her sister. "He certainly is handsome."

"He is married, you know." Cecilia's smile took all criticism from her comment.

"One can still admire."

"Is his wife with him?"

"How would I know?"

"Lady Olivia will join us in the morning. She's retired for the evening." Lord Destry, still seated next to them and blatantly eavesdropping, joined their conversation as if he had been invited.

"Thank you, my lord," Cecilia answered with a

downward cast to her eyes. How much had the marquis overheard?

Reverend Michael Garrett waited until the room was quiet. "It's a pleasure to be invited to read something aloud besides the Bible. The anonymous author of this piece has written a fascinating book and I hope what you hear tonight will encourage you to read it in full. In the meantime, I invite you to discuss each section as I finish reading."

Twilight was settling, which meant it must be close to ten. The half-light added to the mood of the evening. At the piano Miss Wilson played an introduction, certainly something from Bach's Requiem. As the last note faded, Mr. Garrett raised the book and began.

> *"Did I request thee, Maker, from my clay*
> *To mould me man? Did I solicit thee*
> *From darkness to promote me?"*

The anguish in his voice spoke of such deep suffering that Cecilia found herself hoping that the Reverend was simply a talented actor and was not drawing from his own experience.

"But that's from *Paradise Lost*," Miss Wilson said, sounding confused and not particularly entertained.

"Indeed." The countess's word and Mrs. Wilson's "Hush" hung in the air together. Miss Wilson blushed. Cecilia could see that the girl did not know whether to be upset at her mother's rebuke or pleased at the countess's approval.

"Yes, it is," Mr. Garrett confirmed. "The author uses it on the title page of *Frankenstein*, I think to encourage sympathy for the monster, who after all did not ask for his humanity."

"But none of us have asked for our humanity," Lord Belmont countered. "That is no excuse for his brutal behavior."

"You have read the book, my lord," Mrs. Kendrick reminded him. "What do you think is the explanation for his murderous rampage?"

"God save us," Destry whispered to both of the sisters, "this is a much too literary conversation for me."

"Stop pretending that you've never read a book," Beatrice admonished him. Cecilia was shocked at her sister's familiarity and could think of nothing to say.

"As rarely as I can manage," Destry insisted.

"My lord," Beatrice said, "I do believe you would enjoy this one. There is all the action even you could wish for."

"Have you read it?" He addressed his question to Cecilia and she could tell that Beatrice was not going to answer for her.

"My brother Ellis brought the first volume to us," she said in a quiet voice, looking down at her hands.

Beatrice did no more than touch her elbow but Cecilia knew what that meant. *Don't be such a moon face, Ceci. Look at him and tell him what you think of the book.*

Beatrice was right, Cecilia decided, and looked up, smiling at Lord Destry. "It's an amazing story and I do so wish to read the other two volumes."

BEATRICE WAITED FOR the marquis to answer her sister, but he had apparently been struck dumb. It was

Cecilia's smile that had done it. Pure sweetness, it had stopped more than one man in his tracks. Unfortunately Beatrice also knew that the silence would not inspire confidence in her sister, who would be sure she had said the wrong thing. Beatrice chose not to come to the rescue.

Cecilia looked down at her hands again. Now that he was not spellbound by her smile, or maybe it was her eyes, the marquis found his voice. "Shall we ask the countess if we can borrow her copy and read it aloud together?"

"You would ask her? Oh, that is a fine idea!"

They were the first spontaneous words Beatrice had heard Cecilia say to the man who would be a duke.

The marquis's "Excellent" confirmed his own enthusiasm for spending more time together. How long would it take, Beatrice wondered, for her sister to see that Lord Destry was just like all the other men she knew? Besotted by her beauty.

Was there any chance that in the next ten days the marquis would come to appreciate where Cecilia's truest beauty lay?

"Yes, I do have some strong opinions on this book," Lord Belmont said, drawing Beatrice's attention back to the more general discussion of the last excerpt. "But please let us see what other passages have been chosen before we discuss it further."

Mr. Garrett read on. The conversation was amusing and occasionally silly, but once or twice some intriguing ideas came to the fore.

"I think the essential question is whether the monster became so because of the lack of a proper upbringing or because of some natural flaw in his creation."

Lord Belmont spoke carefully and then waited for the company to answer.

"The author, then, is prompting a discussion of the concept that at birth we have a clean slate and our lives are formed by what we experience." Mr. Garrett smiled. "The marquis is looking perplexed."

"Miss Brent has just assured me that this book is very entertaining and full of adventure. Now I am wondering if we are talking about the same book."

"Ah, yes, but do not the best books entertain and encourage thought as well?"

Lord Destry looked unconvinced, but ventured an opinion anyway. "It seems to me that all children need guidance to understand what they are truly put on earth for."

"Then you consider the monster Dr. Frankenstein's child, despite the fact that he was born fully grown?" Mr. Garrett suggested.

"No, no," Destry insisted. "I have no idea about this book but was speaking about children in general, Reverend."

"Sometimes I do believe that my two boys are monsters." That made everyone laugh, and Mr. Garrett went on. "But taking your point and applying it to Dr. Frankenstein's creation, it is clear that the doctor abandoned him when the creature did not meet his expectations. What should he have taught him?"

"That we should all love one another," the marquis answered promptly.

"Bravo, my lord," Beatrice whispered to him. On her other side Cecilia looked over her sister's head at Lord Destry in some confusion.

"We should teach our children to contribute to the common good," Lord Belmont added.

Mr. Garrett nodded again and waited for other answers.

"To obey the Commandments and allow their betters to lead them." Baron Crenshaw sat with his arms folded across his chest, his words bold and insistent.

"Very interesting, my lord. So here in this small group we already have three different schools of thought. One emphasizing love of fellow man, the second an obligation to make a contribution to society, and the third, the need to obey."

"I take issue with the suggestion that we should teach them to let their betters lead them. What if their betters are misguided?" Lord Jess called out from the back of the room. His stance was indolent, leaning as he was against the wall near the door, but his tone belied his relaxed posture. "What if children are misinformed and wrongly taught?"

He straightened and walked to stand at the edge of the rows of chairs, still not part of the group. Not quite. "What if they are raised to believe that physical force is a solution when they are frustrated or angry?" He paused for a long moment. "As the monster demonstrated."

"Many believe physical punishment is necessary." Mr. Garrett offered the sentence for debate, Beatrice thought, not because he believed it himself. His eyes were too kind to allow it.

"In the schoolroom, perhaps," Lord Jess allowed, not at all irritated by the dissent, "but what about physical force among adults?"

"If they are consenting adults then they may fight to

their death." Mr. Brent spoke his piece, turning to look at Lord Jess and then at the countess, who gave a slight smile.

"But, sir, what if they do not consent? What if one is forced to accept physical discipline? As an adult?" Lord Jess addressed his question to the group but Beatrice could see Lord Crenshaw stiffen. He was not looking at Lord Jess. If he had been, Lord Jess would have been singed by the baron's eyes. They burned with rage.

"To force someone to accept physical punishment is wrong." Mrs. Kendrick was the first woman to voice an opinion and Beatrice silently cheered her on. "As the book unfolds the reader sees that even the monster understands right from wrong. If Frankenstein's monster is human enough to know he is doing wrong, then are not men equally intelligent?"

"Slaves are treated without a thought for their humanity," Beatrice said and hoped that her comment would advance the discussion.

"They are property and can be dealt with as the owner sees fit," Crenshaw volunteered from his seat.

"And what of wives?" Lord Jess asked. "Upon marriage, what they own becomes their husband's property, but they themselves do not, even though Saint Paul says that wives must be submissive to their husbands."

Mr. Garrett shook his head. "My wife takes great issue with that passage, and that alone makes me realize that 'submissive' may be the wrong word."

"As a vicar, Mr. Garrett, are you not honor bound to follow the teachings of the Church of England?" Lord Crenshaw demanded.

"Yes, I am, but that does not mean I cannot question their wisdom and suggest other interpretations. Bear in mind that Paul's command to me is 'Love your wife.' How is forcing her submission a loving act?"

"Because it is in her best interest." Crenshaw made the statement as if it were obvious, then sat back. He was relaxed enough that Beatrice did not fear a fist-fight.

"It is in your wife's best interest to do what you wish her to do?" Mr. Garrett addressed his question to the group.

"Yes," said Mrs. Wilson when Crenshaw merely shrugged.

"I often think it is in my best interests to do what Lady Olivia asks of me," Mr. Garrett countered.

There was light, somewhat forced laughter among the company.

"If your wife chooses not to submit, what are your options, gentlemen? Take away her pin money?"

"Would you beat her? Deny her food?" This from Jess.

He spoke without humor. Really, Beatrice thought, he was joking. Wasn't he? But she could feel Lord Destry tense beside her.

"I'm sure the countess agrees with me when I suggest that we should save the theological discussion for Sunday," Mr. Garrett said with a smile, as though he did not feel the tension in the room.

The countess stood up. "I do believe that we must have plumbed the depths of *Frankenstein* to have drifted so far off the subject." She turned toward the piano. "Miss Wilson, will you play the closing piece? I trust that will leave us in a happier frame of mind."

Miss Wilson made a false start, but then settled her mind and her focus on the music. As the servants entered with tea, she played a lively piece that invited everyone to forget the horrors of Dr. Frankenstein's monster and enjoy the last of the lovely summer evening.

Chapter Sixteen

CECILIA ROSE TO find some tea, but Beatrice kept her seat, more puzzled than upset by the drama that had played out before them. It was more, much more than conflicting thoughts on Saint Paul's call for wives to be submissive and husbands to love their wives. Lord Jess had introduced the subject of wives and the need for submission, Lord Crenshaw had been angry, and the marquis had been nervous.

One might call it gossip but Beatrice could not resist asking Lord Destry, "What upset you, my lord?"

The marquis had stood up, but he sat in his chair again, turning it so that he faced Beatrice more directly. He tapped his finger on his knee and finally answered her. "Jess deliberately tried to make someone angry and came very close to succeeding."

"Mr. Garrett? He was not serious about beating one's wife, was he?" Beatrice could hear the dismay in her voice. "I am sorry if I sound like a governess. I did ask."

"Garrett beat his wife? Never. He worships the ground Olivia walks on." Destry hesitated, something so rare in their short acquaintance that Beatrice was afraid for a moment. "Miss Brent, it is not a subject for genteel discussion." He put his head back on his chair and closed his eyes briefly.

"Now *you* sound like *my* governess." She laughed as she spoke.

Destry sat up straight. "If you are going to laugh at me then I will not try to be discreet and will instead shock you with the truth."

"I would value the truth more than your attempts at delicacy, my lord."

He leaned closer. "The truth is that Jess and Crenshaw hate each other."

"But why? They are very different, I grant you that, but they also have so much in common. They are gentlemen. They both enjoy gaming to the extreme." Beatrice paused. "It's the gaming, isn't it? They had some disagreement over a game of chance. Did Lord Crenshaw accuse Lord Jess of cheating?"

Destry's laugh was full of irony and not much humor.

Beatrice nodded. "So that is the tawdry incident to which Papa referred."

"No! No! One has never accused the other of cheating at a game of chance." Destry shook his head. "You will have to ask Jess for the story. It is not mine to tell."

"I should not ask Lord Crenshaw?"

"It might be interesting to ask both of them—not when they are together, mind you. But I do not think the baron will answer you, at least not as honestly as

Jess would. And he may well be affronted by the question."

Lord Destry stood up. "Now I need some tea, though I would prefer something stronger. If you will excuse me, Miss Brent."

It was just short of rude of him to leave her alone, which proved to Beatrice how upset he was. She debated approaching Lord Jess directly but decided that there might be other ways of finding out what she wanted to know.

It was hard to believe that the Lord Crenshaw she knew was less than a gentleman, but she was already realizing that he was more controlling than she had once thought, and much less amiable. Lord Jess, on the other hand, was not just the man of good humor and easy spirits that he pretended to be. There was more to him. When Beatrice looked about for Cecilia, anxious to discuss her confusion, she realized that her sister was no longer among them.

"She went to bed," Papa told her when she sought him out. "Something about needing her beauty sleep."

How ridiculous, Beatrice thought. She must have been upset.

"Are you staying on awhile, Papa?"

He glanced at the countess and the two exchanged a smile. "No," he said with a profound look of disappointment. "The countess has no more tasks for me and I cannot avoid the meetings in town any longer. Roger will have laid the plans before the potential investors but I need to be there to answer their questions."

"Perhaps you will be able to stop here again before the girls actually have to leave," the countess suggested. "Havenhall is only a few hours' travel from London, not such a great detour."

"Please, Papa, insist that Roger come, too," Beatrice added. "He works much too hard." As she spoke Beatrice watched the countess tuck her arm in the crook of Mr. Brent's elbow.

Beatrice closed her eyes. *For the love of God, they are having an affair.* Of a sudden, she was sure of it. The way they looked at each other made her think of the way Lord Destry looked at Cecilia, as though looking was not going to be enough.

"Will I see you at breakfast, Papa?"

"If you are up early."

"I will be there at six o'clock, then."

"No, Beatrice," her godmother countered, "I think nine will be quite early enough."

Papa was always up when the cock crowed. But apparently not tomorrow. What would the others say when they saw him at breakfast? She *must* talk to Cecilia.

With a fond if slightly embarrassed good night to her father and the countess, Beatrice left the room. Mrs. Kendrick and the earl were discussing something in the passage, and were apparently on their way to bed as well.

Beatrice reasoned that if they were going to the same bed they would not need to stand here to converse. Of course they could be discussing whose bed would be more comfortable.

She giggled at the thought. Her level of sophistication would move up several levels before this party was over. Look at her—she was no longer shocked but laughing, all right, giggling, at the idea of a love affair.

Cecilia was still dressed when Beatrice reached their room, though Darwell was in the small dressing room, ready to help her disrobe. Ceci was staring into the mirror, a distant look in her eyes.

Beatrice went into the dressing room. "Darwell, Ceci and I will help each other this evening. You may leave now."

Darwell was shocked.

"Yes, I know it verifies that we are not born with a title or raised to be waited on, but it is only one night. I promise that tomorrow I will be as demanding as a duke's daughter."

Darwell shook her head, even though her lips twitched with a smile. "You are impertinent, Miss Beatrice, but charmingly so. Thank you, miss, I will say good night and be here in the morning."

"We are to meet Papa for a farewell breakfast at nine o'clock."

"Miss Cecilia will not ride in the morning?" They both looked at Cecilia, who had not heard a word they said.

"Perhaps in the afternoon, Darwell," Beatrice spoke for her sister. "It promises to be a cool day."

Darwell nodded and with a worried glance at Cecilia moved toward the door. "I trust you understand your sister well enough to deal with her distress."

"Yes, I do, Darwell. And thank you for your understanding and concern."

"Do not thank me, Miss Beatrice. It is so plebeian."

"Yes, I know, but I keep forgetting that I am not supposed to." Beatrice smiled as the oh-so-proper lady's maid shook her head in resignation and left the room. Darwell was probably more of a lady than she was.

Beatrice walked over to her sister, who had gone from staring into the mirror to looking out the window.

Standing next to her twin, Beatrice said nothing, waiting for Ceci to speak first.

"I know that all I have to offer a gentleman are my looks and a healthy body for bearing children," Cecilia began. "But you know there is still a person inside who worries and loves like everyone else."

When Cecilia turned to face her sister her eyes were glazed with tears. "Yes, the first thing anyone notices about me is that I am pretty," she continued. "Even knowing how meaningless that is, I did virtually the same thing. I judged a man by his rank and appearance."

Beatrice was so taken aback by Cecilia's comment she had no answer. Though she was certain of one thing. "You have far more to offer than a lovely face. You *know* that. You are thoughtful and kind. Your knowledge of flowers and plants is superior. You can speak French even better than our governess, and Mama wanted you to read to her because your voice is so sweet. That is only the beginning of what makes you a treasure to everyone who knows you."

"Bitsy, how could I so misjudge the marquis?" Cecilia exclaimed as though she had not heard a word her sister had said. "I mean, how could I take Lord Destry's measure the way I did, without seeing the man of worth beneath his outlandish behavior?"

"For the love of God, Ceci." Beatrice was confused and just a trifle exasperated. "What brought this on?"

Cecilia moved away from the window and walked into the dressing room, moving as though her gown weighed a hundred pounds. She stopped in front of the great cheval glass and then turned to face her sister, who had followed her.

"Did you hear what the marquis said when Mr. Garrett asked what we should teach our children?"

Beatrice thought back and shook her head, with apology.

"Lord Destry said that we should teach children to love one another." Ceci took her sister's hands. "He is one of the wealthiest men in England, related to the highest ranking nobility, and he thinks nothing is more important than loving one another. Is that not remarkable?" She didn't wait for an answer. "And he said that he did not like intellectual discussions. Silly man."

Silly man? And suddenly Beatrice understood. Her sister's opinion of Lord Destry had changed dramatically.

"Are you developing a *tendre* for him?" Beatrice asked, and then regretted speaking so directly.

"Oh, no! I could never be a duchess."

Now who was being silly? Cecilia would make a wonderful duchess and not because she was beautiful, but how many times could she argue that point in one night? She would pray that Cecilia was able to determine it for herself.

"Are you tired?"

"I wish I was. I am as wide awake as I am in the morning."

"Then let's find out where the gentlemen are gaming, on the pretext of seeing if anyone is riding in the morning. Then perhaps we can join them for a while. We did say we would let them teach us how to game."

"Oh, Beatrice, I don't think we should do that. It does not sound at all proper."

"Of course it is."

"I do not want to see—" Cecilia stopped mid-sentence and then went on. "That is, I do not want to go downstairs again. I want to go to bed."

"But you said you are not at all tired."

"Then we can talk or read to each other. I may not be fatigued but I have had enough of the others for now."

"The others" being the marquis. "All right. We shall be each other's maid like when we were younger. Turn around and let me undo your dress and stays."

Once in bed with a branch of candles lit, Beatrice read a few passages aloud from their favorite poem.

"*The Lady of the Lake* must surely be Scott's most successful poem," Beatrice declared.

They were propped up against their pillows, not looking at each other. In fact when Beatrice glanced at her, Cecilia's eyes were closed.

"I think it's the sort of story that appeals to both men and women," Cecilia mused. "Even more than *Frankenstein*."

"Scott has battles and a love story that everyone can admire." Beatrice set the book on the table next to her bed and blew out all but one candle.

"All right, Ceci. If we were casting it for an amateur theatrical you would be Ellen." She went on before her sister could object. "Who would you choose to play James Fitz-James?"

"I think Lord Jess," Cecilia said, playing along. "Even though Fitz-James was, in fact, King James the Fifth. He liked to visit his subjects in disguise so he must have had a sense of fun. Though I am not sure that Lord Jess has the right gravitas for such a role."

"But the marquis is a more noble rank."

"Oh no, he must be Malcolm Graeme."

"Ellen's beloved?"

"Yes, of course. He and Lord Destry share so many of the same qualities. They both are loyal, and ride like the wind."

Cecilia ended her words with a jaw-cracking yawn and a murmured apology as she relaxed and closed her eyes. Beatrice felt a moment of annoyance. She was still not tired. What were they doing in bed before midnight? With a sigh she blew out the candle. "Good night, sister."

A couple of slurred words that might have been "Sleep well" were Cecilia's only response.

Beatrice settled herself, restaging the cast for *The Lady of the Lake*. If she were Ellen Douglas she would cast Jess Pennistan as Malcolm Graeme. She did not want a lover who was her height. And Destry would make a fine enough James Fitz-James.

Chapter Seventeen

"Is THIS NOT amazing?" Beatrice exclaimed as she and Lady Olivia Garrett circled the base of the ancient, giant lime tree.

"Indeed it is. I've always wanted to see a banqueting platform."

It was hard to believe that this cheerful, diminutive woman was Lord Jess's older sister, though not so hard to believe she was Mr. Garrett's wife. She and her husband shared a similar optimistic view of life. In the three days since Lady Olivia and Mr. Garrett had arrived, Beatrice and Jess's sister had spent enough time together to now qualify as friends. So Beatrice had accepted Olivia's suggestion that they look for the banqueting platform with alacrity.

"The countess said it is no longer stable enough for dinners but that it is safe enough for a few at a time. Do you want to see what the view is like?"

Lady Olivia nodded with enthusiasm, and then

began the climb up the man-made staircase that wound around the trunk of a tree that was easily twenty-five feet in girth.

"Where is your sister?" Olivia paused halfway up and turned to face Beatrice. "Would she not find this fascinating?"

"I expect Cecilia will meet us here eventually, but your time in the kitchen inspired her."

Olivia wrinkled her nose in a way that was half apology, half embarrassment.

"No, no, you have a passion for cooking that we both respect," Beatrice insisted, and stepped ahead of Olivia to take the lead. "It was Cecilia's dearest wish to approach the garden staff. She has made the acquaintance of the head gardener and today she convinced him to show her the greenhouses."

They had reached the platform itself and stopped to take it all in. Fabric had been draped through the branches, giving the platform a fanciful appearance.

"Is that watered silk? How extravagant." Olivia walked over to finger the cream-colored material. There was no table, but there were a chaise longue and two chairs covered in brown and green.

"This is the perfect spot for a couple to meet for a tête-à-tête." Olivia spoke half to herself.

Or something more. Beatrice barely kept herself from voicing that aloud and refused to even think that her father and the countess might have come here together.

Feeling very much an intruder in a spot she now associated with intimacy, Beatrice sat on one of the branches that ran along the edge of the space.

"Doing what one loves is so very satisfying," Olivia assured her, finding her own seat on a nearby branch.

Young ladies were expected to know something of gardening, but Lady Olivia's love of cooking was more than a little unusual for the daughter of a duke. Beatrice mulled over how to ask about it. "When did you realize that you loved working with food?" That was a safe enough way to bring up the subject.

"When I was about twelve. I wondered why some dishes were so excellent and some were not. Mama would never have let me spend time in the kitchen, but she was not well and Tildy, my governess, was easily distracted.

"So I would sneak down and observe. I dressed like one of the servants and by the time Cook figured out who I was she also realized that I was fascinated by food. We were two artists who shared a passion, and there was no stopping me. Or Cook. After a while we discovered that baking was my favorite and I began to help with that exclusively."

"What an amazing tale. If I had tried something like that, Mama would have confined me to my room until I was over the urge." Perhaps she should not have said that. Lady Olivia was so easy to talk to that Beatrice did not censor her words at all around her.

"Yes, it is odd, is it not, that dukes and their families are allowed eccentricities that society would not otherwise tolerate."

"We are all very lucky in your case." The delicious memory was enough to make her mouth water. "Breakfast has been amazing the past two days."

"Cinnamon rolls are popular with everyone," Olivia said, her conspiratorial whisper pleased. "All I have to do is promise that the servants will have their fair share and Cook is pressured unmercifully until she allows me to bake."

"Lucky for Papa that he had a chance to take some with him. And to make your acquaintance." She added the last hurriedly. *For the love of God, why had she brought up Papa's departure?* She had avoided mentioning it before. From the corner of her eye she watched for Lady Olivia's reaction.

"I am so pleased to have met him, even if it was only for a few minutes."

Beatrice felt some relief. At least one of them knew how to make polite conversation.

Papa's send-off had been a private and thoroughly feminine event, surrounded as he was by his daughters and the countess. Then Lady Olivia had come hurrying in from the kitchen, bearing two perfect cinnamon rolls. She was kind enough to wrap them up for Mr. Brent.

"He certainly was in good spirits, and that was even before I made him a gift of the cinnamon rolls."

"I have not seen him this happy in months." Did she sound defensive? She hoped not.

"It's quite obvious that he and the countess are very fond of each other."

"You are not shocked by it?" Beatrice blurted out.

"No," Olivia said. "Never."

Abandoning the pretext of purely social conversation, Beatrice looked directly at Olivia. "Do you think it disloyal of me to be happy for him? Mama has only been gone a little over a year. She wanted us happy more than anything." Beatrice ignored the well of tears.

"Of course it's not disloyal."

Lady Olivia's words were reassuring, but then what else could she have said?

"My own brother fell in love again after the death of his first wife, and it was not nearly as straightforward as your father and the countess."

Beatrice had no idea what to say to that. A dozen questions filtered through her mind.

"And one of my other brothers married a woman who pretended to be a prostitute in order to save lives in France during the war. At least I think she was pretending."

For the love of God, which brother was that?

"And wait until you meet David and Mia. She is forever irritating him and she insists that she does it on purpose because making up is so much fun." Olivia wrinkled her nose, and her cheeks grew pink. "I do not care what Jess says; the love of a good woman makes a man happier than anything else in the world."

"What does Jess say?" Beatrice could not resist that leading statement.

"Jess is a puzzle to all of us," Olivia said, not answering the question. "He gives the appearance of a man given to little more than gaming and women, but when you think of what he did for Annie Blackwood you have to know that there is more to him than he allows most people to see."

"Who is Annie Blackwood?" And what were she and Lord Jess to each other?

"One of my dearest friends. She was the daughter of my governess and like a sister to me. She is still at Pennford and I doubt she will ever leave."

Which did not answer Beatrice's question, or at least the part about Jess. Lord Jess, she reminded herself.

"Mayhap he will fall in love here," Olivia said with a lightness that did not match the wistfulness in her eyes. "I so wish he could be as happy as I am."

"What kind of woman would it take?" Beatrice really hoped Olivia would answer her even if it was an impertinent question.

"He needs someone who can see below the surface and find the man who is loyal to the extreme, is honorable regardless of the consequences, and loves his family even though he is estranged from them. And that last makes no sense at all."

"Yes, it does." Beatrice stood so quickly that the branch that was her seat shook. "You can love someone even when they are irritating. Sometimes Ceci will drive me near mad with her worry about her appearance and her hair and what she should talk about, but I always love her." Having made her point as forcefully as she could, Beatrice sat back down carefully.

"Yes." Olivia slipped off her branch and moved over to sit on one of the chairs, which all but swallowed her. She looked like a doll sitting in her owner's chair. "Sometimes Michael talks to me like I am one of his parishioners."

She lowered her voice in imitation of her husband. "Olivia, the first Commandment means there is no work in the kitchen on Sunday." Olivia made a face again. "Then I ask him why the servants work on Sunday and he shakes his head as if my cooking is no more than a hobby."

It was obvious from her wrinkled brow that even the

memory of the conversation annoyed her. "I love him totally and completely, even then."

They sat in silence awhile. Beatrice watched Olivia's face soften, and looked away as though she had caught the woman in a daydream not meant to be shared. Perhaps she would bring her husband back here later.

To love someone so much that the mere thought of that love could make you happy. Lord Jess came to mind, but she decided that was only because of the way he made her feel. Not because there was any potential for a lasting connection between them.

"Did you see the arrangement of the small figures on the mantel this morning?" Olivia sat up straight and struggled to the edge of the chair. "I mean, the figurines that the countess had made for the first arrivals."

"Yes. They've been rearranged. Who could have done that? And what does it signify?"

"You will have to tell me. For instance, the way Lord Crenshaw is posed between you and Katherine Wilson as if he must make a choice." Olivia moved even closer. "Beatrice, has the baron been courting you?"

"No!" Beatrice said and then reconsidered. "Well, I have been wondering, as he did dance with me twice at the Assemblies, but I thought it might be because he was interested in knowing my father better. Perhaps it is the beginning of a courtship."

"He cannot be very good at it if you have never seriously acknowledged it until now."

That made Beatrice giggle. "It may not be his fault. The truth is I am not all that interested in marriage. I want to study art and focus all my passion on that."

Olivia was silent for a long moment. "That is a subject for a whole different discussion."

"What is?"

"Whether passion for a much-loved profession is sufficient for a woman. Or a man," she added after a moment's pause.

Beatrice could feel a lecture coming. "I am not interested in the baron. I have come to think he is too controlling."

"I am relieved. My family does not think highly of him."

"But why?" This was not the comment she had expected at all.

"I'm sorry, Beatrice, I should never have mentioned it. I wish I could tell you, but it is not something that is ever discussed."

It was a very gentle rebuke but Beatrice could feel her cheeks go blotchy with embarrassment. She stood and wandered over to the edge of the platform. She leaned against the rail and felt it give a little. She stepped back. Looking down from even this modest height made her nervous and excited all at once. Beatrice backed away from the edge and found a spot in the exact middle.

"Please do not be embarrassed. It was my mistake. It's just that you are so easy to talk to and I am surrounded by men at home. Annie has been away caring for her mother, who is failing, so I have had no one with whom to discuss my concerns. The duchess is lovely but years older than I am."

"If Lord Crenshaw does show interest in Miss Wilson, is there any reason to warn her?"

"No, most definitely not."

That was firm enough to be reassuring.

"It would do no good," Olivia added. "Please believe me."

That was not so reassuring, but Beatrice agreed and wished that Olivia had thought twice before bringing up the subject. Now her curiosity was awakened and she wanted to know what the secret was. Too many people had alluded to it, which also made her wonder why, if so many people knew the story, it was still shrouded with secrecy.

"What is there between the Earl of Belmont and the fascinating Mrs. Kendrick? It's obvious, I suppose," Olivia answered the question herself. "Their figures were situated together, very close together."

"They are adults without attachments," Beatrice said, quoting Lord Destry. "The marquis told me at dinner last night that the earl is content to let his brother inherit and Mrs. Kendrick is a widow, which gives her so much more freedom."

"Speaking of William, it did not take the placement of the figures at opposite ends of the mantel for me to notice how completely your sister is avoiding him."

William? The marquis's Christian name is William? Olivia really did know him well. "Yes, Cecilia is pretending he does not exist. She did not go riding the last few mornings, lest she run into him, which makes her restless and irritable."

"He can be a pest when he has an idea he will not let go of."

"I don't think he was pestering her, but they will never make a connection if she keeps on ignoring him." She considered telling Olivia about Cecilia's realization that she had judged the marquis in such a superficial way, but then decided that it was her sister's "secret."

"Do you think they are well suited?"

Now there was a direct question.

"I think they should have the opportunity to find out instead of avoiding each other." She came closer to Olivia. "What is just as bad is that Lord Destry seems to accept the situation. He went to that prizefight with the other gentlemen yesterday when it was the perfect opportunity to stay behind, and I do not know where he was last night when we played charades."

"He was in the small ballroom practicing his juggling," Olivia explained. "It's the skill he is going to demonstrate tonight."

"Juggling?" Beatrice asked, distracted for a moment. "I suppose it does suit someone who has trouble sitting still." As did riding.

"And today the marquis is fishing with Lord Jess and Lord Belmont. Mrs. Kendrick went with them, but no matter how much I begged, the countess would not let us go with them."

Which was a vast disappointment since the countess had always been inclined to favor opportunities that would broaden their experience. Neither she nor Cecilia had any idea how to fish.

Olivia looked at her slyly. "I find it fascinating that you and Jess are placed together. Someone thinks of you as a couple even if you are standing at his back and he is pretending not to know that you are there."

"Pretending?"

"Of course." Olivia's matter-of-fact shrug almost convinced Beatrice, who had originally thought the placement was a hurtful comment. "Jess is fascinated by you."

Beatrice's heart gave a leap. "Me? He is fascinated by me?"

"He was telling me all about your explanation of Rembrandt's drawings, and how clever you were the night of the Frankenstein discussion. A man does not talk about such things unless he is intrigued."

Beatrice wanted to race off to the fishing stream and corner Lord Jess. She wanted answers to all her questions, first and foremost why he was both interested *and* not inclined to even look at her. Was it because he felt the same intense longing that ran through her when they were together? Hardly; the man was far more experienced in the ways of the world than she was.

"Beatrice?" Olivia's tone made it clear that it was not the first time she had called out her name. "I think we must find a way to encourage your sister to at least look at William. He will never force himself on anyone. I know this for a fact since he once proposed to me when he thought I was in need of rescue from disgrace. But he did not seem at all upset when I declined, without much tact I might add.

"Then Mia and William decided to marry without thinking at all about the difference between friendship and marriage. They were much too like-minded, both eager for the next adventure and willing to risk everything to enjoy it. If they had married, it would have been a disaster!"

"Two proposals?" *How many different proposals had the man made?* Two made him sound as though he could not make up his mind. If he was that quixotic, then he would not do at all for her sister, who needed a loving and loyal husband above all else.

Olivia must have read her thoughts for she bounced out of her chair and moved closer, taking Beatrice's hands. "Do not blame William. He was not treated well by his grandfather, who played all sorts of games to convince him to marry me." Olivia sighed and shook her head. "I cannot imagine having a grandfather who told you that the family would be better off if you died and the dukedom went to some distant cousin in the Bahamas."

His grandfather had actually said that? How awful.

"Sometimes," Olivia went on in a voice that was more speculative than certain, "sometimes I think William is so wild because he doesn't think it matters if he lives or dies. Loving the right woman could change that. But the right woman was not me or Mia Castellano."

Olivia's musings made Beatrice see the marquis in a different way, certainly with more sympathy than before.

"Anyway," Olivia said with a shift of mood, "Mia's happy marriage to David proves that she needed someone far more restrained than William. Two men could not be more different than William and David." Olivia laughed out loud at some mental image or comparison. "Excuse me, Beatrice, just a silly memory of the two of them. It still makes me laugh."

Beatrice wondered if she would ever have a chance to meet the rest of Olivia's eccentric family.

"We have to find a way to give William one more chance with your sister. Surely we can come up with an idea that will bring them together. A way neither of them can refuse."

"I suppose," Beatrice agreed, halfheartedly. "But, Olivia, attraction is one thing. Dealing with the ways that a connection like that would change lives is another matter entirely." That seemed an obscure but genteel way to address Cecilia's terror at the idea of being a duchess.

Olivia was lost in thought and did not hear her. "Beatrice, I think I know exactly how to do it."

Chapter Eighteen

"MY LORD, THE fishing expedition must have been very successful. The servants were quite weighed down with the catch."

Beatrice Brent spoke to Destry as she came across the lawn from the summerhouse, a book in her hand. That mischievous smile always made him smile back. Beatrice at her most engaging was a delight. Why could he not be fascinated by her instead of her sister?

William dropped the ball he had been playing with and clapped his hands together. "It was an excellent outing all in all, capped by Jess falling into the river. The fish appreciated the entertainment as much as we did."

"Really? He fell in the river?" Beatrice smiled, though he could see worry in her eyes. As if a man could catch a chill on a day this warm.

The marquis picked up the ball again and began

tossing it into the air and catching it. Then he added a second.

"I see that you juggle," Beatrice said.

"Yes, I do." He did not care how classless she thought the talent. "It's what I am going to demonstrate this evening."

He picked up a third ball and added it to the other two. He managed an impressive string of tosses before he missed one, but made up for it by catching all three and pretending that the display was complete. "I always do better with an audience."

"Do you use an assistant when you perform?"

"I've never performed before, but that's not a bad idea. If she was pretty enough she would distract the audience from my lack of perfection." He cocked his head, considering, and then had a brilliant idea. "Do you think your sister would be willing to help me?" It would be one way of getting Cecilia to talk to him. She had been as elusive as a butterfly these last few days.

Beatrice smiled in approval. Had that been what she was aiming for all along?

"I will go ask her now," she said.

"Excellent." It could only help to have Cecilia's sister in his corner. "If I can have her attention for a few minutes before I perform, that would be adequate."

BEATRICE DID HER best not to run from the lawn and upstairs to find Cecilia. She burst into their bedroom and immediately spotted Cecilia reading in a chair near the window.

"Put that book down, Ceci, and talk to me." Beatrice waited while her sister complied. She had probably not been reading anyway. Pretending to read was just one more way Ceci had of avoiding conversation when she wanted to think through a problem. She should have been dressing for dinner. Now that was odd. Where was Darwell?

"The marquis was telling me today how nervous he is about demonstrating his skill this evening." That was a total and complete lie, but if this worked Ceci would never know.

"What is he going to do?" Her sister's eyes lit with interest.

"He is going to juggle." She did her best to make it sound like a skill to be admired.

"You mean like a performer at a fair?"

"Yes, doesn't it sound like fun?"

"Hmmm" was Ceci's ambiguous response.

"Oh, do not be a snob and say that it sounds common."

"No, never, but juggling is hardly an intellectual endeavor. I do wonder if the marquis was speaking the truth when he said that he had never read before he suggested we read *Frankenstein*."

"His given name is William. Olivia told me."

"His name is William? Very heroic sounding, is it not?"

"Yes, it is." *That's better.* "He said that he could use an assistant this evening and, Ceci, he asked me if I could talk you into helping him."

"He did?" Her amazement was obvious.

"Yes, he said that having you in front of everyone with him would help distract the others from any mistakes he might make."

"Any woman could do that."

"But he asked for you, sister! Not me. Or Katherine. Or Mrs. Kendrick." She could have gone on but felt her point was made. "And you thought he was avoiding you. He clearly is not."

"But I cannot assist. I have excused myself from dinner tonight." Cecilia began to twist her hands together. "I don't feel well."

"Nonsense, Ceci. You are never sick a day. You're just making an excuse to avoid Lord Destry." Beatrice looked around the room. "Where is Darwell?"

"Callan, Lord Jess's valet, came to the door and asked for her assistance with something. She promised to be back in time to help you dress."

"Then we had best start right away since you *are* going to dinner and you *are* assisting Lord Destry."

Beatrice went into the dressing room and opened the clothes press. She hoped Cecilia would follow. Beatrice had no idea what would be the best sort of dress to wear for such a performance.

Cecilia did join her, but she closed the lid on the dresses. "I cannot do it, Bitsy. I hate being the center of attention. You know that."

"They will all be watching him juggle."

"Then why does he need me?"

Ceci did have a point. "I told you, to hand him his various props and look approving." Hoping, praying that what she was about to say would not ruin everything, Beatrice took the risk. "Consider this, Ceci. He is asking for your help. To refuse would be so unkind, would tell him once and for all that you think he is not worthy of your attention." Beatrice lifted the lid of the press again.

"But that's not true at all," her sister said with some

urgency. She eyed the dresses. "I'll be terrified the entire time. But you do have a point. I would never want him to think I find him lacking."

With a resigned sigh, Ceci lifted a dress out. "I think this pale pink. It will not call attention to me the way a bolder color would, and it is a fabric that does not wrinkle much so we can manage without Darwell having to iron it."

Beatrice's dress was already hanging. A blue that was more marine than true blue, it was one of her favorites of the new gowns.

Before they could do more than don clean shifts and tie each other's stays, Darwell was back. She looked as composed as usual, so Beatrice had to rethink the idea that she and Callan were having their own love affair.

She had love on the brain. Not everyone here was falling in love. She was the perfect example of that and so was Mrs. Wilson, though one presumed she was in love with her husband.

Darwell accepted that Cecilia had changed her mind, but did comment to Beatrice as she did her hair. "I knew it was all a hum, but did not even try to convince her. You seem to be the only one who can do that, miss."

Cecilia wanted to wear her hair as simply as possible and, though she did raise her eyebrows at the idea, Darwell did not argue. She just gave Beatrice an arch look, hoping she would work her magic again.

Beatrice shook her head and did not try to discourage her sister. Cecilia thought that the simple style would dim her beauty, which made Beatrice want to laugh out loud. If anything, it made her look even more alluring.

"I hope you know what you are doing, miss," Darwell said to her as they left the room.

Beatrice nodded, trying to look confident but not at all sure she was succeeding.

JESS WATCHED THE performance with more fascination than amusement. The performer he was watching was not Destry, who was doing a creditable job juggling everything from oranges to plates, and even some candleholders that must have been difficult to balance, much less catch.

No, it was Beatrice who had most of his attention. She was as nervous as a mother hen with a new chick out from under her wing. That was an understatement, Jess decided. She was acting as if her entire fate rested on the turn of a single card. She would be the world's worst card player if she could not control her expressions better.

Cecilia, chick to Beatrice's mother hen, was managing quite well as Des's assistant. She concentrated all her attention on the performance, as though Des were dependent on her for good luck.

Cecilia seemed awed by the juggling, but Jess suspected that the audience was as bemused by the vision in pink as they were by the man's dexterity.

Occasionally Cecilia would glance at her sister. Beatrice's worry must have communicated itself because those glances did nothing to bolster her confidence. Someone needed to distract Beatrice if only to save the performance. Nominating himself, ignoring the fact that it was just an excuse to be closer to her, Jess left his spot by the door and joined her where she stood at the back of the group.

"Dinner was a unique experience, was it not?"

"Yes," Beatrice answered absently, as she gave a bright nod to Cecilia.

"To eat the very fish one has caught has a very basic feel to it."

"Yes," Beatrice said again, applauding lightly at a particularly deft catch by Des.

"It made me feel very primitive." He closed the space between them even more.

"Indeed," Beatrice said, ignoring his nearness, but he could feel her heat and she did not move away.

"It made me long to throw you over my shoulder, take you to my cave, and ravish you with kisses until you begged for mercy."

That did draw her attention. She still did not look away from Cecilia but straightened her shoulders. "Begged? I would never beg, my lord. Though I must admit I am curious as to how it feels to be ravished with kisses." She glanced at him. "Now stop trying to shock me and leave me alone until Lord Destry and Cecilia have finished."

Despite the set-down, he had to laugh. Her reaction made him want to kiss her all the more. Not wise. Not wise at all. But then wisdom was not a trait particular to any of the Pennistans. They left that to Olivia's husband, Michael Garrett, who had enough for five men.

"She is not the only one who must have confidence in her. You need to as well. Now is a good time to start."

She stared straight ahead and he could feel her brain working. "You are right," she said, as if a man with insight were the oddest thing in the world. "How did you know that?"

"I've spent my life watching people." Usually at the gaming table but it paid off in other areas as well.

She followed his advice and gave him her full attention. "I'm curious, my lord, where does one go to be ravished with kisses?"

He could tell her, but it would be even more fun to show her.

A hearty round of applause startled her. The other guests moved to the front of the room, giving him an irresistible opportunity.

His rational mind made one loud protest but his impulse won out and he grabbed Beatrice's hand, pulling her into the corridor, which was empty of guests and servants.

He could see surprise but not shock in her eyes as he lowered his mouth to hers. He could feel her smile, taste her sweetness, the gift of youth and innocence she presented to him without guile. Pulling her closer still, he found he wanted to protect and ravish her both at the same time.

Pleasure spiraled between them, ensnaring him with longing if not pure lust, and what began as a teasing kiss became something he could not control. He showed her what a kiss could be, how it promised and teased and tempted.

When he could finally command himself to draw back he was prepared for outrage, but she surprised him. She did look stunned, which was gratifying in a purely masculine way, but raising her hand to her lips, she smiled. A secret smile this time.

"How can it be everything and not enough, both at once?"

Like the urge to protect and ravish, he thought.

She seemed to think better of waiting for an answer and dashed away from him, back into the salon to join the others.

"It was the most exciting experience of my entire life."

"Bitsy, you actually let him kiss you?" Cecilia was not at all sure she had heard correctly. Beatrice was given to impulse, but not wildness.

"He was irresistible." The accompanying shrug was the most nominal apology.

"You barely know him."

"It's not about the length of an acquaintance. There is some kind of magnetism between us. The truth is, Cecilia, kissing him is the least of what I would like to do."

Cecilia shook her head and covered her ears. She did not want to hear any more of this. She had to, though. She had to exhibit some of the sense that her sister had lost.

"He is the only man Papa insisted we have nothing to do with. I fear you are just being difficult."

"No," Beatrice said. "At least I don't think so."

Cecilia could not think of what else to do or say to reach her sister. So she opted for the cold truth, even if she would sound like a prude. "Kissing Lord Jess was wrong and I am heartily disappointed in you, sister. You are behaving like a woman of easy virtue and if the countess finds out she will be very upset. I have no more to say to you right now." She folded her arms and did not try to hide her anger at what felt like a betrayal.

"Ceci!" Beatrice stepped back as if the attack had been physical.

Cecilia wished that Darwell would come in and they could end this discussion. She felt like crying and could see tears in Beatrice's eyes as well.

"I'm sorry you feel that way." Beatrice spoke in a voice stiffened by the effort of holding on to control. "I am going to the art gallery and will leave you to count my sins in peace."

With that, Beatrice left the room. But the hurt lingered in the air and Ceci sat on the edge of the sofa with a graceless thump, letting the tears fall. The sisters never argued and it was small comfort that Beatrice was as upset as she was. The idea that Beatrice might seek out Lord Jess for consolation made the tears disappear, and she was out the door a moment later to make sure that did not happen.

Chapter Nineteen

Jess watched Destry toss back a brandy and pour himself another. Drinking recklessly was not Des's style. Jess watched him drink the second one with equal disregard for the fine liquor it was.

Destry needed to talk, not drink, even though Jess knew exactly what the conversation would be about. Hell, he needed the distraction. The memory of kissing Beatrice was overwhelming even though it was, at best, a mistake in judgment and, at the worst, the first step toward deep and serious trouble. Pushing the issue as far out of his mind as he could, Jess moved the decanter up a shelf and away from Destry's grasping hand.

"Give that bottle back to me!"

Destry tried to reach past him, but Jess merely stepped in his way and let an ineffectual punch land on his arm. The man was already foxed, Jess thought.

How much had Destry had to drink before his performance?

No, he had been stone sober then. No one could juggle that well when drunk.

So he'd come to the game room and started in on the drink in the last hour. That was more than enough time for him to ruin the rest of his evening.

"You're the last one to preach sobriety, Pennistan. Just last week I saw you drunker than five lords and demanding more!"

"In a gaming hell, Des. Not at a house party where ladies are present."

"God, now you sound like a duenna." Destry looked around. "The only lady here is Nora Kendrick, and her husband spent most of his life aboard a ship. She's used to men who stagger." He laughed at his own joke.

Des tumbled into a chair at one of the gaming tables. He tried to put his head in his hands, elbows propped on the table, but one elbow missed the edge and he almost hit his head, which would have done him no good at all.

He sat back and rubbed his forehead with both hands as though the headache had already started.

"It's hopeless." Destry's flat voice was more convincing than the words.

"What is?" Jess sat in the nearest chair and played with the ivory counters, prepared to listen.

"Cecilia Brent will not even look at me, much less talk to me. Much less marry me."

Jess made a face. "Are you not jumping ahead a little? There is something called courtship between talking and marriage."

"Yes, yes." Destry waved a hand in the air as if

courtship and all the attendant formalities of a proposal were mere details. "Yes, but I can't even start a courtship if she ignores me."

"She was in front of the audience with you tonight. And judging by the scared-as-a-rabbit expression in her eyes, that was not a spot she enjoyed."

"Yes, she was." Destry brightened. "And you say she was scared? But she was wonderful."

She did *look* wonderful, Jess remembered. She hadn't had to *do* anything but hand Destry the occasional prop. "She watched you as though the performance was the most impressive display of juggling she had ever seen."

"Yes," Destry agreed. "And the way she handed me each piece with such a reassuring smile. Did you see the little crease between her brows when she thought I might be taking on too much? Even that was adorable."

Listening was one thing, but doing so without laughing was asking too much. Jess disguised it as a cough. "She was a superior assistant," he agreed, fairly sure that agreeing was all he had to do.

"Indeed she was, and like a tempting dessert in that delicious pink dress." Destry's eyes lost their focus and he went somewhere else for a few seconds. But he came back soon enough, his expression morose again. "She disappeared the minute she could, as though she regretted helping me. How do you explain that?" He jabbed a finger at him and Jess leaned back, pushing the finger away. "Jess, she's too beautiful to even consider me."

"Nonsense, Des." This part Jess knew the answer to. "You are going to be a duke. You can have your pick."

"She'll refuse." He looked around for his glass and then shrugged. He paused for a long moment. "It's because I'm too short."

Destry spoke as if height were the most important element in a courtship. But Jess knew what that comment indicated. Destry was wallowing in the well of self-pity. This observation was always at the very bottom. Now the only thing for a friend to do was to find a bed for the man and let him sleep it off.

Destry must have realized it himself. He stood up and staggered over to the long sofa in front of the fireplace. The sofa had a high back and was parallel to the unlit fireplace, the perfect spot for a couple to "talk" without being observed by the rest of the room.

It was also true that anyone lying on it would be invisible to everyone else. If he did not snore.

Destry stretched out with an arm over his face and was asleep, or more likely unconscious, in ten seconds.

Jess headed back to the drinks table, determined to savor the brandy that Destry had drunk so thoughtlessly. He poured himself a small glass, and as he sipped, he surveyed the space.

It was a generous game room with three tables set for play. Despite the size the room had a snug quality to it. Was it because the paintings that dotted the walls did not overwhelm the space? Most were drawings and he imagined that Beatrice Brent would much rather look at them than play cards.

If Cecilia were a confection, then Beatrice was a spicy treat. She was always so alive and she drew a man's attention with her wit and élan as much as her sister did with her beauty. Instead of ending his inter-

est, their shared, very much shared, kiss had only fueled it. It had also fueled an accompanying frustration.

Neither her father nor the countess would consider
allowing him to spend an extended amount of time
with her, even under the guise of a genteel flirtation.
He already knew there would be nothing genteel about
it. One kiss had proved that. She was much too curious, much too passionate to want anything less than a
very thorough lesson. And that would put him on the
road to marriage whether he wanted it or not.

Marriage worked for some, but not for him. As a
bachelor he could wager what he wanted, when he
wanted, without worrying about mouths to feed or a
wife to clothe. He'd seen more than one friend's leg
shackled by marriage.

Jess could not imagine a life without games of
chance, a world where the players were constrained by
wives and money. Where there were no surprises left.

Lord Belmont came into the room and walked
toward Nora Kendrick. Nora's dog, Finch, was nota-
ble for his absence.

"Some wine, my dear?" Belmont asked as he made
straight for the drinks table.

Nora Kendrick nodded and smiled, whispering to
Jess. "Does he never stop drinking? And how is it that
he does not slide from his chair onto the floor? He is
fascinating." She heard her own words and went on.
"Fascinating in many more ways than that, I assure
you."

"I have never seen him in any state but sober," Jess
whispered back, feeling more like a marriage broker
than ever. Was that his role at this party? So far it felt

that way. "And I have never seen him take a drink until well after noon."

"The admiral, my husband, had an impressive capacity but it did seem to affect—" Nora Kendrick stopped abruptly and then her mouth spread into a guilty smile. "My, my," she said, "perhaps it is time for me to slow down as well."

Belmont joined them, handing a glass to Nora Kendrick with a steady hand, and Nora must have decided that one more drink would not be too much after all. She touched her glass to the earl's and took a small sip.

Before the three of them could begin a conversation, Crenshaw came into the room and the ambiance immediately changed from convivial to challenging.

"Time for play," Crenshaw announced.

Destry popped up from his resting spot looking completely recovered; at least, he did once he smoothed his hair back.

Without waiting for agreement, Crenshaw walked to the farthest table, the one with the best light, Jess noted, and picked up the playing cards.

Destry sat next to him, and Belmont and Nora Kendrick took two chairs next to each other, apparently playing as one. The last to take a seat, Jess settled himself opposite Crenshaw.

Tonight he would do what he had come to do. Win back his land. Then he could leave without ever having to explain that misguided kiss to the oh-so-delectable Beatrice Brent.

Chapter Twenty

CECILIA HAD A general idea where the art gallery was but she still made three wrong turns and finally had to ask a footman for the easiest way to find it, hoping that Beatrice would really be there.

The gallery was not lit tonight, and the full moon provided the only illumination. Despite the gloom Cecilia could see Beatrice sitting on an upholstered bench across from some gigantic scene of a man at sea. The sailing ship was fighting the elements and it seemed to be losing.

"This painting is exactly how I feel, Ceci." Beatrice spoke without turning her head as Cecilia sat next to her.

"As though you are struggling against nature?"

"Yes, exactly. I am attracted to the man. There is nothing wrong with that except that he is a gamer and a rake. Perhaps all he needs is the love of a good woman to show him a more righteous path."

Cecilia bit her lip to keep from laughing. While she had no doubt that her sister was a good woman, she did not think Beatrice would ever be completely happy on a "righteous path" herself, no matter how one defined that vague phrase.

"What is a righteous path, anyway?" Beatrice asked, reading her sister's thoughts. "Surely it is enough to hurt no one and be loyal to one's family."

"I do believe there are events in his past that call that loyalty into question," Cecilia added with more timidity than she wished.

"What did happen? And how do I find out?" Finally Beatrice turned away from the painting and looked at her twin. "No one will tell me and that is simply ridiculous. You cannot make a decision without knowing all the facts."

"Papa is trying to protect you, and Darwell will not gossip." Both of those seemed reasonable explanations for their reticence.

"I asked Lady Olivia and she would not tell me, either." With a sigh Beatrice went on, "I will have to ask him directly. Sometime."

"But not tonight."

Beatrice said nothing for a long moment.

"Ceci, I will drop the subject and not ask tonight, unless Lord Jess brings it up, if you do one thing for me."

Cecilia did not like the sound of this bargain. Beatrice's sly smile doubled her worry.

"I think you should be spending more time with Lord Destry."

"That's absurd, Beatrice." Cecilia could not hide her exasperation. "I just spent the evening as his assistant.

How much more friendly do you want me to be?" She did not dare admit that acting as his assistant had been "fun," to use her sister's favorite word.

"But you barely had any time to converse with each other."

How wise was it of her to see more of Lord Destry? He made her forget to think about how she looked, or whether she was saying the right words. He made her feel nervous and excited, when she much preferred calm and collected.

"What is the point in knowing him better?" Immediately Cecilia regretted the question. She should have said "no" firmly. Now they were in for a discussion. In an effort to avoid a possible argument Cecilia decided to be blunt. "I do not want to be a duchess. I want a quiet life in the country with children and a husband who is both sensible and sensitive. Lord Destry is neither."

"You told me the other night that you had misjudged him. Need I remind you that this is the man who said that children should be taught to love one another? What is that if not caring?"

So they were going to have a debate whether she wanted to or not. Cecilia hated debates because she always lost. "I have had a long day and do not want to end it with an argument."

"Here is my idea," Beatrice began, ignoring her sister's complaint. "Listen and admit that it makes sense. It's a compromise. We will find the gentlemen, who are most likely gaming, on the pretext of asking who is going to ride in the morning, just as I suggested last night. If they invite us to join them in the game room we will stay and observe for a few minutes. You do not have to make conversation, only keep me company."

"Lord Destry will be riding. I do not need to ask. He goes out on Jupiter every morning."

"Then come with me and don't ask. I should not go alone in case there are no other ladies with them."

Cecilia knew this was just another way for Beatrice to win exactly what she wanted.

"But I'm going whether you come or not," Beatrice insisted. "It's my turn to have some fun. And after all, we did agree that they could teach us how to game."

If she wanted to avoid an argument, Cecilia knew she had no choice. "All right, but we must go back to our rooms first. I'm sure my hair needs some attention." If she could retreat to their room and enlist Darwell for support, Cecilia was sure she could keep her sister from going.

"It looks fine, Ceci. Not a curl out of place. And yet I wager a guinea that if you come with me you will look in every mirror we pass." Beatrice danced around her with a teasing smile.

"I'm not that vain," Cecilia answered with affront. "I only want to look my best."

Beatrice stopped moving but said nothing, only bending her head slightly, with a challenging look.

"Very well, but no wagering," Cecilia said, rising. There was a mirror behind her and she was amazed how hard it was not to take a quick look.

"Come, let us ask the footman where the gentlemen are playing tonight." Beatrice took her sister's hand and Cecilia held on tight.

"What are a footman's duties, do you suppose?" Beatrice asked, hoping to distract her sister.

"To help ladies and gentlemen up and down the stairs," Cecilia answered promptly. "Or, yes, as you suggested, to tell visitors how to find certain rooms. But they must do more than that." Cecilia thought a moment. "We could ask Darwell. She told me that Callan was a footman for years before he became a valet."

"When did you talk to her about Callan?" She and Darwell never talked about anything personal.

"When she was doing my hair. She is a veritable font of information. I can't decide if she likes talking about him or was trying to keep me from fretting about this evening."

"Both, probably," Beatrice said. "I think they are old friends, and perhaps more now."

"Hmmm" was all Cecilia said, which made Beatrice suspect that her sister knew more than she was letting on. Had Darwell sworn her to secrecy? When?

"Bitsy, she told me that whenever Lord Jess wins he gives Callan a bonus."

"No, really?" Beatrice wondered if Jess won often.

"Yes, Darwell told me that Callan says it more than makes up for the times when Lord Jess is short of funds and cannot pay him in a timely manner."

And how often does that happen? Beatrice wondered. They reached the footman before she could ask her sister, but that was all right since it hardly mattered. It was not as if she and Jess were courting. A flirtation was all they could share—one that involved lots of kisses.

"Would you tell us where the card room is?" Beatrice asked the footman.

"Of course, Miss Brent. The gentlemen are playing

in the smaller of the gaming salons on the third floor in the west wing." He began to give them directions and then suggested he escort them instead.

After the fourth turn Cecilia began wringing her hands. "How will we find our way back?"

"We can always ask another footman, but I believe I can get us back safely. We have passed some remarkable works of art. There was a rather lovely oil by a painter I do not know—I must do a bit of research tomorrow. And here is a type of Gainsborough you do not see very often. We will have no trouble."

Cecilia had not noticed the paintings, but she had counted two mirrors since they'd made their wager. And, yes, except for the wager, she would have looked at herself in each one to make certain that she was still presentable. The thought horrified her. It was as though she were addicted to her appearance or, at least, to making sure she looked as perfect as possible at all times.

The footman opened the door to what must be the small game room and Cecilia was sure they were in the wrong place at the wrong time. For one thing this "small room" was the size of their dining room at home and, even worse, judging by the tension in the room something awful must be afoot. Something of which she would rather not be a part.

The table where the players were gathered sat in a circle of light that left the rest of the room in deep shadow, making for an appearance of impropriety even if it was of the mildest sort. Lord Destry's red scarf was loosened, as was his shirt, and Cecilia could see, even from this distance, that he'd had quite a bit to drink. She could tell by the way he slouched in his chair, and he was far less active than he usually was. *This is exactly what I feared.*

"It's just the shadows," Beatrice whispered. "They would make even you look dangerous."

Cecilia noted that Bitsy herself stayed back and watched with her, waiting for the right moment to announce their presence. All she wanted to do was sneak out without being noticed, a thought that would never occur to her sister.

The gamers included Lord Crenshaw, Lord Jess, the marquis, the Earl of Belmont, and Mrs. Kendrick. Not one of them looked their way. All attention was focused on the hand in play. Only Lord Crenshaw and Lord Jessup were holding cards.

"Lord Jess looks particularly intense," Beatrice whispered.

"Yes," Cecilia breathed back, tearing her eyes away from the marquis. Lord Jessup usually stood back from the rest or was the last to enter a room. But not now. With even more concentration than the rest of them, Jess waited and watched his opponent.

With the play of one card, the entire table reacted. Destry with a whoop of excitement, Mrs. Kendrick with a whispered phrase, and Lord Jess with a smile of such malicious satisfaction it justified the angry expression Lord Crenshaw could not hide.

The elation was such a change of mood that it made Cecilia jump, and she pressed her hand to her mouth for fear she would let out a scream.

Lord Belmont broke the silence. "You've lost, Crenshaw. Well played, both of you," he declared. "As hard as it is to believe, Crenshaw, you now owe Jess two thousand pounds." Lord Belmont was, as usual, the voice of calm.

"Two thousand pounds," Beatrice hissed, her mouth next to her sister's ear. "That's a fortune."

Lord Jessup settled on a neutral, if satisfied expression, and Crenshaw seemed to rethink a tirade of words, settling for only two. "You bastard."

"There is a lady present," Lord Jessup reminded him.

Mrs. Kendrick nodded. "A lady who was married to a sailor for fifteen years. Your language is excused, my lord."

"How do she and Belmont do that?" Beatrice asked. "They are so good at easing difficult situations."

"Shh," Cecilia responded. This was hardly the place for such analysis. She wanted desperately to leave.

"If you prefer," Lord Jessup said silkily, "I will take the land that you won from me the last time we played for high stakes."

"That played-out coal mine?" Crenshaw leaned back in his chair, raising it off its front two legs.

"Lord Crenshaw is acting as though he has the upper hand," Beatrice said.

"Yes. Why? He lost."

Lord Jessup must have realized he'd made a tactical error, for his satisfied expression was replaced with a try for casual indifference.

It almost worked.

Nothing about this exchange was casual. It frightened Cecilia enough that she wanted to close her eyes and cover her ears.

"I know it's worth less than two thousand but it does have sentimental value," Lord Jessup countered.

"I'm not sure I even own those paltry acres any-more."

"You still cannot tell the truth, can you, Crenshaw?" Jess said as he stood up. "You own the mine and it is not played out. I have been keeping my eye on it. And on you. Watch your step, my lord."

"Watch my step? You impertinent bastard!" Lord Crenshaw thundered, rising abruptly and sweeping cards and markers off the table as he leaned across to grab for Lord Jess's cravat. "I swear I will beat you to a pulp if you interfere in my life again."

"Take your hands off me." Lord Jess stood perfectly still, his words and his eyes his only defense.

"This is horrible! Leave, we have to leave," Cecilia insisted, so upset she forgot to whisper.

Beatrice nodded, but did not move.

"This is not some performance," Cecilia began, furious with her sister, who she suspected was thrilled by the display.

"Gentlemen," Lord Belmont began, and Cecilia turned back to listen, "and I remind you that you are both gentlemen, you are to end this now. Crenshaw, take your hands off Pennistan. And you—" He turned to Lord Jess. "You are the son of a duke. Do not dis-credit your family name."

Taking a lesson from the earl, Cecilia turned to her sister and spoke in as forceful a whisper as she could summon up. "We are leaving now. We will not be an audience to this spectacle."

Crenshaw let go of Lord Jessup, ran a hand through his hair, and did not answer at first. The others waited while he collected his temper and his scattered wits.

"For the love of God, Ceci, wait just a minute more.

The 'spectacle' has calmed considerably," Beatrice countered in a matter-of-fact refusal to budge.

Crenshaw ran his hand through his hair one more time and finally spoke. "I will arrange to have the funds transferred to your bank, my lord Jessup. I trust you will be willing to hold my voucher until that can be arranged."

"As I recall you refused to hold mine when you won the land," Lord Jess reminded him, informing everyone present of Crenshaw's unsportsmanlike behavior. "But since this is turning out to be such a lovely house party, I would hate to compel you to leave early." Lord Jess paused a moment and went on. "Of course I will hold your voucher, my lord baron."

"Let's leave, Beatrice. Please let's leave," Cecilia begged, well aware that she had reverted to her usual style, but at least she had grabbed Beatrice's hand as she spoke. "I do not want to be involved in this."

Crenshaw drank the dregs from the glass nearest him and stood, almost knocking over his chair in the process. "If you will excuse me. Mrs. Kendrick." He bowed to her. "And gentlemen. I will go draft the letter to my man of business."

He headed for the door, and at that moment the others looked up and caught sight of Cecilia and Beatrice hovering there.

Chapter Twenty-one

WHAT IN THE name of all that was holy was Beatrice doing here with her sister, Jess wondered. And what did it say about his supposedly nonexistent sense of responsibility that he cared how much she had seen and heard?

"Excellent," Destry announced, jumping up from his seat. "You are like a breath of fresh air." He laughed, hurrying over to them. "Do come join us."

He grabbed Cecilia's hand and pulled her farther into the room. The act was rude in its insistence, and not something any lady would welcome. Beatrice followed with more caution than she'd ever shown before.

Destry's overfamiliarity convinced Jess that while he had been engrossed in play, his friend had decided to keep company with Belmont and Nora Kendrick at the drinks table.

"Come, come," Des urged her. "We were taking a break, and fortifying ourselves for the next game."

"I don't think we will be staying. You see—" Cecilia started to pull her hand from his, but something made her stop. Probably Destry's wounded puppy look, the one he put on when he was disappointed.

"We only stopped in for a moment to see if anyone was planning on riding in the morning," Beatrice said. She stopped moving into the room, pausing only halfway to the table where Cecilia now stood. "Cecilia loves a morning outing, and I will not be able to join her tomorrow."

Beatrice had seen it all, Jess thought with regret. He could tell by the way she would not meet his eyes, the stiffness of her words, and the way she held her body. Or, a new thought occurred to him, was she regretting their impetuous kiss? Oh, he hoped not. She had been much too enthusiastic to regret it. Or perhaps it was the enthusiasm she regretted. Fearing he was being as silly as Destry without even spirits as an excuse, Jess pushed the speculation out of his head.

"Riding? Tomorrow morning? Yes," the marquis said eagerly. "Join me! Come along with me!"

Jess cringed at his friend's overly animated invitation.

"Thank you, my lord," the beauty said, her eyes on the carpet. "But despite my sister's inquiry on my behalf, I do believe we are committed to breakfast with Miss Wilson tomorrow morning."

"Then come join us now," Destry insisted, bowing this time instead of going behind her and pushing her. *Thank God.*

His little Venus, the one who knew no fear, hesitated. "But we are beginners. We would not want to play too deep and we fear that will bore the rest of you. I think we should say good night."

Yes, she had seen it all. He left his spot near the wall and crossed to her, Destry, and Cecilia.

He bowed to the sisters. "Indeed, we have played deep enough for one evening and very unusual play it was. Come, let us introduce you to gaming in a more relaxed manner."

The Earl of Belmont made to leave. Introducing young ladies to some innocent gaming was, apparently, not the way he wanted to spend the rest of the evening. But a slight shake of Mrs. Kendrick's head sent him back to his seat.

Exactly. If they left there would be no one to chaperone the two young women.

Des seated Cecilia, pushing her chair so close to the table that Jess doubted the woman could draw breath.

Beatrice was left to her own devices. Jess came around the table and pulled out a chair for her. Instead of sitting, she turned to him. She gave him a look tinged with desperation.

"He's had too much to drink, my lord. I brought Ceci here to spend time with him, to see how charming he can be. This is a disaster in the making."

"Beatrice, I learned from observing my siblings that when it comes to affairs of the heart, it is wisest to let the lovers find their own course."

"But the marquis is your friend, my lord. Don't you see that this will spoil everything?"

Though he was not sure if "everything" meant anything more than her sister's happiness, Jess nodded.

"Yes. It's pure torture to watch Destry make a fool of himself."

"My lord, do something or I will never let you smother me with kisses." She tugged at his sleeve as if she did not have his full attention. She did.

"It's ravish you with kisses, Beatrice. I want to ravish you with kisses. Smothering is something else entirely, and not nearly as comfortable."

She looked down, but he heard her laugh. She did not respond in any other way, but pushed him toward the game table.

"Do something about Destry. Please!"

Lost in their flirtation, Jess missed Destry's next misstep.

"I thought the markers represented coins, my lord," Cecilia said with a touch of primness.

"They can, but they can represent any item that one is willing to wager. A token perhaps?"

What Destry wanted was a kiss. Did anyone doubt that?

"A penny." Belmont spoke firmly. "You will play for a penny."

"Yes," Jess agreed as Belmont raised his eyebrows, which was as close to censure as the earl came.

With a gracious bow, the earl and Nora Kendrick stood and relinquished their place to Jess. The couple moved to another table to play some two-handed game that Jess was sure would necessitate heads close together and soft words.

"I thought that we could try something that did not involve counting," Destry insisted. "Miss Brent has told me that counting is not her strong suit."

"I am not a dunce, my lord." Cecilia's tone conveyed

more insult than amusement. "I can count to twenty and on a good day even as high as fifty."

"What shall we play?" Beatrice asked, her air of desperation revealing itself in a too-bright smile.

Under most circumstances, Jess would have suggested simply wagering on the cut of the cards, but something that easy would only be taken as an insult to Cecilia's intelligence. Besides, it was terminally boring unless the stakes were high.

"One of my favorites is to wager on the cut of the cards," Destry said, though Jess knew that for a lie. "Each of us puts a marker in the middle." They all did so. Cecilia's abrupt movements all but shouted, "I do not want to be here!"

Jess pressed himself back in his chair as if that would put him out of range of Cecilia's ire.

"Now as dealer, I will cut the deck. And you must state whether you think the next card will be higher or lower than the card I show. For simplicity's sake, let us agree to wager on only whether the card will be higher."

"Oh yes," Cecilia said sweetly, "do keep it as simple as possible."

Jess could see that Beatrice, too, had given up on trying to salvage the evening and was waiting to gather up the pieces.

"Excellent!" Destry gave Cecilia a winning smile, and Jess was sure he had no idea how many insults he was showering on the woman he hoped to marry.

If only to keep his run of bad moves consistent, or perhaps to illustrate how bad his luck was, the card Destry drew was the queen of spades.

"How lucky for me," he said with the enthusiasm no

true gambler would ever express. "You can wager, if you wish, but there are only six chances for you to best me."

Both players shook their heads and Destry won. Similar draws occurred for two more hands. That was when Cecilia decided she had had enough.

"Thank you, my lord, but I find I am fatigued by the play, and must say good night." She stood before Destry could say anything. "Beatrice?"

Without waiting for more than her sister's glance, Cecilia made her way to the door. Beatrice usually led the way, but not tonight. She jumped up from her chair and followed her sister.

How fascinating, Jess thought. So this was Cecilia Brent angry. Very calm, very controlled, but near a boil all the same. No one, except the drunk and completely oblivious Destry, could miss the heat.

Destry ran after her. "Wait, wait, you can't leave."

Cecilia turned to speak and saw that he was about to grab her arm. Again. She moved it and he fell forward. Destry maintained his footing, but ran his head into the wall with a distinct thud.

He staggered back and fell on his ass with his hands raised to his head. There was no blood, but Jess was sure the man was seeing stars.

"Oh dear, the marquis has fallen down," Cecilia announced to the room in general. She stepped around him and out the door without a backward glance. Beatrice did hesitate, glancing at Jess who shook his head. "Leave!" he said.

She nodded and left him with Destry.

"Go after them, Jess." Destry looked up, wincing as

even that movement made his head ache. "Go after them and explain."

"Explain what?" Jess could not help but vent his frustration. "Yes, now that I give it some thought, I could easily explain that you are a buffoon but only when you are drunk, which happens so rarely it's a guarantee of disaster."

Destry nodded, but stopped when a spasm of pain reminded him of his head injury.

"I suspect they will close the door in my face before I even half explain, but I will try." *Only because it matters to Beatrice.* Her sensibilities should not matter to him so much—that they did was proof positive that he was falling deeper and deeper under her spell.

The footman opened the door for Jess, and as he left he could hear Nora Kendrick directing the servant who was ministering to Destry. "Help him up, and make sure that he has a walk in the fresh air."

Relieved that the man's folly was not life-threatening, Jess began the long walk to the front of the house and down a flight to the second floor, where he had seen Beatrice upon his arrival. From what they had said over the last few days, he understood that the twins were sharing one of the finer suites.

He could neither see them nor hear their footsteps or voices. The sisters must be all but running from the game room. Not that he blamed them.

Jess wished that he could resolve the headache that he was facing as he tried to smooth over Destry's mess. If only the apothecary sold a tonic that erased memory. It would solve so many problems. Even some of his own.

Chapter Twenty-two

JESS SAW THE last of Beatrice's green dress as she slipped into her room and closed the door behind her. He did not think about propriety as he knocked. It was Beatrice and not the maid who opened it and she was, naturally, taken aback by his presence.

"Now is not a good time, my lord."

It was an understatement. From what he could hear, Cecilia's temper had finally let loose.

"Does he think I am a simpleton? No more than a pretty face?" Cecilia's back was to the door as she went on, Darwell her very sympathetic audience. The maid did not so much as glance at Jess but he knew she was aware of his presence.

"And I knew exactly what he was hinting at when he suggested a token instead of money. Did he think I was so taken with him that I would use the counters to wager kisses? What if one of the other gentlemen had won? Then I would have had to kiss him, too. The marquis may not care a fig for propriety, but I do!"

"Miss Brent," Jess tried, "I do apologize on the marquis's behalf. Please hear me."

She whirled toward the door and then left the room completely.

"This is one of those times when I still miss Mama dreadfully." Beatrice's confidential whisper was barely audible. "She would know exactly what to do to calm Ceci."

With a glance over her shoulder, Beatrice stepped out into the passage and closed the door behind her.

"I think it is useless to try to be a mediator tonight." She did not wait for his agreement. "Unless he and Cecilia marry in a blaze of romantic sensibility this will not be an evening anyone remembers fondly."

The passage was not the right place to try to cut Destry's losses, but to suggest a place more private would be inviting trouble all his own. Jess took a step into the middle of the corridor and Beatrice followed him.

"The marquis rarely drinks," he began, "and I can hardly think of a time when he has done so to excess."

Beatrice shook her head, rejecting that attempt. "If you tell her that, she will think that she drove him to it."

"She did," Jess said, drawing a glare from her. "Listen to me, please, before you start shouting, too. Destry is convinced she will have nothing to do with him because his size offends her and she would be embarrassed to be seen in public with him."

"That's just stupid. Cecilia knows better than most not to judge people based on appearance."

"Yes, yes, I can see how that would be true."

Beatrice smiled, apparently pleased by his quick grasp of the idea.

"The fact is, my lord, that Cecilia is afraid to allow a courtship because she is sure she could never be a proper duchess. Doing everything as perfectly as she can has always been so important to her."

"She is afraid of failing?" Now he was aghast. "She's already demonstrated her talent for acting regal. That freezing tone she used when she left the room this evening was better than anything my mother ever tried."

Beatrice made a face as she tried to recall that moment and then laughed suddenly. "Yes," she said, then stopped the laugh with a glance at the door, now firmly shut. "The way she looked at me and said 'Beatrice?' made me dare not refuse to accompany her."

Beatrice clapped her hands and then sobered. "But, you see, you are right on one point. She hates to be embarrassed and Lord Destry embarrassed her. One upset like that calls to mind all her worst worries. I've seen it time and again. In this case the worry is that a gentleman will not even try to see beyond her beauty, that she will be married for the money she can bring to a union, that her husband will think jewels and baubles will be all she needs to be happy." Her shoulders slumped and she shook her head. "My lord, the marquis's blunder could not have been worse."

"It could have been much worse. If Crenshaw had still been among us there would have been a fight at least, if not a challenge to a duel."

"Is Lord Crenshaw that hot-tempered?" Beatrice leaned closer and her spicy perfume made him want to tell her what was really on his mind. Instead he answered her question.

"Crenshaw loves nothing better than to savage someone, anyone, with words or fists. Appearing to stand for a lady would make it even sweeter."

"My lord," she began in a tentative style that was not her usual approach. "What is it between you and the baron that created such ill will this evening? I risk a set-down, I know, and understand if you do not wish to speak of it."

Jess hesitated, which was not his usual style, either. The bastard had so many fooled that Jess had long ago abandoned any second thoughts he had about the part he'd played in Crenshaw's divorce. It might not be solely his story but perhaps he could tell it in a way that would leave the innocent protected. And keep this innocent from being misled by Crenshaw's supposed charm, but this was hardly the place for such a conversation.

"Beatrice, what is between Crenshaw and me has nothing to do with Destry's behavior tonight."

"I know, I know, and I understand that there is nothing that can be done about my sister and him until both parties are more themselves." He smiled at the delicate phrasing and she smiled back. "This seems to be a good time for an answer to a question that has plagued me since we first met."

"The only thing good about this moment is that we are alone together, but I am sorry, Beatrice, the corridor is not an appropriate place for me to talk about Crenshaw."

As if proving his point, they heard footsteps coming their way and, much to Jess's relief, Michael Garrett turned the corner and came toward them.

Jess was not sure what Garrett had heard, but he

showed not one ounce of censure. "If you two would like to continue your conversation, you can use our sitting room and Olivia and I will be your chaperones."

He did not wait for an answer but opened the door just next to the Brent sisters' suite.

"Just a moment while I tell Olivia."

It did not take Garrett long, but it gave Beatrice enough time to enter her bedchamber and tell Darwell and Cecilia where she would be. Jess overheard Cecilia's "There is nothing the marquis's ambassador can say that will make me speak with that boor again!"

Jess did not hear how Beatrice replied but apparently she thought what he had to say was more important than calming her sister.

Michael opened the sitting room door and invited them in. Once he had the door closed he explained, "Olivia is already abed as she wishes to bake bread with Cook in the morning, the very early morning, but I have some work left to do on Sunday's sermon."

He ushered them to the fireplace, poured wine for them, plated some biscuits and moved a discreet distance away. He did seem truly busy with his Bible and papers.

The two of them sat and the silence grew and stretched and lengthened. Jess had told this story before, but he still did not know where to begin.

Then he realized that it all began and ended with dear Annie Blackwood.

BEATRICE WAITED IN silence for him to start until she wondered if he had forgotten her. Or changed his mind.

She had been sitting in a chair at a right angle to him and moved to sit beside him on the sofa. "Mr. Garrett has gone to all this trouble, my lord. You have to explain your anger with the baron. Please." Best to add the "please" lest she sound too much like a duchess herself.

He began with a voice full of resignation and pain. "Crenshaw's first wife was a close friend of our family."

Beatrice wondered if he was referring to Annie, the woman whom Olivia had mentioned. Jess took a sip of wine before he continued. "My father, the duke, was her guardian and she grew up as Olivia's dearest friend and remains so to this day."

Beatrice began to sort the players in her head: Lord Crenshaw, Annie, the Duke of Meryon, and Lord Jess.

"How did she come to be part of your household?" *And how well did you know her?*

"Her mother was Olivia's governess until she became too—unwell—to continue."

It sounded as though the word "unwell" was chosen out of kindness or the better part of discretion. Beatrice decided it was best not to give any thought to what compelled this governess to leave the duke's employ.

"When Annie's mother left our household she asked that Annie be allowed to stay. Of course my mother would not have it any other way. And for the rest of her growing years she was as part of the family."

Did Jess realize he had used her given name?

"I have no idea how Crenshaw met her, but he asked for her hand at a point in his life when he had no expectations of inheriting the title. He had a brother who would inherit and this brother had a son. Still, Crenshaw could have married higher than the guardian child of a duke."

The kindness in his voice elevated the woman who held that tentative place in his family to something, someone, dear to his heart.

"I suppose Crenshaw thought an alliance with a ducal family would be to his advantage. And Annie was a woman accustomed to running a large household. Crenshaw had a nice enough estate very near Birmingham." What he said made sense, but wasn't it possible that Crenshaw had fallen in love with the girl? Beatrice kept silent, not wanting to interrupt the story.

Jess looked at Beatrice for the first time. Now the memory suffused his face with anger. "Crenshaw married her with my father's blessing and they came to London." He shook his head as if trying to understand how so great a wrong could have started so innocently.

"That must have been hard for all of you, especially Olivia. To lose her best friend and have her be at a distance where travel was not easy."

"I suppose. I was in London, too, but beyond an initial call I rarely saw them. I sensed that Crenshaw was jealous and I did not want to make Annie's life difficult. Beyond that, the entertainments of married couples are somewhat different from those of bachelors."

He picked up a biscuit and then put it back down.

"To be honest, I wanted no reminders of my family. After my mother's death, the duke, my father, became less and less pleasant. Those of us who could left home, and Olivia escaped to the kitchen. After my father died and my brother Lynford became duke, my life was firmly placed in London. The only time I recall going back to Pennford was for his son's christening."

Did he know how revealing that was? How important his mother had been to his father and perforce to the family as a whole? She would have to think more about that later.

"Olivia tells me there were letters and all was well enough. But then there was the accident that took his brother and the heir's lives and suddenly Annie's husband was Baron Lord Crenshaw."

Grief that brought good fortune could make for a very difficult period in any marriage, Beatrice thought.

Jess was staring at his hands, which he held between his knees in a relaxed way that made Beatrice think of defeat. There was another long silence before he went on.

"The letters from Annie stopped and my brother, who was duke by then, ordered me to call and see if all was well. I put it off for a fortnight just to be difficult."

Jess caught her eye again, and the pain she saw in his gaze made her reach for his hand.

He held on to it with both of his.

"She was unwell?"

"Thin to the point of starvation, with bruises on her arms and a black eye. I asked her what had happened, but I did so in front of the baron and Annie would only say she had been ill and had fallen in a faint.

"I wondered if she had suffered a miscarriage, if you will excuse me for mentioning such a delicate subject. Trusting time would heal her, I left to meet my friends."

Oh dear, that could not have been the right thing to do, Beatrice thought.

"The next day, Annie's lady's maid came to me to

tell me that Crenshaw was off at a meeting and that I must come talk to her mistress. Annie's bruises had haunted my dreams and I went back to his town-house." He shook his head. "I think if I had done no more than write to my brother, she would have been dead within the year."

"But you did not and she is safe now."

"Thanks to Leonie Darwell."

"Our Darwell was Annie's maid?" What a small world they were part of now, but that did explain Darwell's strong defense of Jess and how he knew her Christian name.

"Yes, Darwell was her maid," Jess went on. "She brought me back and insisted that Annie tell me the truth, that whenever Crenshaw was angry he would use his wife as his whipping boy. When they were to go out socially and he did not want her bruises to be seen he would shut her up in her room and not allow her to eat."

Beatrice gasped. "But that sort of treatment is grounds for divorce, is it not?"

"Yes," Jess said, but he was not done. "When Annie finished her story I told her she was coming with me, leaving everything behind, and that I would take her home to the Pennistans' house in London and then escort her to Pennford when she was well enough. She left with me within the hour."

If the story did not involve such pain for Annie, it would have been a very romantic rescue.

"It will tell you how ill and abused she was that she obeyed me without the slightest argument."

Beatrice wanted to comfort him, put her head on his shoulder, but could hear Mr. Garrett rustling his papers. She feared he would think it too intimate a gesture. Instead she whispered, "I am so sorry."

He patted her hand in a fatherly way and she withdrew it from his. "Annie is the one who suffered the most. In every possible way."

Beatrice nodded, but that did not mean his suffering was any less painful.

"When we arrived back at Pennford my brother was sickened by her story."

He drew a deep breath and glanced over her shoulder toward where Mr. Garrett sat working. Whatever passed between them was communicated without words and Jess went on.

"But when my brother the duke confronted Crenshaw, the man insisted that Annie and I had contrived the alleged abuse to cover an affair." He shook his head and actually smiled a little. "I love her, but like a sister, mind you, and my family knew it. More than once my father had hinted that we two should make a match, but neither of us wanted that."

Beatrice wondered if he had ever "wanted" any woman enough to consider marriage. Or was the entire idea of being tied to one woman unappealing to him?

"In the end I told my brother that Crenshaw could apply to the House of Lords for a divorce on the grounds of infidelity and name me as the paramour, even though it was a lie."

Too noble, Beatrice thought. Much too noble.

He looked at her for the first time since he'd started recounting the story, his face all too revealing, a mix of cynical, sober, and sad. "It was the one time in my life that my reputation for wildness was a help and not a hindrance. For Annie it meant the end of her life in society, as much by her own choice as the ton's. She stayed at Pennford and never went to London or even Birmingham again. Among the ton, Crenshaw had all the sympathy any cuckolded husband without an heir could possibly want."

He sighed as if exhausted with the telling. "When another scandal made the rounds in a few months I was forgiven, for the most part, and welcomed back into those corners of society that I enjoyed the most. I never was one for Almack's. And so I expect that when you have your Season we will hardly move in the same circles, my dear Miss Brent."

"It is a tale of heroic proportions, my lord. Your willingness to sacrifice all for the good of a friend. I commend you for it. But then, tell me, why would you still wager with the man?"

"Make no mistake, we avoid each other. I suspect if he had known I would be in attendance here he would have found a way to back out."

There was a tap at the door and Jess went to answer it. Darwell came in and, with a curtsy to the two gentlemen, addressed her. "Miss Beatrice, you must come back to your room now. Your sister needs you."

Beatrice stood and took Jess's hand. "I will keep your words in complete confidence."

Jess smiled. Truly. "Thank you. Leonie Darwell is among the few who know the truth. As does Lord Destry. Your sister must be your dearest confidante, so I will trust your judgment to impart as much of the story to her as you wish."

"To ruin his reputation, if only with Cecilia, is no less than he deserves. Death would be too kind." Beatrice regretted her words immediately. She walked over to Mr. Garrett. "I'm sorry, sir. That is unchristian of me, but anger rules at the moment."

"I forgive you, and please believe that God understands anger better than we do. Crenshaw will have to explain his deeds when he is before God. Even I take great pleasure in thinking about that meeting."

Beatrice nodded and left them with a gracious curtsy, following Darwell. As she and Darwell made their way down the passage, Beatrice told her, "Lord Jessup told me about Annie's marriage to Lord Crenshaw, and the divorce."

Darwell's nod was her only comment but a moment later she could not seem to resist. "Lord Crenshaw does not know the meaning of truth. I think if he were to face death he could not be honest."

Beatrice heard the bitterness and understood it. How awful it must have been to be so close to Annie and not be able to do anything to stop the abuse. The baron's wife was not the only one who had suffered.

"And to think that I welcomed his attentions in Birmingham and even here as well." It made her shiver. She was determined to avoid him. If nothing else, she would have the opportunity to practice the social nicety of being cordial to someone you hated.

"It makes Cecilia's tantrum seem petty." She would not allow herself to feel disloyal for speaking the truth.

"Yes, miss."

As they moved through the sitting room toward her bedchamber and her sister, Beatrice took a moment to contemplate the oddities of life. The story she had just heard had been fascinating and would forever change her opinion of both Lord Crenshaw and Jess Pennistan, and even her understanding of Darwell and what a lady's maid must know and never tell.

How odd that what she had really wanted to know was why Jess and Lord Crenshaw had nearly come to blows over some "paltry acres."

That question had been answered but many more had been born in the explanation. What other secrets were there? Was everyone's life one thing to society and, at its heart, something else entirely? She thought of Mr. Garrett and wondered if even he had secrets he rarely shared. Did she?

Chapter Twenty-three

JESS WALKED OVER to the corner of the bookshelf devoted to spirits. He set the wine aside and poured a brandy.

"Pour me one, if you will, Jess." Michael took off his spectacles and rubbed his eyes. "I imagine that story is not easy to recount no matter how many times you tell it."

Jess took a fortifying drink. "It was a cruel thing to do to such a sweet woman."

Michael was cleaning his lenses but stopped. "Are you speaking of Annie or Miss Brent?"

Jess half shook his head, struck by the question. "I was speaking of Annie but the same can be said of Miss Brent. It has darkened her heart a little. Imagine someone of her gentle upbringing wishing a man dead." He drank some of the brandy. "Even though I know this was all Crenshaw's doing, talking about it makes me feel as tainted as he is."

"Stop right there." Michael set down his spectacles and stood up. "There is no god in the pantheon that would call you tainted."

"The pantheon, Michael? Are you turning heretic?"

"No, not at all." He did not smile at the teasing; his face remained serious, a rare expression for him. "I know your beliefs do not incline you to the god I represent. So just in case Zeus or Yahweh speaks to you more clearly, I include them, too."

"The god of gamers, perhaps." Jess finished off the last of his brandy and went to put the glass back on the table. It was a good excuse to turn away from Garrett's searching eyes.

"The Roman god of gamers is a goddess. Fortuna it is for you."

Did the man know everything? "It hardly matters whether any god thinks I am good or evil. It's true that the people most important to me know why Annie needed a divorce. But beyond that I am not much better than Crenshaw. I would never physically harm a woman but I have won fortunes from their husbands and left them with nothing but worry and ruin."

"And what brings on this confession?"

Jess shrugged. He thought of Beatrice Brent and how ill-suited he and she were. How powerless they were to stay away from each other.

"Beatrice Brent is quite delightful."

Garrett seemed to be reading his mind.

"Did you see how much she wanted to comfort you, Jess? She could hardly stand to see you so upset. You are a hero to her now, you know."

"Yes, compassion fairly radiated from her. That was not what I intended at all."

"If only I had a shilling for every man, woman, and child who said that to me," Michael said, running his hand around the back of his neck as if an ache was starting there. "And as I say to each of them, what we intend is one thing. The consequences are not in our control."

"Damn little is," Jess admitted. He wanted more brandy but denied himself just to prove he had some control somewhere.

"You just said that the people who are most important to you knew the truth about Annie's divorce and that's all that matters to you."

Jess nodded.

"Clearly, Beatrice Brent is now one of those people."

Jess looked stunned at the obvious. "She is not falling in love with me, is she?"

Michael laughed, so sincerely that it took him a minute to control himself. "I have no idea, but the real question is whether you are falling in love with her."

"My life is satisfying as it is. I am not going to complicate it with a chit who is endlessly curious and discontented with anything but the truth. The whole truth." He knew he was warning himself as much as Garrett. Yes, he was wildly attracted to her, but he had enough experience to control his baser urges, and even hers, if necessary.

"Yes, her curiosity could be a trial if it were not offset by the joys of that curiosity in other parts of your life."

It was Jess's turn to laugh. "You sound like the madam in a whorehouse trying to convince me to bed an ugly girl."

Garrett waved away the analogy. "Believe me, the love of a good woman can change your life. I know."

"Yes, I know you know, Michael. But I do not want to change my life."

"Yes, I see that," Michael acknowledged. "How did you ever happen on a life of pleasure for its own sake?" he asked bluntly. "I came on the scene long after that was in play."

"I have no special skills. That was obvious early. Not like the rest of the family. David went into the navy at fifteen and seemed set on a career there. Gabriel became a man of science before he was ten. Even Olivia discovered her love of cooking at an early age, and God knows Lynford behaved like a duke before he was breeched."

"No such clear calling for you, eh? That's something I can understand. You know how far and fast I ran from the priesthood. Odd, that. It eventually caught up with me and here I am."

"And here I am as well. I am good at gaming and even better at whoring. One could say that I am true to the Pennistan idea that one pursues what one excels in."

"I grant you the gaming, Jess. But no one ever hears about your women."

"They call it discretion, Michael. And some charm. I have both. I will not bore you with the details of my conquests. They, in fact, all bore me eventually. Except for the two women whose amazing agility kept me entertained for days."

Michael smiled and shook his head. "You are not going to shock me. I could tell you about a French whore who would have sex with her clients behind a transparent screen so that the men who were waiting would be ready for her."

Jess laughed.

"But this is not a contest, Jess, over which of us has lived a more dissolute life. You would undoubtedly win, I grant you that. But is it not time for a change? To turn your life in a new direction?"

"Spare me the sermon."

"All right, but I will have you consider this one fact. David left the navy and found a new place among the mill owners in Birmingham. Gabriel now works closely with an artist developing a form of instruction for physicians and biologists. Olivia is now more a mother than a cook. I grant you Lynford is every bit a duke, but softened by his marriage."

"And your point is?"

"The point is that they all took one road and found another that suited them once they matured. Could that not be in the cards," he smiled at the pun and continued, "in the cards for you?"

"And Beatrice Brent is the key?"

Garrett laughed. "That would be too easy. Let's call her a signal that change is possible. I am looking beyond this house party. You have a whole life to live, more than one day at a time one would hope."

"Is this how you convert people from a life of sin? By nagging them into surrender?"

"I'm not speaking as a priest, but as a happily married man who would wish the same for you."

"Again, spare me," Jess said, suddenly annoyed with Garrett's endless equanimity and supposed wisdom.

"Very well." With a cordial nod, Garrett made his way to the bedchamber door. He paused to share one more thought. "Live in the moment for as long as you can stand it, Jess. And since we are both in this moment and since Beatrice Brent is here with us as well, let me warn you that if you are truly not interested in her, you must come up with a way to discourage her. And you had better not break her heart in the process. That carries a burden of guilt I would not wish on any man."

"DEAR HEAVEN, BEATRICE, you are telling me the truth, aren't you?" Cecilia waved away the question. "Of course you are." Cecilia had put her face in her hands but Beatrice could still make out the words. She stayed that way awhile. Beatrice knew her sister was envisioning the misery Annie must have endured.

Cecilia had forgone a morning ride for what Beatrice decided were obvious reasons, though she wondered if Lord Destry had felt well enough to go out anyway. Beatrice could not imagine anything more uncomfortable than thumping up and down on horseback in time with a headache from too much wine or brandy or whatever he had been drinking to excess.

Beatrice waited, and finally Cecilia looked up. Tears glistened in her eyes but she managed not to give in to them.

"The poor woman. To be surrounded by servants with no one to turn to."

Cecilia's mood had been much improved by a good night's sleep. Beatrice had sent Darwell on some trivial errand, telling her they wished to linger over their chocolate before dressing. As soon as they were alone Beatrice told her sister the story she had learned the night before. It did the job of changing Cecilia's sensibility from ill-tempered to profoundly sympathetic.

"Bitsy, what a horror. It makes Darwell a veritable heroine for staying on to care for her with no rescue in sight."

They sat in silence, sipping chocolate, until finally Cecilia asked.

"How will we act around Lord Crenshaw now that we know?"

"We cannot act any different."

"But why not shun the man? It is no less than he deserves."

"Because Lord Jess trusted me enough to tell me a story very few know and does, perforce, trust me to be discreet as well. I admit I am not sure I am practiced enough in society's niceties to carry it off, but like everything else here, this will be good practice."

"Very well, we are to tell no one and act as if nothing has changed." Cecilia stopped stirring the chocolate and dropped the spoon on the tray.

"Can you imagine what would happen if Mrs. Wilson heard the story? She loves to be the first to spread any sort of gossip."

Ceci gasped. "Lord Crenshaw has been paying attention to both you and Miss Wilson, Bitsy. What if he asks to court her?"

"Oh, Ceci, stop looking for trouble. It finds us easily enough." Beatrice took a small bite of one of the breakfast rolls. It was another bit of perfection from Lady Olivia's kitchen.

"Isn't it amazing that something as basic as bread would respond so well to genius?" she said, distracted by the treat.

Cecilia took a bit of the roll and dipped it in the now cool chocolate, nibbled it, and nodded at Beatrice. "The chocolate is rather good this way. It helps that the roll has just a little sugar in it. Chocolate and cake are an interesting combination. I wonder if Olivia has ever considered putting the two together." Cecilia took one more taste and her smile faded. "I just hope I am a good enough actress."

"Nonsense, Ceci, you do not have to act. Just be the lady you always are."

Cecilia brushed some crumbs from her night robe while she considered what her sister said.

"Treat Lord Crenshaw the same way you would treat Lord Jess, the earl, and Lord Destry." As soon as Beatrice said the marquis's name she wished she had not.

"Destry! I will be every bit a lady to him, even if he is a stupid man who had too much to drink."

"Bravo for you, Ceci." Jess was right. Her sister, who could not imagine herself a duchess, had the air naturally. "Lord Jess is arranging for the rabbit race today. It is to be held around four on the lawn that slopes to the ha-ha on the west side of the house. The sun, if it decides to come out and play, will make it a lovely spot."

"Oh, I have the perfect dress for that. It's the palest green, edged in flowers. Darwell took it to be pressed. I want to look so beautiful it will make Lord Destry weep."

Chapter Twenty-four

"I DO NOT understand what talent of yours this is meant to showcase, Lord Jess." Beatrice danced around him, more sprite than Venus. Her dress was a tribute to summer, the lightest lawn with an under-skirt of pale yellow that made her look like she was as much a part of the garden as the flowering shrubs along the edge of the grass.

"Then you have no imagination, Beatrice." Jess folded his arms and waited until she stopped fluttering around him. "It demonstrates my ability to provide gaming fun no matter what the situation, age, or means of the participants. I can corrupt anyone."

She made a face at him as if she disagreed but was afraid to say so.

Today he had to do it. Garrett was right. He had to show her how dangerous flirting with a man could be.

"You are the first to know this." Jess leaned closer for a conspiratorial whisper. It was all he could do not to nip the tender part of her neck where she had dabbed the sensuous perfume she favored. "We will be racing chickens instead of rabbits."

"Why the change?" She shivered and he did not think it was because she was chilled.

"I realized that a rabbit race would end much too quickly. Even two or three would only last a few minutes."

"And the entire point is to be outside enjoying the wonderful sun."

"No, my dear Miss Brent," he said, offering his arm as they made their way across the field to where the land dropped off. He'd had the course set up near the ha-ha so that there would be a perfect mix of sun and shade. "The entire point is to wager as much money as possible on as many frivolous things as you can think of. For example, do you see this tree?"

He walked sedately with her until they were behind a giant tree that could have housed a family in its trunk. "I wager a guinea that if we stand here I will be able to sneak a kiss without anyone being the wiser."

She was leaning against the tree now, watching him with a look he thought she must have practiced in the mirror for the last few days.

God forbid that look came naturally. She would be fighting men off with a stick.

Now was the time to do it. To convince her he was no hero. He was no more than a man who lived to please himself. It was all that was expected of him and he would be a fool to try for more.

He pressed her against the tree, straddling her body with a leg on either side so that they were very intimately connected, his hands on either side of her head, the tree at her back.

She gave a little gasp of surprise but showed no sign of fear. Just that damnable curiosity that was both her most outrageous sin and her greatest virtue.

He laughed and bent to kiss her cheek and the tantalizing spot beneath her ear where her scent ignited all manner of impure thoughts. She turned her head in invitation. It took a herculean effort, but he did not touch her lips. Not yet.

"Before the other night, had you ever been kissed, Beatrice?"

"Of course." She raised her hands to his chest and managed to make him completely forget what he was going to say next. He stared at her for a long moment, losing himself in her luminous blue eyes, so like her sister's but with a light in them that was all her own. With an effort he remembered the script he'd prepared.

"Of course? You've been kissed by someone other than your father or your mother? Other than me?" He thought of that man who worked for her father, the one with whom she was such good friends, and felt a surge of absurd jealousy that he had not been the first.

"Yes, I have," she said, so defiantly that he was suddenly certain she was telling a lie.

"By someone other than your brothers, cousin, or sister?"

"Don't be ridiculous." She looked over his shoulder.

"Was I the first man to kiss you, Beatrice?" Her eyes flew back to his. "On the mouth?" As he spoke he looked away from her eyes, at her lips. She had pressed them together as though she was trying not to ready them for his touch.

He framed her face with his hands and leaned into her. She watched as he came closer, then her eyes fluttered closed and her mouth curved to welcome his.

Jess did his best to control the contact. This was all about giving her a disgust of him, frightening her into leaving him alone. At first he was completely in charge.

Then he felt the tip of her tongue tease his mouth.

Lust slammed through him. Instantly he forgot his purpose and took what she offered, giving in return. He ran his hands down to where her hands were still pressed to his chest. He pulled them away so that nothing was between them but the clothes they wore. Their bodies were molded together, pressed against the tree.

The first kiss ended but a second drove them on, his hands in her hair, his mind filled with the taste and feel of her, his body ready to take all she had to give.

A moan, his or hers, was a call to sanity many, too many kisses later.

He ended that last kiss rudely, without a thought to her comfort. Taking a step back he left a good twelve inches between them.

"Dear God, Beatrice," he said, breathing hard, "this is not a contest either one of us can win."

"A contest?" His choice of words seemed to bring her into the moment more effectively than a bucket of cold water. "What does one win? More kisses?"

He could tell by her tone that she knew that was not the right answer.

"Damn it. A broken heart, or worse."

She stepped to the edge of the giant tree trunk and looked back toward the house.

"No one in sight." She stepped back, took his arm. She must have felt the same slap of awareness that went straight to his manhood because she dropped hold of him almost immediately. Stepping out from behind the tree, Beatrice walked toward the path to the ha-ha and waited for him.

"You suggested a wager before, um, we were distracted, my lord. What did you have in mind?"

Since that suggestion had been made before his world was tilted on its axis, it took him longer than it should have to recall what she was talking about. He joined her and pretended he had recovered his equanimity as easily as she had, and finally he found his voice. "Yes, I was going to suggest that your sister would arrive alone but that Destry would be close behind. But now I think that is too obvious and that we might as well keep our guineas for some more meaningful wager."

She glanced at him, eyes full of suspicion, as if wondering if there was a double meaning to his words, which there was not. So she was not as recovered as she pretended. He must remember that she was something of an actress. He tried for the blandest of expressions and waited for her to speak.

She cleared her throat and answered him.

"Yes, just as pointless as my inclination to accept the wager, but only if you agree to wager that Lord Destry will promptly say something he means as a compliment that Cecilia will interpret as an insult."

He laughed aloud at the equally easy win and suddenly they were friends. Her demeanor changed a little and she was once again more girl than woman and eager for the next entertainment. What did it say about the rake in him that he was sorry it did not involve kisses?

"You know, my lord, chickens are not bred to race."
She danced around to the front of him and walked
backward. "I mean, they are more likely to peck the
ground for food than they are to run across a finish
line."

"Exactly. That will give us plenty of time to wager
and enjoy one another's company."

She stopped and gave him a questioning glance.

"Beatrice," he said with a tired sigh, "if I meant a
double entendre you would not doubt it."

Her expression relaxed into a smile, but instead of
enjoying his company she abandoned him to inspect
the racecourse. He watched her as he talked with the
keeper and listened to the man's concerns about what
this activity would do to the hens' laying potential.

Jess had assured the keeper he had the countess's
permission to use the hens, and promised to replace
any that were so traumatized by the experience that
their laying days were over.

The run was about forty feet long, fenced with a
wall of fabric down its length on both sides. Beatrice
studied it as if it were one of her favorite works of art.
Jess wondered what she was really thinking about.

She walked back toward him. Her insouciance was
gone, her footsteps ladylike. Cautious, that's how he
would describe her. It was amusing, but not as appealing as her curiosity.

"I wager a guinea that your sister will exclaim over
the chickens but refuse to actually hold one."

"I wager a guinea that Lord Destry will reach in and
take one out to show her how innocent they are."

It was just as well that neither accepted the other's
wager, as a moment later the newly arrived Cecilia

walked over to the wooden cage and marveled at the contestants. As predicted, Des came hurrying along, almost running to stand beside her. She put her hands behind her back when he lifted a hen out for her to hold.

"A guinea that the chicken will nip Des when he tries to put it back."

"Much too certain, my lord."

"I am going to help whichever one of them needs help the most." Jess gave a bow from the neck and left her laughing.

The chicken did nip Destry. Cecilia handed him a handkerchief to cover his wound, and then she walked toward Lord Jess, leaving Destry with his mouth gaping open.

Cecilia's manner reminded Jess of his mother's when she was disgusted with his behavior. Eventually he'd learned there was no point in trying to explain or apologize. His mother, the duchess, would decide when he was in her good graces again.

Destry was not yet in Miss Brent's good graces. Clearly, while Cecilia's temper might have dissipated it had not cooled completely.

"He will not stop apologizing," she hissed to Jess, more distressed than annoyed with Destry.

They looked on as Destry sought out Beatrice, who took him by the arm and moved him beyond the race-course nearer to the edge of the ha-ha.

Cecilia began to improvise both parts of her sister's conversation.

"Stop apologizing to her, you imbecile." She spoke in a breathy voice amazingly like her sister's.

"But I *am* sorry." Her manly imitation of Lord Destry was less perfect but all the more amusing for it.

"The more often you say it the less credible it is, you idiot."

"Do you think so?"

"I know it's true, you simpleton."

"All right, if you think she will forgive me."

"I never said that, you silly man."

Jess wondered how many more innocent insults Cecilia could think up. He turned his back on Beatrice. It was the only way he could give her sister his full attention.

"Forgive him, Cecilia, and put us all out of our misery." He waited until she looked away from Destry and directly at him. "You know he is in love with you."

She shook her head, one sharp shake. "Nonsense. He is not in love with me. He is infatuated with my looks and has no respect for me as a person. That is not love."

She had her back to Destry now, too.

"Look at him," Jess said. "He is the last man in the world to judge by appearances. He has spent his whole life convincing people he is fully a man despite his lack of height."

"He's the heir to a dukedom," Cecilia reminded him, obviously not at all inclined to sympathy. "The marquis does not have to convince anyone of anything."

"He had to convince his family first and foremost." *Forgive me, Des, but desperate measures are called for.* "He told me once"—he considered adding "when he was very drunk" but decided it wiser to skip that— "that when it was clear he was, despite his size, a healthy boy, his grandfather would take him riding almost every day the old duke was at Bendall Manor, their main estate. Those outings are how Des learned to ride like a madman, as his grandfather would challenge him to all sorts of races and jumps."

"That's easy enough to picture," Cecilia said. "He loves a headlong gallop as much as anything else."

"Indeed he does." How often had she watched him? "One day his grandfather challenged him to take a jump that was quite impossible. Des almost tried it, just to prove he was a man, but then he realized that if he did not make it he would surely break his neck."

Cecilia put her hand on her own neck, engrossed in the story.

"Destry said as much to his grandfather, who merely shrugged. In that moment, he told me, Destry realized that his death was exactly what his grandfather wanted."

"His grandfather did not want him to inherit." Her eyes were wide with shock.

"No." *In for a penny, in for a pound,* Jess thought. "The old duke told him that he would rather have the title pass to his cousin than have Destry inherit."

"Because he is so short?" Cecilia's expression was incredulous. "For no other reason?"

"That's right. I suspect he worried that Destry would taint the bloodline somehow. That all future Bendasbrooks would be short."

She glanced over at Destry and Beatrice, who were still deep in conversation.

"So you see, Miss Brent, you must believe that Destry would never judge anyone solely by their appearance."

"But he treated me as if I was stupid, implying I

could neither count nor add." She was all sympathy now, but still confused by his behavior.

"I ask you, Miss Brent, how anyone could think you stupid when we have seen you discuss and name plants the rest of us think of as simply green and leafy."

Destry and Beatrice came to them. They made a foursome just as the rest of the house party arrived, except for Mrs. Wilson.

Miss Wilson held tight to Lord Crenshaw's arm as they made their way across the lawn and Jess looked at Beatrice. Both she and Cecilia were regarding the newly matched couple with undisguised concern.

"I'd be happy to loan you a few guineas, Crenshaw, if your pockets are to let after last night's loss."

Destry rocked back and forth from heels to toes, his teasing good-natured, but Jess had no idea how Crenshaw would react to this most public reminder of his loss.

"I managed to find a few coins, my lord marquis," Crenshaw replied, more formally than necessary.

"What does he mean, my lord?" Katherine Wilson asked.

In fact, Jess realized, she had not witnessed the throw of the last card. So perhaps Destry's teasing had a point.

"Nothing!" Crenshaw's answer was a command to silence. One that made Miss Wilson blush. Jess could tell that she wanted to move away from him but Crenshaw visibly tightened his hold on her arm. Beatrice stepped forward but before she could interfere, he did.

"Miss Wilson." Jess drew her attention and Crenshaw's suspicion, which was all the better. "As you may recall we are to be ladies against gentlemen. So unless you wish the ladies to question your loyalty, may I suggest you join them and move to your side of the field and leave Crenshaw to us?"

He loved the ambiguity in his words and wished Crenshaw was enough of a coward to fear him. But the baron did not shrink from confrontation, especially if it involved his fists.

With a cautious smile at Crenshaw, Katherine Wilson joined the Brent sisters and Nora Kendrick, moving to one side of the fabric wall. Jess might have been wrong but he thought she looked relieved.

Chapter Twenty-five

FROM THEN ON wagers were tossed back and forth with abandon. Several languished with no one accepting the offer.

"A guinea to the person who can name the breed of our chickens." Lord Jess held up a coin.

No one answered until Nora Kendrick came up behind him and grabbed it.

"They are female Devon Old Pegs!"

"Never heard of 'em." Crenshaw held up a coin. "A guinea says Mrs. Kendrick made it up."

"My lord, they are a relatively new breed. The admiral was fond of chickens so I am more familiar with them than most ladies are." Nora was smiling broadly and Jess could not tell if she was being honest or not.

Lord Crenshaw was convinced and admitted defeat by handing over his coin with a gracious bow.

"I think Crenshaw gave in too soon," Belmont called

out. "I wager two guineas that Nora made up that name after all."

Mrs. Kendrick merely raised her brows and they all turned to the keeper, who rubbed his chin and then spoke.

"Cannot say I ever heard of Devon Old Pegs, my lady," he said, "though they may exist. These are indeed a new breed but they are called Derbyshire Redcaps, madam." He touched his forelock in apology.

"Well, at least I fooled one of you," Nora said, not noticing the spasm of anger that twisted Crenshaw's face before he regained control of himself.

"Let the race begin," Lord Destry bellowed, all impatience. As restless as the chickens, Jess thought.

"No!" Beatrice objected. "First we must pick our team of hens."

The ladies gathered by the cage as they chose their runners. Miss Wilson named them Roxie and Molly.

"Laugh if you dare," Beatrice challenged as the ladies moved behind the fabric wall. "Roxie and Molly will race all the better for having names."

"Not being burdened with names, ours will run like the wind," Destry announced as Jess gestured for the fowl to be released.

"Wait! Wait!" Beatrice called out again and everyone groaned. "Can we turn them toward the finish line if they become confused?"

"Yes, but only if you are willing to touch them yourself with your own hands. No servants allowed." Jess wondered if the will to win would overcome Beatrice's natural wish to avoid a henpeck.

"A guinea that there will be a hen fight the minute

they are released from the cage." Lord Crenshaw won his guinea from Lord Belmont.

"Belmont obviously knows nothing about hens," Destry said to Cecilia.

Jess noticed that while she did not ignore him, she did no more than nod.

Beatrice decided to champion Molly. Jess watched her, not the hens, and grinned at her enthusiasm, the way she wrinkled her brow at Molly's disinterest.

"This is a race, Molly! Money is at stake. Possibly even your life!"

The four chickens responded to the boisterous shouting and encouragement, each in her own way. Molly and Nameless Number One pecked the earth, ignoring the noise. Roxie headed toward the finish line with purpose but was distracted when Lord Destry whistled.

"You can't whistle like that!" Beatrice shouted. "That's not fair, is it, Lord Jess?"

Jess folded his arms, and rocked back on his heels. "Whistling is perfectly acceptable."

"Of course you say so since Lord Destry is on your team."

"Of course," Jess said, holding back a laugh.

She gave him a threatening look, but he was sure she saw the laughter in his eyes.

At that moment Nameless Number Two flew toward the ladies, though she could not make it over the wall. Even so all of the ladies screamed, except Nora Kendrick, but even she took a step back.

Having achieved her wish to wreak terror on the humans, Nameless Number Two settled to the ground and began a prosaic search for seeds and insects.

Molly began to move with significant speed, but in the wrong direction.

With a "No!" Beatrice lifted her skirts to a rather unladylike height and stepped clear over the wall. She grabbed Molly from behind, a move so unexpected, by the hen at least, that Molly was not able to elude her. The hen squawked with such vehemence that once she was facing the right direction Beatrice ran from the course and back to the relative protection of the wall.

Apparently Molly blamed Roxie, the hen nearest her, for the interference and a classic hen fight began. The keeper brushed them apart with a broom, urging them toward the finish line, but the two seemed set on bickering. It took another try for the keeper to separate them successfully.

Then Roxie turned her head and, with one eye, stared at Katherine Wilson. "What did I do? I didn't do anything," she insisted, stepping behind Nora Kendrick.

Suggestions flew back and forth on Roxie's motivations until Lord Belmont called out. "I will pay a shilling to anyone who can stay quiet for one minute."

Murmurs all around before silence settled on the group. Now all that could be heard was the pecking and squawking of the hens. Lord Destry picked up Nameless Number One and set her in the correct direction, a few feet ahead of her starting point.

One of the ladies protested, very quietly, but it was a sound, and Belmont held out his hand for a guinea. Beatrice handed him a marker and pressed her lips together.

As the end of the minute approached one of the chickens moved purposefully and directly for Lord

Crenshaw's boot, the toe of which was under the edge of the fabric. Everyone pressed forward and saw Crenshaw lift his foot and kick the fowl toward the center of the run, without force but without any care, either.

Jess saw Destry draw in a breath to protest, but then Cecilia put a hand on his arm and he stayed silent.

A few seconds later when Lord Belmont called the minute, Destry bowed to Cecilia. "You saved me from myself. I and my shilling thank you."

Cecilia curtsied back to him, her eyes more thoughtful than her smile. "My lord, his anger was barely contained. I was worried about more than your wealth." His huge smile must have made Cecilia rethink her comment. "I mean that I did not want any unpleasantness to upset us again."

Des inclined his head, but Jess could tell by his expression that Destry felt his apology had finally been accepted.

Lord Crenshaw wagered that the ladies would lose interest before the hens ever made it to the finish line. Lord Belmont accepted. Crenshaw lost. For with the return of the noise, or perhaps it was the grain Belmont scattered at the end of the run, three of the contestants moved more or less toward the finish.

Miss Wilson protested when Destry nudged Nameless Number Two toward the finish line and away from an apparently appealing insect hidden in the grass.

Lord Crenshaw wagered a guinea that none of the ladies would be willing to pick up either Molly or Roxie after the race ended. Where had he been when Beatrice had turned Molly around, Jess wondered.

Beatrice promptly accepted as did Cecilia and Nora Kendrick. Then Beatrice spent a hilarious minute chasing the elusive Molly. Finally, breathless, her hair tumbling down her back, she nabbed the hen and returned her to the cage. They both received a reward. Molly's was edible.

Jess had no idea why such a wave of longing washed through him as he watched her. There was something about her that drew him in, and he was just as charmed by her laughter as he was by the way she sobered and quietly handed her guinea to the keeper. All the while she seemed completely unconcerned about her mussed hair and blotchy cheeks.

The last wager was from Lord Belmont. He insisted that Roxie would make it back to the cage in record time to try to claim her part of the prize. Several accepted and Belmont had to pay up when Roxie fell off the edge of the ha-ha, tumbling three feet down, stunned but apparently unharmed.

Roxie's indignant squawks left everyone laughing. The keeper fetched her and Jess hoped that the fall would not mean Roxie went to the stewing pot while still so young.

Jess watched Beatrice as she tried juggling her coins according to Des's instructions. She pressed her lips together and concentrated with a determination that made him aware of exactly how intense this woman could be. Before he could censor his thoughts, he imagined that same intensity in bed and groaned as his body responded to the fantasy.

Roxie's state of health was the least of his worries.

Slowly the group made its way back to the house. Jess did not wait for Beatrice, but at some point she abandoned her attempts to juggle and walk at the same time and caught up with him.

When she reached his side, she stopped and put her hand on a giant beech, as though she still needed to catch her breath.

"Do not even mention this to Lord Destry, or Cecilia, come to think of it, but that was much more fun than last night's experience. Does that mean I would prefer wagering on horse races to games at table?"

"I think you make the most of any opportunity life puts before you. Your curiosity is one of your greatest gifts." He did not mean to sound as serious as he did.

"How kind of you to say so." Her expression showed some surprise. "Mama said it was one of my greatest faults. She did not see it as curiosity but called it my inability to accept life as it is without questioning everything."

Her cheeks were pink now; the blotchy look had faded. She had smoothed her hair at some point but it still spilled down her back, making him wonder why women felt compelled to pin it up. Ah, he realized, *women* didn't, but *ladies* did.

And he knew why. He knew. Right now she was everything he had ever wanted in a woman and completely irresistible.

"Mothers surely see things differently than gentlemen." *Lovers* was what he wanted to say and stopped the word just in time. "Mothers want to protect their chicks, do they not? Gentlemen love the idea of a curious young lady, which I do believe we proved earlier today."

"I suppose we did, but you see, the problem with a kiss like that is it only makes me more curious."

"It cannot happen again, you do understand that?" he insisted.

She nodded, a hand on her mouth as though holding something back. What did it say about how little he understood her that he did not know if it was laughter, tears, or curses?

When Beatrice did not move, he did, heading toward the river with the aim of spending some time in, or at least very near, cold water, because he knew exactly what she had not said. She might understand but it did not mean she would obey.

BEATRICE WALKED SLOWLY back to the house. Her heart was pounding as though the kiss against the tree had just happened. Yes, his kisses had been her first but she could not imagine any other man's kiss inciting more passion. Her body was awakened in ways that were unfamiliar and shocking.

She wished Jess had not stopped, but was relieved that he had. Still, she wondered when they could find a quiet spot and kiss again.

It might not be the wisest thing to wish for but they were both adult enough to stop before it went too far. Hadn't Jess proved that?

She ignored the truth that it had taken her all of five minutes to walk on steady legs after their encounter. Beatrice tried to bury the longing for more in the back of her mind and hurried to the house.

As she reached the patio Beatrice could see Lord Destry and Cecilia coming across the lawn together, deep in conversation. The marquis walked with his hands behind his back and listened to whatever Cecilia was saying with much waving of her hands. Beatrice wondered what they could be talking about, but was thrilled that they *were* talking.

The house party had settled into a lovely rhythm of entertainments, meals, and the occasional outing. The countess knew exactly what was needed to keep her guests from boredom. Was that a natural skill or something she had learned? Beatrice decided that experience helped, but that it could be learned through observation.

Was it not interesting that the same did not apply to every skill? She was sure that making love came from experience and that observation had very little to do with it. And she was sure that Lord Jess had a great deal of experience. She did not, she thought with sudden chagrin.

The kiss to end all kisses was back in her head again and her body reacted with the same shivering want that had enveloped her when she was in Jess's arms. She tried to ignore the restlessness and quickened her pace as if she could outrun the longing.

As she drew close enough to hail her sister and Destry, Beatrice could see it was the marquis's turn to speak. Whatever he was saying was making Cecilia look at him with surprise.

Beatrice decided to walk in a different direction and allow the two some time to finish their conversation, whether it was a beginning of something or the end.

After a week she had some sense of the house. Examining the art had taken her all the way to the attics, where she had discovered some truly terrible examples of sixteenth-century art and some lovely floral sketches, which she had admired so much that the countess had made her a gift of them.

Now she made her way from the main floor to the second and then up to the third, ignoring the statue of a couple in an intimate embrace and the painting of a man and woman who had eyes only for each other.

Where was a landscape when you needed one? Not a wild chaotic sea scene, but a meadow in the afternoon sun with animals grazing. Even in a painting like that there would probably be some dairymaid and shepherd dallying in the woods.

Beatrice found herself in one of the bedroom wings, one that was facing east. It was a section favored by the gentlemen who rose early to ride, or those who welcomed the sun. As she hurried down the corridor looking for a footman to show her the way out, she heard someone crying.

She froze. It was a woman, surely. But what would a woman, other than one of the serving maids, be doing in this wing? Crenshaw popped into her head and she moved more purposefully toward the sound. She came around a corner and saw a couple standing in a doorway.

"What am I to do?"

For the love of God, it was Darwell. Darwell crying was as hard to accept as her father laughing uncontrollably.

"Crenshaw has not actually set his sights on the Wilson girl. This is a house party, Leonie. He is entertaining himself with what is available."

Beatrice had no idea who Darwell was talking to but clearly it was someone she knew well, who called her by her Christian name. Beatrice thought a moment. It was Daniel Callan, Lord Jess's valet, she was almost sure of it. Darwell had mentioned him more than once.

They seemed very close, much as she and Cecilia had suspected.

"He may be only flirting now, but he will soon realize that Miss Wilson is the perfect match. Miss Beatrice would have realized how poorly suited they were eventually. Miss Wilson"—Darwell sighed—"she is too eager to please, too easily led." She lowered her head to Callan's shoulder and his arm came around her. "I watched him ruin one woman's life. I cannot let that happen again."

Beatrice backed up and retraced her steps. She did not need to hear any more to know what had upset Darwell.

Beatrice wondered how she could help, what she could do.

She was so lost in thought that she finally had to ask a footman for help in finding her room.

Chapter Twenty-six

CECILIA WAS WAITING for her. Perfect, Beatrice thought. She could tell her about Darwell, then hear what Ceci and Lord Destry had been talking about.

With effort Beatrice decided she was not going to tell her sister about the kiss to end all kisses. It was the wisest thing to do, considering how Cecilia had reacted last time. Firm in her resolve, she gave Cecilia her complete attention.

"Beatrice, Lord Destry and I are going to have a race." Ceci grinned; that was the only way to describe her smile. She looked as though she had just been given the most wonderful present.

"A race? That's what you're so excited about?"

"What I mean is, Destry and I, we are going to have a cross-country race on horses."

"Really? A horse race?" Beatrice could not control her dismay. "For the love of God, why in the world would you want to do that? He will run rings around you."

"Why are you so sure of that? You're the one who hates to ride. I can handle a horse and they don't scare me." Ceci took a half step away from her sister, her smile vanished.

"I'm sorry if it hurts your feelings but I'm only telling the truth." Beatrice stood her ground.

Cecilia put her hands together and the smile came back, not a grin but a hint of one. "He did agree to give me an advantage."

"I don't care if he gives you a five-minute head start, he will win. And you will not be able to jump or go particularly fast."

"That isn't true." Cecilia looked away from her sister.

"You will not jump. You cannot control a horse properly going over a fence riding sidesaddle the way ladies must. I will never speak to you again if you do." She stood before Cecilia, her arms crossed, trying to look resolute rather than afraid.

"Oh, all right, we will avoid all jumps."

That was too easy, Beatrice thought.

"We already agreed there would be no jumps."

"Good," Beatrice said, her fear easing. "But he can ride astride and you cannot, at least not in company such as this."

"That is just the thing." Ceci clapped her hands. "I cannot ride astride so he has agreed to ride sidesaddle."

"How in the world did you convince him to do that?" Beatrice asked, amazed at what Destry was willing to do to win Cecilia's approval.

Cecilia looked so smug that Beatrice almost did not

care how she had convinced the marquis. Her sister so rarely acted as though she were the one in charge.

"We were having a discussion." She paused. "Well, to be honest, it was more like the beginning of an argument, over the fact that I am beautiful and he is short. I told him that his height does not matter to me at all and he insisted that, while my beauty is a joy to behold—"

"Ceci," Beatrice interrupted, "that is such a poetic way to put it. Romantic even."

"Oh, believe me, there was nothing romantic about his tone of voice. The point was that he knows there is more to me than looks, just as I know he is more than his size."

Darwell came in then. She gave a brief curtsy to the ladies, and went through the sitting room and into the bedchamber without speaking. Beatrice knew why Darwell was upset, but she had her hands full with Ceci right now. Poor Darwell would have to wait.

"So how did this 'almost argument' lead to a cross-country horse race?" Beatrice shook her head. "With Lord Destry riding sidesaddle?"

"We agreed that we are most equal on a horse. His height and my looks have nothing to do with our ability to ride."

"So you are going to race to prove that you are in fact not equal even when it comes to riding?"

"Oh, Beatrice, you are such a spoilsport. We are going to race because it is a way for me to demonstrate something very important without saying it again and again."

"And that is?" Beatrice prompted, completely at a loss.

"I am going to *let* Lord Destry win," Cecilia announced. "And this is why." She recounted the story of his grandfather's plot exactly as she had heard it earlier in the day from Lord Jess.

When Cecilia finished, her sister's reaction was all she could have wished. "That is one of the cruelest stories I have ever heard, and our grandfather was not the kindly sort himself."

"But the Duke of Bendas was ten times worse. To actually wish your grandson dead? That was hideous." Cecilia shook her head. "But the good part of the story is that Destry became a truly skilled horseman. It's one place where he knows he excels and does not have to continually prove himself."

"That's true enough. Lord Jess says he has won a small fortune wagering with people who do not know of his skill."

Distracted, Cecilia held up a finger. "You will wager on me, Beatrice. It is your duty as a sister."

"Yes, of course." They were going to invite everyone to wager? That was just one more element added to the most nonsensical plan Beatrice had ever heard. "But, Ceci, riding is one thing he does take pride in. He does not need to win the race to improve the way he sees himself."

"Of course not, but I need to prove to him that his height and wealth are not important and that his ability to ride is. And I will be so gracious in defeat that it will be all the proof he needs."

Beatrice tried without success to recall another time when her sister had been so inclined to stage-manage an event. Which was a good thing as this event made so little sense. "Cecilia, playing a game like that is not a good way to start a courtship."

"Who has said anything about a courtship?" She looked surprised.

"He has. At least a dozen times to whoever will listen." That was an exaggeration but it was obvious to anyone with eyes.

"This is no more than a flirtation and it is very important for me to leave here on good terms with anyone that I will meet in London."

"So his height and his wealth are not important to you but his title is. And his influence and whoever he can introduce you to."

"You make me sound mercenary." Ceci looked genuinely offended.

"Not so much mercenary as like every other girl in society who is trying to make a match."

"Beatrice, take that back." Annoyance pushed aside hurt feelings. "I am trying *not* to ruin our chances at having a successful Season and finding a match that suits us perfectly. Someone like Lord Destry but without a title."

That's revealing, Beatrice thought. Cecilia just as much as admitted she would want Destry if it were not for his title. The horse race made a tad more sense now. "For one thing, Ceci, I do not need to find a match." Beatrice walked around the room. *I am doing this for you.* "And for another, what do you think the chances are that we will be in the same social circle as the daughters of dukes or a marquis? It's not as though we will be presented at court or be given vouchers to Almack's."

"I think there is a very good chance we will be at

some of the same outings as Destry and Lord Cren-shaw and Katherine Wilson. They are friends of ours now and surely we will be included."

Their conversation had moved a long way away from the horse race. Beatrice wanted to change the subject— talking about their Season would only upset her sister. It was an event that was still months away and very much an unknown.

"When we are in London and the invitations arrive we will know the truth of the matter, Ceci, but for now I think we should talk to Darwell and see what has upset her."

"Darwell is upset? Oh, I hadn't noticed. But yes, we must see what's wrong," Cecilia agreed. She closed the space between them. "Beatrice, I am sorry you think the race is a stupid idea, but I am sure it will be just the thing Destry and I need to be comfortable with each other."

So that was what Cecilia thought this was about. Feeling comfortable with Destry. Ending the tension that had her feeling so uncomfortable when she was with him. All right, she could meet her sister halfway on this. "So you think racing with him will make you two friends so that when you meet in London all will be fine between you?"

"Exactly," Cecilia said with a smile that showed she and her sister shared a perfect understanding.

Yes, it was an incredibly stupid plan, Beatrice thought, but kept it to herself. She wondered what had prompted Destry to agree and then decided his reasons were probably just as half-witted.

Chapter Twenty-seven

"I WILL HAVE time to practice, Jess. The race is not for two days."

"You are insane, Des. I used to think you were adventurous but you have crossed the line."

They were in the stable walking around Jupiter, who was obviously uncomfortable with the strange saddle strapped to his back.

"What I am is a pragmatist." He gave Jupiter a piece of apple and stroked his mane, which went a long way toward making the horse more agreeable. "Listen. Once Cecilia wins this race, she will realize that she is indeed more than her lovely face. That she is my equal no matter what my title is. She will see that I want to make her my wife for all the right reasons."

"You're saddling yourself, pun intended," Jess added, "with unrealistic expectations. It is *one* race. A race in which you will look like a fool."

"Excellent! She will see that I am a man before I am

a marquis and Cecilia Brent will look like a duchess. Definitely worth looking a fool." Destry moved the mounting block closer and made his way to the different saddle.

"You might be able to adjust to this, but what about Jupiter?"

"Right, I'm more concerned about him. I talked to the head groom and he says that Jupiter will have to grow accustomed to the different distribution of weight. Since I do not weigh as much as most gentlemen it is not the problem it might be for someone like you."

Jess considered. It would never be a problem for him, since there was no way in hell he would ever ride sidesaddle. He watched as Des dismounted, then mounted again and just sat for a few minutes. The horse shook his head once but settled soon enough.

In the end Destry managed to stay on the horse for the whole session, which consisted of riding at a slow walk around the ring and then out to the path, up to the house and back. Not even a canter. Who knew that Destry had patience tucked away in that compact body?

"Excellent!" Des joined Jess at the horse ring. "The groom tells me he will have one of his best and smallest grooms take Jupiter out this evening while we are at dinner. Then I will spend a few hours with him tomorrow morning and possibly afternoon as well."

"It sounds Machiavellian to me, Des, but then why should that surprise me? You're heir to the Bendas dukedom after all."

"Yes, I do believe my grandfather would approve."

Destry looked up to the sky and appeared to be listening for the dead man's endorsement.

The mention of his grandfather reminded Jess of the story he'd told Cecilia. Jess had no idea whether that had anything to do with the resolution of differences between them, even if building some sympathy had been his intention. Now he found himself wishing he had kept his mouth shut. The last thing Destry wanted from Cecilia Brent was sympathy.

"DARWELL, PLEASE DO not upset yourself," Cecilia pleaded, handing the maid a handkerchief. Now that they all knew the truth about Crenshaw, Darwell was willing to openly voice her concerns for Miss Wilson. She had not succumbed to tears but Beatrice could see how distressed she was as she twisted the piece of cotton between her fingers.

"Something should be done to protect Miss Wilson," Darwell went on. "In the normal course of events I would speak to her maid, but I know her and she will do nothing to jeopardize her position. She would as soon turn her back as listen."

"You are not to lose sleep over this, Darwell," Cecilia insisted. "Beatrice and I will devise a plan. You were right to tell us of your concerns."

Beatrice had no ideas and doubted that Cecilia did, either, but she nodded bracingly. "I already have a plan, but it is growing time to dress for dinner, is it not?"

"Oh dear," Darwell said, pressing her hands to her cheeks. "Tonight's theme is quite unique and I want to be sure you two are dressed to perfection."

When Darwell left for the dressing room to shake out their gowns, Cecilia whispered, "What happened to the maid who was so superior? Who told us what to do instead of the other way around?"

Beatrice had wondered the same. "I think it's a testament to how much Crenshaw's abuse hurt her as well. Even now, years later, it still upsets her." Beatrice thought about what she had seen this afternoon but decided to respect Darwell's privacy and not mention it to her sister. Besides, if she did tell Ceci what she had seen, then she would have to explain how she came to be in the gentlemen's wing, and it was all much too complicated to go into right now. It was so much easier to worry about Darwell's concerns than her own headaches. "Poor Darwell. I must think of a solution." Beatrice sat on the sofa, pressing her lips together, eyes narrowed in concentration.

"We have to dress. At least pretend you are interested in what you're wearing."

"A dress is not important when I have so much on my mind," Beatrice said.

"Bitsy, Darwell needs the distraction."

"Yes, I know, but I think it would help as much if I could think of a way to convince her that Miss Wilson is not in any immediate danger." Beatrice thought for a moment and realized that she herself was not quite convinced. "Should I go to the countess?"

"And tell her what, sister?" Cecilia asked with her usual practicality. "Lord Jessup asked you to keep his story a secret, and he is already viewed with suspicion by our godmother. Darwell cannot speak to the maid. It's up to Lord Jess to solve the problem."

"That's easy to say, but what can he do? He is, after all, the one whom everyone blames for the incident."

"Ladies," Darwell called from the dressing room. "Come and look at these gowns and let me help you dress."

"We are coming, Darwell," Cecilia said agreeably with an insistent look at her sister.

"I will pretend," Beatrice said with a resigned sigh. Dressing did prove a distraction after all.

"These gowns are better suited to a ball than to a country party dinner, Darwell." Cecilia fingered the exquisite silk, a blue that Beatrice knew was one of her favorite colors, festooned with faux flowers the size of guineas in shades of blue fading to white. The floral trim ran around the neckline, down the sides, and along the edge of the flounces.

"I told you, tonight is special," Darwell reminded her, "and is this not the most special of the gowns you have with you?"

"Yes, it is." Cecilia began to smile. "What is Beatrice going to wear?"

Darwell held up another gown. It was a pale apricot color with gold and peach bead trim around the neck. The beading also circled the dress at the waist and was echoed between the knee and ankle, where Cecilia's dress had ruffles.

"It's perfect for you, Beatrice."

"Yes, but I do wish I could wear ruffles."

Darwell made a sound of frustration. "I've told you before that they do not suit someone of your size. It will have to be one of life's disappointments, miss."

Beatrice smiled and pressed her lips together to keep from laughing. A gown without ruffles was hardly one of life's disappointments. No, not when she was attracted to the wrong man in everyone's eyes but her own.

When they were ready to join the party, Cecilia looked at herself in the glass "one more time" and followed her sister and Darwell, who shepherded them downstairs to the large banquet hall, a space that could seat at least one hundred, maybe more.

The first thing Beatrice noticed was that Jess was at the end of the room that was farthest from the door, talking to Lord Belmont, Nora Kendrick, and Finch.

The four were standing in front of a small orchestra whose members were quietly tuning their instruments.

The conversation was animated and as Beatrice watched, trying to decipher some sense of what they were discussing, Jess looked up and caught her eye.

He bowed to her, but did not immediately end his conversation with the couple to come greet her. Not that she expected him to. Or even wanted him to. Quite the opposite, in fact. They were friends, not lovers, and friends did not abandon all to rush to the other's side. In fact she would do her best to keep this much distance between them for the entire evening, if only because being close to him made her weak in the knees.

With a condescending nod, she raised her eyes from his and gasped. The orchestra was placed under a spectacular painting of Venice—or was it a mural?—that filled the wall from the wainscoting to within a foot of the ceiling.

How could she have missed that when she walked in? It was the only painting in the room. The other walls were windowed and the wall behind her was mostly filled with doors, three sets, with marble statues in between.

"Look at that painting, Ceci. I've never seen a Canaletto done on such a grand scale."

Before Cecilia could comment, the countess came over to them. They curtsied to her.

"Tonight the grand salon is as much dining room as ballroom," she announced, and for the first time Beatrice noticed that dinner tables were arranged around the floor of the ballroom.

"Yes, my lady, it is incredible," Beatrice said.

"The flowers are spectacular," Cecilia added with unfeigned enthusiasm. "One cannot tell the real blooms from the silk."

"I know flowers are a favorite decoration of yours, Cecilia. And Beatrice, I knew you would not mind spending the evening near that magnificent painting."

"How thoughtful of you, my lady, thank you." Beatrice tore her eyes from the masterpiece to survey the rest of the room one more time, avoiding the group near the orchestra. "Am I correct in guessing that there will be other guests with us this evening?"

"Yes, fifty in all. Neighbors, for the most part. I like to invite friends to dinner at least once during a house party so that we do not succumb to boredom."

Beatrice thought about the kiss she had shared with Jess. Boredom was not one of her worries.

Even as the countess explained the guest list, people began to filter into the room.

"Come, let me introduce you to some of my friends," the countess said, taking Cecilia's hand.

The countess led them to a couple whose two sons were attending with them. She introduced them before breaking away to greet another group of newly arrived guests.

Beatrice could see that the two young men were struck speechless by Cecilia's beauty. While she waited for them to recover, she looked about and watched the arriving guests mingle, familiar faces mixed in with the new.

Lord Destry was easy to spot as he was wearing his signature red cravat, though everything else about his attire was perfection. He came up to the group and Beatrice took it upon herself to introduce him, thanking God that all of these guests had the same last name.

The gentleman, his wife, and their sons, all four, avoided looking at Lord Destry at first, as though his height made them uncomfortable, but once his title was revealed they overcame their hesitation and tried for convivial. They were not particularly successful.

Beatrice could see Cecilia's smile become forced. For his part, Destry remained charming. Finally, during a lull in the conversation, Cecilia took Destry's arm and suggested that they examine the flowers more closely.

With a grin of satisfaction, Destry bowed to the family and walked off with the prize of the evening. And incidentally left Beatrice alone without any means of escape.

No one said anything for too long and Beatrice realized that what they wanted to talk about most was her sister and Lord Destry. Beatrice pretended that Mrs. Kendrick was signaling to her and excused herself. She was not out of hearing when the younger son asked, "What does the beauty see in that midge?"

It took real effort not to turn back and heap equal insults on them, but indeed Mrs. Kendrick was signaling to her now and Beatrice wended her way through the small crowd to her side.

Around Finch's neck Mrs. Kendrick had tied a red ribbon, which perfectly matched her garnet-colored gown and jewels. "Good evening, Beatrice. What an amazing surprise this is, is it not?"

"Yes, indeed."

"Belmont insists he is the worst dancer in the house. But I imagine that if he has some wine with his dinner I can entice him to the dance floor."

"I have no doubt of it." Beatrice really liked this woman. She was so full of life and when she wanted something she did not keep it a secret. Did you have to wait to be a widow of means to act like that?

"Have you seen all our fellow houseguests?" Mrs. Kendrick asked.

"All but Lord Crenshaw and Katherine."

"They are over by that statue. Some Greek god, I assume. The statue reminds me of Lord Jess. With a playful look but detached from the company."

Beatrice wanted nothing more than to quiz Mrs. Kendrick about Jess but held her tongue, trying for an air of sophistication she was far from feeling.

"Surely Mr. Garrett and Lady Olivia will be joining us."

"They were invited, and Mr. Garrett tells me that Lady Olivia has agreed to join us and allow the chef the rule of the kitchen this evening." Mrs. Kendrick nodded toward the great doors. "Here they are now."

The countess was welcoming Mr. Garrett while Lady Olivia looked around in awe.

"It's a relief that even Lady Olivia is impressed by

this display," Mrs. Kendrick said. "She is a duke's daughter and grew up in a castle, after all."

Two older ladies approached them. Not bothering with introductions they launched into conversation, and began talking about how close they were to the lady of the house.

"The countess is unequaled as a hostess," one said, her double chin shaking as she spoke. "Always trying something new."

"You are so right, my dear," the other said as the feather on her head kept time with her nod. They then proceeded to recount several other dinner parties they had attended and finished with an uncertain, "But I have never seen anything quite like the way she has placed tables and chairs right in the ballroom."

The lady with the feather turned to Beatrice. "You are preparing for a London Season?"

"Yes, I am."

"Then I hope you never have to attend the same soi-rées as that beauty who is with the gentleman with the red cravat."

Before Beatrice could explain that she and the beauty were sisters, the other nodded. "This will be excellent practice for a ball. Never doubt for a minute that the countess has a reason for everything she does. Tonight I would imagine she wants to give you both a taste of the ballroom."

"How very, very generous of her," Beatrice said, while Mrs. Kendrick pressed her lips together. No res-cue from that quarter.

"Generous, yes." The double-chinned lady tapped Beatrice's fingers with her fan. "But Jasmine always has self-interest lurking somewhere."

Her friend was peering at the door when her expression changed. "Who is the gentleman that just this minute came into the room?"

Without another word, the two hurried away, making straight for the door and an introduction.

Beatrice followed their progress and turned back to Mrs. Kendrick, stunned. "It's Papa."

Chapter Twenty-eight

"INDEED, IT IS Mr. Brent," Mrs. Kendrick said as even Finch gave a quiet bark of agreement. The three of them watched the warmth with which the countess and Beatrice's father greeted each other.

"I think I know what self-interest the countess has at play tonight," Mrs. Kendrick said. "She wants to dance with your father."

"Dance with him? But how extravagant."

"One of the advantages of being a wealthy widow is that you can spend your money any way you choose."

Beatrice nodded, still astounded that the countess might go to such lengths to spend time with her father.

"Bear in mind that once her son and his new wife return from their wedding trip, the countess will no longer be the lady of the house. This is her last opportunity to entertain in the style she has perfected over the years."

Lord Belmont and Jess joined them and any other

thoughts of Beatrice's papa and the countess evaporated.

Jess looked wonderful. His coat was a green superfine wool that reminded her of the colors the old masters used; its deep, deep green hinted at mystery. His eyes were not at all mysterious but he cringed, actually cringed, when his gaze fell on her.

"Miss Brent!" The earl's surprise was genuine. "I wondered to whom Nora was talking."

"Have you noticed that Mr. Brent has just arrived?" Nora brought them into the conversation with practiced skill. Though her father's arrival was something Beatrice herself might have avoided mentioning since he and Jess were not on the best of terms.

"Yes, I saw him in the hall when he first arrived." Belmont barely drew a breath before continuing. "Nora, come look at this wall with me. I think it has a secret door." Belmont drew her away, leaving Beatrice and Jess together.

She watched them walk away as though all the air in the room went with them. She wondered if Jess felt the same way.

JESS COULD TELL Beatrice had seen him hesitate. What did it say about his gamer's face that he had not been able to hide that reaction, which she would surely misinterpret? He had hoped to avoid her but only because being this close was so damn distracting.

Now he could see that she felt abandoned. The weather had been lovely, but she was unable to speak even that conventional courtesy. Despite her discomfort she looked especially lovely tonight, rather like a sprite who had deigned to join the mortals for the evening. The jeweled comb in her hair caught the light from the massive chandeliers and sparkled the way her eyes usually did. He knew just the way to bring that sparkle back.

"We must speak of something, Miss Brent. I am not going to leave you alone with no one to talk to. That would make me even less of a gentleman than I already am."

She opened her mouth, then closed it again.

"Tell me what you are thinking, Beatrice. It is much more entertaining than trying to think of something innocuous to say."

"Why would you think I am hiding the truth, my lord?"

Because your voice is wooden and stiff and that is not at all like you. "Because you have very speaking eyes and at the moment they are not at all taken with my presence."

"Very well," she said firmly, raising her chin. "I was not looking forward to seeing you again after our last encounter."

"Are you referring to our kiss?" He leaned close and whispered the obvious.

"Yes."

"So you are deliberately avoiding me this evening?"

"Only as much as you are trying to ignore me," she tossed back at him, nervous and unsure of how he felt now.

"Yes, I am avoiding you."

That brought her attention back to him with a jerk. When she looked puzzled he reminded her, "Honesty, please."

"All right. I assume you are avoiding me because of my inexperience. My first kisses were with you, and I was a complete failure at it."

Perhaps that was a little more honesty than he needed at the moment. The reminder of that jolt of wanting made him want her all over again. "That is not the reason at all, Beatrice. Not at all."

"Then why?" She stepped closer. The cluster of people behind him prevented him from taking a step back. He did not need to be any closer to her. At least now they were surrounded by chaperones.

"The truth, Jess," Beatrice said, turning the tables on him.

"Think about it, little Venus. If you were not a failure at kissing, tell me, why else would I avoid you?"

When the light did not dawn, he raised her hand and kissed it. She was wearing gloves, of course, but he could feel the shiver run from her fingers up her arm. "That's why." He put his other hand on top of hers so that it was caught between his. "Because your touch does the same thing to me."

She looked at their hands and then into his eyes. He saw confusion in hers. "But we hardly know each other. We have nothing in common."

"Oh, my dearest Venus, what's between us has nothing to do with anything but the desire to hold and be held. We could speak different languages and the wanting would still be there."

"We may not speak different languages but we do live in different worlds."

He could hear the heartache in her tone and would do anything to make her smile, to have her eyes light with curiosity. "And you wish we could meet in the middle, is that it?" Before she could answer an incensed voice came between them.

"I told you not to spend time in this man's company, Beatrice. And what is the first thing I see? That you are practically in his arms. Must you always do the exact opposite of what I ask?"

Abel Brent startled them apart. His words were like a cold-water bath dumped on both of them.

"Good evening, Papa. How wonderful to see you here." Beatrice kissed him on both cheeks, choosing to ignore his reprimand. "Lord Jess, I hope to have the chance to dance with you this evening. If you will excuse us I will help my father find Cecilia."

Nicely handled, Jess thought. He bowed in response to her curtsy, now feeling committed to ask her to dance at least once. Her father gave him a scathing look, as if challenging him to even try to dance with her. He'd wager a guinea that the countess would be able to calm him down and acted on that certainty. It was only one dance, after all.

"It will be my pleasure to dance with you, Miss Brent." Was playing along with her despite her father's annoyance one way for them to "meet in the middle"?

Jess walked away, feeling her father's glare like a dagger in his back. It was the first time in a very long while that he had been in a situation like this. But he was significantly older, if not wiser, now. He found himself looking forward to the dance and, if necessary, the confrontation with her father.

BEATRICE WATCHED JESS walk away and wished the dancing would begin. She hated the idea of arguing with her father among the company. She took his arm and told him as much.

"We will discuss it later," he said firmly. "But you are not to dance with Lord Jessup," her father added, ignoring his own words to "discuss it later." "He has proven over and over that he is not the gentleman he was born to be."

Beatrice pressed her lips together. If she responded to that accusation the discussion would begin here and now and would become an argument. She searched for something else to say.

"Did Roger come with you?"

"No, he stayed in London to discuss a design with one of his mentors," her father said, and then went back to the subject she wished they would drop. "I trust by now you have heard of his involvement in Lord Crenshaw's divorce, as well as his legion of mistresses and the fortunes he has won and lost. His own family does not receive him."

His sister does, Beatrice wanted to say, just one breath away from arguing with him. *Please, someone interrupt us.*

As if in answer to her prayer, the orchestra played a chord calling everyone's attention to the countess, who stood on the musicians' platform.

"Good evening, everyone, and welcome to Havenhall and our first ever dinner and ball." She went on to explain the dinner service, each course to be followed by a period of dancing, and invited her guests to sit down to enjoy the first course and wines.

Beatrice and Cecilia were seated at one of the tables for eight with their father and the countess. The other seats remained empty long enough for her father to berate Beatrice yet again for accepting Lord Jessup's invitation to dance.

"Abel, dancing with Lord Jess is perfectly acceptable," the countess said.

"But you don't want them together any more than I do."

"Yes, but Jess has been the model of propriety this past ten days and we will be nearby."

Neither one of them gave Beatrice any credit for behaving well. Did they think that she would melt into his arms without a thought? Actually, she admitted to herself, that's exactly what had happened; being in his arms made thinking difficult and clear thinking nigh impossible.

Her father considered the countess's words. Before he could comment further, Michael Garrett and his wife took two seats at the table, along with Marquis Destry and an older gentleman whom the countess introduced as Mr. Hogarth, the art curator and librarian of Havenhall. In answer to Beatrice's excited question, the man acknowledged that, yes, he was related to the artist of the same name, but only distantly.

The conversation was general at first, leading Lady Olivia to comment, "I think tables for eight, be they round or square, are the best possible number for a dinner party. It allows for interesting group conversation and one-on-one as well, with no one left feeling neglected."

They continued on in a general manner but soon the conversation became more directed, and Beatrice was so engrossed in her discussion of art with Mr. Hogarth that she could not have said what she ate, although she was quite sure she would have noticed if it had been either salmon or haricots verts.

She did notice that her father and Lord Destry were deep in conversation, but both Cecilia and the countess were listening to them, so it could not have been a discussion of anything too personal, like whether Lord Destry could pay his addresses to her sister.

As Beatrice and Mr. Hogarth finished speaking about the Canaletto mural at the end of the banquet hall, the orchestra struck a chord and the dance master invited, "Ladies and gentlemen, please take the floor for a set of reels."

To her surprise, and a little dismay, her father did not ask the countess to dance, but came directly to her. With a mental groan she accepted his hand. Cecilia and Lord Destry were a couple, as were Michael Garrett and the countess. Lady Olivia explained that she did not enjoy dancing and would be delighted to talk with Mr. Hogarth about any books on cookery with which he might be familiar. Apparently it was a subject he knew well, as they immediately fell into a discussion of the writings of the celebrated chef Antoine Carême.

I want to be with them, Beatrice wailed to herself as she took the floor with her father and steeled herself for a lecture between steps. As luck would have it, each time he began to speak they would change partners. Eventually he realized that he had to pay attention to the dance, and even once asked her to remind him of the next step.

Beatrice realized that dancing was not something

Papa had ever had an interest in, and wondered where and how he had learned so quickly. He performed very well, she thought, and she hoped that the countess appreciated his efforts.

As they progressed through the dance she saw that Lord Crenshaw was dancing with Miss Wilson. The two were spending a significant amount of time together, which was worrisome. What could she do to warn the girl without betraying Lord Jess's confidence?

The others were also paired as one would expect. Destry made Cecilia laugh each time they came together, and Lord Jess had already made a conquest of one of the young lady neighbors whose name Beatrice could not recall.

As they left the floor, Papa held her back a moment. "Watch yourself, young lady."

"Yes, Papa," she answered with as demure a curtsy as she could manage, and then turned to find Lord Destry behind her, asking for the next dance.

"It's going to be a waltz and I much prefer to dance with someone my own size or I will look ridiculous."

"Which is not a very gracious way of explaining why you wish me for a partner, but since I feel the same about dancing in the arms of a tall man like Lord Jess I will make no complaint."

Destry made one of his elaborate bows to her as the music started and the two of them set themselves in position for the dance, far enough apart to be decorous but as close as the dance dictated.

They moved quietly to the music until Beatrice noticed Lord Jess's dancing partner.

"Lord Jess is dancing with Miss Wilson."

Destry looked their way. "And appears to be having a serious conversation with her."

"Where is Lord Crenshaw?" Beatrice asked.

"Dancing with Mrs. Wilson," he answered, his voice sounding just as worried as she felt.

"Do you think Lord Jess is telling her about Lord Crenshaw's," she paused, trying to be discreet, "about his misdeeds?"

"What misdeeds would those be, Miss Brent?" Destry asked with a narrow-eyed interest.

"Um, his evil deeds," she answered with some exasperation. "The way he treated his first wife." She finally decided to be blunt. "Lord Jess told me the story."

"He did?" It took Destry several turns to adjust to the bit of news, and as they danced Beatrice kept her eyes fixed on Jess and Miss Wilson. She looked intense and a little upset, but was keeping a polite smile on her face.

Relieved, Beatrice relaxed too soon, for a moment later Katherine broke away from Jess and left the dance floor, heading from the room.

"What should we do?" Beatrice asked.

"Keep dancing and do not give it any attention. With a waltz very few people will notice since it is such an intimate dance."

They kept on moving but Beatrice was sure that Destry wanted the dance to be over as much as she did. They noticed Lord Crenshaw and Mrs. Wilson leave the floor, too. Crenshaw headed for Jess and Beatrice could not stand the suspense. Fortunately the music ended. At the same moment, Jess turned his back on Crenshaw and headed for the grand doors. Beatrice grabbed Destry's hand and pulled him with her in the same direction.

"We must do something."

"Miss Brent, no! Please stay here."

She let go of his hand but was not about to stay behind.

Chapter Twenty-nine

JESS FOUND KATHERINE Wilson in the passage, some way down from the entrance to the banquet hall, crying quietly but without restraint.

"I am sorry to have caused you to run from me, Miss Wilson. Please." He handed her his handkerchief and prayed that no one would come upon them.

"It's just that I do not want to be the subject of gossip or speculation."

That makes two of us, Jess thought. Crying here was only minimally more private than crying on the dance floor.

"Now I will have to talk to Crenshaw about your story," she complained between hiccoughs, "and he will tell me his version and I will not know whom to believe."

Jess saw an opening for one more caution. "If you do not trust him completely, I would suggest that you think a long time before you allow him more than a passing acquaintance."

"He is going to ask for permission to court me." She sniffed and gave him a miserable smile. "He has spoken with Mama and he is going to see Papa tomorrow."

Before she could continue Crenshaw himself came into the passageway.

"Stop accosting her, right now!"

"I am not accosting her," Jess said wearily. "I am trying to comfort her."

Crenshaw pushed past him and took Katherine's arm. "Stop those waterworks."

His command worked.

"Yes, my lord," Miss Wilson said. With one unladylike sniffle and a deep breath the tears ended.

"Now go back into the dining room and find your mama. Seat yourself for the next course and I will join you shortly."

"I think I should excuse myself and put a cold cloth on my face so I do not look as if I have been crying."

"You may do that, but do not absent yourself for too long."

She nodded and left, eyes downcast.

"You are a pig, Crenshaw, and the sooner she knows it the better. You cannot imagine I would let her marry you without at least trying to warn her family."

Crenshaw grabbed Jess by the cravat and pushed him against the wall. "Listen to me, Pennistan. I hold the upper hand here. You are a disgrace to your name and your family. My name is gold and yours is dross. No one will listen to you."

"Take your hands off me."

Crenshaw ignored him. With the skill he'd learned in

the boxing ring from his brothers, Jess used his hands to force Crenshaw's grip from his cravat and then punched him with a thoroughness that sent the big man staggering back.

"Crenshaw, the only thing that is saving you from a thrashing now is the number of people who would be shocked by violence at such a gathering."

Crenshaw stood up, swayed, but raised his arms, ready to continue. Jess heard the sound of running footsteps and swore. This was not an exchange he wanted anyone else to witness.

Apparently Crenshaw felt the same way. He seemed to think better of continuing the fight.

"This is far from over, Pennistan." The baron made an attempt to straighten his cravat and coat as he walked away from the banquet room. Jess did not care where he was headed as long as it was out of his sight.

Destry emerged from the banquet room, moving quickly. "What happened? Where is Crenshaw?"

"Crenshaw is down the hall wiping his bloody nose. He pushed me one more time and once too far."

"I wish I'd been here. I would have liked to take a swing at him myself."

"Thank you, Des." Jess appreciated the support, even if he was relieved that there had been no witnesses but the footman.

"Des, would you go tell Mrs. Wilson that Lord Crenshaw and her daughter will return shortly, or some other lie? I should kill the bastard and be done with him. It's what he deserves, but I am going to bed. The last thing I need now is a dance with Beatrice Brent."

Destry cleared his throat and nodded toward a shadowed part of the corridor.

"Beatrice?" Jess closed his eyes and hoped she had not heard him.

She marched toward the two of them, her hands fisted at her sides, her expression angry and hurt at the same time. Damn it, she had heard every word.

"I will take your message to Mrs. Wilson." Destry hurried away as though he could not move fast enough. Smart man.

"I heard what you said, that you cannot bear the thought of waltzing with me. Are you determined to make every woman you see tonight cry?"

Jess had no answer for her. He'd used up all his words and most of his civility. He could blame what he did on the anger still roiling through him, or the opposite, his need for something sweet and good, but neither was an excuse.

Jess pushed on a door across the passage from the banquet hall and pulled her through it with him.

Punching the door closed with his foot, he pressed her against it. "You want to know why I dread the thought of dancing with you?"

Now she had no answer for him. Her eyes were big with surprise, and was that a little fear he saw? Good, he thought. Now she was beginning to understand.

Pushing his fingers through the coil of her hair, he felt the luxury of it spill over his hands, the silken length of it one more caress that he took with greedy pleasure.

She closed her eyes. Standing this close he could see the lashes dark against her cheeks. He bent to kiss them and then her mouth, her lips slightly parted and, God help him, welcoming.

No wager he'd ever won had made him feel this powerful. No race he'd ever won had made him feel so elated. No woman he'd ever won had made him feel this complete. All that with no more than a kiss.

Her arms around his neck captured him, torturing him with an urgency that was mutual. Reaching up to take her hands he entwined his fingers with hers and then moved them behind her back so he could kiss her neck, trail his mouth down to the swell of her breasts.

Her heart was pounding, her breath came in short gasps of arousal. He felt his own arousal pressing against the softness of her and knew he was a moment away from taking her.

No, it was more than that. He was a breath away from making love to her and never letting her go, of waltzing with her for the rest of his life, the rest of her life.

The rest of her life? She deserved better. That his brain was still working was a miracle, and he did not ignore the gift. He lifted his head, putting some very small distance between them. Beatrice still had her eyes closed. She waited, her flushed cheeks and breathlessness making him feel like a cad for leaving her in such a state. But he needed to—for her own sake.

"We stop here, Beatrice."

When she opened her eyes, he saw confusion. "What?"

He wanted to explain that this was all they could share. That a marriage between someone with his reputation and someone with her background would guarantee the ton's rejection. She would say she didn't care, but it would never work. He'd thought all week about ways to make her avoid him. Make her hate him. He knew how, and now was the time.

It might be the hardest thing he would ever have to do.

"You are too easy, Beatrice. I could have had you any time these last few days. But sex with a girl like you is much too complicated. A kiss in the dark is the only proof I needed. You would have let me take whatever I wanted, wouldn't you? I'm not falling into that trap, my dear. I have been at this game for far too long."

As his words sank in, her face took on that mottled cast that meant anger. Good. Good, that was what he wanted, even if it made him feel sick.

She pushed him away, straightened her clothes, and felt for her hair, now a mess better suited to the bedroom than the ballroom. Then she slapped him with a strength he had not anticipated.

It barely stung his cheek but it crushed his heart.

With some presence of mind, she avoided the company by crossing the twilit room to a communicating door and disappearing into the next room.

Jess watched her. Beatrice did not look back. She was long gone before he'd regained his sanity and walked back to the ball.

BEATRICE REACHED HER bedchamber just in time. She could not hold the tears back any longer and crashed through the sitting room door, slamming it behind her. Bent double with sobs, she staggered into the bedchamber, slamming that door as well. She held

on to one of the bedposts, trying desperately to control
herself.

"Miss Beatrice!"

*For the love of God, Darwell was here. Why could she
not be off with Callan?* Beatrice knew she could barely
form a coherent sentence and Darwell would want to
know why she was upset.

"Miss, let me undo your dress and stays or you will
faint."

Beatrice began to move to the dressing room but Darwell stopped her. "Stay here, miss, and turn around."

She obeyed. All she wanted to do was climb into bed
and pull the covers over her head. It was too much to
hope she would be asleep before Cecilia came to bed.

"Can you tell me what happened?"

Beatrice shook her head, but tried. "Lord Jess and I
had an argument." Beatrice stopped. She didn't have
the energy to tell the whole story. "Really, Darwell, it
was all my fault. Jess made that perfectly clear. Now I
just want to go to bed."

Darwell made soothing sounds, asking no more
questions. She did insist on brushing the snarls out of
Beatrice's hair, putting it into a quick braid, before letting Beatrice slide under the covers. Beatrice heard
doors opening and closing and a few minutes later
Darwell brought a cool cloth for her eyes.

"Go to sleep, Miss Beatrice. It will all be better by
the light of day."

If only that were true, Beatrice thought. The cool
cloth did help calm her, but she still wished she could
curl into the tiniest ball and disappear. It would be so
much better than ever having to see Jess Pennistan
again.

* * *

"I KNOW YOU weren't asleep when I came up." Cecilia watched her sister with an intensity she hoped would make Beatrice tell the truth. "Darwell told me that you were upset, that Lord Crenshaw had something to do with it, and I should leave you alone until this morning. So I did. Bitsy, it was very hard. Now tell me what happened."

Beatrice sighed and Cecilia knew her firmness had worked. "It was not Lord Crenshaw. But he upset Jess and then Jess and I had a huge, ugly argument."

Beatrice's eyes filled and she stopped speaking, staring at the ceiling until she was able to will the tears not to fall. Cecilia waited. She could feel her twin's pain and her own happiness dimmed a little.

"So," Beatrice went on, "I had to leave the party because my skin was all red and blotchy. You know how it is when I'm angry."

Cecilia nodded. Darwell said Beatrice had been crying, too. There was no doubt that she really had been upset, very upset.

"I'm not sure I feel that much better this morning, but my complexion is back to normal and we have so much to look forward to."

"That's all you're going to say? What did you argue about?"

"Lord Jess was in a foul mood. He'd argued with Crenshaw. They were both so angry at each other. Then Lord Jess said that the last thing he wanted was to dance with me."

"Oh, Bitsy. How awful for you." Cecilia rubbed her sister's back, hoping her sympathy was some comfort.

"That was not the worst." Beatrice looked away, her lips pressed together, and Cecilia was certain she was going to be given only an edited version of the true story.

"Oh, it really does not matter what he said. I understand why Lord Jess was flirting with me and it is not because he found me particularly appealing."

Beatrice pressed her lips together as if the next words were hard to say.

"Lord Jess made it clear that I was a convenient distraction and nothing more."

Tears puddled in her eyes and Beatrice brushed them away with an impatient hand.

"It's stupid for me to cry because I only wanted to practice flirting, not fall in love. Which I haven't," she added urgently. "But I fear it's what Lord Jess thinks."

It was then that Cecilia noted that her sister was calling him Lord Jess again. He had been Jess for the last few days. "Then perhaps Papa was right to warn us away from him." She spoke cautiously, not sure of her sister's true feelings.

"But you know why Papa did that and what a lie that whole story is." Beatrice paused, obviously thinking. "I liked him until last night." She bit her lip and stopped the confidence. "I'm tired of talking about this. Let's dress and find the curator we met last night. Maybe he can tell us about any treasures we have not found ourselves."

"All right," Cecilia agreed, though it sounded like a rather boring way to spend the morning. "Lord Destry will be practicing riding sidesaddle most of the day so I decided not to ride myself. I think if I was in the field it might make him too nervous."

Beatrice smiled, just a little. "Admit it, Ceci, you are the one who would be nervous watching him."

"If I acted nervous in front of him, he would think I do not believe he can do it." She considered her next words. "Only to you would I admit that while I know he can learn to handle Jupiter with a sidesaddle I am still concerned for his safety."

"I know what you mean," Beatrice said. "It's just like the way I worry about you when I think you are taking too many risks on horseback, or riding too fast for safety. I know you are the best rider I have ever met, but I still worry."

Cecilia hoped that Beatrice did not feel as sick as she did at the thought of Destry suffering an injury.

"Ceci, I think that's what love does to us."

"Do not use that word, Beatrice. I am not in love with Destry. I am not."

"But why will you not allow yourself to even entertain the idea? There isn't anything truly keeping you apart."

"My birth. His title. His family would never allow him to marry someone so far outside his social circle."

"Ceci, you do not know that for sure."

"And I do not want to. I am not made for confrontation like you are. Did you know that the old duke, the one who died last year, disinherited his daughter because she would not do what he said? Mrs. Wilson told me about it."

That did give Beatrice pause, but only for a moment. "The old duke was crazed and beyond demanding. And besides, he is dead now. Why would Mrs. Wilson upset you with that story?"

"It was a warning, Beatrice. A warning that the ton

is more demanding than the countess, who is, after all, our godmother."

"So you are going to let one person, a woman neither one of us particularly likes, dictate whom you fall in love with?"

"I am not in love with him!" Cecilia shouted and then put her hands over her ears.

"Try telling that to your heart." Beatrice spoke very quietly and her eyes filled once again.

Chapter Thirty

"THIS IS THE first day that I have not been thoroughly entertained," Beatrice announced to her sister as Darwell helped them undress. "Of course, it could have been my mood. What did you think, Cecilia?"

"Lord Crenshaw's skill at archery was impressive but it was hardly fair to challenge the other gentlemen without advance warning so that they could practice." Cecilia sat at the dressing table and applied some of the face cream that Katherine insisted was the best available. It smelled odd but felt silky soft.

Darwell gathered their dresses and took them into the dressing room.

"And did you notice, Beatrice, that he was not at dinner this evening? The countess said he had a meeting and would be back in the morning. Do you think he went to see Mr. Wilson?"

"Lord Crenshaw is going to offer for her so soon?" So Beatrice was as surprised as she was. "Perhaps he is just asking for permission to court her," Cecilia suggested. "But why would her family agree to that before her Season?"

"Because they have two other daughters to bring out, one in each of the next two years," Beatrice explained as she rolled down her stockings. "Katherine and I were talking about that after dinner. They are all so close in age that her father suggested bringing them out in two groups rather than individually, but Mrs. Wilson said that each must have her own time in London."

"No wonder Mr. Wilson wants to be sure his estates prosper."

"And would be inclined to welcome Crenshaw's courtship, don't you think?"

Darwell came back into the room in time to hear that last and made a sound of disgust. Cecilia thought perhaps this was not something they should discuss around their maid, given her dislike of the man.

"Surely Lord Crenshaw will be back in time for the race," Beatrice ventured. "No one wants to miss that, if only to see the spectacle of the marquis riding side-saddle."

"Lord Jess told me at dinner that—" Cecilia stopped speaking. "I am sorry, Bitsy, I forgot that you made me promise to never say that man's name again."

"I will excuse the lapse but next time I will threaten to make you 'eat soap,' as Mama used to say." She spoke without smiling.

Cecilia's face must have shown her shock, because Beatrice started to laugh.

"Ceci, don't look at me that way. You know how often Mama followed through on that threat."

"Never," Cecilia said, relaxing enough to try one more time. "I wish you would confide in me."

"There is no point." Her sister answered without hesitation, and Cecilia knew it was hopeless to press her further.

"I thought Lord Jess and I did a credible job of being civil to each other."

"Yes, if you consider endless curtsies and bows a sign of civility. Did you even once answer any question he addressed to you?"

"Yes," Beatrice said. "When he asked me if I would like the chicken I told him I would. And another time I accepted the salt to pass to Lord Belmont."

"Charming," Cecilia said, meaning the opposite. "Everyone noticed, you know."

"They did not. I watched and they all had their eyes on the earl and Mrs. Kendrick."

"Not everyone did, Bitsy, believe me. But Nora and the earl were in amazingly good spirits. I swear I saw Mrs. Wilson roll her eyes. As if she had never seen two people falling in love."

Cecilia saw Darwell press her lips together to keep from smiling. The maid gathered up their clothes and took them into the dressing room, leaving them to don their nightgowns.

"Oh, I think it's more than that," Beatrice said. "I think they're sharing a bed."

"Really?" Cecilia's expression of ennui disappeared instantly. "Here in this house?"

"They are not renting a room at the village inn. Yes, here in this house. It is a house party and those sorts of liaisons are common enough." Beatrice held the so- phisticated pose for a few seconds longer and then widened her eyes. "I wonder how they manage it. Does one arrange it beforehand, or just knock on the door?"

"We could ask Darwell." Cecilia was delighted to see her sister's eyes lit with curiosity again.

"No, we cannot ask Darwell. And that's another thing. What about maids and valets? When do they know to disappear and where do they go?"

"Do not ask me." Darwell spoke with disapproval. "I heard you from the other room," she explained.

Darwell took Cecilia's brush from her and finished the last of the strokes that kept her hair so lustrous. "Now change the subject. It is not seemly for two young ladies to discuss such goings-on. You would do better to discuss the plant demonstration that Miss Cecilia will give in two days." She spoke to Cecilia's reflection in the mirror. "You have only one more day to prepare."

"Oh, Darwell," Cecilia moaned. "Why did you remind me? Now I will never be able to fall asleep."

BEATRICE FINISHED BRAIDING her hair and wished that something as innocent as her talk on Rembrandt's drawings would keep her from sleep. All she could do when the lights were out and distractions were gone was think about Jess and the way he'd made her feel.

Worst of all was the niggling fear that he might be right, that she would give in to the next man who tempted her.

No, that wasn't true. She could not imagine lying with anyone but Jess. No other man's touch had ever made her feel wanton and so irresponsible that nothing mattered but being with him in every way possible.

Of course there had not been any other men, but even when she first saw him from the window she had felt a strong attraction. And that had never ever happened to her before.

There were a hundred reasons why being with him would be wrong, not the least of which was that Jess would think her easy and lose any respect that he might still have for her. And she would lose hers for him, she admitted to herself. She sighed.

And tried to redirect her thoughts by counting the number and placement of old master drawings she had seen this past fortnight.

Chapter Thirty-one

"WHAT THE HELL is wrong with you?" Destry asked.

"Concentrate on what you're doing," Jess snapped back. "Or you will land on your ass."

They were riding the racecourse that Destry and Cecilia had laid out earlier.

"Riding sidesaddle requires a little less concentration than it did yesterday, I'm happy to report," Destry announced cheerfully. "Besides, I would have to be without any sensibility at all not to sense your foul mood. Even your horse can sense it and I'm at least as smart as he is."

"Nothing's wrong."

"It has nothing to do with drinking to excess and going to bed the other night drunk as two lords, does it?" Destry asked.

Jess grunted back. His headache was fading. No point in pretending that was an excuse.

"I've decided your ill humor is about one of two

things. Perhaps both. You were not able to win the land from Crenshaw and want another try, or you're upset about a woman."

Jess grumbled. It wasn't the land.

"It's a shame you didn't try for Nora Kendrick sooner. Too late now," Destry babbled on. "She and Belmont are as close as a saddle and a horse. Of course it may not be true love. There's always that chance."

"I don't want a chance at true love, and you know it is not with Nora Kendrick, damn it." *I just want her,* he thought. *Now, today, maybe tomorrow, but not forever.*

They rode for a while until the quiet was broken by the sound of another person on horseback. Lord Crenshaw passed them with no more greeting than a curt glance. Crenshaw was so absorbed in his own thoughts that he did not even seem to notice Destry's strange position on Jupiter.

"I'm leaving after your race," Jess said as he watched Crenshaw ride out of sight. "I don't know why I waited this long. It's not as though I'll have another chance to win the land from him and that is all these last two weeks were supposed to be about. My punch to his face last night put paid to that."

HIS FRIEND WAS not his usual charming self, Destry realized. Jess never drank to excess and to brawl in public was not at all in his nature.

They rode on to the halfway point of the race, the ford across the river, which was not much more than a healthy stream this time of year, even after the rain of the other night.

Destry held back from crossing to assess the depth and speed of the water and to give Jupiter an equal chance to observe. Jess waited with him, lost in thought. He was unaware of the sound of a conveyance approaching.

This couple did notice his unusual position on the horse, and Destry could have cried with embarrassment. Cecilia's father and the countess were riding in a rather elegantly tricked-out dogcart, with the countess holding the reins. In the back of the cart was a basket and blanket. Clearly the two were planning on a picnic.

The couple stopped to greet them. "Lord Jessup. Good morning to you." Mr. Brent hailed them in an unexpectedly friendly way, and then saw how Destry was mounted. "My lord marquis," he said with a careful, seated bow.

"Good morning, my lady and Mr. Brent." Destry could not decide whether to try to explain his awkward seat or pretend that nothing was odd about a man riding sidesaddle. He opted for something in between.

"Mr. Brent, your daughter Miss Cecilia and I were discussing the disadvantage a lady endures because she must ride sidesaddle and I thought I would try it so that I could better understand her perspective." He hoped that the countess at least would think that romantic.

"I see," Mr. Brent said with a dubious nod. After a moment's consideration he added, "Let's just hope she does not convince you to try wearing a gown so that you can see how awkward that can be."

With a laugh, the countess clucked the horse and they moved off, the horses and cart moving confidently over the ford and to the north, the opposite direction from what Destry and Cecilia had established as their racecourse. That he and Jess would not run into them again was the smallest of reliefs.

"That could have gone better."

"That's stating the obvious, Jess. Do you think he has me pegged as odd now?"

"Either that or a man who can be led by the nose," Jess said with the first smile he had tested all day. "So why didn't you tell him everything?"

"Because Cecilia never even suggested I wear a woman's habit."

"Not that, Des. Why did you not tell him about the race?"

"I was afraid he would forbid it and it's too important for me to take that chance. Do I need to explain that to you again?"

"God, no," Jess said with what sounded like an element of horror in his voice. "Let's head back," he suggested. "The last thing I want is to run into any more of the houseguests."

Destry was certain that he was keen on avoiding one houseguest in particular. What had gone on between Jess and Beatrice Brent the other night? Beatrice was acting more subdued than usual and was painfully polite to Jess when compelled to speak to him. It was some relief that even a man as charming as Jess Pennistan found women a puzzle.

"DO I LOOK all right?" Cecilia twisted and turned in front of the cheval glass that dominated the dressing room.

"You look just right for an afternoon of fun." Beatrice prided herself on finding different ways to reassure her sister. Phrases that did not involve the word "beautiful."

"It really is a lovely habit. But I wonder if it is too severe."

"The style suits you, Miss Cecilia." Darwell spoke with the confident voice of one who understood fashion and style completely. "Excessive ruffles would be all wrong. This style announces that you are a confident, capable woman."

On a horse, Beatrice thought.

"Oh, my. That is precisely what I wish to convey." Cecilia left the dressing room and moved around the bedchamber, testing the swirl of skirts.

"I could kiss you, Darwell. You said exactly the right thing."

"Thank you, Miss Beatrice," Darwell said with a rare grin. "No kiss is necessary. Your appreciation is quite enough."

"You will be so valuable to Cecilia in London."

Darwell sobered suddenly.

"What is it?" Beatrice took a step closer. "Is something wrong?"

"Miss, I am so sorry, but I will not be going with you to London."

"Really? Why not? Are the two of us too much work? I could employ a maid of my own."

"No, Miss Beatrice, you and Miss Cecilia are a pleasure to work for." She turned, surveyed herself in the mirror and shook her head. "Daniel Callan and I are going to be married."

"Married! How wonderful. Oh, we must tell Cecilia." Beatrice hurried from the bedchamber into the sitting room where Cecilia was in front of a mirror fiddling with the curls that framed her face.

"Ceci! Darwell and Lord Jess's valet are going to be married!"

Beatrice turned back to Darwell, who had followed her into the sitting room. Her expression was not what one would expect from a woman who had announced her engagement.

"Oh, that is wonderful news. The best."

"I hope so, Miss Cecilia. It is not impulsive. We have known each other forever. I suppose as we grow older and see an end to our years of service it's right to turn to each other for comfort in our later years."

For the love of God, Beatrice thought, *that sounds far more practical than romantic.* She looked at Cecilia, who nodded.

"Do you love him, Darwell?" Cecilia asked, going straight to the point.

"What is love, Miss Cecilia? I think he is kind and patient. I have seen him care for men who are not worth half of what he is, if one is speaking of honor and honesty. We understand that the ton is made up of the same sort of people who are in all levels of society."

It sounded to Beatrice as though Darwell had learned the same lessons that the marquis had: that the ton were like everyone else, just better dressed. Which only proved the point.

Darwell looked from one to the other. "And my world is much brighter when he is near. I can talk to him about every little thing. He listens to me, and that is a wonderful and rare thing in a man."

"Darwell, that sounds like love to us," Cecilia said as Beatrice nodded agreement.

"We are thinking that we will leave service and move to a city like Birmingham or Manchester where we can open a shop to assist men and women who wish to move up in society."

"Like us!" Cecilia said.

"I mean no offense, miss."

"Of course not. The countess knew we needed advice and you are the best."

"How kind of you, but it does leave you without a maid for the Season."

"Oh dear. You cannot wait a year or so?" Cecilia asked, sounding as if she already knew the answer.

"Miss, we are both approaching fifty years of age. You will understand when you are older. We feel there is no time to waste."

"Then we will see you are established quickly, in Birmingham of course, and Ceci and I will be your first customers."

"Thank you, Miss Beatrice. I was worried you would be more upset."

"Oh, I am," Cecilia assured her, with a self-deprecating smile that made Beatrice laugh.

"Sometimes you are too direct, Ceci." She took Darwell's hand and led her to the door. "Go tell your man, one who actually listens to you, that you have broken the news to us and we are happy for both of you."

"Thank you, miss. Both of you." Darwell left the room, but not before Beatrice saw her eyes fill with tears.

Beatrice turned to her sister. "You are not to start worrying about this. I have complete faith that the countess will find us another excellent lady's maid before we go to London."

"Hmmm" was the best that Cecilia could manage.

"Do you recall Mama saying that a husband who listens is the greatest gift a wife can receive?"

"Oh yes," Cecilia said. "It would come up whenever Papa forgot a dinner invitation or asked Mama something she insisted she had told him a hundred times."

"Do you remember how delighted she was that one time Papa actually took her advice? I don't even know what the idea was but she was happy for days and when I asked her why she was in such good spirits her answer was, 'Because he listened to me, really listened.'"

They stood together looking out the window. "I still miss her. Especially now." Beatrice could not help but think that Mama would tell her the best way to go on, to deal with men like Lord Jess, to help Cecilia enjoy herself.

"I know you miss her. We all do."

"Do you think having children, twins, weakened her so much that she died sooner?" It had taken her a whole year to ask that question, one that had haunted her from the day of Mama's death.

"Oh no, Bitsy, I do not." She squeezed her hand.

"How can you be so sure?" Beatrice wanted it so desperately to be true.

"You know Mama was never strong. Remember the countess told us how often she was ill at school?"

Beatrice nodded but that seemed to prove her point that carrying twins had been too much for her delicate body.

"If you must blame someone for losing her too soon,

you can look at Grandfather for allowing her to marry, Father for wanting children, and Mama for agreeing to have them. Bitsy, do you see, the list would be endless."

"Endless, yes, I suppose it is." The urge to cry had evaporated in the face of that truth. She hugged her sister, careful not to crease her habit or disarrange her hair. "Thank you. You are the best sister in the world."

Ceci could not hide her smile or the blush of pleasure that colored her cheeks.

"You go ahead, Ceci. I am going to wash my face, then I want to take this letter to Papa's room so that he can carry it to Roger for me. I will join you before the race begins."

"You are writing to Roger?" Cecilia seemed to find that odd.

"I asked the countess if he could come for a day or so and she encouraged me to invite him."

"Why?"

Beatrice huffed out a breath. "Because I want Lord Jess to see that I have gentlemen friends."

"You wish to make him jealous? Beatrice, I don't think Jess is—"

"No, Cecilia," Beatrice interrupted. "I do not want to make him jealous. Please leave it at that."

"All right, but only because I do not want to upset you again."

Beatrice reassured her sister and pushed her out of the room with the command to ignore all mirrors. Ceci was an amazing combination of insecurity and wisdom. If only she could find someone who could cure her of the one and appreciate the other.

* * *

WORKING FROM HER memory of painting placement, Beatrice found her way to the gentlemen's bedroom wing, only once stopping to ask for help from a footman. The passage was quiet, as most of the guests were gathering outside for the race and, Beatrice surmised, the servants were at their noon dinner, as was the custom in this house.

Her father's room was small, not a suite like the rooms she shared with her sister. There was a writing desk, and Papa's traveling desk was set on top of it. Beatrice tucked her correspondence into one of the pockets and prayed that Roger would come as soon as he could. She so needed to be with someone who valued her as a person, her mind rather than her body, her words rather than her mouth. That was what was important.

Once she was back in the passage, she decided to follow the route she had happened on the other day, the shortcut to the gardens. As she passed the doorway where she had overheard Callan and Darwell's conversation, she noticed the door was opened.

Jess's room, she thought, and with a look up and down the hall, she stepped inside. It was no bigger than her father's bedchamber, with two windows commanding an even less impressive view.

Standing in the middle of the space, she avoided looking at the bed by closing her eyes. She could almost feel Jess's presence. It was not the scent so much as a kind of energy that was trapped by the walls and ceiling, which made her feel as though she were close to him even in his absence.

Stupid girl, she thought. *Why break your heart over a man who does not want you?* She opened her eyes and saw a wooden box sitting on the writing desk. Walking over, she undid the latch and raised the lid. Instead of correspondence, the box was filled with coins and small slips of paper.

She thought about the traveling desk that occupied the same space in her father's room. The two men could not be more different. So much for Mama's insistence that every girl looked for her papa in the man she wanted to marry.

"What are you doing here?"

Beatrice turned around with a gasp, a hand to her throat. Lord Jess stood in the doorway, looking more annoyed than angry.

"Uhm, I . . . ," Beatrice began, and decided on the truth. "I was curious. I came up to leave a letter for my father to take to London and I saw that the door to your room was open."

"Come out now." He did not seem to care what her explanation was. "If someone, even a footman, were to find you here with me there would be hell to pay." He stepped back into the corridor. "Out, now," he demanded.

"I'm coming," she said with a girlish huff of annoyance. "I was not trying to seduce you. I didn't even know you were about."

"Try telling that to your father if he were to find us." He stood back, his arms folded across his chest. "Which way are you going? I will go in the opposite direction."

Before she could answer they both heard the sound of footsteps. They were too far from the door to hide in his room. Apparently noting the same thing, Lord Jess took her arm and urged her to fall into step beside him.

"Since I was coming up to the house anyway." Jess made it sound as though they were in the middle of a conversation as the footman rounded the corner. The footman stepped to the wall so they could pass. As was the habit of the gentlemen of the ton, Lord Jess completely ignored his presence and kept on with his totally fabricated conversation. "Your father asked me to find you and make sure you were not late for the race."

Chapter Thirty-two

"Where are Lord Jessup and Beatrice?" Cecilia looked about from her saddle but could find neither one of them in the small circle of well-wishers or among those making their way across the lawn.

"Jess went back to the house." Destry sat stiffly, Cecilia noticed, and did not even turn his head to look for them as she had.

Their friends had laughed themselves silly at the sight of the marquis riding sidesaddle, and the wagers were now heavily in her favor.

"Is it not odd that our biggest supporters are not here? What will the others say?"

"Nothing, if we do not make an issue of it," Destry insisted.

"I am not making an issue of it."

Michael Garrett came up to them. "I would suggest that you start the race before the horses grow too restless. I am sure Jess and Beatrice will be along presently."

"Yes, we will," Destry said.

Destry was eager to begin so Cecilia decided not to wait any longer.

"Lord Crenshaw? Where is he?" Cecilia asked.

Destry ignored the question as Mr. Garrett held up his hand for attention. "I trust all wagers have been made," he announced. "The course will take Miss Brent and the marquis two miles cross-country. They will span the ford, but there will be no jumps. Then they will cross back over the river at the bridge nearest the main gate, returning up the drive, and circle the house. The racecourse ends to your left. The yellow ribbon is the finish line. I will fire the starting pistol on the count of three!"

The small crowd cheered and in an amazingly loud voice Mr. Garrett counted, "One, two, three." He pulled the trigger and they were off.

Cecilia's horse needed no urging, and she concentrated on the race ahead of her without one more worry for her sister.

"YOU ARE QUIET." Beatrice was not happy. Jess might be a fool but even a fool could see that. He knew from Callan, who knew from Darwell, that Miss Beatrice had slept well enough.

That was a plus. On the minus side, she had spent the whole of yesterday "preparing for her talk" on the art at Havenhall, a talk she could have easily given without preparation at all. She had not been at dinner last night and Cecilia had excused herself early as well.

"I have nothing to say to you, Lord Jess."

Beatrice did not spare him a glance but continued over the grass, watching her step as though there were rabbit holes at every turn.

"I understand that." Indeed, he had avoided her so as not to witness the distress he had caused. For all his faults, he had never spoken to a woman as cruelly as he had spoken to Beatrice. But then he had never felt his life a waste before he had met her and realized how little he had to offer any woman of worth. He might not be able to change that, but he could do one thing to make her happier in this moment. "Beatrice, I want to apologize."

"It is forgotten, my lord." Her tone said the opposite.

"I have not forgotten it. And I want to apologize."

"For what, my lord?" She raised her eyebrows. Those dark-swept brows were a very effective weapon. But she gave him, however unintentionally, the opening he wanted.

"For our conversation the night of the ball, and for hurting you with words that were nothing but lies."

"Our conversation?" Beatrice furrowed her brow as she pretended to try to recall what he was talking about. "Really, being called a slut—"

"I did not call you a slut. That is too extreme."

"Perhaps, but 'slut' is what I heard."

"Beatrice," he tried again, despite the feeling that the conversation was passing from his control to hers.

"Perhaps I can pose nude for an artist and make certain the description."

"Stop it." He took her by the arms and she froze, a look of such panic in her eyes that he released her at once. "It's true that I wanted to drive you away. For the last two days I had exactly what I thought I wanted. But I was wrong."

"Don't you dare—" She stopped herself, pressed her lips together, and turned from him, running, not toward the racecourse, but toward the trees in the opposite direction.

He took off after her. It did not take him long to overtake her but by then they were both breathless.

She whirled to face him. "I do not want to hear anything you have to say, be it truth or lies. Why can you not leave me alone?"

"Because you will not let me leave you alone." Which was not what he meant to say, even if it was the truth. "You are always there, those eyes, those damnably beautiful eyes, mirroring your endless curiosity about every little thing." He pulled her closer to him. "Curious about everything until there was one thing that my head could not let go of."

She did not pull away from him this time and was about to speak when he raised his hand and covered her lips with his fingers. "And your mouth. Word upon word, about art, gaming, people, ideas, on and on endlessly until I wanted to be the only word on your lips, those perfectly shaped pretty pink lips. Until I wanted those lips on mine."

Now she was stunned, there was no hiding that.

"Beatrice, everyone knows, even I know, that Jess Pennistan is the wrong man for you. That your goodness and sweetness deserve more than a dandy who games as his life's work. That your fine, bluestocking mind deserves more than a man who cares most about where the best game of chance is played."

There were tears in her eyes.

"I will seduce any woman willing. Do you hear me?" He wanted to shout but whispered instead.

Beatrice opened her mouth but said nothing. He waited, giving himself credit for patience. It took a moment but when she spoke her voice was steady. "Do not forget your arrogance."

She might have tears in her eyes but she was thinking clearly.

"Really, Jess, do you not see that you are so much more than a profligate? You are kind to everyone, no matter if they can improve your lot in life or not. You play only with those who can afford to lose. You seduce only the willing. There is not a mean bone in your body." She stood on tiptoes and leaned close enough to touch her lips to his but did not. "And now you must listen. You have not seduced me. For the love of God, I was willing.

"At first I thought that this house party would be the safest place in the world to experiment with someone dangerous, but I think that was terribly unfair to you."

"Pure torture," he agreed, but with a smile.

They both jumped at the sound of the gun and the start of the race.

"I'm sorry. Now you are late for the race," he said, not sorry at all.

"It doesn't matter. The finish is what matters." She took a step away from him. "So now you're telling me that what you said the other night was a lie?"

"Yes," he said firmly. "God, I've thought about this endlessly and I can explain my behavior a dozen ways, but I will settle on two."

"I don't mind long stories." Her smile meant forgiveness and the rebirth of curiosity. Jess could not help but be relieved. He sobered almost as fast. "Crenshaw had made me angry as a hornet and I vented it on you."

"That's what Cecilia told me that Destry told her, but I was not ready to believe it."

"And the other reason is that I wanted to scare you away. You are right, you were too great a temptation. Your very presence makes me want to make love to you."

"How many women have you told that same thing?" she asked as she leaned back against the tree behind her.

"Too many."

"You are all braggadocio. I have seen no proof that you are such a rake. None of the servants run from you. Nora Kendrick is a widow, a wealthy widow, and you never approached her."

"As you said yourself, Beatrice, this house party is a protected world. It is not London. Once you are there you will hear the truth. There have been too many," he repeated, "but never someone as young and untouched as you are."

"Untouched is such an unappealing word." She angled her head and looked up from under her lashes. "Could we not touch a little so that I am not quite such a threat to unmarried men?"

He shook his head and, with one finger, raised her chin.

"You are impossible." He pressed a gentle kiss to her mouth.

"Not really," she whispered against his lips. "Only curious."

He was the one who was seduced. He had been so

determined not to take but now found it was so much easier to give. Her joy and his surrender took them far beyond the touch of lips and tongues. The trees and shrubs around them were every bit a bower, he thought, nature's summerhouse where they could be as private as they needed or wanted.

"I want to lie on the grass with you, right here," he murmured between kissing her neck, then her throat. "I want to unpin your hair." He did so as he buried his face in it and she wrapped her arms around him, pressing them closer to each other.

"I want to see you dressed only in the shade and shadows of summer." He cupped her breast through gown and stays and then reached to rub the tip of it with his thumb. He ran his hand down to the soft spot between her legs and pressed his fingers, through her dress and shift, into her just enough that she pressed her legs together to hold him there and gasped with the pleasure of it. He scooped her up and carried her. She buried her face in his neck, pressing kisses, licking him and pressing her teeth against the vein that throbbed.

The summerhouse was buried in the shade. A table and chairs sat on one side of the room, and a long sofa that was more of a day bed with scrolled ends and no back was on the other. He laid her down on it and she raised her arms to draw him over her. They kissed and touched and soon his fall was undone, his manhood upright and hard with arousal. Beatrice's dress was pushed up to her waist, the sweet tangle of hair between her legs wet with welcome.

Lying beside her he used his hand again to bring her to pleasure without costing her the virginity that, to the ton at least, was her most valuable asset. She turned her head into his chest to smother the cry as waves of sensation pulsed through her, and then gave in to the final sweep with her back arched as if she wanted every last bit of what he gave her.

Afterward, they lay in each other's arms for a long while. It did little to ease the ache in his loins but she held tight to him and he wanted only to make her happy.

And when had he ever thought that before? *You love her*, a little voice whispered and he let the truth flood through him.

He moved to sit up. She shivered and held him to her.

"No, Jess, I cannot leave you so frustrated."

"You can and you will." He pushed away from her, smoothing her dress down around her legs.

"Let me—" she began.

"No!" He stood up and turned from her, welcoming the chill of separation. His body began to recover. He was not sure his heart ever would.

"I feel so very selfish and I do not feel quite so complete without you holding me."

He turned to look at her. "You know this is only headed for disaster."

She opened her mouth and then bit her lip in that gesture she had of holding back more. Standing up, she brushed her skirts down and pushed her hair back and looked exactly like what she was, a woman who now understood the pleasure of sex.

"There is no point in discussing this with you when you are not quite yourself," she said. "And since you will not allow me to do anything about it I am going to the house for a few minutes to try to tidy myself." She was going to say more but he did not let her.

"Come to the racecourse as soon as you can. They are sure to ask where you are."

"I hate the way you dictate terms to me. You are as bad as Papa." She let out her breath in a huff and then stopped, as though just then struck by something. She shook her head and began to the walk back to the house.

Jess watched her. She turned back once, waiting for him to move from the tree.

Finally she made a dismissive gesture with her hands. "Stop watching me!" she called back and he obeyed her, heading to join the others, where he hoped to find sanity. What did it say about the state of his mind that he was looking to Destry's exploits as the sane moment in his day?

Chapter Thirty-three

THIS IS DECIDEDLY *odd*, Destry thought as he turned to see exactly where Cecilia was. Right behind him, but definitely moving at a pace that kept her there when he was moving at the perfect pace for her to pass him.

If she was in front of him he could admire her seat, how beautiful she looked in the dark blue habit, and daydream about spending every morning riding the land with her after spending every night together in bed. Instead he was trying to devise a way to lose without falling off his horse.

They had truly raced for the first half, neck and neck the whole way. He could have gone faster but did not want to endanger her. Or himself, to be honest. Destry knew every time she glanced his way, as she knew when he looked at her. Occasionally they looked at the same time, which made them both grin and push their mounts a little more.

At the ford, which she reached first, she let loose a triumphant laugh even as they both slowed to cross safely. Back on land they moved on barely at a canter, her golden hair no longer streaming behind her, now barely stirred by the afternoon breeze, which looked to be bringing rain their way.

Cecilia was acting as though she did not want to win.

Which was impossible.

Winning was as important to her as it was to him.

Destry slowed his horse a little more and Cecilia did the same. Totally confused by her behavior, he slowed even more, settling into a walk. She came up beside him but did not pass him.

"What are you doing?" Because of the sidesaddle she had to look over her shoulder at him even though they were side by side.

"What are *you* doing?"

"Move a little ahead of me, my lord, so I do not have to twist so far to see you," she ordered.

"No, you come around to the other side and move a little ahead." Two could play this game.

"Do you want me to win this race?"

"No more than you want me to win." *Genius,* he thought. That was the perfect non-answer.

"That makes no sense. What do you mean?"

"The same thing you mean." That sounded more evasive than clever.

"Oh, stop, Destry. This is not some verbal puzzle. Answer my question."

"Only if you will answer mine."

"All right," she said with such vehemence that he thought she was barely hanging on to her patience.

"Are you letting me win? That is, are you *trying* to let me win?"

"Yes," he said, amazed at how hard it was to admit it.

"You are willing to lose deliberately to make me . . ." Her voice trailed off. "To make me do what?" she finished, confusion evident.

"That is two questions. I should be allowed one of mine first. Are you trying to let me win?"

"Yes," she bit out and then asked again, "Why do you want me to win?"

"So you can see that you have everything it takes to be a duchess." He wanted to ask his next question but waited to see how she would react to that declaration.

"I do not see how winning a horse race is proof of that. It's hardly one of the more practical aspects of what a duchess does."

"But it does represent who a duchess is. That is, someone who is capable and excels."

She had nothing to say to that but considered his words. Their horses were barely moving now.

"Cecilia," he began, grabbing what he hoped was the advantage. "There is nothing that separates you from me other than the obvious man-versus-woman difference, and thanks be to God for that.

"You are as equal to the task of being a duchess as I am equal to the task of being a duke. I thought that if you won the race it would go one more step toward proving that."

Her anger disappeared. Her expression softened to a slight smile. "I do question your logic, my lord."

He leaned closer. "I would prefer you call me Des, or even William."

She shook her head.

"Come a little closer."

"Why?" she asked.

"So I can kiss you without falling off this damn horse."

Startled, she drew back.

You idiot, now you have scared her off. But she did not race away so he asked her a question of his own.

"Why did *you* want *me* to win?"

"Because winning at everything is the way you prove yourself worthy and winning in a horse race is the most important win of all. I did not want to compromise your confidence."

He was struck by her understanding of him but she was not completely right. "Cecilia, winning this race, any race, is no longer the most important win. Not anymore."

"And what is?"

"Winning you."

The smile blinked out and she looked away from him, down the path ahead. "My lord?"

Did she not understand him? He'd thought it was rather romantic, and entirely unplanned.

Her horse moved ahead a few steps and it struck him that Cecilia Brent was sincerely not interested in him, whether he be duke or Dutchman.

"William," she said. "What is that? On the path. Up ahead."

"The banqueting platform."

"No, not that," she said, cutting him off and pointing. "That lump in the road. It looks like, uhm, a person."

They both urged their horses into more than a walk and Des moved ahead of Cecilia, wanting to spare her sensibilities if blood was involved. Concern warred with alarm when he saw it was a person, a man, though the body's back was turned to them, hiding the man's identity.

Destry slid off the horse and ran to the still form, turning the body over as soon as he reached it.

"Crenshaw!" Cecilia gasped. She was still seated on her horse and Destry hoped she could not see how awkwardly Crenshaw's head sat on his shoulders.

Though his body was still warm, there was no doubt that he was dead. No one could be alive with his neck at that angle.

"He's dead, isn't he, William?"

Destry could hear no tremor in Cecilia's voice but ran over to her in case she should feel faint. He jumped up on a fallen log nearby. "Do not faint before you dismount, Cecilia."

"I am not going to faint, my lord. Not at a time like this." She slid off the horse and into his arms. She was very pale but her eyes were clear.

"Do not look at him again."

She nodded, swallowing hard.

"One of us must go for help, Cecilia."

"I will," she volunteered promptly. "I can ride faster in sidesaddle than you can. Will you be all right, here alone with the," she paused, apparently unable to say "dead body," and then went on, "with Lord Crenshaw?"

"Yes," he said.

She nodded again as she remounted her horse. "Do you think you will be safe here?" she asked with a wavering voice. "What if he was murdered and his killer comes after you?"

"He probably just fell from his horse." Though her suggestion did give him pause.

Cecilia pointed to the banqueting platform, which had a broken railing. "I don't think so, William."

"All the more reason for you to go for help right away. I can defend myself, if necessary." He showed her the pistol he always carried, tucked into the waist of his pants.

"All right." Cecilia urged her mount on. "I will be back as soon as I can. With help."

"Do not come back yourself. There is no need for you to see this again."

She raised a hand in understanding.

"Cecilia!" Destry called. She stopped and looked his way. "One more thing. There is one thought that keeps running through my head. I know it is the wrong time and place but I am still going to say it."

She waited, still watching him.

"I love you."

Cecilia's expression of disbelief was not the response he had been hoping for.

Idiot. It was beyond the wrong time and place to make such a pronouncement. It was bizarre. But as he looked at Crenshaw, his face even now losing color and any tinge of life, he knew that if his world were to end in the next five minutes, telling Cecilia he loved her was the one thing he would regret leaving undone.

He stood up and scanned the surrounding area. No sounds came to him. Even the birds were quiet. His horse was grazing a few yards away and Jupiter's lack of concern convinced him as surely as anything that he was safe.

What had happened? Obviously Crenshaw had fallen

from the banqueting platform. He walked to the steps and was debating going up when he heard a horse, or was it two, coming toward him. Jess. He hoped it was Jess. Come to think of it, where had he been? As Belmont and Michael Garrett rode into sight, Destry took another look at the stairs and wondered where Jess had spent the last hour.

TIME PASSED IN a haze for Cecilia. She did everything she could to be helpful, refusing to allow herself to be unwell or to cry. All the while she tried to balance the truth with what she *wished* was the truth.

She expected to see Crenshaw come walking up the path to the finish line where she waited with the others and was shocked to the point of nausea when he went by in the back of a wagon, inelegantly posed on a pile of burlap. According to the land steward, Destry was in charge at the scene with Mr. Garrett and Lord Belmont assisting him.

Cecilia had decided that the most she could do to help now would be to stay out of the way. She was sitting on the ground against the base of a tree waiting, feeling stupidly female. Tears filled her eyes and she remembered why she'd experienced a moment of déjà vu when she had first seen Crenshaw.

Nora Kendrick came to sit next to her, patting her hand, a gesture for which Cecilia would be eternally grateful.

"I have seen someone dead with a broken neck before," Cecilia tried to explain, her eyes closing as she spoke. "Our brother. He died after falling from a horse."

"My dear, that *would* be upsetting." Nora continued to pat her hand. "However were you able to handle yourself so well today?"

"I did what had to be done." Cecilia opened her
eyes. "A hysterical woman would have been no help at
all. But I must admit that now I am feeling less than
capable."

"It happens that way sometimes. We are fine in the
emergency and then are overwhelmed by the shock.
Just stay here and soon someone will bring a conveyance for you."

"What is happening? Do you know anything?"

"I can go and see, if you do not mind being alone."

"I will be fine alone, and would rather know than sit
here and wonder." And surely Beatrice would be along
shortly.

With a final pat, Nora Kendrick stood and headed
down the path to the scene of Lord Crenshaw's accident. That's what it was. An accident. Cecilia was sure
of it now that she'd had some time to think about what
had happened. Gentlemen were not murdered at country house parties. He'd had too much to drink and had
fallen off the platform. She did not try to answer the
question as to why he had been up there in the first
place.

With that explanation in place she concentrated on
the other event that had taken her by surprise.

William had said, "I love you." That was part of the
reason she was upset. How could it be true? How
could he know so soon?

He was too impulsive. Even the countess had warned
her of that. Beatrice would sometimes act without

much forethought and it was almost always amusing, but Cecilia did not feel the same about Destry's spontaneous declaration.

Might he decide he did not love her with equal impulse?

After they were married?

Nora Kendrick came back before Cecilia thought herself into a bout of crying.

"The countess is still out on the property somewhere with your father. The land steward has sent for the coroner."

"But why the coroner?"

"The coroner will determine whether or not it was an accident."

"Lord Belmont could do that, could he not?"

"Yes, but Destry says there should be an official investigation." Nora shrugged. "I have no idea why. It was clearly an accident."

"Do you think so, too?" Cecilia wanted it to be an accident quite desperately. The alternative was too terrible to contemplate.

"Who would want him dead?" she asked, as if that were answer enough.

Lord Jess, Cecilia thought, but kept the horrible thought to herself. Nora Kendrick did not know the truth behind Crenshaw's divorce, nor had she heard Jess's threat the other night. The one Beatrice had told her about.

The wind gusted through the trees and Cecilia felt a rush of cooler air.

"I think it is about to rain," Nora said, pulling her shawl closer to her body. "Are you well enough to walk to the house? I would hate for you to be rained upon. It would not do you any good after such a shock."

"I think I am better." Cecilia stood up and felt much restored. The freshening wind was at their back and together they hurried across the lawn to the house. Beatrice met them just as they arrived at the steps to the terrace.

"Did you win?" Beatrice asked, all smiles, until she took in their somber faces. "Is everything all right? Is the marquis all right?"

"William is fine, but Lord Crenshaw is dead," Cecilia said bluntly. She explained how the baron had been found and that the men were still at the scene. It began to rain as she finished her story. She ended with, "The coroner has been sent for," as they all hurried to the side door.

"Why the coroner? He only comes if it is thought to be other than an accident," Beatrice said, concern more than curiosity coloring her words.

"The marquis sent for him," Mrs. Kendrick said, which really did not answer the question.

"The men are still at the banqueting platform? Is Jess with them, too?" Beatrice asked, pressing her lips together.

"I don't know. I have not seen him at all today," Ceci said. "Have you, Mrs. Kendrick?"

"He was with the other gentlemen. Lord Destry said he came walking up from the river."

They fell silent as the footman opened the door for them.

"What can we do? What should we do?" Beatrice asked.

"I'm sure Mr. Garrett has some experience with this

sort of thing." Mrs. Kendrick spoke with a conviction that surprised Cecilia.

"He has known people who have been murdered?" Beatrice asked, amazed at the idea.

"He was not always a vicar," Mrs. Kendrick explained. "He fought Napoleon, and not in the conventional way."

Is everyone but me extraordinary in some way? Cecilia wondered.

The housekeeper met them in the passage and urged them into one of the small salons. A fire had been lit, and Cecilia warmed her hands in front of it, surprised at how cold they were despite the relative warmth of the August day.

One of the maids bustled in with tea and sweets. There was a bottle of brandy on the tray and Mrs. Kendrick insisted on adding a drop to Cecilia's tea. "She is upset. Finding Lord Crenshaw reminded her of your brother."

"Of course it did." Beatrice sat on the sofa next to her sister and hugged her.

After holding herself together all day, Cecilia at last began to cry. "Lord Crenshaw was not a very nice man, but I did not wish him dead. And what if it was murder? Who would want to kill him?" Her words were compromised by tears, but she felt her sister stiffen beside her.

Beatrice stood up. "Can you stay with her, Mrs. Kendrick? I need to find Jess. I will be back as soon as I can."

"He's with the other gentlemen and it's raining, Beatrice."

"I will take an umbrella." She shook out her skirts and made for the door.

"Beatrice, this is carrying your curiosity entirely too far," Cecilia insisted. "It is not seemly for you—' There was no point in even finishing the sentence— Beatrice was already gone.

Chapter Thirty-four

As Beatrice hurried across the lawn, she saw the party of gentlemen crossing toward her. Jess was with Lord Belmont, the marquis, Mr. Garrett, and a gentleman she did not recognize. Could the coroner have arrived already?

Please no, not before she had the chance to talk to Jess.

Jess saw her first. Beatrice was not sure what she expected. Not a loving greeting, but surely not the distress that caused him to rub his brow and squeeze his eyes shut for a moment. Just as quickly he was himself again, at the back of the group, with a noncommittal expression on his face.

"Miss Brent, there is no need for you to be out in the rain." Lord Belmont took her arm in a more forceful gesture than usual and she had no choice but to turn and allow him to escort her back to the house.

"I want to speak with Lord Jessup." Beatrice decided that a direct approach was best.

"In a while. I want you to go inside, find Nora and your sister, and stay with them for now." As he told her what he expected, he escorted her one way and the others headed in the opposite direction. "Miss Wilson and her mother will join you, I am sure. They will have all sorts of questions for your sister and she will need your support."

"Was that other man with you the coroner? How did he arrive so quickly?"

"No, it was the land manager. The coroner has been sent for."

"Then I need to speak with Jess, my lord, right away." She tried to pull her arm from his.

"No, you do not, Beatrice." His firm tone of voice left her no option until he added, "Unless you do not trust Lord Jess's honor."

"Of course I do. I don't care what anyone says. He is innocent."

That stopped the earl in his tracks. "Innocent of what?" he asked, his expression hard and not at all forgiving.

Realizing her mistake, Beatrice tried to think of something Jess could be innocent of besides Lord Crenshaw's death.

"He was with me." She was not going to have hysterics, so she did her best to lower her voice to a reasonable tone. "I don't care what he tells you. He was with me for a good bit of time before Crenshaw was found dead."

"Thank you, Miss Brent." The earl bowed to her quite formally. "I will bear that in mind."

"You believe me, do you not?"

"Yes, I do, Beatrice. But I am not the one who needs to be convinced. Let me see what is needed, and I will come back for you if necessary."

Beatrice let the earl go and went back into the small salon. All the ladies were gathered there now, though the countess was not among them.

With a nod to the others, Beatrice walked over to sit next to her sister. "You've told them everything." Beatrice was sure she had, given how pale Cecilia was. She wished her sister would take a little more tea with brandy.

"Yes." Cecilia shook her head. "It was very difficult."

Beatrice nodded and was sorry that she could not have been in two places at once. "The countess is not back yet?"

"Not that I know of."

"That means that she and Papa are trapped somewhere by the rain, or traveling back to the house in an open cart."

"They will be fine. The countess is not nearly as delicate as Mama was. A little rain will do no more than dampen her dress."

Beatrice nodded. Still, it was one more thing to worry about.

They all sat in silence. The only person crying was Mrs. Wilson. Katherine Wilson sat very still, staring into some future that was entirely different than it had been a few hours ago.

"If her heart was engaged," Cecilia whispered, "then she is behaving far more stoically than one would expect."

"Everyone is different. But it could be that Lord Jess's conversation with her last night has made her see things differently. As awful as his death is, it did rescue her from a difficult choice."

"Oh, did you find Lord Jess?"

"Actually, I talked to Lord Belmont and hope that will suffice."

"Why? What was so important?"

"I was alone with Jess before the start of the race. For quite a while, actually."

"Beatrice! What were you doing? No, wait, don't tell me. I do not want to know." She covered her ears, which drew the attention of everyone else in the room.

Beatrice did not look away, well aware that this was probably the beginning of the end of her London Season. And Cecilia's.

"THE CORONER IS in Scotland and will not be back for a month." The land manager spoke directly to Lord Destry but his voice was loud enough for the rest of the gentlemen to hear. Jess wondered if they would have to wait for the coroner or if someone else could conduct the investigation. It was absurd to think they all must remain until he returned.

He assessed the group. Garrett was still attending to Lord Crenshaw's spiritual needs, whatever they could be, given that the man was already dead. That left him, Belmont, and Des with drinks in hand and death very much in the room with them.

Jess tasted the wine, but then set his glass down and pushed it away. He, more than anyone, needed a clear head.

"Thank you," Destry said to the land manager, speaking as formally as if he were seated in the House of Lords. "I would appreciate it if you would stay awhile, unless there are urgent demands on your time."

Destry was very much in control of the situation. In fact, this was the first time Jess had ever seen him behave like a titled gentleman.

"I can remain as long as you have need of me, my lord." The land manager moved away from the center of the room, hat in hand, and waited.

Destry paced as he spoke, hands behind his back. "It's my understanding that we need only wait for the coroner if we suspect foul play." He stared at the floor a moment. "Do I?" he said very quietly to himself and then shook his head. "I'm too close," he murmured again, seemingly to himself.

He looked up and spoke to all three of them. "I believe we should ask the Earl of Belmont to investigate the incident, and to decide whether there is a need to inform the coroner." Destry looked up at Belmont. "My lord earl, are you willing to take this on?"

"Yes, my lord." Belmont bowed formally.

With a nod and a gesture, Destry passed the investigation over to Belmont. The earl and the land agent spent a few minutes discussing arrangements for the preservation of Lord Crenshaw's body.

"What difference does it make?" Jess whispered to Destry, feeling as curious as Beatrice.

"If murder is suspected, the body cannot be buried until the coroner sees it."

"How do you know all this?"

"Part of the training to be a duke," Destry responded

with a wry smile. "Never knew I would actually use this bit."

They stood silent while the others talked, until Des spoke for Jess's ears alone. "I told Cecilia that I love her."

Yes, he was used to Destry's inclination to change the subject without preamble, but this declaration gave him a moment's pause.

"What did you say?" Jess held up his hand. "I heard you. I heard you. Des, that's tantamount to a proposal. What were you thinking?"

"I was looking at Crenshaw and thinking how death can come knocking any minute and that there's no time to waste. It was not impulse. I do love her and I would be delighted if she considered that a proposal."

"You're right about how life can change. When we came here we both wanted nothing more than a few weeks of gaming, fishing, and flirting. Now you are ready for marriage and I am the prime suspect in a death." That, if anything, would drive Beatrice away. What had she been doing walking up to him like that? Her curiosity must be driving her near mad.

"No one has said that, Jess."

"Belmont will. Crenshaw and I have had two confrontations since the house party started, and last night I said I should have killed him. And I said it in front of witnesses."

"But you didn't kill him," Destry said with conviction, then compromised that by asking, "Where were you anyway?"

This was the moment when he had to make a choice. If he told the truth, Beatrice's reputation would be in tatters. Hell, it could be so ruined that a London Season among the ton would be impossible.

For Beatrice, then, he decided.

"I was walking down by the river. I told you that."

"That makes no sense, Jess. You never go for walks and we were in the middle of one of the better gaming opportunities of these few weeks."

"I know it's odd but that is where I was."

"Where was Beatrice? She was missing, too."

"Do you think she could push a man to his death?" Jess imbued the question with as much sarcasm as he could muster.

"No, of course not, but it is odd that the two of you were missing at the same time from an event that should have been of keen interest to you both." Destry looked away, shook his head, and then added, "Unless you were more interested in each other."

Before Jess could find the words to distract Destry from that truth, Belmont came to them. "If you two gentlemen would join the ladies, I will make a few other inquiries and come to you shortly."

"What 'other inquiries' is he talking about?" Destry asked as they trooped down the passage to the salon where the ladies were gathered.

"I would guess he wants to talk to the servants. The footmen are everywhere. It was not only you and Beatrice who heard me wish Crenshaw dead the night of the ball. At least one footman was standing nearby."

"Yes, the footmen. I don't even notice them in the normal course of events."

"Which, I do believe, makes them valuable sources of information."

One of said footmen opened the door to the salon.

Destry paused and gave the servant his full attention. "How many footmen are employed here?"

"I think you would have to ask the majordomo, my lord."

"Because you do not know or would rather not be talking to me?" Destry warned, but with a smile.

"Both, my lord." His face reddened.

"Is that so? Very good." Destry watched him a moment more and then walked into the room with Jess. "Now the question is are all the footmen as honest as this one? I'm going to find Belmont."

"Des, he told us to stay here."

"Yes, I know," Destry replied blithely, and headed down the passage.

Jess watched him go, thinking he could be hell to live with. Destry needed someone to tamp down his impulsiveness. He wondered if Cecilia Brent was up to that challenge.

Once in the salon, he looked for Beatrice and found her seated next to her sister, with Mrs. Kendrick nearby. He saw the fear in her eyes and tried to think of a way to organize a private moment so he could reassure her.

Jess headed across the room, taking stock of the rest of the guests. Mr. Garrett was already there, talking with Mrs. Kendrick. Lady Olivia sat next to Mrs. Wilson, who was twisting a handkerchief and dabbing at tears.

Cecilia and Beatrice both rose as he came farther into the room.

Jess explained to everyone what was happening and they all sat down again or found seats, except for Beatrice, who wandered over to a window, away from the others.

He wanted to talk to her more than anyone else and she wanted the same, he could tell that, but he decided it would attract too much attention if he went directly to her. He approached Garrett first to ask about Crenshaw's body and was assured that it was being preserved in the icehouse until it could be returned to his estate for burial.

How many times had the icehouse been used for something like that? He made a mental note to avoid any ices for the rest of his stay.

He paused to tell Cecilia where Destry was, which he phrased as "conducting some inquiries of his own," and to ask Nora Kendrick if Belmont had given her any special directions. He had not.

Finally, Jess wandered over to the window where Beatrice was waiting with barely concealed impatience.

"I told them I was walking by the river. You have nothing to worry about, Beatrice. You will not be compromised."

"Jess, listen to me." Beatrice spoke quietly, with a sad smile as if she was seeking comfort instead of discussing perjury. "You will not lie for me. I will not allow it. You know they will suspect you. It is inevitable. I urge you to simply tell the truth."

"No. It will make your chance for a Season very difficult to manage."

"Oh, what does that matter?" She glanced over at Mrs. Wilson. "Cecilia's beauty is all the entrée she needs. And the only reasons I was hoping for a Season were to have fun and to help Cecilia find a match." She took his arm. "Do not lie to save me."

He closed his eyes. Not seeing her intense blue eyes

would make it easier to think clearly. But the feel of her hand on his arm reminded him that she was watching and waiting for him to answer.

"Dear friends!" The countess and Mr. Brent burst into the room. "I am so sorry!" The countess was dressed in the same clothes she had worn out that morning. She had not even taken time to change or freshen up. She went from one guest to another expressing sympathy and affection while Mr. Brent stood at the door looking awkward and very wet.

"Go to your father," Jess said. "Do not let him see you standing here with me."

"No. I want him to know that you have my complete support."

"But I do not want your support, Beatrice. It only makes life more complicated."

"Yes, I know, but I expect I am going to spend my life under my father's roof and I want him to understand that it will be on my terms."

Her words shocked him. She did not expect an offer of marriage in exchange for his ruination of her? Did this woman think of everyone's best interests but her own?

The countess left the room, promising she would return as soon as she had changed. Jess did not know how significant it was that the countess did not even look at Abel Brent.

Mr. Brent watched the door close without expression. If ever there was a fish out of water it was Abel Brent caught with his secret out. He and the countess had been gone for most of the day. Jess guessed it was one of the rare moments in his life when Brent was not in command of a situation.

Brent turned to have a few words with Cecilia, who had run to his side and was urging him to change before he caught a chill. Garrett offered Mr. Brent a brandy, which he accepted gratefully and drank in one swallow.

Fortified by the drink, he seemed to realize that there was one situation he *was* in command of. He came up to Beatrice with Cecilia trailing behind, her face full of anxiety.

"Beatrice, this is a nightmare. You should be as far from this man as possible. Come with me now."

"No, Papa. I am staying here as Lord Belmont asked."

"There is a real possibility that murder has been done," Brent said, looking at Jess, accusing him with his eyes if not his words. "If you do not come with me now, I swear I will not allow you to leave home ever again."

"Father, I am staying in this room, right here."

Brent drew a breath to speak but Beatrice beat him to it. "You are the one making a scene. Please go change from your wet clothes."

Cecilia's "Please, Papa" was the last poke he needed.

"You have not heard the last of this, young lady."

"Yes, Papa," both girls chorused. Cecilia took his arm and walked with him to the door. They had a quiet conference there and he left the company. Cecilia came right back to her sister.

"He is angry and upset."

"He is embarrassed," Beatrice said.

"Bitsy, he is adamant about removing you from this—um—situation." Cecilia did not look at him, but Jess was sure he was the "situation."

"I don't care what he wants. I am going to do what is right."

"What are you talking about? Obeying your father is what is right." Now Cecilia did look at Jess, a question in her eyes.

"I have told her the same thing. Not in so many words but I do agree with you."

"I am as adamant as Papa, Cecilia. I am sorry you are caught in the middle."

Cecilia threw up her hands. She must know as well as anyone how stubborn her sister could be.

Jess would wager on Beatrice to win this contest, but he was not at all sure who would be the biggest loser.

Chapter Thirty-five

LORD BELMONT AND the marquis returned to the salon just as Beatrice was thinking that they should go change for dinner. Whatever the countess had planned would probably be postponed, but she had not yet returned to tell them what to expect.

It would hardly do to continue their entertainments when one of the guests had died that very day. Not that they needed to go into mourning; after all, none of them was related to Baron Crenshaw. But it would be a gesture of respect to maintain no more than a quiet presence.

"Ladies and gentlemen," the earl began, "I thank you for your patience. I have a few questions to ask, then you may be excused to your rooms. The countess will be along shortly but she asked me to advise you that the ladies will have trays sent to their rooms. The gentlemen will gather in the small dining room, where their meal will be served."

"A tray in our room is exactly the right thing, is it not?" Beatrice asked her sister. "The countess always knows what to do."

"I suppose so. It has the added benefit of keeping you and Papa apart until you both calm down."

"You mean until you can convince me to do as he wishes."

"I hate it when the two of you are at odds. Please calm yourself."

"I do want to be calm," Beatrice insisted in a reasoned voice that almost hid her annoyance. "There is always the chance Papa will come to our room. Well, it won't be the first time I have pretended a headache and gone to bed before dark."

"If I could have your attention, please." Lord Belmont waited until the quiet conversations stopped. "The ladies are free to leave if they wish. There is no reason to involve any of you in this discussion."

Lady Olivia and Miss Wilson stood, and Cecilia took a step toward the door. Mrs. Wilson and Nora Kendrick did not move a muscle. That was a relief, as Beatrice had no intention of going, either.

"Before you leave, ladies, Mr. Garrett will be holding a service tomorrow before dinner if you would like to spend some time in prayer and reflection for the repose of Baron Crenshaw's soul."

Lord Belmont's announcement awakened Miss Wilson from the shocked sensibility that had held her in thrall for the last few hours. "Mama," she whimpered and began to cry. Her mother put her arm around her shoulders and escorted her from the room. Lady Olivia followed them.

"The poor thing." Cecilia came back to sit beside

her sister. "It's as though she did not believe it was real until that moment."

Cecilia drew a deep breath and Beatrice wondered if her sister was about to start crying, too. There was not a tear in her own heart, Beatrice thought. All that rested there right now was worry for Lord Jess.

"I hope she knows how fortunate she is to have her mama at a time like this." No sooner were the words out of Cecilia's mouth than the footman opened the door and Mrs. Wilson and the countess came in together.

"Lady Olivia is staying with Katherine until this business is finished," Mrs. Wilson announced to the room. She sat down next to Mr. Garrett, while the countess came to sit next to her goddaughters.

"Are you all right, dear girls?" the countess asked. In Beatrice's opinion the countess showed more tenderness for her goddaughters in that one sentence than Mrs. Wilson had given to her own daughter. Beatrice looked at Cecilia and without words they both agreed to lie.

"Yes," they chorused together.

"Is Papa all right?"

The countess smiled. "He is very fine, Cecilia, though he is upset that our outing kept me from my guests at such a difficult time."

And embarrassed, Beatrice thought again. The countess did not seem to be at all.

"He is a gentleman in all the ways that count. I want you never to forget that, no matter what the gossips say." She looked from one to the other. "Do you understand me?"

"Yes, my lady," they chorused again, though Beatrice was privately thrilled that Papa had such staunch support in the countess. It was exactly the way she wished to support Jess, regardless of what Mrs. Wilson, or those like her, might think or, worse, say.

"The gentlemen's whereabouts are accounted for with one exception," Lord Belmont said.

A hum of conversation came on the heels of the earl's announcement. Beatrice raised her chin as Cecilia took hold of her hand.

Jess stood at the back of the room as he usually did, looking only vaguely interested in the proceedings.

"It feels like an official inquiry, does it not?" Cecilia asked, sotto voce. "I mean, even without the coroner present, the earl is being very careful in his choice of words."

"Your attention, please." Belmont waited a beat after everyone stopped talking. "I am asking the following question in the presence of others so that I will have witnesses when I speak with the coroner."

Jess was going to lie to protect her reputation. That could not be allowed to happen. She raised her hand and waited until the earl noticed it.

"No," Jess began, taking a step toward her, but Beatrice spoke as fast as she could summon the words.

"I was with Lord Jess for almost an hour right before Lord Crenshaw's body was discovered."

"Thank you, Miss Brent." Belmont looked at Jess. "That is corroborated by one of the footmen who told me that he saw the two of you in the corridor near Lord Jessup's room."

"We met there quite by accident and then spent the next hour together, but out of doors, not in the house."

She bit her lip and could not look away from the earl, afraid of what she might see in the others' faces.

"Can anyone verify that, Beatrice?" Belmont asked in such a kind voice that she knew he suspected the worst.

"No one but Lord Jess. We were alone." She felt Cecilia squeeze her hand so hard that it hurt, heard Mrs. Wilson gasp, and was almost certain that she heard Jess swear. The countess was shaking her head, obviously upset.

Belmont shifted to face Jess. "Is that true, my lord?"

Jess hesitated for so long the others began to shift uncomfortably. Finally, he spoke. "Yes." Jess imbued the word with regret.

"One of you should say that nothing of an intimate nature had occurred, or something like that," Cecilia whispered.

"Ceci, that would be a lie," Beatrice whispered back.

"Shh," Cecilia said, even though she was the one who'd brought up the subject.

"Thank you, again, Miss Brent. Your honesty comes at some cost to yourself, but I am sure in the end that virtue will be rewarded." The earl bowed to her and then to the marquis.

"Lord Destry, I appreciate your request that I solve this unfortunate puzzle. From what I have learned about everyone's whereabouts, I conclude that no one in the party or on staff had the opportunity to commit a crime against the baron. So it appears that Lord Crenshaw's death was an accident. Though why he chose to view the race from the banqueting platform and quite alone will remain a mystery."

Marquis Destry came to the center of the room to

stand next to Belmont. "Thank you, my lord." He nodded to Belmont and announced, "We are finished."

If only that were true, Beatrice thought.

Jess did not move as the others rose, maintaining his favored spot on the edge of the crowd. There was nothing remote about the way he was watching her. His eyes considered her with a speculation that showed anger and frustration. She wished it thrilled her heart. Instead it frightened her.

Chapter Thirty-six

JESS STARED INTO the empty fireplace as he considered his options. He needed to make a decision before Mr. Brent joined him. Michael Garrett stood by the window, waiting.

Jess's thoughts went in five different directions but at the bottom of it all *What is best for Beatrice* held sway.

"Do you think I've lost all chance to buy the land back?" Jess asked as he turned from the fireplace and walked toward Garrett.

"I imagine that your chances are better now. Those acres are not part of the entail and since Crenshaw had a debt to settle with you, his trustees might consider it. Is the coal deposit worth more than the two thousand pounds you won from him?"

"Potentially, but it will take money to make it profitable. Money that Crenshaw was unwilling or unable to invest. Besides that, I doubt that he wrote to his man of business. He would first try to win enough to pay off the debt to me."

"There's one other thing, Jess, gaming debts are usually forgiven when a man dies."

"Not by me, Michael. There was enough ill will between us that no one will be surprised when I press for payment."

"Is it worth the opprobrium if that becomes public?"

"To have the land back? To be able to show the deed to my brother the duke? Yes, it is worth another bit of scandal."

"All in the name of family. You have an odd way of earning your brother's respect."

Jess shrugged. "I have a long way to go to earn his respect. I want the land back so that I have something, other than my ability to game, to show that I am a man of means."

"It will be an added benefit then."

Which brought Beatrice to front and center. Jess supposed he wanted the land back as much for her as for his mother.

"I do not have to offer for Beatrice." Jess started with the easiest solution to his problem. "If I do not offer marriage it will mean she returns to Birmingham without entrée to society. Her reputation will survive as I do not expect anyone here will gossip. I do think even Mrs. Wilson could be prevailed on to exercise some control if Beatrice never comes to London." He walked back across the room and leaned on the mantel, staring at the top edge of the fire screen and the empty grate behind it, seeing Beatrice honest and stalwart, speaking the truth at the cost of her reputation.

"But not offering to marry her is the coward's way out."

"Not really," Michael said.

Jess turned back to the man and raised his eyebrow.

"It's only flying in the face of convention, and the two of you have already shown a certain propensity for that." Michael waited a moment and then went on. "Cecilia will be welcome among the ton. Her beauty will override her sister's supposed disgrace. And Cecilia's successful Season is what is important to Beatrice."

Jess was still caught up in the idea that Beatrice cared as little for the ton as he did and, besides that, she had made it clear that she never expected a proposal.

"Do you recall stories of the Gunning sisters?" Michael asked.

Jess shook his head.

"They were Irish beauties," Michael explained, "with little but their beauty to recommend them. They came to London at the end of the last century and walked away with prize matches. Much has changed, but Cecilia Brent's reputation is intact. She will not be at a loss for suitors."

"Unless Destry beats them off."

"Or wins her hand first."

"Yes," Jess agreed. "That's more likely. That ridiculous horse race where each was willing to lose to bolster the other's confidence is proof there is more between them than friendship. Or could be." Jess wondered if Destry might be talking with Mr. Brent right now.

"I didn't hear about that. Is that why the race took so long?"

"No," Jess said. "Destry explained it all to me. Before they found Crenshaw they were at a standstill because each intended for the other to win."

Garrett laughed, a sincere laugh. "It sounds as though the only person Destry must now convince is Cecilia's father. I expect that will be a fairly easy conversation. Surely the absurdity of his sidesaddle ride has faded in the light of all that has followed. And the man will be a duke someday."

"That sounds convincing. How about if you speak for me when Brent arrives?"

"I think not, brother." Garrett shook his head slowly but with conviction.

"So," Jess began, returning to his own personal headache. "I do not have to offer for Beatrice Brent simply because we spent an hour alone together and I touched her intimately."

Garrett pursed his lips but managed to restrain any comment.

"To walk away from her is in keeping with my general reputation for avoiding responsibility of any kind." But it felt all wrong. He shrugged. "If I thought Beatrice and I could make a marriage of convenience and then live separate lives it might work, but she is so damn curious about every little thing, I have this unholy picture of her as queen of every gaming hell from here to London within the year."

"Why does that bother you? It's been your life's work."

Garrett could hit with true aim when he wanted to. "It bothers me because she is a terrible gamer and I would spend all my time making money to cover her losses."

"So why not stop making wagers on cards and find something else on which to gamble?"

"What the hell does that mean?" Jess turned away from Garrett, uncomfortable with the direction of their conversation.

Garrett came over to stand closer to him.

"Your brother David is taking a huge chance on his cotton mill. It opened last month."

"David spent years lost in Mexico. He is hardly a model for conventional living." There was that word again. Now that he thought about it none of the Pennistans were conventional.

"I'm not suggesting that you go into partnership with him, but he has set a precedent for a Pennistan going into business."

"So you think I should let her return to Birmingham when her father's aim has been to raise his daughter's position in society?"

Garrett laughed and then coughed to cover it. "Yes, after all, what level are you going to raise her to? At least her father makes some contribution to the world. Jess, not to put too fine a point on it, but Olivia contributes more to the world than you do."

Jess felt his face redden. What did it say about his life that this confidant thought he was wasting it?

"Think about it awhile." Garrett put a hand on Jess's shoulder and Jess felt some of his embarrassment ease. "Think about why making a change in order to save Beatrice from a gaming hell matters to you."

He didn't want to, because it would mean that he loved her. Why should the truth hurt so much?

"Think about taking a chance on something bigger than the turn of a card."

He had no idea what that could be. Was there any point in trying to talk to David about it?

"Brent will not come to you this evening. He will see you in the morning when both the countess and I hope that cooler heads will prevail."

"Why did you not tell me that when you came into the room?"

"I wanted to hear your thoughts on the subject when you were under pressure. There is so much less opportunity to prevaricate."

"Your life as a spy bleeds through, Michael."

"Yes, the experience does have its uses."

"I HAVE HEARD the story from the countess. Beatrice, you have disgraced yourself beyond all imagining." Her father towered over her, his anger only adding to his stature. Her own upset made her feel as though she were shriveling before his eyes.

"I am sorry, Papa, but I could not allow Lord Jessup to lie to protect me."

"And why not?"

"Because he might have been accused of murder. Is that not obvious?"

"Do not talk to me that way or I will take a switch to you. Something I should have done a long time ago."

"Papa, please," Cecilia began.

He raised his hand in a familiar "say no more" gesture. "Leave the room, Cecilia. Your sister does not need your protection."

"Papa, you just this minute threatened to take a

switch to her," Cecilia protested, and her father looked at her as if she had sprouted feathers and was squawking.

"What happened to my biddable daughter? I see you are taking lessons from your sister, when it should be the other way around."

"I love you, Papa, and I am sorry that you are upset," Cecilia began, but her father cut her off.

"Upset does not begin to cover the rage I feel at Beatrice and at Pennistan. If we were equals I would challenge him to a duel for his insult to my daughter's virtue."

"It was not his fault," Beatrice insisted, but in a small voice that did not carry conviction. She cleared her throat and went on. "He warned me away more than once. Truly he did." It was her own fascination that had been her undoing. "I never thought about the consequences if he lost his control."

"How honest of you to admit that you are that selfish. You do realize that your behavior may have cost your sister her chance to marry well."

This brought tears to her eyes. "I know everyone is upset right now, but I am praying that in time everyone will see that it was my fault and not Cecilia's."

"I want your promise, your word, Beatrice, that you will stay in your room until we leave for home, and when we return to Birmingham you will behave as your mother taught you." He was angry still, and though he was not precisely shouting at her, his tone was hardly civil.

Bringing up Mama was the final knife in her heart. Her tears spilled onto her cheeks. She looked at Cecilia, who was tearful as well, her eyes begging Beatrice to agree. "Yes, Papa, I will come home with you as soon as you wish."

"And I have your word that you will stay in this room and think about your failings?"

She had been hoping he would forget that. "Yes, Papa, but sir, I would ask that you speak with Lord Jess." She stepped back, afraid of how he might react to that.

"Oh, I will speak to him, but if you happen to see him you will ignore him, shun him to the point of rudeness. Do you understand?"

"Yes, sir," Beatrice replied without argument, anxious to make her point. "But, Father, there is so much more to the story of his involvement in Lord Crenshaw's divorce. Cecilia, tell him that I am speaking the truth."

Before Cecilia could answer, her father made a sound of disgust. "Good God, I had forgotten all about that."

He had? And she was the one who had reminded him. What a dismal failure she was as a peacemaker.

"All the more reason to refuse to consider him if he does the right thing and offers for you."

"If he what?" She understood the words but it took a moment for them to sink in. "I do not want to marry him if he only proposes because it is expected of him!"

"Enough!" her father bellowed. "You will marry him if I tell you to! Come, Cecilia, I do not want you influenced by your sister any more than necessary."

Cecilia started. "Yes, Papa." With a last look at Beatrice, her eyes spoke for her. *I will champion you, sister, I promise.*

Beatrice nodded, understanding the unspoken pledge.

Her father and sister left the room, though his shouted words still bounced off the walls.

Stay in her room? She would obey him on that. Sitting down again, Beatrice did what any woman so estranged from her family would do. She began to cry.

"NOW IS NOT a good time to speak with my father, William." He had stopped her in the hall. It was an awkward place to converse, but public enough. Cecilia tried to stop wringing her hands. "What do you want to say, anyway?"

"Did you not hear what I told you today?"

"Yes," she said, staring at the marble floor, which was far easier than looking him in the eyes.

"And does the thought of me courting you fill you with disgust?"

"No!" She looked at him now. "But to declare yourself when it is one-sided is too impulsive."

"Is it that you cannot love me or that it's too soon to know?"

"Too soon," she whispered. Someone had to control this impulsiveness. Between her sister, Jess, and William it seemed to be an epidemic around here.

"But not impossible?"

She knew her hesitation was a mistake. He pounced on it.

"Then I want to speak to your father today. Tell him of my interest at least." Destry was trying to vent his energy by pacing the hall. "The house party is over. We will all be leaving as soon as we can make arrangements."

"And it would be too inconvenient for you to travel to Birmingham to talk to him at some future date?"

"If I wait a month and call on you at home, I fear you will have forgotten me."

"Do not be absurd. Forgetting you would be like forgetting that the sun rises every day."

William brightened at that analogy. Perhaps she should not have said that, but it had erased the wounded look that made his smile disappear and his eyes grow sad.

"Listen to me, William. Papa is not in the mood to honor the wishes of anyone with connections to society." Cecilia paused and reconsidered, then tried again. "What I mean is that as much as he wants me to marry well, Papa would not be receptive right now. Not after the way Mrs. Wilson treated him at breakfast this morning."

When her father had come in and wished the group "Good morning," Mrs. Wilson had set her cup in the saucer with a clank that should have broken it, stood up, and left the room without a word.

William paused in his pacing and made a noise suspiciously like a snort. "Mrs. Wilson was unforgivably rude to your father and that is the first thing I will tell him."

"It would be better not to mention it." Cecilia forced herself to stop wringing her hands.

"All right, I'll do as you suggest and not mention it," he agreed, not pausing in his movement from one end of the hall to the other. "I will even wait to speak to him if you think it better."

"You will do as I ask?" How amazing. No one ever did what she suggested.

"And if you are worried about Jane Wilson spoiling your entrée into society, she will not. She is only one. The support of the other guests here will be all you need." He stopped his constant pacing and stepped onto the hearth so they were eye-to-eye. "It pains me to say that." He paused and then hurried on. "The truth is that I fear if you have a Season you will find someone you like better." His warm brown eyes were intent and he was smiling but she could sense his uncertainty.

"That would be impossible, William. Where else could I find a man willing to ride sidesaddle or allow me to win a race? Or one who will actually listen to what I am saying?" Oh dear, that sounded too much like a declaration and she was sure, almost sure, it was too soon to know her feelings, or even his.

"I almost believe you, Cecilia, but then I remember that I am barely five feet tall and think that, yes, indeed, I am hard to forget. Though easy to ignore."

"William, feeling sorry for yourself will draw no sympathy from me. Your height is no more important than my beauty. You have convinced me of that."

"I have?" His anxiety disappeared, replaced by a smile that lit his whole face.

"Yes, you have." She loved it when he smiled, the way it lit his eyes and dimpled his cheeks.

"Then let me move on to the next conviction that I wish you to share."

"Oh dear," she said with a little laugh. "Is this list very long?"

"No. As a matter of fact, if I can convince you of this first one then the rest will most likely evaporate."

"Do begin."

She sat on the sofa and composed herself. He stepped down from the hearth and stood in front of her.

"The way you handled our discovery of Lord Crenshaw was masterful. Most women would have swooned. And if they did not faint dead away, they would have argued with me about what to do. You did not. You kept your head, did what I asked, and made a very difficult situation a little more manageable."

"Thank you. It was simply the right thing to do. I did lose my composure later." Honesty compelled her to admit that.

"No one would expect less of a woman with even the slightest sensibility."

"Thank you again, but you know a compliment like that is not hard to accept."

"Cecilia, this next one might be. You behaved exactly as a duchess should."

She closed her eyes, feeling as though she had been led into a trap.

"Do you want me to list the ways you have proved your worth?"

She shook her head, eyes still closed.

"Wait, I have a better way to prove it."

Cecilia smiled a little, wondering what his next proof would be. Then she felt the press of his lips on hers. His hands were on her shoulders holding her still as though he was afraid she might push him away.

His kiss was the sweetest touch she'd ever felt. More than sweet. It was perfection. She felt as if she had come home and found everything she had ever longed for.

She made some sound, or he did, and pressed her lips

to his lest he think she wanted him to stop. His hands slid down her arms and hers went round his waist.

William kissed her again and again, his mouth never leaving hers. The tingling in her head and heart moved lower, until she could not hold him close enough.

When the kiss ended, as all kisses must, he drew back and looked into her eyes. "Did that help convince you, my dearest darling Cecilia?"

"Almost," she said. "I think one more kiss, or perhaps two, might be needed."

He sat beside her. "I hope you will think of this when you are overwhelmed with attention during your Season."

Cecilia leaned down to him and took the initiative. This time he tasted her lips with his tongue and she did the same, flustered that she was so unschooled in the art of love. He did not seem to mind teaching her, though. When they moved apart, putting some distance between them on the sofa, she laughed.

"I do know one thing, my lord."

When he finished straightening his red cravat he looked at her with raised eyebrows.

"Papa will find a match in you when it comes to a man who wants his way."

Chapter Thirty-seven

BEATRICE HURRIED TO answer the tap at the door. Darwell had gone to the village with Callan on her half day, which suited Beatrice perfectly. She was doing her best to honor her father's demand that she stay in her rooms, but without Cecilia to talk to it was a challenge.

She tried to settle with a book but kept staring out the window instead. The only movement in the drive marked the comings and goings of the other guests. Michael and Olivia Garrett were out walking. Her sister and the marquis were riding, and Mrs. Wilson was sitting on a bench near the gate finding as little interest in her book as Beatrice did in hers.

Of Jess there was no sign. Could he have left? That would be so ungallant, so unkind, that she could not believe it possible. When the tap at the door came it was not imperative enough to be Jess, but she hurried to answer nonetheless.

Nora Kendrick stood there with Finch tucked under her arm. Today he was wearing a miniature cravat that matched the ribbons on his mistress's elegant green gown.

Nora gave a nod of greeting, her usual smiling demeanor absent. Finch gave a cheerful "woof" which was at odds with his mistress's serious expression.

"Beatrice," she began, "Miss Wilson has asked to speak to both of us."

"Of course," Beatrice said, giving only a moment's thought to her promise. Surely Papa would make an exception for a request of this type. Miss Wilson was grieving, after all, and Beatrice doubted her mother was much comfort.

"Do you know why she wishes to see us?" Beatrice asked as they walked the short distance to Katherine's bedchamber.

"I can guess, but only because Nicky mentioned the possibility."

Nicky? Of course, Nora was referring to the Earl of Belmont.

"It's very gratifying that I can help him in his inquiry," Nora said, with a small smile that quickly disappeared. "And very small of me to find pleasure in someone else's misery."

Beatrice was not sure how to respond to that. She opted for direct. "This is a difficult time for anyone connected to Lord Crenshaw, but you are not the only one entertained by the investigation. You cannot doubt that for all his solemnity the earl is having as much fun as I would have if I discovered a previously unknown Rembrandt drawing."

"Thank you, Beatrice. That is very kind of you. And observant," she added with an appreciative smile.

"So, you think this invitation has something to do with Lord Crenshaw's death?"

"Nicky insisted that I come without any sort of opinion," she replied demurely.

Beatrice nodded, intrigued by the mystery. Her intrigue changed to distress when they turned the corner and saw Jess lounging against the wall outside of Katherine's room.

"What is he doing here?" she hissed.

"Miss Wilson asked for him to attend as well." Nora stopped walking. "Is that a problem? I realize that you and Jess have a somewhat undecided relationship at the moment, but I was hoping you could rise above your concerns. Was I wrong?"

"No, no." She thought about explaining her father's insistence that she stay in her room and have nothing to do with Jess, but she was not sure it was something a woman as independent as Nora would understand. "I was just surprised to see him, that's all." The insane beating of her heart made that a gross understatement.

He looked as wonderful as he ever did. No circles under his eyes from a sleepless night. No blotchy complexion from crying. The thought of him crying into his pillow made her smile a little. He must have quite misinterpreted that because he smiled back, not that devilish I'm-looking-for-trouble-and-here-she-is smile that would always be her undoing, but a cynical I've-seen-it-all twist of the lips that made her feel they could never be friends again.

Oh, how she wished that they could be friends, more than friends. She closed her eyes against the force of his presence and made herself face the truth and not what she wished was the truth. Their interlude had been a moment of weakness on her part, on both their parts, probably. It was not true love but lust, a word that sounded no prettier than what it meant. She kept the word in mind as she opened her eyes and curtsied to him.

He bowed in return, then the three took a moment to compose themselves before Jess knocked on the door.

Katherine herself opened it, holding it back so they could enter. Her room was not a suite like the one Cecilia and Beatrice shared, but it was a generous space with some lovely paintings and a large sitting area around the fireplace. There was a small fire burning gently on the grate, despite the overall warmth of the day.

Beatrice and Nora sat at Katherine's invitation. Jess remained standing a little away from the rest of them. He nodded to Nora, and the understanding that she would be in charge of the discussion passed between them.

Apparently prompted by the earl's behavior in other parts of the investigation, Nora waited for Katherine Wilson to speak. In the little while that took, Beatrice noticed Katherine's red-rimmed eyes and red-tipped nose. She was no prettier than any other woman who had been crying her heart out.

Beatrice never would have guessed that Katherine's heart had become involved so quickly. Yet it was possible, as she had seen with Cecilia and the marquis. If she was being totally honest, she would admit that she would cry her heart out, too, if it had been Jess who had fallen to his death.

Did that mean she was in love with him? She straightened a little. What else would you call this feeling of loss, of incompleteness? But love was such an important word, so significant, and it would hurt too much if it was one-sided.

No, yes, no. She had been thinking in circles since yesterday. It did not help at all that this was the first time she had seen him today. Should she try to talk to him about what he intended to do? Her father had made her swear she would not. Oh, it was so hard to be a dutiful daughter when your life, your future hung in the balance.

Beatrice turned to look at him and found him staring at her, at her back to be more precise.

His expression was intense, as though he could read something in her posture that was an answer to a question he had been considering for hours, days, years even. Then Jess shook his head, looking like he'd decided she was not, after all, the answer for which he'd been searching.

Stung, she showed him her back and tried to give Katherine her complete attention.

Katherine opened her mouth, but before she could speak, she was overcome with sobs. Finch jumped out of Nora's arms and leaned against the girl's leg, offering the canine version of comfort.

Beatrice moved to sit next to her on the small sofa. "Do stop crying, Katherine. You will make yourself sick."

"It's what I deserve. It's what I deserve," she said

over and over again. Finally she explained. "I killed Lord Crenshaw."

A stunned silence filled the room.

"That's not possible, Katherine," Beatrice said after a quick look at Nora, who looked more puzzled than shocked. "You are too gently bred to hurt anything or anyone. The other day you saw a mouse and would not hear of calling the housekeeper."

As Beatrice spoke she stroked a hand down Katherine's back and could not help but notice how tense she was. "If you do not stop crying, you will not be able to give us the true account of what happened. Clearly it weighs on you and we want to help."

Nora leaned forward and took the girl's other hand. "Tell us what happened, Katherine."

Katherine sniffed, finally calmed by Nora's gentle voice.

Jess had moved over to stand closer to the fireplace, his expression one of casual interest. Beatrice could tell by the way he held his fist tight by his side that his composure was all an act. She could almost hear him thinking, *Here is one more life that Crenshaw has damaged.*

"Lord Crenshaw sent me a note asking me to meet him at the banqueting platform in order to watch Cecilia and Lord Destry's race. I thought it rather unusual and asked Mama what I should do. It was she who decided it was all right for me to go without a chaperone. That we would be out in public with others near enough. She was very anxious to promote our acquaintance."

Her mother was anxious, Beatrice thought. It did not sound like the girl had been as interested.

"Lord Crenshaw and I waited and waited for the race to come our way, but it was taking the longest time and he grew annoyed as he tended to do when time failed to march to his plan." Katherine paused and dabbed at the last of the tears running down her cheeks. "Then he asked me to marry him."

Beatrice and Nora exchanged startled glances. That was not what they expected.

"I was surprised. It was so soon. I was flattered, of course, and told him so, but asked if I could think about it awhile."

That was sensible. Beatrice leaned a little closer, and Finch dashed back to Nora. Even Jess straightened and focused more fully on Katherine, who began to twist her handkerchief.

"You see, I'd had a conversation with Lord Jess, and it gave me pause." She looked up at Jess. "If you will forgive me, my lord. Mama said that you could only be expected to speak ill of him, but when I spoke to Mr. Garrett after our conversation he assured me that you were telling the truth when you said that Lord Crenshaw was not always kind where ladies were concerned."

Not always kind? Beatrice was amazed at his choice of words. Crenshaw had used and abused his wife to the point of death.

Instead of being offended by this part of her story, Jess bowed a little. "How wise of you to find someone as sensible as Mr. Garrett with whom to speak."

She shrugged off his words and went on. "I wanted some time to make sure that even considering a courtship, much less agreeing to marry Lord Crenshaw, was the right decision."

She never would have counted sensibleness as one of Katherine's virtues. Beatrice was impressed.

Finally Katherine turned from Jess to look at Beatrice, then Nora Kendrick. "When I asked for time to consider, Lord Crenshaw changed before my eyes. He was furious with me. His anger was out of all proportion to my request. I did not reject him," she said urgently. "I may be inexperienced, but I do understand a man's pride is at stake in a situation like this. But it was too soon." She almost wailed the last.

"Of course, you handled a difficult situation very well," Nora said, though Beatrice wondered how she could know that when they had not heard the end of the story yet.

"He grabbed me and began shouting, insisting he would shake some sense into me. I was afraid that he was going to hit me and I pulled myself from his grip, backing away until I was leaning against the railing of the platform. I had no place to go." She stopped and drew a breath to fortify herself.

Beatrice was desperate to know what had happened and was annoyed that Katherine had to stop to breathe.

"Crenshaw lunged for me, and I stepped out of his reach. He fell against the railing where I had been standing, and it gave way. Lord Crenshaw tumbled to the ground before I could do anything to save him."

Beatrice was about to point out that if Katherine had reached for him, she would have fallen also, quite possibly to her death as well. But before she could say anything Nora asked, "What did you do then?"

"I ran down the steps, and saw by the way his head was bent that his neck was broken. His eyes were open, but staring without anger or any other emotion. I knew he was dead." Tears poured from her eyes, but she was unaware of them. "I was afraid I would be ruined if I was found with the body, so I ran back to the house."

"Have you told anyone else?" Nora asked.

Her mother, Beatrice thought.

"No," she said firmly. "When I came back, I managed to stay calm and told Mama that I'd decided not to go to the platform, and that if Lord Crenshaw wanted to spend time with me he could do it someplace more conventional. She was annoyed, but at that point there was nothing she could do."

She dropped her head. It was sad to see all the happiness drained from her. Katherine was a shadow of the young woman whose company she and her sister had enjoyed over the last two weeks.

"I could not live with it anymore," she admitted. "I had to tell someone. I thought of the two of you," she glanced at Nora and Beatrice, "since you both have been so kind to me. And Lord Jess is here because he can verify our previous conversation."

Did she think she was going to be accused of pushing Lord Crenshaw over the edge of the platform? Beatrice supposed it could have happened that way, but it was, as she had observed at the beginning of this conversation, not at all in Katherine's nature.

She herself might do it, Beatrice thought, to save her life or her sister's. Nora Kendrick might, but still only to save someone else. Or to save Finch, who was clearly as important to her as any human being. Even Mrs. Wilson could probably bring herself to do it, if it meant her life or possibly her daughter's, but Katherine herself would hesitate a moment too long.

Nora drew Beatrice's attention, and they changed seats. The older woman took Katherine's hands in hers, compelling Katherine to look her in the eye.

"I must tell Belmont your story, which is what I assume you intended when you invited me to hear it."

Katherine nodded, looking relieved that she would not have to recount it again.

"I can tell you now that it will make no difference to his inquiry. You were a witness and a completely innocent party."

"Thank you." Katherine breathed the phrase as if finally releasing a burden that was growing increasingly difficult to bear.

"What do you want to happen now, Katherine?"

Beatrice loved the way Nora phrased that question and looked at Jess for his reaction. There was a gentle smile on his face which Beatrice read as compassion. It made her appreciate, not love, him all the more.

"Please, I beg of you. Do not tell Mama."

"Of course not," Nora said.

"You may rest assured that we will keep this story in confidence," Jess said. It was the first time he had spoken, and Katherine accepted his male voice as law.

"When this is all settled, I want to go home. I want to see my old governess. She is still caring for my sisters who are not yet out. She will understand."

They talked for a few more minutes, making plans that might not survive the hour, but Katherine was all the better for it. When the three of them left the girl, her maid had returned with tea. She had a caring air that reassured Beatrice that Katherine was in good hands.

When they were in the passage, Beatrice turned to go back to her room when Nora stopped her.

"Please. Both of you, come with me. Belmont may have some questions and your insights might prove helpful."

Once again, Beatrice did not hesitate. But for the love of God, let her father be somewhere else on the property. He might not have Lord Crenshaw's temper, but she did not want to make life more difficult for any of her family.

Chapter Thirty-eight

THEY FINISHED THEIR meeting with Belmont just in time to attend the service for Lord Crenshaw in Havenhall's tiny chapel. Jess watched as the various guests and some of the staff entered and took seats in the short rows that seated four on each side of the center aisle.

The countess took the first row on the right with Destry as her escort. The row behind her was empty.

Across the aisle the Earl of Belmont and Mrs. Kendrick sat in front of Mrs. Wilson and her daughter. Olivia came in at the last minute, trailing a scent of apples and cinnamon that made Jess hope there might be cake this evening. When she saw him sitting in the last row, she slid in next to him, pressing a kiss to his cheek.

"I feel a fraud being here," she whispered. "I barely knew the man, but hated him more than I hate yeast that fails."

"Lollie," Jess said, using a childhood nickname that still suited her, "there are times when I wonder how you can be married to a man of God."

"I am just being honest, which Michael would applaud, and I assure you that I am going to pray for Crenshaw's soul."

"Don't you think it's too late to spare him the fires of hell?"

"Michael would say he may have repented at the last moment and no prayers are ever wasted." She wrinkled her nose. "That has burdened me with an image of God, or maybe St. Peter, busy all the time routing prayers to where they are needed most."

She settled herself, closing her eyes, her brow furrowed in concentration. Jess watched her, wishing that prayers were all that were needed to right his world.

Beatrice came in with her father and sister and they moved toward seats in the second row, directly behind the countess as Mervis directed. Beatrice lagged behind her family, turning to look at Jess. She seemed weighed down with a distress that he was sure had little to do with Crenshaw. He nodded to her. It was not pride or some high opinion of himself that convinced him that he was the cause of her upset. It was the ache in his own heart.

She neither turned away from him nor responded to his gesture, but continued to stare at him with a sadness that was painful to see.

He wished there was something he could do to make her curious again, to make her exclaim, "What fun!," to make her understand that in another world he would have loved her forever. In this world, in the life he had created for himself, his love would corrupt her until she hated him and he hated himself even more.

Several of the senior staff and gentlemen of the house, like the curator, Mr. Hogarth, filled in the empty rows. The chapel was full when the Reverend Michael Garrett came into the sanctuary, dressed in a simple purple vestment perfectly suited to the occasion.

Jess watched Beatrice's back. He loved reading her by the way she angled her head. At the moment it was bent low, most likely in prayer, and he could see the sweet curve of her neck, so vulnerable, so untouched.

"Not all of us here mourn the passing of Arthur Crenshaw."

That drew everyone's attention. Jess watched as Beatrice raised her head abruptly, angling it to one side as if she was not sure she had heard correctly.

"It's as though he is speaking directly to me," Olivia whispered. "I'm not sure if I hate or love the way he can do that."

Jess nodded absently, well aware that Garrett was speaking directly to him. What did Olivia have to regret? Some unkind thoughts? Had any other person in this chapel wished Crenshaw dead? Thought killing him was the best possible solution? And though it was one more thing that would damn him to hell, Jess felt no remorse.

"We are each created in God's image and likeness. That may become distorted as we age. But you and I, the living, should find joy in the chance we still have to rediscover that blessing of goodness. The blessing that came with us into the world and is with us always."

Garrett paused as though he wanted everyone to think about his words. Jess watched Beatrice lean forward in her pew, seemingly engrossed in what Michael was saying.

"Arthur Crenshaw has no more time to prove himself. May God have mercy on his soul."

Jess supposed that was as close as the Reverend Mr. Garrett would come to saying that Crenshaw deserved to burn in hell.

"But!" Garrett made the word an exclamation. "There is no rule that says we who are still embracing the joy of life must continue on the road we have chosen so far."

Beatrice wiggled in her seat, and Jess understood the discomfort those words could arouse.

"We are free to choose another path at this moment, tomorrow, or at the moment of death." He paused and added, "All those choices are the same to God, who does not measure time as we do."

To Jess, Olivia whispered, "But what if you think you are on the right path? How do you know for sure?"

"My wife has asked me more than once how we can know if we are on the right path. The answer is very, very simple. Do you love life and what you are doing with it? Are you happy? Do you make others happy? Then you are doing exactly what God wills. If not, then what would it take to make you happy?"

Beatrice, Jess thought, before he could control his answer. Her sweetness, her love of life, her intensity. All those qualities that made the world new for him when he saw it through her eyes.

He loved Beatrice Brent.

There was no point in lying to himself. And then he marveled at his selfishness. She might be able to save him, but what could he offer her?

He watched her bend her head, resting her forehead on her folded hands, in a pose of prayerful intensity.

Jess could not take his eyes from her, could not hear anything but his heart's insistence that he loved her, and his head shouting that he had nothing to offer her but a jaded heart.

He did not hear any of the rest of the short service. When it was over, he stood and, before anyone could capture his attention, left the chapel. It was amazingly stuffy and the smell of incense was making his eyes water.

"WE HAVE HAD the loveliest weather these past two weeks." Cecilia made a face at her inane attempt at conversation. She and William should be beyond such commonplace topics.

William turned in his saddle. "Even the rain has come mostly at night. How convenient for us."

They rode on, not side by side, but with Cecilia following. The groom was almost out of sight. The trail was narrow here and the horses walked languidly, all of them enjoying the shade. There was a reason one rode in the morning like this, especially in summer. It was warm, and would grow warmer still, judging by the angle of the sun and the merest scattering of clouds.

Cecilia could not even *think* an original thought. All her original thoughts settled on one thing. Kissing William. Again. And again.

They had reached the ford, which was now exposed without water running over it, the river at its summer low. There were one or two pools in the shade of the hawthorns with ferns along the edge. The trout would be there, she thought, waiting for cooler temperatures and stronger currents.

The river as a topic of discussion was marginally better than the weather. But when she raised her head to speak to William, he was watching her with such longing that "kissing William" was the only phrase that she could think of.

"Cecilia," he began, and before he could say another word, she urged her horse across the ford and up the hill at a pace that would preclude conversation. *Please do not bring up marriage again*. As much as she might want it, the thought terrified her. She was not ready to say yes, but the last thing she ever wanted was to hurt him.

He followed her, caught up, and paced himself beside her horse, both moving faster than was safe in an open field with which neither was familiar.

"You can run, but eventually I will catch you," he shouted over the pounding hooves. "Cecilia, stop and talk to me before one of our horses finds a rabbit hole."

He was right. She did not want to hurt him in any way, but avoiding him was just as bad.

Slowing, Cecilia turned back to the quiet river and one of those pools where they could be comfortable while she ruined his day, if not his life.

"This glade is flawless," she announced, fascinated. She tried to concentrate on the way the sun filtered through the leaves, casting light but not heat. "I've passed this spot once or twice before and never stopped to study it. Do you think these stones and that boulder were moved here deliberately?"

"By some landscape architect bent on creating a

haven even better than nature could?" William asked as they dismounted and let their horses drink.

"Yes, but he did his work too perfectly." She twirled around, her head raised heavenward. "If the weather was always like this I think I could live here."

"It would be the perfect setting for you. I should like someone to paint you seated on that rock, surrounded by one of the few beauties that are comparable to yours."

"No one paints portraits like that," she said, trying to steer the conversation to something less personal.

"Only because they have not yet thought of it. Or seen you sitting here." He walked around her as though he were an artist considering the pose. "If I could, I would have such a haven as this created for you, but our gardens at home are not this verdant. The climate is not welcoming. Even in the summer." He considered the idea for a moment. "There is a house in the Lake District that would suit. We could live there."

So he was simply going to pretend that he had already proposed and ignore the truth. She was not going to play that game. "My lord," she said formally, "you have not even spoken to my father yet."

"Because I listened to you and, on your advice, I am waiting until he is in better humor. And a sound suggestion it was, because it later occurred to me that I should see if the lady is willing before I approach her father."

She shook her head. "William, I cannot marry you." Which was not the truth but was easier than trying to explain how she felt.

"You are already married? You are mad for another? Your sister is older and must marry first?"

She shook her head at the absurd questions.

"Then tell me, Cecilia, because I do not believe you."

"We have not known each other long." That sounded tentative even to her own ears and, as expected, he waved her excuse away without comment.

"You are impulsive, even your best friends say that, and I am afraid you only think you love me because I am beautiful and you want it to be true." There. She had told him the truth and it actually felt good to have it in the open so she went on. "Once you have time and distance to think about it you will realize that it was only an infatuation."

William jumped off the rock, anger radiating from him in waves. "Do not tell me what I feel, Cecilia Brent. Do not tell me that this all-consuming need to be with you is not love. Do not tell me that I am too impulsive when this feeling has driven me since the moment I met you, until I drink hoping to forget it, ride too hard hoping to escape it." He shook his head. "I love you."

The way he spoke the words made it sound more like damnation than his salvation.

She had never seen him angry before. Now that she thought about it, she'd never even seen him a trifle annoyed. He was always in good humor—until now. It was more reassuring than frightening.

"My apologies, William. Your unfailing good spirits tricked me into thinking that you are not serious about anything. I see that I am wrong."

He exhaled, a short, sharp breath, but said nothing. She could see the anger was still with him in the set of his mouth, the rigid way he held his body, and the fact that he was standing perfectly still.

She stood straight, too. "I still cannot marry you." She swallowed. He was not the only one who could give a speech, so she began. "You are the finest man I have ever met. I must love you. I must, because I am miserable without you and your anger does not frighten me. The fact that you are several inches shorter than I seems to be the ideal size and I want to kiss you as much as I want to bury my face in the sweetest roses."

He took her hand and kissed it, but was wise enough to wait for the "but" that was coming.

"And I am so afraid that it cannot last forever. It is too great a gift from God to be true."

"Of course it cannot last forever."

She stopped.

"It will only grow stronger and better. Can you doubt that being together in every way is better than kissing? That sharing children is more complete than anything we have yet experienced?"

Oh dear, she thought. He was winning. She could feel her doubts fading, her longing invading her, overtaking her wisdom and banishing it to the back of her mind.

"Cecilia, my dearest, if you are not sure, then I will not propose to you. I will wait. And if that is not a gesture of the purest love then nothing is."

That was true, she thought. Patience was not often his to command.

"I will speak to your father for his permission to court you, but I will not propose until you wish it."

That would please Papa. At least she hoped it would.

"You can enjoy the Season, dance with every man who asks. It will be a trial for me, but I give it to you with all the love my heart can hold."

"Oh, William." She was lost now and could not regret it.

"My impulse bows to your sensibility."

They kissed, each reaching for the other at the same moment. It was as much a commitment as any words could be. And the embrace lasted far longer than their conversation had.

When they were apart and breathing more normally, William reached out for her hand.

"I ask only two things in return."

Her natural caution was not completely forsaken. "And those are?"

"First, if you do find someone more to your liking, you will tell me in a private meeting before it is announced to the rest of society."

"Oh, William, of course I would, but I do not see how that could ever happen." There could never be anyone else. "And the other?"

"That you come wading with me."

Cecilia remembered that earlier meeting, one of their first, when he had made the same invitation. She had been shocked at the time. This time she gave in to the impulse. For now she understood that this was a man who would listen to her, allowing her words to calm him just as his sense of adventure would brighten her world.

"What a perfect spot for wading." She gave him her hand. "Yes. Let's wade in, my lord. But not too deep this first time."

Chapter Thirty-nine

BEATRICE STOOD AT the window, watching the drive, feeling sorry for herself. There really was no other way to describe her mood.

What a dismal end to what had started as a fabulous adventure.

Papa was not speaking to her. Cecilia had been moved to another room so that Beatrice could not even have the comfort of her support. Even Darwell had abandoned her, off to find their trunks so she could begin packing for their return to Birmingham.

Beatrice's bedchamber felt like prison, most likely what her father intended. Would Jess have to leave before she was allowed out of her room? What would it take for her father to reconsider his punishment?

The answer came in the form of a horse and rider ambling up the drive. There was a flat case perched on the back of the horse. That alone would identify the rider as Roger Tremaine. She pushed open the window and leaned out, not caring that she looked like a house-maid about to shake out a dust rag.

"Roger! Roger!" she called out, waving madly. "How wonderful to see you."

He looked around, behind, and finally up, and returned her wave with a simple, much less enthusiastic gesture. That was Roger, always calm and ordered. Beatrice knew he was as thrilled to see her as she was to see him.

It took all of fifteen minutes to send one of the footmen for her father. The countess came with him and Beatrice was sure it was entirely due to her presence that her father allowed her to welcome Roger.

Beatrice reached the hall just as her friend entered it. She threw her arms around his neck, certain that he was the exact medicine she needed right now.

"Beatrice! Do behave." Despite the snub, he hugged her back and then held her at arm's length.

"Let's go for a walk, please," she said with such urgency she knew he would realize it was important for them to talk.

"Yes, let's walk. It's exactly what I need after hours in the saddle. Shall I take time to freshen up or is it so urgent that you can tolerate the smell of horse?"

"No need to freshen up for me," she said with a forced gaiety, suddenly realizing that the footmen were silent but very much present.

Roger took her arm and with a word to the porter about his bags they were out the door again. They walked in silence at first, Beatrice finding comfort in his very presence.

There was a bench under a tree within sight of the drive so it was a perfectly acceptable place for an unchaperoned couple to sit. It had the added benefit of being in the shade, which she hoped would give them some relief from the heavy heat of the day.

"Roger," Beatrice began without preamble. "I am in such trouble. Really. Father is furious with me and he will not even let Cecilia talk to me. It's as though he has disowned me."

The ache in her heart eased a little when Roger took her hand. She leaned against his shoulder. She could feel his heart beating steadily. That's what Roger was. Steady as a sheltered flame. She knew that she would find that steadiness monumentally boring in a mate, but right now it was exactly what she needed.

"You know he will see reason, Beatrice."

"I have not even told you what I did."

"It does not matter what you did. He is your father and he loves you."

His confidence bolstered hers a little. But she wanted an informed opinion, not a sentimental one. "He says I ruined Ceci's chance at a successful Season."

"Nothing is going to compromise Cecilia's Season, for reasons too often recounted for me to repeat." He patted her hand. "But, my dear girl, you are to have a Season as well, find a match, and enjoy every art gallery in town."

"You know it was always more important to Cecilia than it was to me."

"What else is there, Beatrice?"

"So much it will take awhile to explain." Beatrice drew a breath and recounted the details relevant to her confession of spending time alone with Jess.

"So the earl is certain Lord Crenshaw's death was an accident?"

"Yes." Beatrice thought for a moment about how to phrase the next. "There was a witness who wishes to remain unnamed but before any of that came to light, Lord Jess was a prime suspect. So I had to tell everyone that we were alone together, for almost an hour. And you know how Papa feels about Jessup Pennistan."

Roger pursed his lips and nodded. "Yes, and your father would see it as a deliberate effort on your part to disobey him." He leaned away so he could see her face. "Was it something more?"

She looked down and nodded. "It was for me. It still is."

"But not for Lord Jessup?" Roger said with the tiniest edge to his voice.

"Yes. No. I'm not sure, but I think so. Roger," she said, turning to him so he could see how serious she was. "Despite his reputation, Jess is very much a gentleman. I know that in my heart. I have seen him at his best." *And his worst.* But she kept that to herself.

"Then you will wait and see what he and your father decide."

That was not comforting. Not at all. "I will not marry someone who offers because my father insists. I cannot imagine anything more humiliating."

"Then you will spend the rest of your life in Birmingham, in your father's house. But we will always be friends, Beatrice. No matter what happens."

"Thank you, Roger." She put her head on his shoulder again. Beatrice wished his heart would beat a little faster when she was near or her heart would give that little leap the way it did when she saw Jess. But it never would.

Roger had been right. They were friends, dear and

good friends, and would never be anything more. Or less.

JESS WATCHED THE cozy scene from the window of the room where he was waiting for the countess.

Who *was* that man with Beatrice? Roger Tremaine, the name swam up from his memory. A good friend, she had said. He could see that. How good a friend exactly, he wondered.

He was so engrossed in trying to decipher what they were discussing that he did not hear the countess come into the room.

"Good day, Jess."

He turned around, feeling caught out like a schoolboy. The countess came to the window anyway.

"What are you looking at?" She followed the line of his gaze. "I see," the countess said. "It's not what you're looking at but whom."

"Beatrice is talking with her friend Roger Tremaine."

"A fine young man," the countess said. "His father is General Tremaine, one of the heroes of the Battle of Corunna. Of course he was only a captain then."

What was Tremaine's connection to the family? Oh yes—he was not in the army at all, but he worked for Mr. Brent. Not that it mattered to Jess.

God help him, he couldn't even lie convincingly to himself anymore. Of course it mattered. He didn't want anyone closer to Beatrice than he was. If this was love then it was a damn painful state.

The countess's quick glance from the corner of her eye told him she had the same thought. "He works for, or perhaps I should say he works with, Mr. Brent. He designs machines and machine parts for Mr. Brent's mills."

"Yes, I do recall. She introduced me to him that first night." Which now seemed about a hundred years ago. "The only thing he has designs on right now is Beatrice."

The countess laughed and pulled him away from the window. "They are friends, Jess. They could have been well on the road to marriage long ago if either of them wanted it."

The countess took a seat in front of a desk that was laden with objets d'art and not a single ledger or book. Jess leaned against the edge of the desk, too restless to sit down himself.

"It's time for you to decide what you are going to do about this mess with Beatrice, Jess."

He stiffened, even though he'd known that was what the countess had on her mind. "I am not a schoolboy who needs to be led through the moves on a chessboard."

"This is not a game, Jessup Pennistan." The sternness in her voice was resoundingly maternal. "You have compromised a young woman's reputation."

"Yes, yes, I have, to my great and lifelong regret."

"Though I can guess it was a mutual effort."

Jess could not believe those words had come out of the lady's mouth.

"Beatrice's curiosity about life, and now love, is the bane of her father's existence. He might be more understanding of your situation than you think. He told me once that he found Beatrice attempting to run one of the devices at his first mill. It fouled the machine for hours and she nearly lost her hand, all because she was curious about how it worked."

"I am going to offer for her."

The countess closed her eyes and shook her head. "Of course you are. The girl deserves at least that show of respect."

"We agree on that, my lady. I am going to find her father now."

The countess stood up and made for the door. "Love makes fools of us all. For men like you, being a fool comes with serious complications."

Her words hung in the room even after she left. Jess was going to find Brent as soon as he pulled his thoughts together, as soon as he found a way to word his offer as the apology it was.

Chapter Forty

BEFORE JESS COULD decide whether he should bow to Mr. Brent or offer to shake his hand, the door burst open and Destry and Cecilia exploded into the room, filling the space with excitement. More than excitement. Pure joy.

"We have been looking everywhere for you, my lord," Cecilia said as she gave an artless curtsy and then hurried over to embrace him.

He was so taken aback he did not respond, but instead looked at Destry with "What the hell?" in his eyes.

"Yes, Cecilia has caught some of my impulsiveness," Des said to him. To her he spoke with a voice of gentle, if somewhat sickening, affection. "Dearest, I think you are embarrassing Jess."

With an expression of good-humored apology she stepped back and came to take Destry's arm.

"Cecilia and I have come to an understanding." He

kissed her hand. "We wanted you to be the first to know that we are *not* engaged."

Cecilia giggled and kissed Destry on the top of his head.

"Cecilia is going to stun society with her charm, good nature, and all-too-obvious beauty during the Season. Then, and only then, she will decide if I am worthy to be her husband."

To Jess, blinded by their smiles, it looked like that choice was already made.

They beamed at each other.

"God help me. Will you two stop torturing me with your good humor?"

"We wanted you to be the first to know that we have no announcement to make."

"Wonderful. I am very happy for you. Or should I say that I am not at all happy to hear your non-announcement. Now unless you can solve my problem, go away and leave me alone."

"You have a problem?" Cecilia said.

"Of course, we can help." Destry strode farther into the room.

Cecilia took Jess's arm and led him to the sofa that the countess had just vacated. "Sit next to me and tell us all about it."

What had he done? What could be more stupid than asking two lovesick fools how to make a proposal that was really an apology?

Destry wandered over to the window and peered out of it. "Who is Beatrice talking to?"

Cecilia rose from the sofa and joined him at the window, resting her hand on Destry's shoulder. "Oh! Roger is back."

Destry turned to look at Jess. "Aha, so he is your problem."

Cecilia came back to the sofa but did not sit down.

"You have nothing to worry about. He already refused Beatrice's proposal. They are merely very good friends."

"Beatrice proposed to him?" Jess made sure he had heard that correctly.

"Just before the party started. She and Papa had an argument. He wanted her to find a match and she said this house party was about preparing for London and not about finding a match. So she decided to make it impossible by attending the house party already betrothed to someone. But Roger was not about to ruin his alliance with Papa's company, even for Beatrice."

"Wonderful, but Roger is not my problem. Beatrice is."

"Yes, I can see how it will be a challenge for you to find a way to have Papa accept you. He is so set against you and so angry with Beatrice for finding such trouble that I cannot believe he would consider you even if you offered him the business opportunity of a lifetime."

"I am not going to do that."

"Of course not. If and when you reclaim that land it is family property. But, I was thinking that you could offer to lease him the mine, just as Roger gives him exclusive use of his creative work."

"Why would your father be interested in that?" he said, his mind spinning. "Why would a mill owner want to lease a coal mine?"

"Because it would give him more control. If there is one thing Papa does not like, it is surprises. If he knew where the coal to power the mills was coming from, and any problems there might be with supply, then he would have more control, would he not?"

Destry and Jess exchanged looks of amazement. "You thought of this yourself?" Jess asked.

"It is obvious, is it not? It's like a lady having a seamstress on her staff, and a draper's shop that always calls when new fabric arrives, and a milliner who saves the best hats for her. Darwell and I have been talking about how to create that sort of coterie when one is new to town."

Destry shook his head, kneeled on the sofa beside her, and kissed her. "Of course you are right." He jumped down and came to stand in front of Jess. If William tried to kiss him, there was a punch coming his way.

"Jess, you could apply the same concept to almost anything that interests you. Horses! If you want a horse to win races you must control the breeding, the training, and the track. It makes perfect sense."

"I'm so happy I could help," Cecilia said, her smile now self-satisfied as well as joyous. "Now when you talk to Papa you have something to offer him that will make him rethink his opposition to a match."

"Thank you. You both have been so helpful. But making a match is not my problem."

"We're ready for the next one, then," Cecilia said encouragingly, "but I only have a few minutes before I must change for dinner."

Jess shook his head. How to explain that a marriage to him was not what was best for her sister. "I think this problem is something that only I can resolve."

He was surprised when they did not insist, but left

him, taking their happiness with them. Perhaps there were more people with whom they wanted to share their non-announcement. Jess went back to the window. Beatrice was gone. Off to dress for dinner, too, he guessed.

Michael Garrett came in as he headed for the door.

"That meddling fool Destry sent you, didn't he? I do not need his help, or yours or God's for that matter. Now leave me alone."

"Destry suggested the same, that I leave you alone, but Olivia wanted me to tell you that we will be leaving in the morning. I consider that a divine message of sorts. Not that we're leaving but that she sent me to tell you. Jess—"

Jess had had enough. Enough angry women, happy couples, and well-meaning idiot vicars. With no warning and hardly any forethought he lashed out at Garrett with a blow that would have downed a lesser man.

Garrett staggered back, shook his head to stop what had to be ringing in his ears, and pulled his cravat back into place. "So that's the kind of prayer you're wanting. I'm not sure that's what Jesus meant but I've turned a few moneylenders on their ass in my day. Let me see if I still have what it takes."

He didn't. Jess knew violence had been no part of Michael Garrett's life for too long, so he gave the village vicar the opening he needed, did not defend himself, and let Michael floor him with a swing that had heat if not power.

"Thinking about suicide, are you?" Michael was panting, more in anger, Jess suspected, than exertion. "You cabbage-headed fool."

Garrett pulled Jess off the floor, dropped him onto

the sofa, and towered over him. "You Pennistans are all idiots when it comes to love. Every one of you except Olivia, who knew what she wanted and near had me killed before she was done." That gave him pause. "Of course, it could be that it's not just Pennistans but men in general." Garrett sat in the wingback chair that was at a right angle to the sofa and thought for a moment.

"That would mean Destry's the exception that proves the rule," Jess suggested.

"William is the exception to almost every rule," Garrett said, and Jess had to laugh.

"He surely knew he wanted Cecilia straight off and no one was going to deny him."

"And when did you know that Beatrice was what you wanted?"

Jess pulled himself up on the sofa, put his booted feet on the floor and wished for drink. Instead he put his head in his hands. "When Des and Cecilia came in. Who knew that lovesickness was contagious?" He wiped his face and looked at Garrett, whose expression all but shouted "Liar!"

"Or when I saw her with that man who works for her father an hour ago. Out the window over there." He gestured with his chin.

Now Jess smiled. He could not help it. He knew. If he was being totally honest, he knew. "Not the first time I saw her. That just lit the fuse. It was a long fuse but it burned very fast. It was not when I stepped on her spectacles, not when we trooped through the secret passage or flirted our way through dinner." His memory was amazingly good with cards but apparently even better where Beatrice Brent was concerned.

"I knew when I kissed her the first time," he admitted, thinking about the way she had touched her tongue to his mouth. *The complete trust of her kiss, the truest gift of her heart.* "The way she made me feel complete."

"Thank God, Jess, and welcome to the club." Garrett tilted his head back and closed his eyes, as if what had just transpired had been as much work for him as honesty had been for Jess.

"But—" Jess began, and this time Garrett interrupted him.

"You are not the wrong person for her. Listen to me. She is the right person for you. You are not going to ruin her, she is going to be the making of you."

He heard Garrett's words from the service. *You can change now, tomorrow, next week, or at the point of death.* Why wait?

"Believe me when I tell you that with Beatrice by your side even the old experiences will be new."

Making love, for one, Jess thought, suddenly restless with wanting.

"Now all you have to do is convince her father that you are the man for his daughter."

Jess suffered a moment of panic, and then smiled. "I think I know a way to do that."

Chapter Forty-one

"AN INTERESTING PROPOSAL, my lord." Abel Brent rubbed his chin. "Almost as interesting as realizing that you have some brains in that head of yours."

Jess swallowed the insult and waited, wondering if he should admit it was all Cecilia's idea. Hell, no. It might have been her idea but he was the one who *had brains enough* to see it as a viable business idea.

The silence between them stretched. Finally Brent began to nod, as though he was almost convinced. "The idea of controlling a fuel source is new to me. I'd thought of investing in a ship but your suggestion expands that concept and opens up other opportunities." Brent leaned back in his chair. "Mr. Garrett and his wife took me aside this afternoon and told me the truth about Crenshaw's divorce."

Just could not let me handle this myself, could you two? That's what families did, he guessed. He would call it meddling. They would respond, "For your own good."

"It does not change my disgust with you for taking advantage of my daughter. I know she can be provocative but I would have thought you were worldly enough to resist that particular temptation."

"I thought so, too, Mr. Brent. We were both wrong. Beatrice is an amazing woman, curious and inquisitive, generous and loving. But I am sure you know all that already."

"Harumph" was Brent's only reply.

Jess knew he should apologize for his behavior but it would be a lie to say he was sorry for it. "I'm sorry for the pain I caused her, sir. I apologize for the embarrassment I caused you and her sister and the countess. I was hoping that you would accept my apology and we could move on."

"So you have the land back from Lord Crenshaw's estate?"

"Not yet, sir," Jess admitted, "but I have already taken steps in that direction and am assured that the land is not part of the entail."

"Hmmm, we'll see."

"But I do not need to wait for the eventuality. My family owns other land that is mined and I am sure that something can be worked out to our families' mutual advantage."

"Does not your brother have first claim on that?"

"Not if I think of it before him."

Brent made a sound that was part laughter and part respect.

"For how long would you be willing to lease the property, my lord? And the mining rights?"

Here was the hard part, Jess thought. "For as long as Beatrice will allow it."

"What does that mean?"

"I want to marry your daughter, sir. I would have said that I will lease the land to you as long as our marriage lasts, but since I have been involved in a divorce already, that might not convey the depth of my commitment to her."

"You want to marry her? Or is it that you feel compelled to offer for her after she provided you with an alibi?"

"My behavior with your daughter has not been admirable. But as someone pointed out to me recently, I can change any time I choose to. I choose to now, and with Beatrice at my side I know that change will last."

Mr. Brent shook his head and Jess's heart fell. Was he going to say no?

"The girl is willful and opinionated, my lord."

"Two things I love about her, sir."

Brent looked at him with interest, as his whole body relaxed a little. "She is endlessly curious."

"What I love best." Jess could not help smiling at the thought.

"You will give up gaming," the older man commanded. Jess's smile had apparently darkened Brent's mood again.

"That I cannot do," Jess said.

Brent's face went from dark to stormy.

"I will always take chances in life, but I will no longer do it in gaming hells. I took a chance when I offered you the coal mine."

Brent nodded and even smiled a little. There was no doubt in Jess's mind that Brent liked to gamble in his own way. How else to explain the man's willingness to let his daughter marry someone who only hoped to be able to provide the coal mine he had promised?

"I will gamble with you on the mining operation, on the ship-owning adventure. And I will take the biggest gamble of all."

"And that is?" Brent stood up.

"That Beatrice will accept my proposal and the two of us will take a chance on a future together. Forever."

"I am almost convinced."

Jess suspected that Beatrice's father had a sentimental streak ten feet wide.

"If you can convince my girl then I will permit it. But I warn you that if you break her heart, I will break you down to a man with no money, no reputation, and nothing but air to live on."

"If I hurt her, sir, it will be no less than I deserve."

JESS WANTED A drink to bolster his courage. He washed his face with cold water instead. He wanted to wait until evening when he would have a better sense of how she felt about him today. Instead he went to look for her right away.

At least he knew how to draw her attention and how to convey his feelings for her in a language she would understand.

Nora Kendrick had agreed to help him, telling him where and when he might run into her and Beatrice. He found the two walking through the art gallery, discussing various paintings.

Beatrice did not seem surprised to see him, which made Jess ever so grateful that Nora was on his side.

Nora excused herself, and Beatrice gave Finch back to his mistress reluctantly. "I think I shall have to find myself a puppy when I return home."

"The right sort can be amazingly good company," Nora agreed. "I can see if any of Finch's littermates have pups, if you would like."

"Thank you, the thought that I will hear from you once we leave Havenhall is delightful."

"Of course! I am sure we will be seeing each other as well. In London during the Season." She looked from Jess to Beatrice. "I have no doubt of it."

Nora Kendrick set Finch on the floor and he scampered ahead of her, out of the gallery, leaving Beatrice and Jess alone in the cavernous space that echoed a hundred other conversations.

"Beatrice Brent."

It was all he had to say for a blush to fly up from her neck to her cheeks.

"Yes, my lord."

"Will you take my arm and examine that Rembrandt drawing we discussed our first evening here?"

"If you wish."

"No, Beatrice," he said firmly, "if *you* wish."

She hesitated and he cursed himself. She could not leave before he even started.

"What I wish and what I can have are two very different things, my lord."

"Your father said that I could seek you out for this conversation."

"He did? And that gives you confidence enough to approach me?"

He laughed; he could not help it. "If I look confident

it is only because I have perfected a gamer's face these last years."

She cast her eyes to heaven but took his arm.

"Whereas you have a face as easy to read as a headline in *The Morning Post*." They began to walk. "Have you seen your sister and Des?"

Beatrice smiled. "Yes. They are so silly, acting as though they are the happy ending of a farce, but so in love you cannot laugh at them but must laugh with them."

"If they are a farce, what are we?"

"A failed production. Not a tragedy, too predictable to be a drama. I suffer too much heartache for it to be a comedy."

"But the end is not written yet."

"Yes, it is."

"Your version of the end sees you cozy in Birmingham with a dog for company, the loving aunt to as many children as Destry and Cecilia are blessed with."

"Studying and writing on the great artists. Do not forget that. My life will have purpose."

"My version of the end is somewhat different." They had reached the simple drawing she had used to explain Rembrandt's genius that first night, the small landscape with cottages and the distant windmill.

"This drawing has the most astounding simplicity that reveals its little world in detail." He wanted to say that it was just like her, but was not sure she would take it as the compliment he meant it to be.

"Do you recall when you explained to me what made a Rembrandt drawing a masterpiece?" On the chance that she did not, he repeated back the lesson. "The path to the cottage is a brown wash and the grasses beside it are really just five or six lines. But they convey to the eye a meaning beyond that."

"Yes." Beatrice gave a jerky nod that made him think her hands were probably shaking. He realized of a sudden that she was as tense as a string pulled tight. It would be best to put them both out of their misery.

"Beatrice." He took her hands and turned so he was facing her, the drawing at his back. "The phrase 'I love you' is nothing more than three words strung together in a sentence. I hope that when I say them to you, you can believe that they can mean as much as a hundred lines Rembrandt draws."

She bit her lip and shook her head just a little. She did not believe him.

"When I say 'I love you, Beatrice' it means I want to be a part of your life forever, that I want to die with your touch as the last thing I feel on this earth."

Her face drained of color and she did not smile.

"Between now and my last breath, I hope I can become the kind of person you could love, that I can someday earn the same respect from you that you have for your father, the same friendship you feel for Roger Tremaine, and the same love for me that I have for you."

Silence stretched between them. Did it take her that long to understand his words or to prepare a gracious rejection?

"Do you mean what you are saying, Jess, or are you just being polite?"

He kissed each of her hands before he went on. He truly had work to do to earn her trust. "Here I am being as much of a poet as I can be, putting my heart before you with nothing to protect it, and you want to know if I am being polite? No, my darling girl, I am being honest. I love you. I began to love you the tiniest little bit when you raised your hand to me from your bedchamber window. I have loved you a little more each day, but thought the ache around my heart was from something I ate or the land that I wanted to have back so desperately."

She relaxed the littlest bit. That, more than the smile, gave him hope. He went on, praying she was one step closer to accepting him.

"I thought a flirtation was just what you needed and all I could offer. It would prepare you for the less honorable gentlemen who would as soon seduce you as dance with you.

"It wasn't until the other day when you so sweetly welcomed my kiss that I knew I did not want another man to dance with you, much less kiss you."

"Are you proposing to me, Jess?"

"I was rather hoping you might propose to me, since then I would know you are in no way forced to accept me."

"I would marry you in an instant if I thought there was no way you were being forced to marry me."

"How can we convince each other that there is no puppet master pulling strings?"

"How did you convince Papa?"

"I made him a business offer he could not refuse."

"Really? That was very clever of you, my lord." Finally animation lit her voice.

"I think there is one more way we can convince each other." He tipped her chin up and kissed her. Nothing existed beyond the two of them and the way they became one.

It was a sweet kiss. They both knew it was wiser to keep it at that.

"Why do I feel no doubt at all when we are together like this?" Beatrice mused.

"I wish I knew. All my much-discussed experience did not prepare me for this. When it comes to loving someone, you and I start as equals."

They kissed again, not as a test but because they wanted to, and when that kiss ended, they both knew the answer.

"Because I love you. That's what makes all the doubts disappear."

He pressed his forehead to hers. "Because it is right."

"My lord?" Beatrice began and cleared her throat before the next phrase. "Will you marry me?"

"If you will marry me," Jess said, and they melted into each other's arms to seal their commitment with a kiss that carried their hopes and their future in one sweet caress.

Epilogue

THE WEATHER WAS atrocious. Wind-driven rain made travel so hideous it was just as well that all the guests for Jess and Beatrice's wedding had arrived at Pennford Castle earlier in the week.

But while the weather might be miserable, it was the only thing that was. The duke's salon overflowed with the Pennistan family—men, women, and children—as well as the bride's family and some close friends.

Lynford Pennistan, the fifth Duke of Meryon, grinned at his wife. "Having Jess here makes us a family again. Having everyone here for his wedding to Beatrice completes us."

"Yes, Lyn, dearest, and your happiness has given us all permission to relax and enjoy every moment." Elena took his arm. "You will notice that all of us, including your son and heir, are decidedly not on our best behavior."

Rexton, the next Duke of Meryon, was teasing one

of his girl cousins. At his young age that consisted of racing around her and trying to make her dizzy. The girl, one of Gabriel's brood, would have no part of it. She plopped herself on the floor and buried her face in the neck of the cat that she always had with her.

"Do you think it wise of Lynette to allow Marie to have that cat with her all the time?" Elena asked her husband.

"My dear duchess, that is not our problem. We have our three to worry about and that is quite enough." He gazed at the rest of Gabriel and Lynette's brood. "Who would have thought that the two of them would take to parenting so happily?"

Or marriage, Lyn thought. He knew how brutal Lynette's first marriage had been, and it was a testament to the power of love that she and Gabriel were as one in almost all things from their work to raising their children.

Gabriel came up to them, a cherubic boy tucked under his arm like a sack of grain and a girl of six or so at his side. "Do you need another boy to work in the garden, Your Grace? Owen can crawl with amazing agility and find all the lowest-hanging fruits and vegetables."

"No, Papa, Owen is too small. The other boys will trample him."

"Do you think so, Angela?" He raised the boy over his head and Owen laughed with delight.

"Papa, that will make him spit up on you," the little girl said with alarm.

At which point Lynette joined them and took Owen from his father's grasp. "He is excited enough already, Gabriel. I am going to take him to the nursery now."

"Before you go, Lynette," the duke intervened. "Have you had time for a thorough discussion of art with Beatrice?"

"There is not enough time in the world to do that, Duke, but they will be coming south on their wedding trip and I plan to let Gabriel and Jess go fishing with the boys. Then Beatrice and I can discuss art all day long. I gave them a cut-paper transparency of Haven-hall as a wedding gift. They seemed delighted with it."

The three watched her walk away with the children. "Do you think she will ever relax enough to call me by name?" the duke asked diffidently.

"You are Lynford and she is Lynette. She says two Lyns in the family are one too many. I think she considers 'Duke' your given name. At least she has abandoned the curtsy and 'Your Grace.' Besides," Gabriel finished with a smile, "she has many names for you whenever you tell us that you are not going to support her latest charity."

The duke raised his eyebrows but did not ask for more.

"Look at Olivia," Elena said. "She would so much rather be in the kitchen."

It was as though Olivia had heard them. She came back from whatever interior thought had held her and walked over to them. "Do you think the apples at breakfast were sufficiently sweet or did they need more sugar?"

"Apples? Those were apples?" Gabriel said, trying for a straight face.

Olivia punched her brother in the arm and went on. "I am determined to come up with a way to prepare salmon that Beatrice will like."

"An admirable goal, my dear," the duke said, just as Annie Blackwood came over.

"Lollie," she began, "I am going to take the boys upstairs to the nursery. The night is awful and the wedding is first thing in the morning. They can stay here tonight. All right?"

"What a good idea. I'll help you. Where is Michael? He promised to show Gabriel's children some magic tricks if they behaved."

"And you call that behaving?" Annie asked, just as two boys nearly toppled a bust on a stand.

"I do indeed," Olivia said without pause. "The statue did not fall and no one was injured."

Olivia and Annie went to collect the children, leaving the duke and his duchess alone again.

Elena leaned close to her husband and whispered, "Look at Mia. She is saying something for David alone. You know he is going to give her one of those chastening looks and she is going to do nothing but laugh at him, which will make him laugh in turn. I have never known a couple who could make bickering seem romantic."

"When will she tell everyone she is increasing?" the duke asked, wishing his wife would whisper something shocking to him.

"She does not want to take away from Jess and Beatrice's day but I do believe most have guessed. Fashion is not so forgiving these days. The more natural waist makes any weight gain obvious."

Indeed, the duke noticed a delicate little bump at Mia's waist when she turned to respond to something the Marquis Destry said.

"You know, Lynford, you and I could—" The duch-

ess stopped and whispered her suggestion, which con
vinced the duke that the gods did sometimes listen.

"Did you mean now or later, Elena?"

BEATRICE WATCHED THE duchess laugh at something
her husband said and smiled along with them. Her fa
ther and the countess were standing next to her, talk
ing with the Earl of Belmont and Nora Kendrick
leaving her free to observe the others.

Jess had left to collect a glass of sherry for her, but
William had stopped him and the two of them were
now in an animated conversation with David Penni
stan and his wife, Mia. Jess found her with his eye
and held up the glass, so she began to move across the
room toward him.

Cecilia caught her before she had taken three steps
She hugged her sister for the fifth time that evening.

Beatrice beamed at her. "I am so excited, Ceci
Twelve hours from now I will be married to the most
wonderful man in the world."

Cecilia scanned the crowd. "I do believe there are
women here who would disagree with you and main
tain that they are married to the most wonderful man
in the world."

Beatrice laughed. "Then I will amend my declara
tion to the most perfect man in the world *for me*."

"Much more diplomatic." Cecilia took her sister's
hand and pulled her toward a quiet part of the room
"Wasn't it thoughtful of the duke to bring the Rem
brandt painting to this room so you could enjoy it?"

When they were out of hearing, Cecilia changed the
subject immediately. "I wanted to let you know that

William and I are going to be married by special license next week."

"Ceci! You and Destry are marrying? That is the most wonderful news in the world. Really it is." Beatrice looked over at Jess and raised a hand. "Just a minute more!" she mouthed and he nodded with a knowing grin. Had William already told him?

"It is wonderful, but Bitsy, do not tell anyone yet. I do not want to take anything from your day but I had to let you know."

"Why special license? You could have a ceremony just like this, small and only family."

"I'm pregnant and we don't want to wait."

"Pregnant!" Beatrice hoped she had not shouted the word. She put her hand to her mouth and stayed quiet while the shock dissipated. Finally she was able to whisper, "For the love of God, Cecilia, what has happened to you?" Beatrice bit her lip and tried again. "I am delighted for you, dearest, but do not tell Papa."

"Of course not. He will find out in due course, as will William's family. You and Jess will be our witnesses, won't you?"

"Of course we will. Where are you going to have the ceremony?"

"At the house in the Lake District that Destry's family owns. Really it is their favorite and now that I have seen them all I have to agree. The pile in Northumberland may be the duke's official residence but there is nothing appealing about it. And I thought that Lake District house would work since you and Jess are headed to Sandleton, which is only a day's travel away."

She must have still looked dazed by the news be
cause Cecilia gave her another hug.

"You did tell me to have some fun. And oh, Beatrice
we are!" Cecilia kissed her sister and walked ove
toward Destry just as Jess came to join her.

"Cecilia told you?" he asked as he handed her th
glass of sherry.

"Yes." Beatrice widened her eyes deliberately. "Sh
told me they are marrying and why it will be by specia
license."

Jess raised her hand and kissed it. "They will be fine
little Venus."

"Please tell me that she has calmed William's impul
siveness, because it sounds to me as though she ha
caught it from him."

"Beatrice, I have never seen him so happy or so con
tent. Let that be enough."

"Oh, it is," Beatrice said. She watched her sister a
Cecilia stood with Destry. They were talking to Mi
chael Garrett and he was nodding as though intereste
and not at all surprised. Beatrice was fairly certair
that everyone important to them would know thei
"secret" well before their wedding.

"Just think, twelve hours from now we will be hus
band and wife and everyone will expect us to sleep
together."

"Odd, is it not, that a few words make it accept
able?"

"But just as much fun, don't you think?" Beatrice
asked with the littlest bit of concern.

"More fun, I am sure, Beatrice. You will no longer
need to worry that someone will come upon us, which

will be a relief to me, too." He leaned down and pressed a quick kiss on her lips.

"But you know the best part?" All smiles, Beatrice Brent waited for Jess Pennistan to shake his head. "After tomorrow, and for as long as we live, there will always be time for one more kiss."

Author's Note

In *One More Kiss,* William Bendasbrook—Viscount Bendasbrook and Marquis Destry—finally gets all the attention he and readers have demanded. More than one person wanted to know what happened to William after his engagement to Mia ended off-page between *Stranger's Kiss* and *Courtesan's Kiss.* I hope his happily ever after meets all your expectations.

Once again I acknowledge Lois McMaster Bujold's character Miles Vorkosigan as the inspiration for William. Miles is from the far future and William the recent past, but certain personality traits transcend time and place.

One historical detail that may be of interest is the Regency concept of coroner. The coroner was appointed by the court and one of his responsibilities was to represent the Crown in matters having to do with unexplained deaths. His appointment was for life. As such the coroner was expected to be a man not influenced by title and wealth, one who commanded the respect of the entire community.

It was up to the coroner with his jury, rather like a grand jury, to examine the evidence and determine if a murder had been committed. I have no idea what would actually happen if the coroner was unavailable as is the case in *One More Kiss,* but since Crenshaw's death was not murder, and was eventually explained by Katherine Wilson, I made up what I thought would probably happen in that situation. Let's call it artistic license, well researched.

My thanks to Meg Grasselli, assistant curator of prints and drawings at the National Gallery of Art, for her explanation of the genius of Rembrandt's drawings. It is a conversation we had years ago and I have never forgotten it and was delighted to share the insight in this book.

The discussion of the fake Rembrandts that Beatrice has with Lord Belmont reflects a true historical fact and is not to be confused with twentieth-century discussions of Rembrandt forgeries. Her "clever construct" for stealing a Rembrandt drawing was my own creation.